EVERYMAN,

I WILL GO WITH THEE,

AND BE THY GUIDE,

IN THY MOST NEED

TO GO BY THY SIDE

EVERYMAN'S POCKET CLASSICS

DETECTIVE STORIES

EDITED BY PETER WASHINGTON

EVERYMAN'S POCKET CLASSICS
Alfred A. Knopf New York London Toronto

THIS IS A BORZOI BOOK

PUBLISHED BY ALFRED A. KNOPF

This selection by Peter Washington first published in Everyman's Library, 2009

A list of acknowledgments to copyright owners appears at the back of this volume.

 Published in the United States by Alfred A. Knopf, a division of Random House, Inc., New York, and in Canada by Random House of Canada Limited, Toronto. Distributed by Random House, Inc., New York. Published in the United Kingdom by Everyman's Library, Northburgh House, 10 Northburgh Street, London EC1V 0AT, and distributed by Random House (UK) Ltd.

US website: www.randomhouse.com/everymans

ISBN: 978-0-307-27271-3 (US)
978-1-84159-604-4 (UK)

A CIP catalogue reference for this book is available from the British Library

Typography by Peter B. Willberg

Typeset in the UK by AccComputing, North Barrow, Somerset

Printed and bound in Germany by GGP Media GmbH, Pössneck

DETECTIVE STORIES

Contents

SARA PARETSKY

THE TAKAMOKU *JOSEKI*

Written for S. Courtenay Wright
Christmas Day, 1982

I

MR AND MRS Takamoku were a quiet, hardworking couple. Although they had lived in Chicago since the 1940s, when they were relocated from an Arizona detention camp, they spoke only halting English. Occasionally I ran into Mrs Takamoku in the foyer of the old three-flat we both lived in on Belmont, or at the corner grocery store. We would exchange a few stilted sentences. She knew I lived alone in my third-floor apartment, and she worried about it, although her manners were too perfect for her to come right out and tell me to get myself a husband.

As time passed, I learned about her son, Akira, and her daughter, Yoshio, both professionals living on the West Coast. I always inquired after them, which pleased her.

With great difficulty I got her to understand that I was a private detective. This troubled her; she often wanted to know if I were doing something dangerous, and would shake her head and frown as she asked. I didn't see Mr Takamoku often. He worked for a printer and usually left long before me in the morning.

Unlike the De Paul students who formed an ever-changing collage on the second floor, the Takamokus did little entertaining, or at least little noisy entertaining. Every Sunday afternoon a procession of Asians came to their apartment, spent a quiet afternoon, and left. One or more Caucasians would join them, incongruous by their height and color.

After a while, I recognized the regulars: a tall, bearded white man, and six or seven Japanese and Koreans.

One Sunday evening in late November I was eating sushi and drinking sake in a storefront restaurant on Halsted. The Takamokus came in as I was finishing my first little pot of sake. I smiled and waved at them, and watched with idle amusement as they conferred earnestly, darting glances at me. While they argued, a waitress brought them bowls of noodles and a plate of sushi; they were clearly regular customers with regular tastes.

At last, Mr Takamoku came over to my table. I invited him and his wife to join me.

'Thank you, thank you,' he said in an agony of embarrassment. 'We only have question for you, not to disturb you.'

'You're not disturbing me. What do you want to know?'

'You are familiar with American customs.' That was a statement, not a question. I nodded, wondering what was coming.

'When a guest behaves badly in the house, what does an American do?'

I gave him my full attention. I had no idea what he was asking, but he would never have brought it up just to be frivolous.

'It depends,' I said carefully. 'Did they break up your sofa or spill tea?'

Mr Takamoku looked at me steadily, fishing for a cigarette. Then he shook his head, slowly. 'Not as much as breaking furniture. Not as little as tea on sofa. In between.'

'I'd give him a second chance.'

A slight crease erased itself from Mr Takamoku's forehead. 'A second chance. A very good idea. A second chance.'

He went back to his wife and ate his noodles with the noisy appreciation that showed good Japanese manners. I had another pot of sake and finished about the same time as the Takamokus; we left the restaurant together. I topped them by a good five inches and perhaps twenty pounds, so I slowed my pace to a crawl to keep step with them.

Mrs Takamoku smiled. 'You are familiar with Go?' she asked, giggling nervously.

'I'm not sure,' I said cautiously, wondering if they wanted me to conjugate an intransitive irregular verb.

'It's a game. You have time to stop and see?'

'Sure,' I agreed, just as Mr Takamoku broke in with vigorous objections.

I couldn't tell whether he didn't want to inconvenience me or didn't want me intruding. However, Mrs Takamoku insisted, so I stopped at the first floor and went into the apartment with her.

The living-room was almost bare. The lack of furniture drew the eye to a beautiful Japanese doll on a stand in one corner, with a bowl of dried flowers in front of her. The only other furnishings were six little tables in a row. They were quite thick and stood low on carved wooden legs. Their tops, about eighteen inches square, were crisscrossed with black lines which formed dozens of little squares. Two covered wooden bowls stood on each table.

'Go-ban,' Mrs Takamoku said, pointing to one of the tables.

I shook my head in incomprehension.

Mr Takamoku picked up a covered bowl. It was filled with smooth white disks, the size of nickels but much thicker. I held one up and saw beautiful shades and shadows in it.

'Clamshell,' Mr Takamoku said. 'They cut, then polish.' He picked up a second bowl, filled with black disks. 'Shale.'

He knelt on a cushion in front of one of the tables and

rapidly placed black and white disks on intersections of the lines. A pattern emerged.

'This is Go. Black play, then white, then black, then white. Each try to make territory, to make eyes.' He showed me an 'eye' – a clear space surrounded by black stones. 'White cannot play here. Black safe. Now white must play someplace else.'

'I see.' I didn't really, but I didn't think it mattered.

'This afternoon, someone knock stones from table, turn upside down, and scrape with knife.'

'This table?' I asked, tapping the one he was playing on.

'Yes.' He swept the stones off swiftly but carefully, and put them in their little pots. He turned the board over. In the middle was a hole, carved and sanded. The wood was very thick – I suppose the hole gave it resonance.

I knelt beside him and looked. I was probably thirty years younger, but I couldn't tuck my knees under me with his grace and ease: I sat cross-legged. A faint scratch marred the sanded bottom.

'Was he American?'

Mr and Mrs Takamoku exchanged a look. 'Japanese, but born in America,' she said. 'Like Akira and Yoshio.'

I shook my head. 'I don't understand. It's not an American custom.' I climbed awkwardly back to my feet. Mr Takamoku stood with one easy movement. He and Mrs Takamoku thanked me profusely. I assured them it was nothing and went to bed.

II

The next Sunday was a cold, gray day with a hint of snow. I sat in front of the television, in my living-room, drinking coffee, dividing my attention between November's income and watching the Bears. Both were equally feeble. I was trying to decide on something friendlier to do when a knock sounded on my door. The outside buzzer hadn't rung. I got up, stacking loose papers on one arm of the chair and balancing the coffee cup on the other.

Through the peephole I could see Mrs Takamoku. I opened the door. Her wrinkled ivory face was agitated, her eyes dilated. 'Oh, good, good, you here. You must come.' She tugged at my hand.

I pulled her gently into the apartment. 'What's wrong? Let me get you a drink.'

'No, no.' She wrung her hands in agitation, repeating that I must come, I must come.

I collected my keys and went down the worn, uncarpeted stairs with her. Her living-room was filled with cigarette smoke and a crowd of anxious men. Mr Takamoku detached himself from the group and hurried over to his wife and me. He clasped my hand and pumped it up and down.

'Good. Good you come. You are a detective, yes? You will see the police do not arrest Naoe and me.'

'What's wrong, Mr Takamoku?'

'He's dead. He's killed. Naoe and I were in camp during World War. They will arrest us.'

'Who's dead?'

He shrugged helplessly. 'I don't know name.'

I pushed through the group. A white man lay sprawled on the floor. His face had contorted in dreadful pain as he died, so it was hard to guess his age. His fair hair was thick and unmarked with gray; he must have been relatively young.

A small dribble of vomit trailed from his clenched teeth. I sniffed at it cautiously. Probably hydrocyanic acid. Not far from his body lay a teacup, a Japanese cup without handles. The contents sprayed out from it like a Rorschach. Without touching it, I sniffed again. The fumes were still discernible.

I got up. 'Has anyone left since this happened?'

The tall, bearded Caucasian I'd noticed on previous Sundays looked around and said 'No' in an authoritative voice.

'And have you called the police?'

Mrs Takamoku gave an agitated cry. 'No police. No. You are detective. You find murderer yourself.'

I shook my head and took her gently by the hand. 'If we don't call the police, they will put us all in jail for concealing a murder. You must tell them.'

The bearded man said, 'I'll do that.'

'Who are you?'

'I'm Charles Welland. I'm a physicist at the University of Chicago, but on Sundays I'm a Go player.'

'I see . . . I'm V. I. Warshawski. I live upstairs. I'm a private investigator. The police look very dimly on all citizens who don't report murders, but especially on P.I.'s.'

Welland went into the dining-room, where the Takamokus kept their phone. I told the Takamokus and their guests that no one could leave before the police gave them permission, then followed Welland to make sure he didn't call anyone besides the police, or take the opportunity to get rid of a vial of poison.

The Go players seemed resigned, albeit very nervous. All of them smoked ferociously; the thick air grew bluer. They split into small groups, five Japanese together, four Koreans in another clump. A lone Chinese fiddled with the stones on one of the Go-bans.

None of them spoke English well enough to give a clear account of how the young man died. When Welland came back, I asked him for a detailed report.

The physicist claimed not to know his name. The dead man had only been coming to the Go club the last month or two.

'Did someone bring him? Or did he just show up one day?'

Welland shrugged. 'He just showed up. Word gets around among Go players. I'm sure he told me his name – it just didn't stick. I think he worked for Hansen Electronic, the big computer firm.'

I asked if everyone there was a regular player. Welland knew all of them by sight, if not by name. They didn't all come every Sunday, but none of the others was a newcomer.

'I see. Okay. What happened today?'

Welland scratched his beard. He had bushy, arched eyebrows which jumped up to punctuate his stronger statements, kind of like Sean Connery. I found it pretty sexy. I pulled my mind back to what he was saying.

'I got here around one-thirty. I think three games were in progress. This guy' – he jerked his thumb toward the dead man – 'arrived a bit later. He and I played a game. Then Mr Hito arrived and the two of them had a game. Dr Han showed up, and he and I were playing when the whole thing happened. Mrs Takamoku sets out tea and snacks. We all wander around and help ourselves. About four, this guy took a swallow of tea, gave a terrible cry, and died.'

'Is there anything important about the game they were playing?'

Welland looked at the board. A handful of black-and-white stones stood on the corner points. He shook his head. 'They'd just started. It looks like our dead friend was trying one of the Takamoku *josekis*. That's a complicated one – I've never seen it used in actual play before.'

'What's that? Anything to do with Mr Takamoku?'

'The *joseki* are the beginning moves in the corners. Takamoku is this one' – he pointed at the far side – 'where black plays on the five-four point – the point where the fourth and fifth lines intersect. It wasn't named for our host. That's just coincidence.'

III

Sergeant McGonnigal didn't find out much more than I did. A thickset young detective, he had a lot of experience and treated his frightened audience gently. He was a little less kind to me, demanding roughly why I was there, what my connection with the dead man was, who my client was. It didn't cheer him up any to hear I was working for the Takamokus, but he let me stay with them while he questioned them. He sent for a young Korean officer to interrogate the Koreans in the group. Welland, who spoke fluent Japanese, translated the Japanese interviews. Dr Han, the lone Chinese, struggled along on his own.

McGonnigal learned that the dead man's name was Peter Folger. He learned that people were milling around all the time watching each other play. He also learned that no one paid attention to anything but the game they were playing, or watching.

'The Japanese say the Go player forgets his father's funeral,' Welland explained. 'It's a game of tremendous concentration.'

No one admitted knowing Folger outside the Go club. No one knew how he found out that the Takamokus hosted Go every Sunday.

My clients hovered tensely in the background, convinced that McGonnigal would arrest them at any minute. But they could add nothing to the story. Anyone who wanted to play was welcome at their apartment on Sunday afternoon. Why should he show a credential? If he knew how to play, that was the proof.

McGonnigal pounced on that. Was Folger a good player? Everyone looked around and nodded. Yes, not the best – that was clearly Dr Han or Mr Kim, one of the Koreans – but quite good enough. Perhaps first *kyu*, whatever that was.

After two hours of this, McGonnigal decided he was getting nowhere. Someone in the room must have had a connection with Folger, but we weren't going to find it by questioning the group. We'd have to dig into their backgrounds.

A uniformed man started collecting addresses while McGonnigal went to his car to radio for plainclothes reinforcements. He wanted everyone in the room tailed and wanted to call from a private phone. A useless precaution, I thought: the innocent wouldn't know they were being followed, and the guilty would expect it.

McGonnigal returned shortly, his face angry. He had a bland-faced, square-jawed man in tow, Derek Hatfield of the FBI. He did computer fraud for them. Our paths had crossed a few times on white-collar crime. I'd found him smart and knowledgeable, but also humorless and overbearing.

'Hello, Derek,' I said, without getting up from the cushion I was sitting on. 'What brings you here?'

'He had the place under surveillance,' McGonnigal said, biting off the words. 'He won't tell me who he was looking for.'

Derek walked over to Folger's body, covered now with a sheet, which he pulled back. He looked at Folger's face and nodded. 'I'm going to have to phone my office for instructions.'

'Just a minute,' McGonnigal said. 'You know the guy, right? You tell me what you were watching him for.'

Derek raised his eyebrows haughtily. 'I'll have to make a call first.'

'Don't be an ass, Hatfield,' I said. 'You think you're impressing us with how mysterious the FBI is, but you're not, really. You know your boss will tell you to cooperate with the city if it's murder. And we might be able to clear this thing up right now, glory for everyone. We know Folger worked for Hansen Electronic. He wasn't one of your guys working undercover, was he?'

Hatfield glared at me. 'I can't answer that.'

'Look,' I said reasonably. 'Either he worked for you and was investigating problems at Hansen, or he worked for them and you suspected he was involved in some kind of fraud. I know there's a lot of talk about Hansen's new Series J computer – was he passing secrets?'

Hatfield put his hands in his pockets and scowled in thought. At last he said, to McGonnigal, 'Is there some place we can go and talk?'

I asked Mrs Takamoku if we could use her kitchen for a few minutes. Her lips moved nervously, but she took Hatfield and me down the hall. Her apartment was laid out like mine and the kitchens were similar, at least in appliances. Hers was spotless; mine had that lived-in look.

McGonnigal told the uniformed man not to let anyone leave or make any phone calls, and followed us.

Hatfield leaned against the back door. I perched on a bar stool next to a high wooden table. McGonnigal stood in the doorway leading to the hall.

'You got someone here named Miyake?' Hatfield asked.

McGonnigal looked through the sheaf of notes in his hand and shook his head.

'Anyone here work for Kawamoto?'

Kawamoto is a big Japanese electronics firm, one of Mitsubishi's peers and a strong rival of Hansen in the mega-computer market.

'Hatfield, are you trying to tell us that Folger was passing Series J secrets to someone from Kawamoto over the Go boards here?'

Hatfield shifted uncomfortably. 'We only got onto it three weeks ago. Folger was just a go-between. We offered him immunity if he would finger the guy from Kawamoto. He couldn't describe him well enough for us to make a pickup. He was going to shake hands with him or touch him in some way as they left the building.'

'The Judas trick,' I remarked.

'Huh?' Hatfield looked puzzled.

McGonnigal smiled for the first time that afternoon. 'That man I kiss is the one you want. You should've gone to Catholic school, Hatfield.'

'Yeah. Anyway, Folger must've told this guy Miyake we were closing in.' Hatfield shook his head disgustedly. 'Miyake must be part of that group, just using an assumed name. We got a tail put on all of them.' He straightened up and started back toward the hall.

'How was Folger passing the information?' I asked.

'It was on microdots.'

'Stay where you are. I might be able to tell you which one is Miyake without leaving the building.'

Of course, both Hatfield and McGonnigal started yelling at me at once. Why was I suppressing evidence, what did I know, they'd have me arrested.

'Calm down, boys,' I said. 'I don't have any evidence. But now that I know the crime, I think I know how it was done. I just need to talk to my clients.'

Mr and Mrs Takamoku looked at me anxiously when I came back to the living-room. I got them to follow me into the hall. 'They're not going to arrest you,' I assured them. 'But I need to know who turned over the Go board last week. Is he here today?'

They talked briefly in Japanese, then Mr Takamoku said, 'We should not betray guest. But murder is much worse. Man in orange shirt, named Hamai.'

Hamai, or Miyake, as Hatfield called him, resisted valiantly. When the police started to put handcuffs on him, he popped a gelatin capsule into his mouth. He was dead almost before they realized what he had done.

Hatfield, impersonal as always, searched his body for the microdot. Hamai had stuck it to his upper lip, where it looked like a mole against his dark skin.

IV

'How did you know?' McGonnigal grumbled, after the bodies had been carted off and the Takamokus' efforts to turn their life savings over to me successfully averted.

'He turned over a Go board here last week. That troubled my clients enough that they asked me about it. Once I knew we were looking for the transfer of information, it was obvious that Folger had stuck the dot in the hole under the board. Hamai couldn't get at it, so he had to turn the whole board over. Today, Folger must have put it in a more accessible spot.'

Hatfield left to make his top-secret report. McGonnigal followed his uniformed men out of the apartment. Welland held the door for me.

'Was his name Hamai or Miyake?'

'Oh, I think his real name was Hamai – that's what all

his identification said. He must have used a false name with Folger. After all, he knew you guys never pay attention to each other's names – you probably wouldn't even notice what Folger called him. If you could figure out who Folger was.'

Welland smiled; his busy eyebrows danced. 'How about a drink? I'd like to salute a lady clever enough to solve the Takamoku *joseki* unaided.'

I looked at my watch. Three hours ago I'd been trying to think of something friendlier to do than watch the Bears get pummeled. This sounded like a good bet. I slipped my hand through his arm and went outside with him.

IAN RANKIN

WINDOW OF OPPORTUNITY

An Inspector Rebus Story

BERNIE FEW'S JAILBREAKS were an art.

And over the years he had honed his art. His escapes from prison, his shrugging off of guards and prison officers, his vanishing acts were the stuff of lights-out stories in jails the length and breadth of Scotland. He was called 'The Grease-Man', 'The Blink', and many other names, including the obvious 'Houdini' and the not-so-obvious 'Claude' (Claude Rains having starred as the original *Invisible Man*).

Bernie Few was beautiful. As a petty thief he was hopeless, but after capture he started to show his real prowess. He wasn't made for being a housebreaker; but he surely did shine as a jailbreaker. He'd stuffed himself into rubbish bags and mail sacks, taken the place of a corpse from one prison hospital, squeezed his wiry frame out of impossibly small windows (sometimes buttering his naked torso in preparation), and crammed himself into ventilation shafts and heating ducts.

But Bernie Few had a problem. Once he'd scaled the high walls, waded through sewers, sprinted from the prison bus, or cracked his guard across the head, once he'd done all this and was outside again, breathing free air and melting into the crowd . . . his movements were like clockwork. All his ingenuity seemed to be exhausted. The prison psychologists put it differently. They said he wanted to be caught, really. It was a game to him.

But to Detective Inspector John Rebus, it was more than a game. It was a chance for a drink.

Bernie would do three things. One, he'd go throw a rock through his ex-wife's living-room window. Two, he'd stand in the middle of Princes Street telling everyone to go to hell (and other places besides). And three, he'd get drunk in Scott's Bar. These days, option one was difficult for Bernie, since his ex-wife had not only moved without leaving a forwarding address but had, at Rebus's suggestion, gone to live on the eleventh floor of an Oxgangs tower block. No more rocks through the living-room window, unless Bernie was handy with ropes and crampons.

Rebus preferred to wait for Bernie in Scott's Bar, where they refused to water down either the whisky or the language. Scott's was a villains' pub, one of the ropiest in Edinburgh. Rebus recognized half the faces in the place, even on a dull Wednesday afternoon. Bail faces, appeal faces. They recognized him, too, but there wasn't going to be any trouble. Every one of them knew why he was here. He hoisted himself on to a barstool and lit a cigarette. The TV was on, showing a satellite sports channel. Cricket, some test between England and the West Indies. It is a popular fallacy that the Scots don't watch cricket. Edinburgh pub drinkers will watch *anything*, especially if England are involved, more especially if England are odds on to get a drubbing. Scott's, as depressing a watering hole as you could ever imagine, had transported itself to the Caribbean for the occasion.

Then the door to the toilets opened with a nerve-jarring squeal, and a man loped out. He was tall and skinny, loose-limbed, hair falling over his eyes. He had a hand on his fly, just checking prior to departure, and his eyes were on the floor.

'See youse then,' he said to nobody, opening the front door to leave. Nobody responded. The door stayed open longer than it should. Someone else was coming in. Eyes flashed from the TV for a moment. Rebus finished his drink and rose from the stool. He knew the man who'd just left the bar. He knew him well. He knew, too, that what had just happened was impossible.

The new customer, a small man with a handful of coins, had a voice hoarse from shouting as he croakily ordered a pint. The barman didn't move. Instead, he looked to Rebus, who was looking at Bernie Few.

Then Bernie Few looked at Rebus.

'Been down to Princes Street, Bernie?' Rebus asked.

Bernie Few sighed and rubbed his tired face. 'Time for a short one, Mr Rebus?'

Rebus nodded. He could do with another himself anyway. He had a couple of things on his mind, neither of them Bernie Few.

Police officers love and hate surveillance operations in more or less equal measure. There's the tedium, but even that beats being tied to a CID desk. Often on a stakeout there's a good spirit, plus there's that adrenal rush when something eventually happens.

The present surveillance was based in a second-floor tenement flat, the owners having been packed off to a seaside caravan for a fortnight. If the operation needed longer than a fortnight, they'd be sent to stay with relations.

The watchers worked in two-man teams and twelve-hour shifts. They were watching the second-floor flat of the tenement across the road. They were keeping tabs on a bandit called Ribs Mackay. He was called Ribs because he was so skinny. He had a heroin habit, and paid for it by pushing drugs. Only he'd never been caught at it, a state of affairs Edinburgh CID were keen to rectify.

The problem was, since the surveillance had begun, Ribs

had been keeping his head down. He stayed in the flat, nipping out only on brief sorties to the corner shop. He'd buy beer, vodka, milk, cigarettes, sometimes breakfast cereal or a jar of peanut butter, and he'd always top off his purchases with half a dozen bars of chocolate. That was about it. There had to be more, but there wasn't any more. Any day now, the operation would be declared dead in the water.

They tried to keep the flat clean, but you couldn't help a bit of untidiness. You couldn't help nosy neighbours either: everyone on the stairwell wondered who the strangers in the Tully residence were. Some asked questions. Some didn't need to be told. Rebus met an old man on the stairs. He was hauling a bag of shopping up to the third floor, stopping for a breather at each step.

'Help you with that?' Rebus offered.

'I can manage.'

'It wouldn't be any bother.'

'I said I can manage.'

Rebus shrugged. 'Suit yourself.' Then he climbed to the landing and gave the recognized knock on the door of the Tullys' flat.

DC Jamphlar opened the door a crack, saw Rebus, and pulled it all the way open. Rebus nipped inside.

'Here,' he said, handing over a paper bag, 'doughrings.'

'Thank you, sir,' said Jamphlar.

In the cramped living-room, DC Connaught was sitting on a dining chair at the net curtain, peering through the net and out of the window. Rebus joined him for a moment. Ribs Mackay's window was grimy, but you could see through the grime into an ordinary-looking living-room. Not that Ribs came to the window much. Connaught wasn't concentrating on the window. He was ranging between the second-floor window and the ground-floor door. If Ribs left the flat,

Jamphlar went haring after him, while Connaught followed Ribs's progress from the window and reported via radio to his colleague.

Initially, there'd been one man in the flat and one in a car at street level. But the man at street level hadn't been needed, and looked suspicious anyway. The street was no main thoroughfare, but a conduit between Clerk Street and Buccleuch Street. There were a few shops at road level, but they carried the look of permanent closure.

Connaught glanced up from the window. 'Afternoon, sir. What brings you here?'

'Any sign of him?' Rebus said.

'Not so much as a tweet.'

'I reckon I know why that is. Your bird's already flown.'

'No chance,' said Jamphlar, biting into a doughring.

'I saw him half an hour ago in Scott's Bar. That's a fair hike from here.'

'Must've been his double.'

But Rebus shook his head. 'When was the last time you saw him?'

Jamphlar checked the notebook. 'We haven't seen him this shift. But this morning Cooper and Sneddon watched him go to the corner shop and come back. That was seven-fifteen.'

'And you come on at eight?'

'Yes, sir.'

'And you haven't seen him since?'

'There's someone in there,' Connaught persisted. 'I've seen movement.'

Rebus spoke slowly. 'But you haven't seen Ribs Mackay, and I have. He's out on the street, doing whatever he does.' He leaned closer to Connaught. 'Come on, son, what is it? Been skiving off? Half an hour down the pub, a bit of a thirst-quencher? Catching some kip on the sofa? Looks comfortable, that sofa.'

Jamphlar was trying to swallow a mouthful of dough which had become suddenly dry. 'We've been doing our job!' he said, spraying crumbs.

Connaught just stared at Rebus with burning eyes. Rebus believed those eyes.

'All right,' he conceded, 'so there's another explanation. A back exit, a convenient drainpipe.'

'The back door's been bricked up,' Connaught said stiffly. 'There's a drainpipe, but Ribs couldn't manage down it.'

'How do you know?'

'I know.' Connaught stared out through the curtain.

'Something else then. Maybe he's using a disguise.'

Jamphlar, still chewing, flicked through the notebook. 'Everyone who comes out and goes in is checked off.'

'He's a druggie,' said Connaught. 'He's not bright enough to fool us.'

'Well, son, that's just what he's doing. You're watching an empty flat.'

'TV's just come on,' said Connaught. Rebus looked out through the curtain. Sure enough, he could see the animated screen. 'I hate this programme,' Connaught muttered. 'I wish he'd change the channel.'

'Maybe he can't,' said Rebus, making for the door.

He returned to the surveillance that evening, taking someone with him. There'd been a bit of difficulty, getting things arranged. Nobody was keen for him to walk out of the station with Bernie Few. But Rebus would assume full responsibility.

'Damned right you will,' said his boss, signing the form.

Jamphlar and Connaught were off, Cooper and Sneddon were on.

'What's this I hear?' Cooper said, opening the door to Rebus and his companion.

'About Ribs?'

'No,' said Cooper, 'about you bringing the day shift a selection of patisseries.'

'Come and take a look,' Sneddon called. Rebus walked over to the window. The light was on in Ribs's living-room, and the blinds weren't shut. Ribs had opened the window and was looking down on to the night-time street, enjoying a cigarette. 'See?' Sneddon said.

'I see,' said Rebus. Then he turned to Bernie Few. 'Come over here, Bernie.' Few came shuffling over to the window, and Rebus explained the whole thing to him. Bernie thought about it, rasping a hand over his chin, then asked the same questions Rebus had earlier asked Jamphlar and Connaught. Then he thought about it some more, staring out through the curtain.

'You keep an eye on the second-floor window?' he asked Cooper.

'That's right.'

'And the main door?'

'Yes.'

'You ever think of looking anywhere else?'

Cooper didn't get it. Neither did Sneddon.

'Go on, Bernie,' said Rebus.

'Look at the top floor,' Bernie Few suggested. Rebus looked. He saw a cracked and begrimed window, covered with ragged bits of cardboard. 'Think anyone lives there?' Bernie asked.

'What are you saying?'

'I think he's done a proper switch on you. Turned the tables, like.' He smiled. 'You're not watching Ribs Mackay. *He's* watching *you*.'

Rebus nodded, quick to get it. 'The change of shifts.' Bernie was nodding too. 'There's that minute or two when one shift's going off and the other's coming on.'

'A window of opportunity,' Bernie agreed. 'He watches, sees the new shift arrive, and skips downstairs and out the door.'

'And twelve hours later,' said Rebus, 'he waits in the street till he sees the next shift clocking on. Then he nips back in.'

Sneddon was shaking his head. 'But the lights, the telly . . .'

'Timer switches,' Bernie Few answered casually. 'You think you see people moving about in there. Maybe you do, but not Ribs. Could just be shadows, a breeze blowing the curtains.'

Sneddon frowned. 'Who *are* you?'

'An expert witness,' Rebus said, patting Bernie Few's shoulder. Then he turned to Sneddon. 'I'm going over there. Keep an eye on Bernie here. And I *mean* keep an eye on him. As in, don't let him out of your sight.'

Sneddon blinked, then stared at Bernie. 'You're Buttery Bernie.'

Bernie shrugged, accepting the nickname. Rebus was already leaving.

He went to the bar at the street's far corner and ordered a whisky. He sluiced his mouth out with the stuff, so that it would be heavy on his breath, then came out of the bar and weaved his way towards Ribs Mackay's tenement, just another soak trying to find his way home. He tugged his jacket over to one side, and undid a couple of buttons on his shirt. He could do this act. Sometimes he did it too well. He got drunk on the method.

He pushed open the tenement door and was in a dimly lit hallway, with worn stone steps curving up. He grasped the banister and started to climb. He didn't even pause at the second floor, but he could hear music from behind Ribs's door. And he saw the door was reinforced, just the kind dealers fitted. It gave them those vital extra seconds when the drug squad came calling, sledgehammers and axes their invitations. Seconds were all you needed to flush evidence away, or to swallow it. These days, prior to a house raid, the drugs squad opened up the sewers and had a man stationed there, ready for the flush . . .

On the top-floor landing, Rebus paused for breath. The door facing him looked hard done by, scarred and chipped and beaten. The nameplate had been hauled off, leaving deep screw holes in the wood. Rebus knocked on the door, ready with excuses and his drunk's head-down stance. He waited, but there was no answer. He listened, then put his eyes to the letterbox. Darkness. He tried the door handle. It turned, and the door swung inwards. When he thought about it, an unlocked door made sense. Ribs would need to come and go in a hurry, and locks took time.

Rebus stepped quietly into the short hallway. Some of the interior doors were open, bringing with them chinks of streetlight. The place smelt musty and damp, and it was cold. There was no furniture, and the wallpaper had peeled from the walls. Long strips now lay in wrinkled piles, like an old woman's stockings come to rest at her ankles. Rebus walked on tiptoe. He didn't know how good the floors were, and he didn't want anyone below to hear him. He didn't want Ribs Mackay to hear him.

He went into the living-room. It was identical in shape to the surveillance living-room. There were newspapers on the floor, a carpet rolled up against one wall. Tufts of carpet lay scattered across the floor. Mice had obviously been taking bits for nesting. Rebus went to the window. There was a small gap where two pieces of cardboard didn't quite meet. Through this gap he had a good view of the surveillance flat. And though the lights were off, the streetlight illuminated the net curtain, so that anyone behind the curtain who moved became a shadow puppet. Someone, Sneddon or Cooper or Bernie Few, was moving just now.

'You clever little runt,' Rebus whispered. Then he picked something up off the floor. It was a single-lens reflex camera, with telephoto lens attached. Not the sort of thing you found lying in abandoned flats. He picked it up and focused on the window across the street. There was absolutely no doubt in his mind now. It was so simple. Ribs sneaked up here, watched the surveillance through the telephoto while they thought they were watching him, and at eight o'clock walked smartly out of the tenement and went about his business.

'You're as good as gold, Bernie,' said Rebus. Then he put the camera back just the way he'd found it and tiptoed back through the flat.

'Where is he?'

Stupid question, considering. Sneddon just shrugged. 'He had to use the bathroom.'

'Of course he did,' said Rebus.

Sneddon led him through to the bathroom. It had a small window high on one wall. The window was open. It led not to the outside, but merely back into the hall near the flat's stairwell door.

'He was in here a while, so I came looking. Banged on the door, no answer, managed to force the thing open, but he wasn't here.' Sneddon's face and neck were red with embarrassment; or maybe it was just the exercise. 'I ran downstairs, but there was no sign of him.'

'I don't believe he could have squeezed out of that window,' Rebus said sceptically. 'Not even Bernie Few.' The window was about twelve inches by nine. It could be reached by standing in the rim of the bath, but the walls were white tile, and Rebus couldn't see any signs of scuff marks. He looked at the toilet. Its lid was down, but didn't sit level with the pan. Rebus lifted the lid and found himself staring at towels, several of them, stuffed down into the pan.

'What the . . .?' Sneddon couldn't believe his eyes. But Rebus could. He opened the small airing cupboard beneath the sink. It was empty. A shelf had been lifted out and placed upright in the back of the cupboard. There was just about room inside to make for a hiding place. Rebus smiled at the disbelieving Sneddon.

'He waited till you'd gone downstairs.'

'Then what?' said Sneddon. 'You mean he's still in the flat?'

Rebus wondered. 'No,' he said at last, shaking his head. 'But think of what he just told us, about how Ribs was tricking us.'

He led Sneddon out of the flat, but instead of heading down, he climbed up a further flight to the top floor. Set into the ceiling was a skylight, and it too was open.

'A walk across the rooftops,' said Rebus.

Sneddon just shook his head. 'Sorry, sir,' he offered.

'Never mind,' said Rebus, knowing, however, that his boss would.

At seven next morning, Ribs Mackay left his flat and walked jauntily to the corner shop, followed by Sneddon. Then he walked back again, enjoying a cigarette, not a care in the world. He'd shown himself to the surveillance team, and now they had something to tell the new shift, something to occupy them during the changeover.

As usual the changeover happened at eight. And exactly a minute after Jamphlar and Connaught entered the tenement, the door across the street opened and Ribs Mackay flew out.

Rebus and Sneddon, snug in Rebus's car, watched him go. Then Sneddon got out to follow him. He didn't look back at Rebus, but he did wave an acknowledgement that his superior had been right. Rebus hoped Sneddon was better as a tail than he was as a watcher. He hoped they'd catch Ribs with the stuff on him, dealing it out perhaps, or taking delivery from his own supplier. That was the plan. That had been the plan throughout.

He started the ignition and drove out on to Buccleuch Street. Scott's Bar was an early opener, and John Rebus had an appointment there.

He owed Bernie Few a drink.

RUTH RENDELL

PEOPLE DON'T DO SUCH THINGS

Gwendolen and me out to dinner, then we had him over at our place, and after that we became close friends.

Writers and the way they work hold a fascination for ordinary chaps like me. It's a mystery to me where they get their ideas from, apart from constructing the thing and creating characters and making their characters talk and so on. But Reeve could do it all right, and set the whole lot at the court of Louis Quinze or in medieval Italy or what not. I've read all nine of his historical novels and admired what you might call his virtuosity. But I only read them to please him really. Detective stories were what I preferred and I seldom bothered with any other form of fiction.

Gwendolen once said to me it was amazing Reeve could fill his books with so much drama when he was living drama all the time. You'd imagine he'd have got rid of it all on paper. I think the truth was that every one of his heroes was himself, only transformed into Cesare Borgia or Casanova. You could see Reeve in them all, tall, handsome and dashing as they were, and each a devil with the women. Reeve had got divorced from his wife a year or so before I'd met him, and since then he'd had a string of girl friends, models, actresses, girls in the fashion trade, secretaries, journalists, schoolteachers, high-powered lady executives and even a dentist. Once when we were over at his place he played us a record of an aria from *Don Giovanni* – another character Reeve identified with and wrote about. It was called the 'Catalogue Song' and it listed all the types of girls the Don had made love to, blonde, brunette, redhead, young, old, rich, poor, ending up with something about as long as she wears a petticoat you know what he does. Funny, I even remember the Italian for that bit, though it's the only Italian I know. *Purche porti la gonnella voi sapete quel che fa.* Then the singer laughed in an unpleasant way, laughed to music with a seducer's sneer, and Reeve laughed too, saying it gave him a fellow-feeling.

I'm old-fashioned, I know that. I'm conventional. Sex is for marriage, as far as I'm concerned, and what sex you have before marriage – I never had much – I can't help thinking of as a shameful secret thing. I never even believed that people did have much of it outside marriage. All talk and boasting, I thought. I really did think that. And I kidded myself that when Reeve talked of going out with a new girl he meant going out with. Taking out for a meal, I thought, and dancing with and taking home in a taxi and then maybe a good-night kiss on the doorstep. Until one Sunday morning, when Reeve was coming over for lunch, I phoned him to ask if he'd meet us in the pub for a pre-lunch drink. He sounded half-asleep and I could hear a girl giggling in the background. Then I heard him say:

'Get some clothes on, lovey, and make us a cup of tea, will you? My head's splitting.'

I told Gwendolen.

'What did you expect?' she said.

'I don't know,' I said. 'I thought you'd be shocked.'

'He's very good-looking and he's only thirty-seven. It's natural.' But she had blushed a little. 'I am rather shocked,' she said. 'We don't belong in his sort of life, do we?'

And yet we remained in it, on the edge of it. As we got to know Reeve better, he put aside those small prevarications he had employed to save our feelings. And he would tell us, without shyness, anecdotes of his amorous past and present. The one about the girl who was so possessive that even though he had broken with her, she had got into his flat in his absence and been lying naked in his bed when he brought his new girl home that night; the one about the married woman who had hidden him for two hours in her wardrobe until her husband had gone out; the girl who had come to borrow a pound of sugar and had stayed all night; fair girls, dark girls, plump, thin, rich, poor . . . *Purche porti la gonnella voi sapete quel che fa.*

'It's another world,' said Gwendolen.

And I said, 'How the other half lives.'

We were given to clichés of this sort. Our life was a cliché, the commonest sort of life led by middle-class people in the Western world. We had a nice detached house in one of the right suburbs, solid furniture and lifetime-lasting carpets. I had my car and she hers. I left for the office at half-past eight and returned at six. Gwendolen cleaned the house and went shopping and gave coffee mornings. In the evenings we liked to sit at home and watch television, generally going to bed at eleven. I think I was a good husband. I never forgot my wife's birthday or failed to send her roses on our anniversary or omitted to do my share of the dishwashing. And she was an excellent wife, romantically-inclined, not sensual. At any rate, she was never sensual with me.

She kept every birthday card I ever sent her, and the Valentines I sent her while we were engaged. Gwendolen was one of those women who hoard and cherish small mementoes. In a drawer of her dressing table she kept the menu card from the restaurant where we celebrated our engagement, a picture postcard of the hotel where we spent our honeymoon, every photograph of us that had ever been taken, our wedding pictures in a leather-bound album. Yes, she was an arch-romantic, and in her diffident way, with an air of daring, she would sometimes reproach Reeve for his callousness.

'But you can't do that to someone who loves you,' she said when he had announced his brutal intention of going off on holiday without telling his latest girl friend where he was going or even that he was going at all. 'You'll break her heart.'

'Gwendolen, my love, she hasn't got a heart. Women don't have them. She has another sort of machine, a combination of telescope, lie detector, scalpel and castrating device.'

'You're too cynical,' said my wife. 'You may fall in love yourself one day and then you'll know how it feels.'

'Not necessarily. As Shaw said –' Reeve was always quoting what other writers had said '–"Don't do unto others as you would have others do unto you, as we don't all have the same tastes." '

'We all have the same taste about not wanting to be ill-treated.'

'She should have thought of that before she tried to control my life. No, I shall quietly disappear for a while. I mightn't go away, in fact. I might just say I'm going away and lie low at home for a fortnight. Fill up the deep freeze, you know, and lay in a stock of liquor. I've done it before in this sort of situation. It's rather pleasant and I get a hell of a lot of work done.'

Gwendolen was silenced by this and, I must say, so was I. You may wonder, after these examples of his morality, just what it was I saw in Reeve. It's hard now for me to remember. Charm, perhaps, and a never-failing hospitality; a rueful way of talking about his own life as if it was all he could hope for, while mine was the ideal all men would aspire to; a helplessness about his financial affairs combined with an admiration for my grasp of them; a manner of talking to me as if we were equally men of the world, only I had chosen the better part. When invited to one of our dull modest gatherings, he would always be the exciting friend with the witty small talk, the reviver of a failing party, the industrious barman; above all, the one among our friends who wasn't an accountant, a bank manager, a solicitor, a general practitioner or a company executive. We had his books on our shelves. Our friends borrowed them and told their friends they'd met Reeve Baker at our house. He gave us a cachet that raised us enough centimetres above the level of the bourgeoisie to make us interesting.

Perhaps, in those days, I should have asked myself what it was he saw in us.

It was about a year ago that I first noticed a coolness between Gwendolen and Reeve. The banter they had gone in for, which had consisted in wry confessions or flirtatious compliments from him, and shy, somewhat maternal reproofs from her, stopped almost entirely. When we all three were together they talked to each other through me, as if I were their interpreter. I asked Gwendolen if he'd done something to upset her.

She looked extremely taken aback. 'What makes you ask?'

'You always seem a bit peeved with him.'

'I'm sorry,' she said. 'I'll try to be nicer. I didn't know I'd changed.' She had changed to me too. She flinched sometimes when I touched her, and although she never refused me, there was an apathy about her love-making.

'What's the matter?' I asked her after a failure which disturbed me because it was so unprecedented.

She said it was nothing, and then, 'We're getting older. You can't expect things to be the same as when we were first married.'

'For God's sake,' I said. 'You're thirty-five and I'm thirty-nine. We're not in our dotage.'

She sighed and looked unhappy. She had become moody and difficult. Although she hardly opened her mouth in Reeve's presence, she talked about him a lot when he wasn't there, seizing upon almost any excuse to discuss him and speculate about his character. And she seemed inexplicably annoyed when, on our tenth wedding anniversary, a greetings card arrived addressed to us both from him. I, of course, had sent her roses. At the end of the week I missed a receipt for a bill I'd paid – as an accountant I'm naturally circumspect about these things – and I searched through our wastepaper basket, thinking I might have thrown it away. I found it, and I also found the anniversary card I'd sent Gwendolen to accompany the roses.

All these things I noticed. That was the trouble with me – I noticed things but I lacked the experience of life to add them up and make a significant total. I didn't have the worldly wisdom to guess why my wife was always out when I phoned her in the afternoons, or why she was for ever buying new clothes. I noticed, I wondered, that was all.

I noticed things about Reeve too. For one thing, that he'd stopped talking about his girl friends.

'He's growing up at last,' I said to Gwendolen.

She reacted with warmth, with enthusiasm. 'I really think he is.'

But she was wrong. He had only three months of what I thought of as celibacy. And then when he talked of a new girl friend, it was to me alone. Confidentially, over a Friday-night drink in the pub, he told me of this 'marvellous chick', twenty years old, he had met at a party the week before.

'It won't last, Reeve,' I said.

'I sincerely hope not. Who wants it to *last*?'

Not Gwendolen, certainly. When I told her she was incredulous, then aghast. And when I said I was sorry I'd told her since Reeve's backsliding upset her so much, she snapped at me that she didn't want to discuss him. She became even more snappy and nervous and depressed too.

Whenever the phone rang she jumped. Once or twice I came home to find no wife, no dinner prepared; then she'd come in, looking haggard, to say she'd been out for a walk. I got her to see our doctor and he put her on tranquillizers which just made her more depressed.

I hadn't seen Reeve for ages. Then, out of the blue he phoned me at work to say he was off to the South of France for three weeks.

'In your state of financial health?' I said. I'd had a struggle getting him to pay the January instalment of his twice-yearly income tax, and I knew he was practically broke till he got the advance on his new book in May. 'The South of France is a bit pricey, isn't it?'

'I'll manage,' he said. 'My bank manager's one of my fans and he's let me have an overdraft.'

Gwendolen didn't seem very surprised to hear about Reeve's holiday. He'd told me he was going on his own – the 'marvellous chick' had long disappeared – and she said she thought he needed the rest, especially as there wouldn't be any of those girls to bother him, as she put it.

When I first met Reeve he'd been renting a flat but I persuaded him to buy one, for security and as an investment. The place was known euphemistically as a garden flat but it was in fact a basement, the lower ground floor of a big Victorian house in Bayswater. My usual route to work didn't take me along his street, but sometimes when the traffic was heavy I'd go through the back doubles and past his house. After he'd been away for about two weeks I happened to do this one morning and, of course, I glanced at Reeve's window. One always does glance at a friend's house, I think, when one is passing even if one knows that friend isn't at home. His bedroom was at the front, the top half of the window visible, the lower half concealed by the rise of lawn. I noticed that the curtains were drawn. Not particularly wise, I thought, an invitation to burglars, and then I forgot about it. But two mornings later I passed that way again, passed very slowly this time as there was a traffic hold-up, and again I glanced at Reeve's window. The curtains were no longer quite drawn. There was a gap about six inches wide between them. Now whatever a burglar may do, it's very unlikely he'll pull back drawn curtains. I didn't consider burglars this time. I thought Reeve must have come back early.

Telling myself I should be late for work anyway if I struggled along in this traffic jam, I parked the car as soon as I could at a meter. I'll knock on old Reeve's door, I thought, and get him to make me a cup of coffee. There was no answer. But as I looked once more at that window I was almost certain those curtains had been moved again, and in the past ten minutes. I rang the doorbell of the woman in the flat upstairs. She came down in her dressing gown.

'Sorry to disturb you,' I said. 'But do you happen to know if Mr Baker's come back?'

'He's not coming back till Saturday,' she said.

'Sure of that?'

'Of course I'm sure,' she said rather huffily. 'I put a note through his door Monday, and if he was back he'd have come straight up for this parcel I took in for him.'

'Did he take his car, d'you know?' I said, feeling like a detective in one of my favourite crime novels.

'Of course he did. What is this? What's he done?'

I said he'd done nothing, as far as I knew, and she banged the door in my face. So I went down the road to the row of lock-up garages. I couldn't see much through the little panes of frosted glass in the door of Reeve's garage, just enough to be certain the interior wasn't empty but that that greenish blur was the body of Reeve's Fiat. And then I knew for sure. He hadn't gone away at all. I chuckled to myself as I imagined him lying low for these three weeks in his flat, living off food from the deep freeze and spending most of his time in the back regions where, enclosed as those rooms were by a courtyard with high walls, he could show lights day and night with impunity. Just wait till Saturday, I thought, and I pictured myself asking him for details of his holiday, laying little traps for him, until even he with his writer's powers of invention would have to admit he'd never been away at all.

Gwendolen was laying the table for our evening meal when I got in. She, I'd decided, was the only person with whom I'd share this joke. I got all her attention the minute I mentioned Reeve's name, but when I reached the bit about his car being in the garage she stared at me and all the colour went out of her face. She sat down, letting the bunch of knives and forks she was holding fall into her lap.

'What on earth's the matter?' I said.

'How could he be so cruel? How could he do that to anyone?'

'Oh, my dear, Reeve's quite ruthless where women are concerned. You remember, he told us he'd done it before.'

'I'm going to phone him,' she said, and I saw that she was shivering. She dialled his number and I heard the ringing tone start.

'He won't answer,' I said. 'I wouldn't have told you if I'd thought it was going to upset you.'

She didn't say any more. There were things cooking on the stove and the table was half-laid, but she left all that and went into the hall. Almost immediately afterwards I heard the front door close.

I know I'm slow on the uptake in some ways but I'm not

stupid. Even a husband who trusts his wife like I trusted mine – or, rather, never considered there was any need for trust – would know, after that, that something had been going on. Nothing much, though, I told myself. A crush perhaps on her part, hero-worship which his flattery and his confidences had fanned. Naturally, she'd feel let down, betrayed, when she discovered he'd deceived her as to his whereabouts when he'd led her to believe she was a special friend and privy to all his secrets. But I went upstairs just the same to reassure myself by looking in that dressing table drawer where she kept her souvenirs. Dishonourable? I don't think so. She had never locked it or tried to keep its contents private from me.

And all those little mementoes of our first meeting, our courtship, our marriage, were still there. Between a birthday card and a Valentine I saw a pressed rose. But there too, alone in a nest made out of a lace handkerchief I had given her, were a locket and a button. The locket was one her mother had left to her, but the photograph in it, that of some long-dead unidentifiable relative, had been replaced by a cut-out of Reeve from a snapshot. On the reverse side was a lock of hair. The button I recognized as coming from Reeve's blazer, though it hadn't, I noticed, been cut off. He must have lost it in our house and she'd picked it up. The hair was Reeve's, black, wavy, here and there with a thread of grey, but again it hadn't been cut off. On one of our visits to his flat she must have combed it out of his hairbrush and twisted it into a lock. Poor little Gwendolen . . . Briefly, I'd suspected Reeve. For one dreadful moment, sitting down there after she'd gone out, I'd asked myself, could he have . . . ? Could my best friend have . . . ? But, no. He hadn't even sent her a letter or a flower. It had been all on her side, and for that reason – I knew where she was bound for – I must stop her reaching him and humiliating herself.

I slipped the things into my pocket with some vague idea of using them to show her how childish she was being. She hadn't taken her car. Gwendolen always disliked driving in central London. I took mine and drove to the tube station I knew she'd go to.

She came out a quarter of an hour after I got there, walking fast and glancing nervously to the right and left of her. When she saw me she gave a little gasp and stood stock-still.

'Get in, darling,' I said gently. 'I want to talk to you.'

She got in but she didn't speak. I drove down to the Bayswater Road and into the Park. There, on the Ring, I parked under the plane trees, and because she still didn't utter a word, I said:

'You mustn't think I don't understand. We've been married ten years and I daresay I'm a dull sort of chap. Reeve's exciting and different and – well, maybe it's only natural for you to think you've fallen for him.'

She stared at me stonily. 'I love him and he loves me.'

'That's nonsense,' I said, but it wasn't the chill of the spring evening that made me shiver. 'Just because he's used that charm of his on you . . .'

She interrupted me. 'I want a divorce.'

'For heaven's sake,' I said. 'You hardly know Reeve. You've never been alone with him, have you?'

'Never been alone with him?' She gave a brittle, desperate laugh. 'He's been my lover for six months. And now I'm going to him. I'm going to tell him he doesn't have to hide from women any more because I'll be with him all the time.'

In the half-dark I gaped at her. 'I don't believe you,' I said, but I did. I did. 'You mean you along with all the rest . . . ? My wife?'

'I'm going to be Reeve's wife. I'm the only one that understands him, the only one he can talk to. He told me that just before – before he went away.'

'Only he didn't go away.' There was a great redness in front of my eyes like a lake of blood. 'You fool,' I shouted at her. 'Don't you see it's you he's hiding from, *you*? He's done this to get away from you like he's got away from all the others. Love you? He never even gave you a present, not even a photograph. If you go there, he won't let you in. You're the last person he'd let in.'

'I'm going to him,' she cried, and she began to struggle with the car door. 'I'm going to him, to live with him, and I never want to see you again!'

In the end I drove home alone. Her wish came true and she never did see me again.

When she wasn't back by eleven I called the police. They asked me to go down to the police station and fill out a Missing Persons form, but they didn't take my fear very seriously. Apparently, when a woman of Gwendolen's age disappears they take it for granted she's gone off with a man. They took it seriously all right when a park keeper found her strangled body among some bushes in the morning.

That was on the Thursday. The police wanted to know where Gwendolen could have been going so far from her home. They wanted the names and addresses of all our friends. Was there anyone we knew in Kensington or Paddington or Bayswater, anywhere in the vicinity of the Park? I said there was no one. The next day they asked me again and I said, as if I'd just remembered:

'Only Reeve Baker. The novelist, you know.' I gave them his address. 'But he's away on holiday, has been for three weeks. He's not coming home till tomorrow.'

What happened after that I know from the evidence given at Reeve's trial, his trial for the murder of my wife. The police called on him on Saturday morning. I don't think they suspected him at all at first. My reading of crime fiction has taught me they would have asked him for any information he could give about our private life.

Unfortunately for him, they had already talked to some of his neighbours. Reeve had led all these people to think he had really gone away. The milkman and the paper boy were both certain he had been away. So when the police questioned him about that, and he knew just why they were questioning him, he got into a panic. He didn't dare say he'd been in France. They could have shown that to be false without the least trouble. Instead, he told the truth and said he'd been lying low to escape the attentions of a woman. Which woman? He wouldn't say, but the woman in the flat upstairs would. Time and time again she had seen Gwendolen visit him in the afternoons, had heard them quarrelling, Gwendolen protesting her love for him and he shouting that he wouldn't be controlled, that he'd do anything to escape her possessiveness.

He had, of course, no alibi for the Wednesday night. But the judge and the jury could see he'd done his best to arrange one. Novelists are apt to let their imaginations run away with them; they don't realize how astute and thorough the police are. And there was firmer evidence of his guilt even than that. Three main exhibits were produced in the court: Reeve's blazer with a button missing from the sleeve; that very button; a cluster of his hairs. The button had been found by Gwendolen's body and the hairs on her coat . . .

My reading of detective stories hadn't been in vain, though I haven't read one since then. People don't, I suppose, after a thing like that.

H.R.F. KEATING

INSPECTOR GHOTE AND THE MIRACLE BABY

WHAT HAS SANTA Claus got in store for me, Inspector Ghote said to himself, bleakly echoing the current cheerful Bombay newspaper advertisements, as he waited to enter the office of Deputy Superintendent Naik that morning of December 25th.

Whatever the DSP had lined up for him, Ghote knew it was going to be nasty. Ever since he had recently declined to turn up for 'voluntary' hockey, DSP Naik had viewed him with sad-eyed disapproval. But what exact form would his displeasure take?

Almost certainly it would have something to do with the big Navy Week parade that afternoon, the chief preoccupation at the moment of most of the ever-excitable and drama-loving Bombayites. Probably he would be ordered out into the crowds watching the Fire Power demonstration in the bay, ordered to come back with a beltful of pickpocketing arrests.

'Come,' the DSP's voice barked out.

Ghote went in and stood squaring his bony shoulders in front of the papers-strewn desk.

'Ah, Ghote, yes. Tulsi Pipe Road for you. Up at the north end. Going to be big trouble there. Rioting. Intercommunity outrages even.'

Ghote's heart sank even deeper than he had expected. Tulsi Pipe Road was a two-kilometres-long thoroughfare that shot straight up from the racecourse into the heart of a densely crowded mill district where badly paid Hindus, Muslims in hundreds and Goans by the thousand, all lived in prickling closeness, either in great areas of tumbledown hutments or in high tottering chawls, floor upon floor of massed humanity. Trouble between the religious communities there meant hell, no less.

'Yes, DSP?' he said, striving not to sound appalled.

'We are having a virgin birth business, Inspector.'

'Virgin birth, DSP sahib?'

'Come, man, you must have come across such cases.'

'I am sorry, DSP,' Ghote said, feeling obliged to be true to hard-won scientific principles. 'I am unable to believe in virgin birth.'

The DSP's round face suffused with instant wrath.

'Of course I am not asking you to believe in virgin birth, man! It is not you who are to believe: it is all those Christians in the Goan community who are believing it about a baby born two days ago. It is the time of year, of course. These affairs are always coming at Christmas. I have dealt with half a dozen in my day.'

'Yes, DSP,' Ghote said, contriving to hit on the right note of awe.

'Yes. And there is only one way to deal with it. Get hold of the girl and find out the name of the man. Do that pretty damn quick and the whole affair drops away to nothing, like monsoon water down a drain.'

'Yes, DSP.'

'Well, what are you waiting for man? Hop it!'

'Name and address of the girl in question, DSP sahib.'

The DSP's face darkened once more. He padded furiously over the jumble of papers on his desk top. And at last he found the chit he wanted.

'There you are, man. And also you will find there the

name of the Head Constable who first reported the matter. See him straightaway. You have got a good man there, active, quick on his feet, sharp. If he could not make that girl talk, you will be having a first-class damn job, Inspector.'

Ghote located Head Constable Mudholkar one hour later at the local chowkey where he was stationed. The Head Constable confirmed at once the blossoming dislike for a sharp bully that Ghote had been harbouring ever since DSP Naik had praised the fellow. And, what was worse, the chap turned out to be very like the DSP in looks as well. He had the same round type of face, the same puffy-looking lips, even a similar soft blur of moustache. But the Head Constable's appearance was nevertheless a travesty of the DSP's. His face was, simply, slewed.

To Ghote's prejudiced eyes, at the first moment of their encounter, the man's features seemed grotesquely distorted, as if in some distant time some god had taken one of the Head Constable's ancestors and had wrenched his whole head sideways between two omnipotent god-hands.

But, as the fellow supplied him with the details of the affair, Ghote forced himself to regard him with an open mind, and he then had to admit that the facial twist which had seemed so pronounced was in fact no more than a drooping corner of the mouth and of one ear being oddly longer than the other.

Ghote had to admit, too, that the chap was efficient. He had all the circumstances of the affair at his fingertips. The girl, named D'Mello, now in a hospital for her own safety, had been rigorously questioned both before and after the birth, but she had steadfastly denied that she had ever been with any man. She was indeed not the sort, the sole daughter of a Goan railway waiter on the Madras Express, a quiet girl, well brought up though her parents were poor enough;

she attended Mass regularly with her mother, and the whole family kept themselves to themselves.

'But with those Christians you can never tell,' Head Constable Mudholkar concluded.

Ghote felt inwardly inclined to agree. Fervid religion had always made him shrink inwardly, whether it was a Hindu holy man spending twenty years silent and standing upright or whether it was the Catholics, always caressing lifeless statues in their churches till glass protection had to be installed, and even then they still stroked the thick panes. Either manifestation rendered him uneasy.

That was the real reason, he now acknowledged to himself, why he did not want to go and see Miss D'Mello in the hospital, where she would be surrounded by nuns amid all the trappings of an alien religion, surrounded with all the panoply of a newly found goddess.

Yet go and see the girl he must.

But first he permitted himself to do every other thing that might possibly be necessary to the case. He visited Mrs D'Mello, and by dint of patient wheedling, and a little forced toughness, confirmed from her the names of the only two men that Head Constable Mudholkar – who certainly proved to know inside-out the particular chawl where the D'Mellos lived – had suggested as possible fathers. They were both young men – a Goan, Charlie Lobo, and a Sikh, Kuldip Singh.

The Lobo family lived one floor below the D'Mellos. But that one flight of dirt-spattered stairs, bringing them just that much nearer the courtyard tap that served the whole crazily leaning chawl, represented a whole layer higher in social status. And Mrs Lobo, a huge, tightly fat woman in a brightly flowered western-style dress, had decided views about the unexpected fame that had come to the people upstairs.

'Has my Charlie been going with that girl?' she repeated after Ghote had managed to put the question, suitably wrapped up, to the boy. 'No, he has not. Charlie, tell the man you hate and despise trash like that.'

'Oh, Mum,' said Charlie, a teenage wisp of a figure suffocating in a necktie beside his balloon-hard mother.

'Tell the man, Charlie.'

And obediently Charlie muttered something that satisfied his passion-filled parent. Ghote put a few more questions for form's sake, but he realized that only by getting hold of the boy on his own was he going to get any worthwhile answers. Yet it turned out that he did not have to employ any cunning. Charlie proved to have a strain of sharp slyness of his own, and hardly had Ghote climbed the stairs to the floor above the D'Mellos where Kuldip Singh lived when he heard a whispered call from the shadow-filled darkness below.

'Mum's got her head over the stove,' Charlie said. 'She don't know I slipped out.'

'There is something you have to tell me?' Ghote said, acting the indulgent uncle. 'You are in trouble – that's it, isn't it?'

'My only trouble is Mum,' the boy replied. 'Listen, mister, I had to tell you. I love Miss D'Mello – yes, I love her. She's the most wonderful girl ever was.'

'And you want to marry her, and because you went too far before –'

'No, no, no. She's far and away too good for me. Mister, I've never even said "Good morning" to her in the two years we've lived here. But I love her, mister, and I'm not going to have Mum make me say different.'

Watching him slip cunningly back home, Ghote made his mental notes and then turned to tackle Kuldip Singh, his last comparatively easy task before the looming interview at the nun-ridden hospital he knew he must have.

Kuldip Singh, as Ghote had heard from Head Constable Mudholkar, was different from his neighbours. He lived in this teeming area from choice not necessity. Officially a student, he spent all his time in a series of antisocial activities – protesting, writing manifestoes, drinking. He seemed an ideal candidate for the unknown and elusive father.

Ghote's suspicions were at once heightened when the young Sikh opened his door. The boy, though old enough to have a beard, lacked this status symbol. Equally he had discarded the obligatory turban of his religion. But all the Sikh bounce was there, as Ghote discovered when he identified himself.

'Policewallah, is it? Then I want nothing at all to do with you. Me and the police are enemies, bhai. Natural enemies.'

'Irrespective of such considerations,' Ghote said stiffly, 'it is my duty to put to you certain questions concerning one Miss D'Mello.'

The young Sikh burst into a roar of laughter.

'The miracle girl, is it?' he said. 'Plenty of trouble for policemen there, I promise you. Top-level rioting coming from that business. The fellow who fathered that baby did us a lot of good.'

Ghote plugged away a good while longer – the hospital nuns awaited – but for all his efforts he learned no more than he had in that first brief exchange. And in the end he still had to go and meet his doom.

Just what he had expected at the hospital he never quite formulated to himself. What he did find was certainly almost the exact opposite of his fears. A calm reigned. White-habited nuns, mostly Indian but with a few Europeans, flitted silently to and fro or talked quietly to the patients whom Ghote glimpsed lying on beds in long wards. Above them swung frail but bright paper chains in honour of the feast day, and these were all the excitement there was.

The small separate ward in which Miss D'Mello lay in a broad bed all alone was no different. Except that the girl was isolated, she seemed to be treated in just the same way as the other new mothers in the big maternity ward that Ghote had been led through on his way in. In the face of such matter-of-factness he felt hollowly cheated.

Suddenly, too, to his own utter surprise he found, looking down at the big calm-after-storm eyes of the Goan girl, that he wanted the story she was about to tell him to be true. Part of him knew that, if it were so, or if it was widely believed to be so, appalling disorders could result from the feverish religious excitement that was bound to mount day by day. But another part of him now simply wanted a miracle to have happened.

He began, quietly and almost diffidently, to put his questions. Miss D'Mello would hardly answer at all, but such syllables as she did whisper were of blank inability to name anyone as the father of her child. After a while Ghote brought himself, with a distinct effort of will, to change his tactics. He banged out the hard line. Miss D'Mello went quietly and totally mute.

Then Ghote slipped in, with adroit suddenness, the name of Charlie Lobo. He got only a small puzzled frown.

Then, in an effort to make sure that her silence was not a silence of fear, he presented, with equal suddenness, the name of Kuldip Singh. If the care-for-nothing young Sikh had forced this timid creature, this might be the way to get an admission. But instead there came something approaching a laugh.

'That Kuldip is a funny fellow,' the girl said, with an out-of-place and unexpected offhandedness.

Ghote almost gave up. But at that moment a nun nurse appeared carrying in her arms a small, long, white-wrapped, minutely crying bundle – the baby.

While she handed the hungry scrap to its mother Ghote stood and watched. Perhaps holding the child she would –?

He looked down at the scene on the broad bed, awaiting his moment again. The girl fiercely held the tiny agitated thing to her breast and in a moment or two quiet came, the tiny head applied to the life-giving nipple. How human the child looked already, Ghote thought. How much a man at two days old. The round skull, almost bald, as it might become again toward the end of its span. The frown on the forehead that would last a lifetime, the tiny, perfectly formed, plainly asymmetrical ears –

And then Ghote knew that there had not been any miracle. It was as he had surmised, but with different circumstances. Miss D'Mello was indeed too frightened to talk. No wonder, when the local bully, Head Constable Mudholkar with his slewed head and its one ear so characteristically longer than the other, was the man who had forced himself on her.

A deep smothering of disappointment floated down on Ghote. So it had been nothing miraculous after all. Just a sad case, to be cleared up painfully. He stared down at the bed.

The tiny boy suckled energetically. And with a topsy-turvy welling up of rose-pink pleasure, Ghote saw that there had after all been a miracle, The daily, hourly, every-minute miracle of a new life, of a new flicker of hope in the tired world.

GEORGES SIMENON

MADEMOISELLE BERTHE AND HER LOVER

I

'MONSIEUR LE COMMISSAIRE,

'I am fully conscious of my boldness in disturbing you in your retirement, the more so since I have heard speak of your charming home on the banks of the Loire.

'But surely you will forgive me when I tell you that it's a matter of life or death for me. I live alone, in the heart of Paris, surrounded by its busy crowds. I go about my business like any other girl, and yet at any moment disaster may strike; maybe a bullet fired from heaven knows where, or a stab in the back? The crowd will see me fall; my body will be carried into some pharmacy before being taken to the morgue. The incident will only rate a few lines in the newspaper, should it deserve mention at all.

'And yet, Monsieur le Commissaire, I want to live, don't you understand? I am young and strong, I long to taste all the joys of life!

'You will no doubt be surprised to receive this letter in your country retreat, the address of which is not easily procured. Let me tell you, then, that I am the niece of a man who for a long time was your colleague in the Police Judiciaire, and who died by your side shortly before your retirement.

'I implore you, Superintendent, answer my call for help:

give up a few days or a few hours for me! Listen to the heartfelt plea of a girl who appeals to you because she does not want to die.

'At 10 a.m. on Tuesday and Wednesday I shall be on the terrace of the Café de Madrid. I shall be wearing a small red hat. In any case, if you come I shall recognize you, since I have a photograph of you with my uncle.

'S.O.S.!... S.O.S.!... S.O.S.!...'

Maigret was furious. For one thing, because his first reaction, whenever he had allowed his feelings to be stirred, was always one of self-critical anger. For another, because he had irrationally chosen not to mention the letter to his wife, and he was slightly ashamed of having invented a pretext for coming to Paris. Thirdly, because the way he had hurried to keep this appointment was a proof that he was less happy in his garden retreat than he tried to make out, and that like any beginner he had become thoughtlessly involved in the first mystery that had cropped up.

And finally, as so often happens in life, there was a material reason for his anger, a trivial and ridiculous one. When he left Meung-sur-Loire at seven that morning there had been an icy fog hanging over the valley, and Maigret had put on his heavy winter overcoat.

Now, as he was sitting on the terrace of the Café de Madrid, the Grands Boulevards were bathed in bright spring sunshine, and lightly clad figures were strolling past.

'In the first place,' he reflected, 'that letter smacks too much of literature. As for the colleague killed at my side shortly before my retirement it can only have been Sergeant Lucas, and he never mentioned any niece...'

The terrace was deserted. He was sitting all alone at a small table, and, not knowing what to drink, since he had him ridiculous, tapped on the table with a coin, and he noticed as they left the terrace that the young man in the fawn coat was also summoning the waiter.

It was no. 67b, not far from the Place Constantin-Pecqueur, between a bakery and an Auvergnat's bar. A typical Montmartre house, with the porter's lodge next to the front door, a worn reddish stair-carpet, walls of yellowish imitation marble and two doors with brass knobs on each landing.

'I'm very sorry to make you climb so high . . . It's right at the top, sixth floor, and there's no lift . . .'

Once on the doormat, she drew a key from her bag, and almost at once a magical sight was revealed. Spring in the Grands Boulevards was pale and insipid compared with the spring that one beheld from this dwelling perched high above the roofs of Paris. Down below, the Rue Caulaincourt was like a dark river along which buses and lorries drifted by, and one felt sorry for the people whose lives went on so far from the air and sunlight.

A french window was open on to a long iron balcony. All along this balcony geraniums were glowing red in the sunlight, and a canary was hopping about in a cage that still contained a little of its morning birdseed.

'Take off your coat, Superintendent . . . Do you mind if I just go and tidy myself up? I dressed in such a hurry, wondering if you would come . . .'

All the doors were standing open, and the whole of the flat was visible. It consisted of three rooms, prettily furnished and meticulously clean, their cheerfulness enhanced by piles of brightly coloured dress materials. Mademoiselle Berthe, who had taken off her jacket, now appeared wearing a close-fitting yellow blouse patterned with tiny flowers.

'Let me take your coat . . . Do sit down . . . I'm all in a

muddle . . . I'm so happy, you see! I feel that the nightmare's over . . .'

And indeed she was looking radiant. Her eyes were glistening; her full rosy lips were parted in a smile.

'You shall understand . . . I don't know where to start, but that doesn't matter, does it? for you're used to such things . . . When you saw this room with my sewing machine and all these bits of stuff you must have guessed that I'm a dressmaker . . . I'm even going to confess something else: I chiefly make dresses which my customers, who are all very nice ladies, ask me to copy from patterns which they bring me and which come from leading fashion houses. You won't give me away?'

She was so overflowing with life that she gave one no time to think, barely time to watch her changing facial expression. And Maigret once again felt somewhat embarrassed at being there, in that atmosphere of femininity and youthfulness, like a respectable married man on the loose.

'Now I've got a more serious confession to make . . . I'm ashamed, but it's got to be done . . . I could never have told my uncle Lucas . . . You see, Superintendent, I'm not a virtuous young person . . . I've got a boy friend, or rather I did have one . . . And it's precisely on his account . . .'

Maigret's embarrassment turned to confusion. Had he been fool enough to believe for one moment that something serious was involved, whereas this was just a case of a romantic girl being threatened by her boy friend in the hope of getting her to come back to him?

She chattered on: 'I met him last summer at Saint-Malo, where I was on holiday. He's a young man of good family, the son of an industrialist who had gone bankrupt. He'd always led the pampered life of a rich boy and then suddenly, at twenty-three, he had to earn his living . . .'

'What does he do?' Maigret asked sceptically.

'At Saint-Malo he was selling cars for a big garage . . . Or rather he was trying to sell them, for things weren't going too well . . . And Albert, that's his name, hates pestering people. Soon after I got back to Paris he came here too and looked for a job . . .'

'Excuse me! Did he live here?'

And Maigret cast a glance towards the open door of the bedroom, where he could see a wardrobe with a mirror and a carefully polished parquet floor.

'No . . .' she said. 'I didn't want him to . . . He had a small room in a hotel in the Rue Lepic. He often came here, but only in the daytime . . .'

'He was your lover?'

She reddened and nodded, then she got up to offer Maigret a glass of wine.

'I've only got some sweet white Bordeaux . . . I don't even know where I've put it . . . My life's in such confusion . . . Listen! I'll be brief, if I may, for I feel I'm going to get all worked up again . . . I found out I'd been wrong about Albert. I soon realized that he wasn't seriously looking for a job and that he spent most of his time in disreputable bars . . . I've several times seen him shaking hands with some very shady-looking characters . . . You see what I mean? . . .'

She was walking backwards and forwards. Her voice grew muffled; tears were clearly not far away.

'A week ago there was that business . . . you may have read about it in the papers but you probably didn't pay much attention to it . . . Four young men robbed a radio dealer's shop in the Boulevard Beaumarchais. They weren't after the stock, which was too unwieldy, but the money, which they'd somehow discovered was in the safe. They took away sixty thousand francs. As they were making off they were seen by the police. One of the youths fired a shot which killed a policeman.'

Maigret had suddenly regained his self-possession, and his figure seemed to have become more substantial, his gaze firmer. Automatically, he lit his pipe, which hitherto he had not ventured to take from his pocket.

'And then?' he said in a tone which was as yet unfamiliar to Mademoiselle Berthe.

'Two of the thieves were arrested . . . two men well known to the police, one who's heavily pock-marked, the other who's known as the Marseillais . . . They were young fellows, practically beginners, and their headquarters is near the Place Blanche, where Albert often went . . .'

'Who fired the shot?' asked Maigret, staring through tobacco smoke at the canary.

'It's not known . . . Or rather, the gun was found on the pavement and it was Albert's . . . It was easy to recognize as he'd borrowed it from his father, whose name was on it. The father came forward when he read about it in the papers. He was questioned at Police Headquarters . . .'

'And Albert?'

'They're looking for him . . . You know better than I do how these things are done. I suppose they've sent out his description. And that's why . . .'

She wiped her eyes and went over to stand for a moment at the balcony, with her back to Maigret, who saw her shoulders shaken by a sob.

When she turned round again she was pale and tense-featured.

'I could have gone to the police and told them the truth, but I was afraid to . . . I trust you, Monsieur Maigret, because I know you won't betray me . . . Look at this!'

She raised the lid of a soup tureen of imitation Rouen

pottery standing on the sideboard, and took out a letter which she showed Maigret. It was written in violet ink in an irregular hand:

> Dear Berthe,
>
> As you'll see from this letter I'm at Calais, and I've got to get across the frontier as quickly as possible. But I'm determined not to leave without you. So I shall expect you. All you've got to do is put an ad. in the *Intransigeant* saying: 'Albert, such and such a day, such and such a time,' and I'll be at Calais station. I'd better warn you right away that if you were to show this letter to a nark I'll have my revenge. What I've done has been for your sake. So you know where your duty lies.
>
> I hold you responsible for whatever may happen to me. I warn you, moreover, that sooner than go off alone I shall prevent you from ever belonging to someone else.
>
> Understand this if you can.
>
> Your Albert

'Why didn't you go to Calais?' Maigret asked with seeming innocence.

'Because I don't want to be the wife or mistress of a murderer. I thought I loved Albert. I took him for a decent boy who was down on his luck. I helped him as much as I could.'

Her lower lip was quivering. Tears were imminent.

'Now I know that all he wanted, all he still wants is my money. For he's well aware that I've got some put by, over fifteen thousand francs in the Savings Bank!'

She burst into tears:

'He's never loved me, you see! And I'm so unhappy! I'm

frightened! I don't want to go there . . . The thought that he . . . that he . . .'

Maigret got up awkwardly and patted Berthe's shoulder as she sat weeping with her elbows on the table and her face buried in her hands. She quickly pulled herself together.

'Somebody from the police came to question me . . . They very nearly took me off as an accomplice. I didn't tell them about the letter, because I was sure that would have meant trouble for me . . . But I'm frightened! I'm sure he'll come back and do me some harm! . . . Once when the cat was rubbing against his legs he picked it up so roughly that the poor thing has been lame ever since . . . I'd have done anything for him . . . If you had seen him you'd have believed, as I did, that he was . . .'

'And you really don't know the young man who was sitting near us at the Café de Madrid?' interrupted Maigret.

'I swear I don't!'

'That's odd . . .'

'Why?'

He had gone on to the balcony, from which he could see out over the Place Constantin-Pecqueur. And there, just at the corner of the Rue Caulaincourt, he saw the familiar fawn-coloured raincoat pacing up and down.

'I don't know . . . just an idea . . .'

'What's in your mind? . . . Tell me! . . . Reassure me! . . . Promise me, Superintendent, that you're going to protect me . . . I've got to know where Albert is . . . If only I was sure that he'd crossed the frontier! . . .'

'What would you do?' he growled.

'I should breathe more freely. Otherwise I'm sure he'll kill me, as he . . .'

His present surroundings seemed to Maigret an epitome of the humble workaday life of Montmartre, with its delight in simple things. On a kitchen table he saw the cutlet which was to provide the girl's lunch and a carton of *céleri rémoulade* from a dairy shop, together with a cream cheese in a blue earthenware dish.

Beside the sewing machine was a half-made dress, an evening dress of organdie dotted with spring flowers. In a china cup there were pins and buttons, a pencil, some tailor's chalk and a few stamps.

And this modest existence was brightened by the sunlight streaming in from the balcony that overlooked the city.

Mademoiselle Berthe was sniffling, unashamedly showing a reddened nose and tear-smeared cheeks.

'I know I'm a blunderer, I say things too straightforwardly, just as they occur to me . . . All the same, unless you help me, I'm sure, I tell you, that one of these days you'll come and identify my body at the morgue . . . He's my first lover, Superintendent . . . There had never been anyone else before, believe it or not . . . I wanted to get married and have children . . . Specially to have children! And now . . .'

'I'll see what I can do, my dear,' Maigret promised somewhat haltingly, for he hated emotional effusions.

But even before he had finished speaking she seized his hand and kissed it.

'Thank you, Superintendent! But tell me one thing more . . . I'm not a monster, am I? I did love him, it's true . . . But what I loved was the decent boy I took him for . . . I'm not betraying him deliberately . . . The proof of that is that I've said nothing to the police . . . It's different with you . . . I appealed to you to protect me, because I'm afraid, because I'm too young to die . . .'

He had moved away from her again and was standing on the balcony with his back to her, his head haloed by tobacco smoke.

'What shall you do?' she went on. 'Of course I'll stand the expenses. I'm not rich, but I told you I had a little money . . .'

'Isn't that a hotel over the way?'

'Yes, the Hôtel de Concarneau . . .'

'Well, I shall probably go and take a room there . . . One piece of advice: don't go out any more than you can help.'

'I won't go out at all if you like except to buy food . . .'

'Can't you get the concierge to do that?'

'I'll ask her . . .'

'I shall come back and see you this evening . . . A pity you don't know that young man . . .'

'Which young man?'

'The one who followed you to the Café de Madrid and who's keeping watch at the corner of the pavement.'

'Unless . . .' she began, her eyes widening.

'Unless?'

'Unless he's an accomplice of Albert's . . . Suppose, instead of coming himself, he's got one of his friends to . . .'

'I'll see you later!' growled Maigret, making for the door.

He was not satisfied. He did not know why. On the landing he picked a piece of white cotton off his sleeve. And as he went down the six floors he was wondering what he should do.

On seeing him, the young man in the raincoat dived into a bistro at the corner of the square, and Maigret followed him, ordered a large glass of beer, made sure the phone booth was in the bar-room itself and went into it, deliberately leaving the door ajar.

'Hello! . . . P.J.? Get me Inspector Lacroix, please . . . Yes, Jérôme Lacroix. It's his uncle Maigret . . . Hello! That you, son? How are things? What's that? Well, can't be helped, it'll have to wait . . . Jump into a taxi and come to see me here in the Rue Caulaincourt . . . Wait a minute.'

He leaned out of the phone booth and asked the *patron*:

'What's your place called?'

'The Zanzi-Bar.'

Maigret spoke into the phone once more: 'At the Zanzi-Bar . . . Yes . . . I'll be expecting you . . . No, no, your aunt's as fit as a fiddle . . . So'm I . . . See you soon . . .'

As he returned to the bar counter he thought he noticed an ironic flicker in the grey eyes of the young man, who was wearing a light-coloured suit, two-toned shoes and a snakeskin belt.

'Like a game of poker-dice?' he asked the *patron*.

'No time . . .'

'What about you, monsieur? Play you at poker-dice for the next drink?'

Maigret hesitated, and finally picked up the dice-box with a gesture as menacing as though he had already slipped the handcuffs on to the young man's wrists.

II

'Three kings at a throw!' the young rascal announced, adding, after a glance at the Superintendent who was picking up the dice:

'Your throw, Monsieur Maigret!'

Maigret threw two nines and a ten, then queried as he made a second throw: 'You know me?'

'We all know the cops!' the other retorted smoothly. 'Three jacks! You're staying in? What's your drink? You can't have been offered much up there, apart from that sweet wine that tastes like gooseberry syrup.'

On such occasions there is only one thing to do: to keep calm and not betray one's irritation. Maigret went on smoking his pipe in brief puffs, and picked up a second match, for his opponent, with angelic suavity, had just turned up three queens.

'You really don't remember me? After grilling me that night from nine o'clock till five in the morning!'

He was jauntier than ever. He was a good-looking scamp and he knew it. Above all, he had such a candid smile when he chose that it was difficult to be angry with him.

'Something to do with dope . . . You're not there yet? It was a few years back . . . I was a messenger at the Célis in the Rue Pigalle, and you were set on getting me to talk . . . Three kings in two throws! That's better. Good! Two nines . . . Pass me a match.'

And after ordering an apéritif with the same nonchalant and good-humoured air, he attacked:

'Well, what d'you make of my little sister?'

The bistro was practically empty, save for one drunk who was obstinately playing with the fruit machine, and the *patron* took advantage of this to fill up his carafes with the dregs of his bottles.

'You surely cottoned on from the start, didn't you?'

It was over four years since Maigret had heard the familiar accent of the underworld, and he almost broke into a smile, like an exile meeting a compatriot.

'With all due respect, between you and me, I hope you didn't let yourself be taken in?'

Softly, softly! To gain time Maigret could always drink a mouthful of beer, or knock out his pipe and fill another.

'I knew she'd be at it again one of these days. You can always tell when that sort of attack is coming on. But I'd not have expected her to bother a big shot like yourself . . . Careful, Monsieur Maigret! You're taking a queen for a jack . . . Four jacks! You're staying in?'

He shook the dice.

'Four kings! You're not in luck, are you? As for little sister, it's not her fault if she's a bit crazy . . . When she was only a kid she was a bit odd, used to walk in her sleep.'

And, glancing at the door, he exclaimed:

'Why, here comes your mate . . . Better perhaps leave you two alone together.'

He drew back to let in Jérôme Lacroix, who had just alighted from a taxi. The two men stared at one another, the young rascal still wearing his engaging smile and the policeman from the Quai des Orfèvres with a puzzled frown.

'Morning, Uncle . . . What's that fellow doing here?'

'Who is he?'

'Louis the Kid . . . You must have known him when he was a pageboy in the Montmartre nightclubs . . . He thinks he's a joker, but I'm going to get him one of these days . . .'

Jérôme Lacroix, whom Maigret had brought into the Police Judiciaire, was a big bony fellow with thick hair and a stubborn expression. He had a long nose, small eyes, huge hands and feet, and he gave the impression of being morose, obstinate, ready to let himself be cut in pieces rather than fail in his duty in the least degree.

'Come and sit over here, son!' said Maigret, choosing a table from which he could see no. 67b. 'Do you know his sister?'

'Whose? Louis the Kid's? Actually I called on her just lately.'

The news did not please Maigret, but he showed no reaction.

'You do mean Mademoiselle Berthe, don't you?'

'Yes. A dressmaker who lives over the way . . . Is my aunt quite well?'

'You asked me that over the telephone.'

'So I did . . . I'm sorry . . .'

'What d'you know about this Mademoiselle Berthe?'

And Maigret observed with some satisfaction that his nephew was somewhat at a loss to reply.

'She's a dressmaker.'

'So you've just told me.'

'She's the mistress of a man called Albert Marcinelle, who's wanted for the murder of a policeman in the Boulevard Beaumarchais.'

'Anything more?'

'Well, that's all I managed to get out of her. Her place seems well kept. Her concierge speaks highly of her. Apart from that Albert she never has a man to visit her, not even her brother, whom she's thrown out once and for all... But... By the way... That's not what brings you to Paris?'

'It is.'

Jérôme, surprised, stared thoughtfully at his glass. He could not understand what interest such a case could have for his uncle, who had repeatedly refused to get involved in more serious affairs.

'You know... In my opinion... We shall pick him up one of these days and that'll be the end of it... A lowdown little scoundrel who's not worth bothering about. We've sent out his description everywhere, and I'd be most surprised if...'

'You ought to put an advertisement in the *Intransigeant*.'

Jérôme was becoming increasingly puzzled.

'To try and find him?'

'Make a note of the wording: "Albert Wednesday 3.17 p.m." Arrange to have a policeman at Calais station at that time. If our Albert turns up...'

'Is that all?'

'That's all.'

'D'you think he'll be there?'

'I bet you ten to one he won't.'

‘So what then?’

‘So nothing! Kiss your wife and son for me . . . By the way, if anything new turns up, give me a call at the Hôtel de Concarneau, will you? It’s three houses further on . . .’

‘Goodbye, Uncle.’

As Maigret paid for the drinks, he was already looking sprightlier than he had been earlier that morning, for he felt things had begun to move.

Roughly speaking, his impression was that the police were over-simplifying the situation and Mademoiselle Berthe was complicating it. Not far off there was a small restaurant favoured by taxi-drivers, with a couple of tables on the terrace, and as one of them was free he sat down and discovered on the menu *fricandeau à l’oseille*, veal with sorrel, one of his favourite dishes.

The atmosphere was so redolent of spring, with light puffs of air so warm and fragrant that, particularly after a bottle of Beaujolais, he felt light-headed and wanted nothing better than to lie down on the grass with a newspaper over his head.

By two o’clock he was at the Hôtel de Concarneau and, not without some difficulty, secured a room on the sixth floor front, exactly opposite Mademoiselle Berthe’s balcony.

When he went up to the window he almost blushed, for the girl was busy trying a dress on a customer whose figure, more than partially undressed, could be made out in the bluish darkness of the room.

He asked himself repeatedly if she was doing this on purpose, and even if she might not have caught sight of him in his room. But the warmth of the day was enough to account for her open window.

Maigret practically never took his eyes off her, and he saw nothing in her behaviour which was not absolutely natural.

When the first customer's fitting was over she set to work on a blue dress, patiently removing pins from between her lips one by one, kneeling for a long while in front of a tailor's dummy covered with black cloth. Then she poured herself a glass of water, did some stitching on her machine, raised her head when she heard a knock on the door and let in a second customer, who was bringing her some dress material. From Maigret's observation post it was almost possible to guess the words spoken from the movements of the women's lips, and he realized that they were arguing about prices and that the customer had to give way in the end.

Not until four o'clock or thereabouts did Maigret think of letting his wife know that he would not be home that night nor, possibly, for the next few days, and he rang for the chambermaid to hand her a telegram and at the same time to order a bottle of beer, since the Brie with which he had followed up his *fricandeau* had made him thirsty.

'Either that girl's very astute,' he muttered to himself, chewing the stem of his pipe, 'or else ...'

Or else what? Why had he got involved in this business? Why had he not gone home by the eleven o'clock train as, at one point, he had thought of doing?

'Let's assume that she's speaking the truth, as seems plausible.'

If that were the case, what was he to do? Act guardian angel, like those American private detectives who are hired to follow nurses and children to protect them from gangsters?

It might go on for a long time. Albert seemed in no hurry to return to Paris to kill his mistress, and Maigret suddenly realized that he did not even know the man by sight.

And suppose it were not true? What had made her appeal to him? Why had she lured him out of his quiet country home into this drab corner of Paris?

He left his heavy overcoat in his room and went down. He stopped to ask the concierge at no. 67b if Mademoiselle Berthe was in.

'She is . . . As it happens I'm just going out to do her shopping for her, as she's got too much work . . . Would you be kind enough to take up this letter for her, while you're about it?'

He recognized Albert's writing and saw the stamp, postmarked Boulogne.

'So there!' he muttered as he climbed the stairs, in answer to an objection he had raised to himself.

He knocked. He was kept waiting for a moment on the landing and, when she opened the door to him, he had to go into the kitchen, since there was still a customer being fitted. The kitchen was as spotless as the rest of the flat. In one corner there was an opened bottle of white Bordeaux and a dirty plate. He overheard:

'A little tighter at the waist . . . Yes, like that . . . It's younger looking . . . When can you let me have it?'

'By next Monday . . .'

'You can't manage sooner?'

'With the best will in the world, no . . . At this time of year everybody's in a hurry.'

Then Mademoiselle Berthe released him, with a sad smile.

'You see how it is!' she said. 'I do my utmost to look cheerful. Life has to go on, in spite of everything. But if you knew how scared I am! or rather how scared I was, because now that you're here . . .'

'I have a letter for you.'

'From him?'

He gave it to her. She read it, dry-eyed but with trembling lips. Then she handed him the paper.

My darling,

I'm beginning to get worried. I warn you my patience is running out. I dare not stay all the time in Calais, where I'd be spotted eventually. I have to keep moving about. I had lunch in Boulogne today and I don't know where I shall sleep. But I know that if you don't turn up I shall do what I said, at the risk of being caught.

It's up to you.

Albert

'You see!' she said dejectedly.

'What does your brother have to say about it?'

She gave no start; she did not even show surprise, only an increased sadness.

'He's spoken to you?'

'We had a drink together.'

'I ought to have told you everything this morning! He's not really a bad lot, but he was left on his own too young... He tries to act like a tough guy, although he wouldn't hurt a fly. All the same I had to stop him coming here because of the way he behaves...'

'All the same, too, you lied to me this morning...'

'I was afraid you might think...'

'Think what, for instance?'

'I don't know... That I was a girl of the same sort!... You might have refused to help me.'

She pointed to the letter: 'You've read that... It's dated yesterday... There's no proof that he hasn't taken the train since then.'

It was beginning to get cooler and the sun had set behind the houses. Mademoiselle Berthe went to close the french window and then returned to Maigret.

'Can I give you a cup of tea? No?... As you realize, I work

for my living . . . I've always worked on my own, to try and establish myself in a job. When I met Albert I thought that meant happiness . . .'

She swallowed her sobs as she mechanically set about tidying the scraps of material strewn about.

'Haven't you any girl friends?' he asked, glancing at the photograph of a fair-haired young woman on the mantelpiece.

Her glance followed his.

'I had Madeleine, but she's married now . . .'

'You don't see her any more?'

'She lives outside Paris . . . Her husband is an important person . . . What Albert meant for me was . . .'

'Couldn't you let me have a picture of him?'

She did not hesitate for a moment.

'It's true that you wouldn't recognize him if you saw him!' she said. 'Wait a minute . . . I've got a photo we had taken at Saint-Malo. It was on the beach . . .'

And she took it from the soup tureen, which evidently served as her treasure-chest. It was a little snapshot taken by some holiday photographer. Albert, in white trousers, bare-armed, a linen cap on his head, looked like any young fellow one might meet at the seaside. As for Mademoiselle Berthe, she was clinging to him as though anxious not to let her happiness escape.

'It's dark, isn't it? As soon as the sun goes down the apartment is very dark. I'll put on the light.'

Just as she switched it on there came a knock at the door. It was the concierge with a basket of provisions.

'Here you are, Mademoiselle Berthe . . .'

'Just put it all in the kitchen, Madame Morin . . .'

'The lettuce is very nice. But as for the Gruyère, I had to . . .'

'I'll see you by and by! . . .'

And when she was once more alone with Maigret, she sat down, threaded a needle and put on her thimble.

'What did the police tell you? I hope you didn't mention that letter?'

Deliberately, he delayed answering, and she looked up and went on speaking more rapidly:

'I'm afraid I'm not very sure how these things are done . . . When I wrote to you . . . I suppose, you see, that when I consulted you it was rather as a lawyer . . .'

'What do you mean?'

'I mean about professional secrecy . . . I've been telling you everything, showing you letters . . . Oh, it wouldn't worry me if they arrested him, in fact it would be the best way to set my mind at ease! But I wouldn't want it to be my responsibility . . . So if they were to start investigating at Calais and Boulogne now . . .'

He gave her no assistance, and she was finding explanations difficult. She hemmed a dress with exaggerated assiduity.

'Which would you rather?' Maigret asked her slowly.

'What d'you mean?'

'That he should be caught or that he should get across the frontier?'

She looked at him with calm, trustful eyes.

'What do you think about it?'

'What would happen to him if he were caught? What danger is he in, exactly?'

'If it's proved . . . If he fired the shot, there's a risk of the death penalty . . .'

She averted her head and bit her lips.

'Then . . . I'd sooner he got across the frontier . . . Although, one of these days, he'll come back to fetch me . . . And if I refuse he'll . . .'

Maigret was holding the photograph of the two lovers, studying chiefly the young man's face, a fairly ordinary face with a mop of curly hair.

'Obviously you haven't written to him yourself...'

'How could I have written to him, since I don't know his address?... And what could I have told him?'

It was hard to imagine that tragedy lay just round the corner, so peaceful was the atmosphere. There were moments when Maigret could have fancied himself sitting at home opposite Madame Maigret as she stitched or darned his socks, for there was the same sense of calm, the same subdued light, the same order and neatness everywhere.

The only difference was that Mademoiselle Berthe was younger and prettier, and dressed with a certain fastidious good taste.

'Has he ever slept here?' he asked just to say something.

To which she replied, with quaint naïveté: 'Never at night...'

'On account of the concierge?'

'And the neighbours. Next door there's an old couple who are sticklers for propriety. There used to be a young woman on the fourth floor who had a great many visitors, and they wrote to the landlord to get her thrown out...'

She recalled her duties as hostess:

'Will you really not take anything? What do you usually drink?'

'I don't want anything, I promise you... I'm beginning to think you've been worrying unnecessarily...'

Now he was walking about as he used to when he was questioning somebody in his office at Police Headquarters, in the days when he was still Superintendent Maigret. He kept touching things automatically, fiddling with the most trifling objects, playing with the pins in the china bowl, setting the soup tureen exactly in the centre of the sideboard.

'In my opinion, when he sees there's no hope, he'll try to cross the Belgian frontier, and it'll be all over . . .'

'Do you think he'll succeed?'

'That depends. Obviously customs officers and policemen all have his description. But if he can get out by some smugglers' route . . .'

'How easy would that be?'

'I think it would be very difficult, because that's the sector where tobacco smuggling is carried out on a large scale. Come now, admit that you're still in love with him . . .'

'No!'

'At any rate that you'd be unhappy if you heard he was caught . . .'

'Isn't that natural? . . . It's ten months since . . .'

'An old married couple, evidently! . . .' he sighed, his voice softening a little. 'Now I'm going to leave you . . .'

'Already?'

'You needn't be afraid! I shan't be far off; just over the way, in fact, on the fifth floor of the Hôtel de Concarneau. I must confess that this afternoon I saw your customers in their slips, and even one of them without . . .'

'I didn't know . . .'

Mademoiselle Berthe's hand, when he grasped it, was soft and warm.

'I trust you . . .' she sighed rather sadly. 'This is the first evening I shall go to bed with my mind at ease.'

Going down the narrow staircase, Maigret felt like a clumsy giant. On the pavement, where it was still daylight, he almost collided with Louis the Kid, who raised a finger to his grey felt hat and said in a bantering tone:

'Excuse me, Superintendent, sir!'

Then Maigret had a sudden attack of ill humour. He felt he was floundering about in a hopeless bog. He wanted to get out of it at all costs, above all to extricate himself from the absurd position he had got into.

'Come here, you . . .'

'Do you want your return match at poker-dice? At your service!'

'What about paying a little visit to the Quai des Orfèvres?'

'That's not a very good idea . . .'

'Whatever you think, I'd like you to follow me there and answer a few questions which Inspector Lacroix will put to you.'

Louis was not enthusiastic.

'Are we going by métro?' he asked.

'We're taking a taxi.'

Maigret had never known a more ridiculous affair, and he reflected that if his wife had seen him a few minutes earlier in Mademoiselle Berthe's apartment she would scarcely have believed that he was there in a professional capacity. He was hardly sure of it himself!

'In you get. To the Quai des Orfèvres, yes, Police Headquarters . . .'

Jérôme would worm things out of the impertinent young rascal, and then they'd see what would happen. As for Mademoiselle Berthe, it was difficult to believe that she was in any real danger, seeing that Albert was still on the run between Calais and Boulogne.

'You know the way . . . Right, now . . . Last room at the end of the passage . . .'

A room which Maigret had occupied at the start of his career, when there was still no electric light in the building.

'Wait for me a moment . . .'

Jérôme was there, drawing up a report.

'Would you like to grill the young scamp I've brought you? He knows more than he appears to...'

'Right, Uncle...'

The scamp still wore his jaunty air, and he had deliberately kept on his hat. He treated himself to a cigarette, which Maigret removed from his lips.

'Tell me now, kid... Where were you on the night of the burglary in the Boulevard Beaumarchais?'

'What night was that?'

'A Monday night...'

'Which month?'

He was acting the simpleton. Maigret found himself longing for the old days when one could stamp on such a fellow's toes to teach him to be serious.

'Where I was?... Wait a sec... I think there was a Marlene Dietrich picture at the cinema in the Rue Rochechouart...'

'And then?'

'And then? Wait a sec! There was a cartoon and then something about the plants that grow at the bottom of the sea...'

Jérôme would have had sufficient patience to keep on questioning him for hours on end. Maigret, however, had had enough of it.

'Were you in on it?'

'On what?'

'That job!'

'What job?'

Maigret felt like punching him in the face. He restrained himself in time.

'Have you got an alibi?'

'A good one! I was in bed...'

'You were at the cinema or you were in bed?'

'I was at the flicks first... Then I went to bed...'

Maigret had brought many others to heel, but here he had no authority to act, and his nephew seemed ill at ease.

'You wouldn't by any chance be the fourth guy, the one they didn't catch?'

The youth solemnly spat on the floor, declaring: 'I swear I wasn't!'

At that same moment the telephone bell rang. Jérôme lifted the receiver and knit his brows:

'What's that? . . . You're sure? . . .'

He hung up again, rose to his feet, and not knowing what to do with Louis left him in the office while he dragged Maigret into the passage.

'That was Emergencies: a woman has just been attacked on the sixth floor of . . .'

'67b Rue Caulaincourt!' his uncle completed the sentence.

'Yes. The concierge declares she saw a man leave the house, bleeding profusely. There's blood all over the stairs . . . What are we going to do with *him*?'

For Jérôme, who had a great respect for regulations, was embarrassed by the somewhat unofficial presence of Louis the Kid.

III

Jérôme Lacroix could not resist constantly turning to Maigret and murmuring uneasily: 'What do you think about it, Uncle?'

And the ex-Superintendent would reply, while the shadow of a smile made his words even more enigmatic:

'You know, son, I never think . . .'

He was taking up as little room as possible. For a long time he sat quite still in a corner beside the dressmaker's dummy, smoking his pipe with an absent-minded air.

Nonetheless his presence embarrassed everyone. The local police superintendent, fearful of appearing ham-fisted in front of the famous Maigret, sought the latter's approval incessantly.

'That's what you would do in my place, isn't it?'

Every landing was crowded, and a policeman was with difficulty preventing people from entering the apartment. Another, at the front door of the house, was vainly repeating: 'Since I tell you there's nothing to see!'

Many inhabitants of the Rue Caulaincourt went without their dinner that evening so as to remain on the watch in the street or at their windows. The weather, as a matter of fact, was ideal, and from time to time one could see shadows passing behind the drawn blinds of the room on the sixth floor.

Down below an ambulance had drawn up. It stood waiting for about an hour and then, to everyone's surprise, drove off again empty.

'What do you think about it, Monsieur Maigret?'

A problem had arisen. Mademoiselle Berthe, who had recovered consciousness, refused to let herself be taken to hospital. She was weak, for she had lost a great deal of blood through a scalp wound. But she displayed the intensity of her feeling by her gaze and by the nervous clenching of her moist hands.

'It's up to the doctor,' said Maigret, who did not wish to assume any responsibility.

And Inspector Lacroix consulted the doctor.

'Do you think we can leave her here?'

'I think that when I've put in a few stitches she can be left to sleep till tomorrow morning...'

All this was taking place amidst the usual confusion. Only the injured girl's eyes remained obstinately fixed on Maigret, and seemed to be appealing to him fervently.

'You heard what the concierge said, Uncle? As I see it, things must have occurred after this fashion: Mademoiselle Berthe went downstairs, probably to buy a few provisions . . .'

'No!' Maigret said quietly.

'You don't think so? Then why did she go down?'

'To post a letter . . .'

Jérôme wondered how Maigret could be so certain of this detail, but he put off the question until later.

'It's unimportant . . .'

'It's very important. But carry on . . .'

'She had scarcely left the house when the concierge saw a man come into the building. The corridor was dark. The concierge assumed he was a friend of one of the tenants. Mademoiselle Berthe came back almost immediately . . .'

'There's a letter-box a hundred metres away, in the Place Constantin-Pecqueur,' specified Maigret, dotting his i's for his own satisfaction.

'All right! . . . She came back . . . She found the intruder in her flat. He attacked her and she defended herself. The man, seriously injured, to judge by the traces of blood on the stairs, hurried down, and the concierge caught sight of him running off, clutching his stomach . . .'

Jérôme looked round somewhat uneasily, and added with less assurance:

'The trouble is that the weapon has not been found . . .'

'The weapons!' Maigret corrected him. 'One blunt instrument with which Mademoiselle Berthe was struck, and another, probably a knife, used to wound the intruder . . .'

'Perhaps he took them away with him?' ventured Jérôme.

And Maigret turned his head away to hide a smile.

Orders had been given to look for an injured man throughout the neighbourhood. The doctor finished dressing the wound on the girl's head; in spite of the pain she strove not to take her eyes off Maigret.

'Do you believe, Uncle, that it may have been her lover?'

'Who did what?'

'Who came here and attacked her . . .'

Why did Maigret reply with such surprising certainty:

'I'm sure it was not!'

'What would you do in my place?'

'Since I'm not in your place I find it hard to answer.'

The local superintendent came up next, in quest of encouragement or approval:

'This is what I've decided; the doctor's going to send a nurse round presently to stay with the patient. Meanwhile I'll put an officer on duty below. Tomorrow we'll consider whether it is possible to question her, and whether there's any point in doing so . . .'

The girl had overheard. She was still looking at Maigret, and she had the impression that he gave her a slight wink. Then, reassured, she yielded to the torpor that was engulfing her.

The two men, uncle and nephew, walked past the inquisitive spectators on the neighbouring doorsteps, and Maigret filled a fresh pipe.

'Suppose we go for a bite?' he suggested. 'It strikes me that we haven't had any dinner yet. There's a brasserie along the street, and I must say a *choucroute garnie* would . . . You've just got to ring up your wife . . .'

During the whole meal Jérôme never ceased to watch his uncle, like a schoolboy in dread of being caught out. And little by little this was making him bad-tempered, even resentful towards Maigret for being too calm, too self-assured.

‘Anyone would think you find this case amusing!’ he remarked, helping himself to sausage.

‘It is amusing, you’re quite right!’

‘It may be amusing for the person who’s not responsible for finding the solution.’

Maigret was enjoying his meal: thickset, broad-shouldered, he picked up his glass of beer with such obvious greedy delight, that he might have served as a brewer’s advertisement.

As he wiped his lips, he treated himself to the sly pleasure of remarking:

‘I’ve found it . . .’

‘What?’

‘The solution . . .’

‘You know who attacked Mademoiselle Berthe?’

‘No!’

‘Well then?’

‘That isn’t important . . . I mean that it isn’t important either for her or for me . . .’

Jérôme’s face grew longer still and, but for the respect he felt for Maigret, he would have been red with anger.

‘Thanks a lot!’ he grumbled, bending over his plate.

‘Why?’

‘Because, instead of helping me, you’re making fun of me. If you’ve really discovered something . . .’

But he tried in vain to provoke his uncle; Maigret had relapsed into stolid impassivity. He ordered a second helping of *choucroute*, with a couple of frankfurters, and a third beer.

‘But look here, do you think I’ve done all I had to do?’

‘You did what you thought you had to, didn’t you?’

‘There’s a nurse in the room . . .’

‘Yes . . .’

'And a policeman at the door . . .'

'Of course!'

'What d'you mean?'

'Nothing . . .'

Maigret paid for the meal; he refused his nephew's invitation to go home with him for coffee. And half an hour later he was at his window in the Hôtel de Concarneau.

On the other side of the street he could see Mademoiselle Berthe's room, where a dim light shone behind the blinds, and he could glimpse the figure of the nurse, huddled in an armchair reading. Down below on the pavement a policeman was pacing up and down, and looking at his watch every quarter of an hour.

'It's up to her to manage now,' Maigret muttered as he closed his window.

And just as he was pulling off his socks, sitting on the edge of the bed, he remembered his nephew, and added:

'It's up to him to work out his plan!'

The room was full of sunlight at nine o'clock next morning as he went up to Mademoiselle Berthe's bedside, while the nurse was tidying up the room.

'I've come to say goodbye to you,' he announced, assuming a falsely innocent air. 'Now that wretched Albert has failed in his attempt, I suppose you're no longer in danger . . .'

Then he read anxiety and almost panic in the wounded girl's eyes. She tried to raise herself up to find out where the nurse was. Then she stammered:

'Don't go yet . . . I implore you!'

'You're really anxious I should stay here?'

'Yes . . .'

'And you're not afraid, for instance, of my giving a few hints to my poor bewildered nephew?'

There was something both gruff and fatherly about Maigret that morning. And yet he was well aware that Mademoiselle Berthe was hesitating between smiles and tears. She was watching him. The previous evening she had been feverish and she might have misunderstood.

The presence of the nurse complicated things still further, for the girl could not speak as openly as she would have liked.

'By the way,' Maigret asked, 'you didn't get a letter this morning?'

She shook her head, and he declared confidently:

'You'll get one tomorrow... Yes, you will!... A letter postmarked Calais or Boulogne... And I can give you one detail: there'll be a couple of pinpricks in the stamp...'

He was smiling. Standing up in the sunlight, he was playing, just as on the previous day, with the china bowl that held pins, buttons and stamps.

He did not need to press his point, for Mademoiselle Berthe's blushes showed that she had understood.

Once more she looked round anxiously, for she was afraid of the nurse overhearing, but Maigret's glance told her that the woman was in the kitchen, where the hissing of the gas stove could now be heard.

'Do you know your next door neighbours?' he asked, changing the subject suddenly. 'You mentioned an old couple, didn't you? Have they a servant?'

'No. The wife does her own housework.'

'And her shopping too?'

'Yes. Every morning about nine or ten o'clock... I know she goes to the market in the Rue Lepic, for I've met her there several times.'

'And the husband?'

'He goes out at the same time and spends his morning

hunting in secondhand book shops in the Boulevard Rochechouart.'

'So that their apartment is empty!' Maigret concluded in an unnecessarily loud tone of voice.

And once again the injured girl hesitated between smiles and tears. She was still uncertain whether Maigret was for her or against her. She dared not decide.

'Just fancy,' he said in a friendly tone, though still speaking very loud, 'they've put a policeman on duty on the pavement. And do you know what orders he's been given?'

He did not even seem to be addressing Mademoiselle Berthe. He had turned to face the opposite direction.

'To prevent you from going out, if the fancy should take you. And to prevent your enemies from coming in. I said coming in, mind you! The police, you see, are afraid they might come and attack you in bed...'

Thereupon he went to open the window wide, knocked out his pipe against his heel and filled another.

There was a longish silence. It seemed as if the girl, as well as the Superintendent, were waiting for something. Maigret paced anxiously up and down the balcony, leaning over to peer into the street, then shrugging his shoulders impatiently.

He even muttered between his teeth: 'The young fool!'

Suddenly he stood motionless, looking down into the street. Mademoiselle Berthe seemed on the point of getting up, in spite of her weak state. The nurse was watching both of them, wondering what it all meant and probably thinking they were a bit crazy.

'There's a métro station at the corner of the street,' sighed Maigret. 'And a bus stop fifty metres away!... And a taxi cruising by, into the bargain. So why?...'

This time Mademoiselle Berthe could not resist questioning him:

'Has he gone?'

And Maigret grumbled:

'He's taking long enough about it, at any rate! . . . You'd think he was tied on by elastic . . . At last!'

'By bus?'

'By métro . . .'

Then Maigret came back into the room, went into the kitchen to fetch the bottle of white wine, and sighed as he poured himself a drink:

'If only it had been dry!'

Mademoiselle Berthe was weeping uncontrollably. She was weeping her heart out, as they say, while the nurse tried to comfort her:

'Calm down, Mademoiselle! You'll do yourself an injury . . . I promise you your wound isn't serious . . . You mustn't be unhappy . . .'

'Idiot!' growled Maigret.

For that goose of a nurse had not understood that these were tears of joy that Berthe was shedding so wildly, while the sunbeams played over her sheets.

IV

When the doctor came, Maigret had taken his hat and left without a word. With the nonchalant air of one who has nothing better to do, he had gone to the Zanzi-Bar, and shortly afterwards had seen his nephew pass by on his way to subject Mademoiselle Berthe to close questioning.

Suddenly Louis the Kid had come in; he tried to draw back on seeing the Superintendent, who, however, called out:

'I've come to take my revenge at poker-dice . . . Give us the dice, *patron*. An anis for this gentleman . . . that's what you like, isn't it, Louis? . . . Your turn to start . . . Three queens . . . I'm afraid that's not good enough . . . What did I tell you? Three kings . . . One up to me . . .'

And without a change of tone he went on, bending towards his companion, who was trying hard to keep his countenance:

'Was the money in the soup tureen?'

Louis the Kid shook his head.

'Was it in Albert's pocket?'

A fresh, even more vigorous shake of the head, and finally Louis confessed:

'He ran off along the embankment and threw the notes into the Seine . . .'

'You're sure of that?'

'I swear it's true!'

'Then why did someone come yesterday?'

'Because he didn't believe me . . .'

Maigret smiled. It was a very special moment, not only on account of the spring weather, the sunshine, the lively atmosphere of the Rue Caulaincourt and his cool beer, but because a single remark had just now reassured him.

It was such a relief that he felt a sudden hot flush of retrospective fear.

Now he could go ahead. He was in a strong position.

'Who fired?'

'The Marseillais . . . Albert had given him his gun . . .'

And Maigret laughed to himself as he watched his nephew gloomily emerging from no. 67b and waiting for the bus a few metres away from the Zanzi-Bar.

'What are you going to do?' asked Louis the Kid, anxiously, still clutching the dice-box.

'Me? I'm going to say goodbye to your sister and catch my train.'

The bus passed, carrying away Jérôme Lacroix. Maigret

crossed the street, and on the sixth floor found the nurse packing up her things.

'I'm not needed any more,' she announced. 'The doctor's going to call once a day and the concierge will look in from time to time . . .'

Maigret's eyes were gleaming with merriment. He paced about the room as though he were at home, waiting for the nurse to leave. Seldom had an inquiry given him as much delight, and yet it was a trivial affair about which, into the bargain, he would never be able to talk.

He recalled his reaction on receiving the letter from Mademoiselle Berthe at Meung-sur-Loire.

'It's odd,' he had observed, 'it seems sincere and yet at the same time it doesn't . . .'

And the young woman in the red hat who had joined him on the terrace of the Café de Madrid had given him the same impression. She was really frightened, that was obvious. But it was obvious, too, that she was lying when she spoke of being terrified of her lover. She did not put on the right tone of voice when she uttered Albert's name. Against her will she spoke it too gently, too tenderly.

Then why had this determined young person ventured to disturb ex-Superintendent Maigret in his rural retreat? And why had she shown him, rather than the police, those letters sent from Boulogne and Calais?

He had not understood to begin with, particularly since he had watched her for hours on end through the window, calmly carrying on her fittings like someone who is not in the least afraid of a vindictive attack. The stamps in the china bowl had given him an idea, and he had pierced them with a pin.

'Why are you smiling, Superintendent?'

'And why are you?'

They were alone together now. The nurse had left. The noise of the street rose towards them, somewhat diminished, with the first hint of that smell of heated asphalt that is typical of Paris in the summer.

Maigret, nonetheless, tried to put on a serious air and assumed his most ominous voice to say:

'Do you know that if the sixty thousand francs had been here and if it was Albert who'd taken them I'd have had you arrested?'

'And yet you were, so to speak, acting on my behalf...'

'That's just it! That's what I realized... I realized that you had sent for me not to protect you against your Albert but to protect Albert against himself... And if you had loved him a tiny bit less, I give you my word that last night I'd have hauled him out of his hiding-place...'

'I don't see what my love...' she murmured, reddening.

'You may not see it, perhaps, but that's how it is. I argued thus: here's a young person who's got plenty of cheek, but who seems to me straight enough. She's trying to save a boy who's got into a bad fix, she tries to save him out of love. And I'm convinced that if the boy had really committed a murder she'd have been revolted...'

'He gave me his solemn word that he never fired, Superintendent. In any case, it was all my fault in a way. I knew he was friendly with my brother Louis, and that some of Louis's associates were shady people. Albert had been unable to find work in Paris, and he was eager to marry me; so he was easily persuaded. The others, whom I don't want to know, took him along to keep watch. One of them borrowed Albert's revolver in case anything should happen. When the police turned up and they all ran away, they left the gun on the spot and they thrust the money into Albert's hands as they went by...'

'I know.'

'How did you guess where he was?'

'To begin with, I made sure there was no cellar or attic here. Then I noticed that, when you spoke to me you sometimes raised your voice, as though you wanted to be heard by someone else . . . Originally there was only one apartment on this floor. When they subdivided it they left the communicating door, but made it a double one, I mean that there's a door on each side of the wall with a gap between the two . . . Albert was in there . . . Only . . .'

'Only I was sure that the police, who had already come once, would search the house a second time. I didn't know if it was being watched. In order to find out . . .'

'You appealed to me, knowing that I would keep you informed as to the course of the official inquiry. I was here to serve as a screen . . . I prevented suspicion from falling on your home and at the same time I provided you with information . . . I came to realize this . . . Do you know it was extremely bright of you?'

'Oh! Superintendent,' she murmured, shamefaced, 'I had to save Albert, didn't I? His accomplices would never have confessed the truth . . . He'd have taken the rap . . . Particularly as they were convinced that we'd kept the money . . . I learned that from my brother . . .'

'Who was trying to protect you! . . . Yesterday evening you went out to post the double letter you sent to your girl friend in Boulogne' (he pointed to her photograph) '. . . that Madeleine, whose job it was to send back the threatening letters to you. Meanwhile one of the accomplices took the opportunity to slip in here and look for the money. You came back, and he knocked you out with a bludgeon. Albert came out of his hiding-place and rushed at him with a knife in his hand . . . That's it, isn't it?'

He had anticipated her story. And he knew, furthermore, that it was Albert who had taken the two weapons into his hiding-place.

'I bet they're still there!' he growled. He opened the communicating door and, as he had expected, found a rubber bludgeon and a blood-stained knife.

'Where are you planning to meet him?' he asked, looking round for his hat.

She hesitated, then stammered:

'Must I tell you? Can I be quite sure that . . .'

Then he laughed outright.

'That I won't have you both arrested at the frontier? Is that what you're trying to imply?'

'No . . . But . . .'

'But you love your Albert so much, don't you? that the very idea that somebody else might . . .'

He was close to the door, had his hand on the knob.

'Actually, you're jealous . . . Yes indeed, Mademoiselle Berthe! . . . And jealous of me, moreover, because you'd wanted to save him all by yourself . . . Come to that, I can't prevent you, as soon as my back's turned, from getting up in spite of your injuries and taking the train to Brussels . . . I'm even willing to bet that a boutique selling Paris models will open there shortly. Goodbye, Mademoiselle Berthe!'

And because he wanted some small revenge after all, he called out as he left the room:

'I shall send you my bill . . .'

J. L. BORGES

DEATH AND THE COMPASS

OF THE MANY problems which exercised the reckless discernment of Lönnrot, none was so strange – so rigorously strange, shall we say – as the periodic series of bloody events which culminated at the villa of Triste-le-Roy, amid the ceaseless aroma of the eucalypti. It is true that Erik Lönnrot failed to prevent the last murder, but that he foresaw it is indisputable. Neither did he guess the identity of Yarmolinsky's luckless assassin, but he did succeed in divining the secret morphology behind the fiendish series as well as the participation of Red Scharlach, whose other nickname is Scharlach the Dandy. That criminal (as countless others) had sworn on his honour to kill Lönnrot, but the latter could never be intimidated. Lönnrot believed himself a pure reasoner, an Auguste Dupin, but there was something of the adventurer in him, and even a little of the gambler.

The first murder occurred in the Hôtel du Nord – that tall prism which dominates the estuary whose waters are the colour of the desert. To that tower (which quite glaringly unites the hateful whiteness of a hospital, the numbered divisibility of a jail, and the general appearance of a bordello) there came on the third day of December the delegate from Podolsk to the Third Talmudic Congress, Doctor Marcel Yarmolinsky, a grey-bearded man with grey eyes. We shall never know whether the Hôtel du Nord pleased him; he accepted it with the ancient resignation which had allowed him to endure three years of war in the Carpathians and three thousand years of oppression and pogroms. He was given a room on Floor R, across from the suite which was occupied – not without splendour – by the Tetrarch of Galilee. Yarmolinsky supped, postponed until the following day an inspection of the unknown city, arranged in a *placard* his many books and few personal possessions, and before midnight extinguished his light. (Thus declared the Tetrarch's chauffeur who slept in the adjoining room.) On the fourth, at 11:03 a.m., the editor of the *Yidische Zaitung* put in a call to him; Doctor Yarmolinsky did not answer. He was found in his room, his face already a little dark, nearly nude beneath a large, anachronistic cape. He was lying not far from the door which opened on the hall; a deep knife wound had split his breast. A few hours later, in the same room amid journalists, photographers and policemen, Inspector Treviranus and Lönnrot were calmly discussing the problem.

'No need to look for a three-legged cat here,' Treviranus was saying as he brandished an imperious cigar. 'We all know that the Tetrarch of Galilee owns the finest sapphires in the world. Someone, intending to steal them, must have broken in here by mistake. Yarmolinsky got up; the robber had to kill him. How does it sound to you?'

'Possible, but not interesting,' Lönnrot answered. 'You'll reply that reality hasn't the least obligation to be interesting. And I'll answer you that reality may avoid that obligation but that hypotheses may not. In the hypothesis that you propose, chance intervenes copiously. Here we have a dead rabbi; I would prefer a purely rabbinical explanation, not the imaginary mischances of an imaginary robber.'

Treviranus replied ill-humouredly:

'I'm not interested in rabbinical explanations. I am

interested in capturing the man who stabbed this unknown person.'

'Not so unknown,' corrected Lönnrot. 'Here are his complete works.' He indicated in the wall-cupboard a row of tall books: a *Vindication of the Cabala*; *An Examination of the Philosophy of Robert Fludd*; a literal translation of the *Sepher Yezirah*; a *Biography of the Baal Shem*; a *History of the Hasidic Sect*; a monograph (in German) on the Tetragrammaton; another, on the divine nomenclature of the Pentateuch. The inspector regarded them with dread, almost with repulsion. Then he began to laugh.

'I'm a poor Christian,' he said. 'Carry off those musty volumes if you want; I don't have any time to waste on Jewish superstitions.'

'Maybe the crime belongs to the history of Jewish superstitions,' murmured Lönnrot.

'Like Christianity,' the editor of the *Yidische Zaitung* ventured to add. He was myopic, an atheist and very shy.

No one answered him. One of the agents had found in the small typewriter a piece of paper on which was written the following unfinished sentence:

The first letter of the Name has been uttered

Lönnrot abstained from smiling. Suddenly become a bibliophile or Hebraist, he ordered a package made of the dead man's books and carried them off to his apartment. Indifferent to the police investigation, he dedicated himself to studying them. One large octavo volume revealed to him the teachings of Israel Baal Shem Tobh, founder of the sect of the Pious; another, the virtues and terrors of the Tetragrammaton, which is the unutterable name of God; another, the thesis that God has a secret name, in which is epitomized (as in the crystal sphere which the Persians ascribe to Alexander of Macedonia) his ninth attribute, eternity that is to say; the immediate knowledge of all things that will be, which are and which have been in the universe. Tradition numbers ninety-nine names of God; the Hebraists attribute that imperfect number to magical fear of even numbers; the Hasidim reason that that hiatus indicates a hundredth name – the Absolute Name.

From this erudition Lönnrot was distracted, a few days later, by the appearance of the editor of the *Yidische Zaitung*. The latter wanted to talk about the murder; Lönnrot preferred to discuss the diverse names of God; the journalist declared, in three columns, that the investigator, Erik Lönnrot, had dedicated himself to studying the names of God in order to come across the name of the murderer. Lönnrot, accustomed to the simplifications of journalism, did not become indignant. One of those enterprising shopkeepers who have discovered that any given man is resigned to buying any given book published a popular edition of the *History of the Hasidic Sect*.

The second murder occurred on the evening of the third of January, in the most deserted and empty corner of the capital's western suburbs. Towards dawn, one of the gendarmes who patrol those solitudes on horseback saw a man in a poncho, lying prone in the shadow of an old paint shop. The harsh features seemed to be masked in blood; a deep knife wound had split his breast. On the wall, across the yellow and red diamonds, were some words written in chalk. The gendarme spelled them out.... That afternoon, Treviranus and Lönnrot headed for the remote scene of the crime. To the left and right of the automobile the city disintegrated; the firmament grew and houses were of less importance than a brick kiln or a poplar tree. They arrived at their miserable destination: an alley's end, with rose-coloured walls which somehow seemed to reflect the extravagant sunset. The dead man had already been identified. He was Daniel Simon Azevedo, an individual of some fame in the old northern suburbs, who had risen from wagon driver to political tough, then degenerated to a thief and even an informer. (The singular style of his death seemed appropriate to them: Azevedo was the last representative of a generation of bandits who knew how to manipulate a dagger, but not a revolver.) The words in chalk were the following:

The second letter of the Name has been uttered

The third murder occurred on the night of the third of February. A little before one o'clock, the telephone in Inspector Treviranus's office rang. In avid secretiveness, a man with a guttural voice spoke; he said his name was Ginzberg (or Ginsburg) and that he was prepared to communicate, for reasonable remuneration, the events surrounding the two sacrifices of Azevedo and Yarmolinsky. A discordant sound of whistles and horns drowned out the informer's voice. Then, the connexion was broken off. Without yet rejecting the possibility of a hoax (after all, it was carnival time), Treviranus found out that he had been called from the Liverpool House, a tavern on the rue de Toulon, that dingy street where side by side exist the cosmorama and the coffee shop, the bawdy house and the bible sellers. Treviranus spoke with the owner. The latter (Black Finnegan, an old Irish criminal who was immersed in, almost overcome by, respectability) told him that the last person to use the phone was a lodger, a certain Gryphius, who had just left with some friends. Treviranus went immediately to Liverpool House. The owner related the following. Eight days ago Gryphius had rented a room above the tavern. He was a sharp-featured man with a nebulous grey beard, and was shabbily dressed in black; Finnegan (who used the room for a purpose which Treviranus guessed) demanded a rent which was undoubtedly excessive; Gryphius paid the stipulated sum without hesitation. He almost never went out; he dined and lunched in his room; his face was scarcely known in the bar. On the night in question, he came downstairs to make a phone call from Finnegan's office. A closed cab stopped in front of the tavern. The driver didn't move from his seat; several patrons recalled that he was wearing a bear's mask. Two harlequins got out of the cab; they were of short stature and no one failed to observe that they were very drunk. With a tooting of horns, they burst into Finnegan's office; they embraced Gryphius, who appeared to recognize them but responded coldly; they exchanged a few words in Yiddish – he in a low, guttural voice, they in high-pitched, false voices – and then went up to the room. Within a quarter hour the three descended, very happy. Gryphius, staggering, seemed as drunk as the others. He walked – tall and dizzy – in the middle, between the masked harlequins. (One of the women at the bar remembered the yellow, red and green diamonds.) Twice he stumbled; twice he was caught and held by the harlequins. Moving off towards the inner harbour which enclosed a rectangular body of water, the three got into the cab and disappeared. From the footboard of the cab, the last of the harlequins scrawled an obscene figure and a sentence on one of the slates of the pier shed.

Treviranus saw the sentence. It was virtually predictable. It said:

The last of the letters of the Name has been uttered

Afterwards, he examined the small room of Gryphius-Ginzberg. On the floor there was a brusque star of blood, in the corners, traces of cigarettes of a Hungarian brand; in a cabinet, a book in Latin – the *Philologus Hebraeo-Graecus* (1739) of Leusden – with several manuscript notes. Treviranus looked it over with indignation and had Lönnrot located. The latter, without removing his hat, began to read while the inspector was interrogating the contradictory witnesses to the possible kidnapping. At four o'clock they left. Out on the twisted rue de Toulon, as they were treading on the dead serpentines of the dawn, Treviranus said:

'And what if all this business tonight were just a mock rehearsal?'

Erik Lönnrot smiled and, with all gravity, read a passage (which was underlined) from the thirty-third dissertation of the *Philologus*: *Dies Judacorum incipit ad solis occasu usque ad solis occasum diei sequentis.*

'This means,' he added, '"The Hebrew day begins at sundown and lasts until the following sundown."'

The inspector attempted an irony.

'Is that fact the most valuable one you've come across tonight?'

'No. Even more valuable was a word that Ginzberg used.'

The afternoon papers did not overlook the periodic disappearances. *La Cruz de la Espada* contrasted them with the admirable discipline and order of the last Hermetical Congress; Ernst Palast, in *El Mártir*, criticized 'the intolerable delays in this clandestine and frugal pogrom, which has taken three months to murder three Jews'; the *Yidische Zaitung* rejected the horrible hypothesis of an anti-Semitic plot, 'even though many penetrating intellects admit no other solution to the triple mystery'; the most illustrious gunman of the south, Dandy Red Scharlach, swore that in his district similar crimes could never occur, and he accused Inspector Franz Treviranus of culpable negligence.

On the night of March first, the inspector received an impressive-looking sealed envelope. He opened it; the envelope contained a letter signed 'Baruch Spinoza' and a detailed plan of the city, obviously torn from a Baedeker. The letter prophesied that on the third of March there would not be a fourth murder, since the paint shop in the west, the tavern on the rue de Toulon and the Hôtel du Nord were 'the perfect vertices of a mystic equilateral triangle'; the map demonstrated in red ink the regularity of the triangle. Treviranus read the *more geometrico* argument with resignation, and sent the letter and the map to Lönnrot – who, unquestionably, was deserving of such madnesses.

Erik Lönnrot studied them. The three locations were in fact equidistant. Symmetry in time (the third of December, the third of January, the third of February); symmetry in space as well. . . . Suddenly, he felt as if he were on the point of solving the mystery. A set of calipers and a compass completed his quick intuition. He smiled, pronounced the word Tetragrammaton (of recent acquisition) and phoned the inspector. He said:

'Thank you for the equilateral triangle you sent me last night. It has enabled me to solve the problem. This Friday the criminals will be in jail, we may rest assured.'

'Then they're not planning a fourth murder?'

'Precisely because they *are* planning a fourth murder we can rest assured.'

Lönnrot hung up. One hour later he was travelling on one of the Southern Railway's trains, in the direction of the abandoned villa of Triste-le-Roy. To the south of the city of our story flows a blind little river of muddy water, defamed by refuse and garbage. On the far side is an industrial suburb where, under the protection of a political boss from Barcelona, gunmen thrive. Lönnrot smiled at the thought that the most celebrated gunman of all – Red Scharlach – would have given a great deal to know of his clandestine visit. Azevedo had been an associate of Scharlach; Lönnrot considered the remote possibility that the fourth victim might be Scharlach himself. Then he rejected the idea. . . . He had very nearly deciphered the problem; mere circumstances, reality (names, prison records, faces, judicial and penal proceedings) hardly interested him now. He wanted to travel a bit, he wanted to rest from three months of sedentary investigation. He reflected that the explanation of the murders was in an anonymous triangle and a dusty Greek word. The mystery appeared almost crystalline to him now; he was mortified to have dedicated a hundred days to it.

The train stopped at a silent loading station. Lönnrot got off. It was one of those deserted afternoons that seem like dawns. The air of the turbid, puddled plain was damp and cold. Lönnrot began walking along the countryside. He saw dogs, he saw a car on a siding, he saw the horizon, he saw a silver-coloured horse drinking the crapulous water of a puddle. It was growing dark when he saw the rectangular belvedere of the villa of Triste-le-Roy, almost as tall as the black eucalypti which surrounded it. He thought that scarcely one dawning and one nightfall (an ancient splendour in the east and another in the west) separated him from the moment long desired by the seekers of the Name.

A rusty wrought-iron fence defined the irregular perimeter of the villa. The main gate was closed. Lönnrot, without much hope of getting in, circled the area. Once again before the insurmountable gate, he placed his hand between the bars almost mechanically and encountered the bolt.

The creaking of the iron surprised him. With a laborious passivity the whole gate swung back.

Lönnrot advanced among the eucalypti treading on confused generations of rigid, broken leaves. Viewed from anear, the house of the villa of Triste-le-Roy abounded in pointless symmetries and in maniacal repetitions: to one Diana in a murky niche corresponded a second Diana in another niche; one balcony was reflected in another balcony; double stairways led to double balustrades. A two-faced Hermes projected a monstrous shadow. Lönnrot circled the house as he had the villa. He examined everything; beneath the level of the terrace he saw a narrow Venetian blind.

He pushed it; a few marble steps descended to a vault. Lönnrot, who had now perceived the architect's preferences, guessed that at the opposite wall there would be another stairway. He found it, ascended, raised his hands and opened the trap door.

A brilliant light led him to a window. He opened it: a yellow, rounded moon defined two silent fountains in the melancholy garden. Lönnrot explored the house. Through anterooms and galleries he passed to duplicate patios, and time after time to the same patio. He ascended the dusty stairs to circular antechambers; he was multiplied infinitely in opposing mirrors; he grew tired of opening or half-opening windows which revealed outside the same desolate garden from various heights and various angles; inside, only pieces of furniture wrapped in yellow dust sheets and chandeliers bound up in tarlatan. A bedroom detained him; in that bedroom, one single flower in a porcelain vase; at the first touch the ancient petals fell apart. On the second floor, on the top floor, the house seemed infinite and expanding. *The house is not this large*, he thought. *Other things are making it seem larger: the dim light, the symmetry, the mirrors, so many years, my unfamiliarity, the loneliness.*

By way of a spiral staircase he arrived at the oriel. The early evening moon shone through the diamonds of the window; they were yellow, red and green. An astonishing, dizzying recollection struck him.

Two men of short stature, robust and ferocious, threw themselves on him and disarmed him; another, very tall, saluted him gravely and said:

'You are very kind. You have saved us a night and a day.'

It was Red Scharlach. The men handcuffed Lönnrot. The latter at length recovered his voice.

'Scharlach, are you looking for the Secret Name?'

Scharlach remained standing, indifferent. He had not participated in the brief struggle, and he scarcely extended his hand to receive Lönnrot's revolver. He spoke; Lönnrot noted in his voice a fatigued triumph, a hatred the size of the universe, a sadness not less than that hatred.

'No,' said Scharlach. 'I am seeking something more ephemeral and perishable, I am seeking Erik Lönnrot. Three years ago, in a gambling house on the rue de Toulon, you arrested my brother and had him sent to jail. My men slipped me away in a coupé from the gun battle with a policeman's bullet in my stomach. Nine days and nine nights I lay in agony in this desolate, symmetrical villa; fever was demolishing me, and the odious two-faced Janus who watches the twilights and the dawns lent horror to my dreams and to my waking. I came to abominate my body, I came to sense that two eyes, two hands, two lungs are as monstrous as two faces. An Irishman tried to convert me to the faith of Jesus; he repeated to me the phrase of the *goyim*: All roads lead to Rome. At night my delirium nurtured itself on that metaphor; I felt that the world was a labyrinth, from which it was impossible to flee, for all roads, though they pretend to lead to the north or south, actually lead to Rome, which was also the quadrilateral jail where my brother was dying and the villa of Triste-le-Roy. On those nights I swore by the God who sees with two faces and by all the gods of fever and of the mirrors to weave a labyrinth around the man who had imprisoned my brother. I have woven it and it is firm: the ingredients are a dead heresiologist, a compass, an eighteenth-century sect, a Greek word, a dagger, the diamonds of a paint shop.

'The first term of the sequence was given to me by chance. I had planned with a few colleagues – among them Daniel Azevedo – the robbery of the Tetrarch's sapphires. Azevedo betrayed us: he got drunk with the money that we had advanced him and he undertook the job a day early. He got lost in the vastness of the hotel; around two in the morning he stumbled into Yarmolinsky's room. The latter, harassed by insomnia, had started to write. He was working on some notes, apparently, for an article on the Name of God; he had already written the words: *The first letter of the Name has been uttered.* Azevedo warned him to be silent; Yarmolinsky reached out his hand for the bell which would awaken the hotel's forces; Azevedo countered with a single stab in the chest. It was almost a reflex action; half a century of violence had taught him that the easiest and surest thing is to kill. . . . Ten days later I learned through the *Yidische Zaitung* that you were seeking in Yarmolinsky's writings the key to his death. I read the *History of the Hasidic Sect*; I learned that the reverent fear of uttering the Name of God had given rise to the doctrine that that Name is all powerful and recondite. I discovered that some Hasidim, in search of that secret Name, had gone so far as to perform human sacrifices. . . . I knew that you would make the conjecture that the

Hasidim had sacrificed the rabbi; I set myself the task of justifying that conjecture.

'Marcel Yarmolinsky died on the night of December third; for the second "sacrifice" I selected the night of January third. He died in the north; for the second "sacrifice" a place in the west was suitable. Daniel Azevedo was the necessary victim. He deserved death; he was impulsive, a traitor; his apprehension could destroy the entire plan. One of us stabbed him; in order to link his corpse to the other one I wrote on the paint shop diamonds: *The second letter of the Name has been uttered.*

'The third murder was produced on the third of February. It was, as Treviranus guessed, a mere sham. I am Gryphius-Ginzberg-Ginsburg; I endured an interminable week (supplemented by a tenuous fake beard) in the perverse cubicle on the rue de Toulon, until my friends abducted me. From the footboard of the cab, one of them wrote on a post; *The last of the letters of the Name has been uttered.* That sentence revealed that the series of murders was *triple*. Thus the public understood it; I, nevertheless, interspersed repeated signs that would allow you, Erik Lönnrot, the reasoner, to understand that the series was quadruple. A portent in the north, others in the east and west, demand a fourth portent in the south; the Tetragrammaton – the name of God, JHVH – is made up of *four* letters; the harlequins and the paint shop sign suggested *four* points. In the manual of Leusden I underlined a certain passage: that passage manifests that Hebrews compute the day from sunset to sunset; that passage makes known that the deaths occurred on the *fourth* of each month. I sent the equilateral triangle to Treviranus. I foresaw that you would add the missing point. The point which would form a perfect rhomb, the point which fixes in advance where a punctual death awaits you. I have premeditated everything, Erik Lönnrot, in order to attract you to the solitudes of Triste-le-Roy.'

Lönnrot avoided Scharlach's eyes. He looked at the trees and the sky subdivided into diamonds of turbid yellow, green and red. He felt faintly cold, and he felt, too, an impersonal – almost anonymous – sadness. It was already night; from the dusty garden came the futile cry of a bird. For the last time, Lönnrot considered the problem of the symmetrical and periodic deaths.

'In your labyrinth there are three lines too many,' he said at last. 'I know of one Greek labyrinth which is a single straight line. Along that line so many philosophers have lost themselves that a mere detective might well do so, too. Scharlach, when in some other incarnation you hunt me, pretend to commit (or do commit) a crime at A, then a second crime at B, eight kilometres from A, then a third crime at C, four kilometres from A and B, halfway between the two. Wait for me afterwards at D, two kilometres from A and C, again halfway between both. Kill me at D, as you are now going to kill me at Triste-le-Roy.'

'The next time I kill you,' replied Scharlach, 'I promise you that labyrinth, consisting of a single line which is invisible and unceasing.'

He moved back a few steps. Then, very carefully, he fired.

ERLE STANLEY GARDNER

LEG MAN

MAE DEVERS CAME into my office with the mail. She stood by my chair for a moment putting envelopes on the desk, pausing to make little adjustments of the inkwell and paper weights, tidying things up a bit.

There was a patent-leather belt around her waist, and below that belt I could see the play of muscles as her supple figure moved from side to side. I slid my arm around the belt and started to draw her close to me.

'Don't get fresh!' she said, trying to pull my hand away, but not trying too hard.

'Listen, I have work to do,' she said. 'Let me loose, Pete.'

'Holding you for ransom, smile-eyes,' I told her.

She suddenly bent down. Her lips formed a hot circle against mine – and Cedric L. Boniface had to choose that moment to come busting into my office without knocking.

Mae heard the preliminary rattle of the door-knob, and scooped up a bunch of papers from the desk. I ran fingers through my hair, and Boniface cleared his throat in his best professional manner.

I couldn't be certain whether I had any lipstick on my mouth, so I put my elbow on my desk, covered my mouth with the fingers of my hand and stared intently at an open law book.

Mae Devers said, 'Very well, Mr Wennick, I'll see that it gets in the mail,' and started for the door. As she passed

Boniface, she turned and gave me a roguish glance, as much as to say, 'Now, smartie, see what you've got yourself into.'

Boniface stared at me, hard. His yellowish eyes, with the bluish-white eyeballs, reminded me of hard-boiled eggs which had been peeled and cut in two lengthwise. He was in a vile humor.

'What was all the commotion about?' he asked.

'Commotion?' I inquired raising my eyes, but keeping my hand to my mouth. 'Where?'

'In here,' he said.

Mae Devers was just closing the door. 'Did you hear anything, Miss Devers?' I asked in my most dignified manner.

'No, sir,' she said demurely, and slipped out into the corridor.

I frowned down at the open law book on the desk. 'I can't seem to make any sense out of the distinction between a bailment of the first class and a bailment of the second class.'

That mollified Boniface somewhat. He loved to discourse on the academic legal points which no one else ever gave a damn about.

'The distinction,' he said, 'is relatively simple, if you can keep from becoming confused by the terminology. Primarily, the matter of consideration is the determining factor in the classification of all bailments.'

'Yes, sir,' I said, my voice muffled behind my hand.

Boniface stared at me. 'Wennick,' he said, 'there's something queer about your connection with this firm. You're supposed to be studying law. You're supposed to make investigations. You're a cross between a sublimated law clerk and a detective. It just happens, however, that in checking over our income tax, I find that the emoluments which have been paid you during the past three months would fix your salary at something over fifteen thousand dollars a year.'

There was nothing I could say to that, so I kept quiet.

Mae Devers opened the door and said, 'Mr Jonathan wants to see you at once, Mr Wennick.'

I got out of the chair as though it had been filled with tacks and said, 'I'm coming at once. Excuse me, Mr Boniface.'

Mae Devers stood in the doorway which led to the general offices and laughed at me as I jerked out a handkerchief and wiped lipstick from my mouth. 'That,' she told me, 'is what you get for playing around.'

I didn't have time to say anything. When old E.B. Jonathan sent word that he wanted to see me at once, it meant that he wanted to see me at once. Cedric L. Boniface followed me to the door of my office and stared meditatively down the corridor as though debating with himself whether or not to invade the sanctity of E.B.'s office to pursue the subject further. I popped into E.B.'s private office like a rabbit making its burrow two jumps ahead of a fox.

Old E.B. looked worse than ever this morning. His face was the color of skimmed milk. There were pouches underneath his tired eyes as big as my fist. His face was puckered up into the acrimonious expression of one who has just bit into a sour lemon.

'Lock the door, Wennick,' he said.

I locked the door.

'Take a seat.'

I sat down.

'Wennick,' he said, 'we're in a devil of a mess.'

I sat there, waiting for him to go on.

'There was some question over certain deductions in my income tax statement,' he said. 'Without thinking, I told Mr Boniface to brief the point. That made it necessary for him to consult the income tax return, and he saw how much you'd been paid for the last three months.'

'So he was just telling me,' I said.

'Well,' E.B. said, 'it's embarrassing. I need Boniface in this business. He can spout more academic law than a college professor, and he's so damn dumb he doesn't know that I'm using him for a stuffed shirt. No one would ever suspect him of being implicated in the – er, more spectacular methods which you use to clean up the cases on which he's working.'

'Yes,' I conceded, 'the man's a veritable talking encyclopedia of law.'

E.B. said, 'We'll have to handle it some way. If he asks you any questions, tell him it's a matter you'd prefer to have him discuss with me. Wennick! Is that lipstick on the corner of your mouth?'

Mechanically, I jerked a handkerchief out of my pocket to the corner of my mouth. 'No, sir,' I said, 'just a bit of red crayon I was using to mark up that brief and . . .'

I stopped as I saw E.B.'s eyes on the handkerchief. It was a red smear. There was no use lying to the old buzzard now. I stuck the handkerchief back in my pocket and said, 'Hell, yes, it's lipstick.'

'Miss Devers, I presume,' he said dryly.

I didn't say anything.

'I'm afraid,' he said, 'it's going to be necessary to dispense with her services. At the time I hired her, I thought she was just a bit too – er, voluptuous. However, she was so highly recommended by the employment agency that –'

'It's all right,' I said. 'Go ahead and fire her.'

'You won't mind?'

'Certainly not,' I told him. 'I can get a job some other place and get one for her at the same time.'

'Now, wait a minute, Wennick,' he said, 'don't misunderstand me. I'm very well satisfied with your services, if you could only learn to leave women alone.'

I decided I might as well give him both barrels. 'Listen,' I said, 'you think women are poison. I think they're damned interesting. The only reason I'm not going to ask you whether the rumor is true that you're paying simultaneous alimony to two wives is that I don't think I have any business inquiring into your private life, and the only reason I'm not going to sit here and talk about my love life is that I know damned well you haven't any business prying into mine.'

His long, bony fingers twisted restlessly, one over the other, as he wrapped his fists together. Then he started cracking his knuckles, one at a time.

'Wennick,' he said at length, 'I have great hopes for your future. I hate to see you throw yourself away on the fleeting urge of a biological whim.'

'All right,' I told him, 'I won't.'

He finished his ten-knuckle salute and shook his head lugubriously. 'They'll get you in the long run, Wennick,' he said.

'I'm not interested in long runs,' I told him. 'I like the sprints.'

He sighed, unlaced his fingers and got down to business. 'The reason I'm particularly concerned about this, Wennick, is that the case I'm going to send you out on involves a woman, a very attractive woman. Unless I'm sadly mistaken, she is a very vital woman, very much alive, very – er, amorous.'

'Who is she?' I asked.

'Her name is Pemberton, Mrs Olive Pemberton. Her husband's Harvey C. Pemberton, of the firm of Bass & Pemberton, Brokers, in Culverton.'

'What does she want?' I asked.

'Her husband's being taken for a ride.'

'What sort of a ride?'

He let his cold eyes regard me in a solemn warning. 'A joy ride, Pete.'

'Who's the woman?'

Old E.B. consulted a memo. 'Her name is Diane Locke – and she's redheaded.'

'What do I do?'

'You find some way to spike her guns. Apparently she has an iron-clad case against Pemberton. I'll start Boniface working on it. He'll puzzle out some legal technicality on which he'll hang a defense. But you beat him to it by spiking her guns.'

'Has the redhead filed suit?' I asked.

'Not yet,' E.B. said. 'At present it's in the milk-and-honey stage. She's getting ready to tighten the screws, and Mrs Pemberton has employed us to see that this other woman doesn't drain her husband's pocketbook with this threatened suit. Incidentally, you're to stay at the Pemberton house, and remember, Mr Pemberton doesn't know his wife is wise to all this and is trying to stop it.'

'Just how,' I asked, 'do I account for my presence to Mr Harvey C. Pemberton?'

'You're to be Mrs Pemberton's brother.'

'How do you figure that?'

'Mrs Pemberton has a brother living in the West. Her husband has never seen him. Fortunately, his name also is Peter, so you won't have any difficulty over names.'

'Suppose,' I asked, 'the real brother shows up while I'm there at the house?'

'He won't,' E.B. said. 'All you have to do is to go to the door at seven-thirty this evening. She'll be waiting for your ring. She'll come to the door and put on all the act that's necessary. You'll wear a red carnation in your left coat lapel so there'll be no mistake. Her maiden name, by the way, was Crowe. You'll be Peter Crowe, sort of a wandering ne'er-do-well brother. The husband knows all about you by reputation.'

'And hasn't seen any pictures or anything?' I asked.

'Apparently not,' E.B. said.

'It sounds like a plant to me,' I told him dubiously.

'I'm quite certain it's all right,' he said. 'I have collected a substantial retainer.'

'O.K.,' I told him, 'I'm on my way.'

'Pete,' he called, as I placed my hand on the door.

'What is it?'

'You'll be discreet,' he warned.

I turned to give him a parting shot. 'I certainly hope I'll be able to,' I said, 'but I doubt it,' and pulled the door shut behind me.

I looked at my wrist watch, saw I had three minutes to go, and put the red carnation in the left lapel of my coat. I'd already spotted the house. It was a big, rambling affair which oozed an atmosphere of suburban prosperity. I took it that Bass & Pemberton, Brokers, had an income which ran into the upper brackets.

I jerked down my vest, adjusted the knot in my tie, smoothed the point of my collar, and marched up the front steps promptly at seven-thirty. I jabbed the bell. I heard slow, dignified masculine steps in the corridor. That wasn't what E.B. had led me to expect. I wondered for a moment if there'd been a hitch in plans and I was going to have to face the husband. The door opened. I took one look at the sour puss on the guy standing in the doorway and knew he was the butler. He was looking at me as a judge looks at a murderer when I heard a feminine squeal and caught a flying glimpse of a woman with jet-black hair, dusky olive complexion and a figure that would get by anywhere. She gave a squeal of delight and flung her arms around my neck.

'Pete!' she screamed. 'Oh, Pete, you darling. You dear! I knew you'd look me up if you ever came near here.'

The butler stepped back and coughed. The woman hugged me, jumped up and down in an ecstasy of glee, then said, 'Let me look at you.' She stepped back, her hands on my shoulders, her eyes studying me.

Up to that point, it had been rehearsed, but the rest of it wasn't. I saw approval in her eyes, a certain trump-this-ace expression, and she tilted her head to offer me her lips.

I don't know just what E.B. referred to as being discreet. I heard the butler cough more violently. I guess he didn't know she had a brother. I let her lead. She led with an ace. I came up for air, to see a short-coupled chap with a tight vest regarding me from brown, mildly surprised eyes. Back of him was a tall guy fifteen years older, with fringes of what had once been red hair around his ears. The rest of his dome was bald. He had a horse face, and the march of time had done things to it. It was a face which showed character.

Mrs Pemberton said, 'Pete, you've never met my husband.'

The chunky chap stepped forward and I shoved out my hand. 'Well, well, well,' I said, 'so this is Harvey. How are you, Harvey?'

'And Mr Bass, my husband's partner,' she said.

I shook hands with the tall guy. 'Pete Crowe, my rolling-stone brother,' Mrs Pemberton observed. 'Where's your baggage, Pete?'

'I left it down at the station,' I told her.

She laughed nervously and said, 'It's just like you to come without sending a wire. We'll drive down and pick up your baggage.'

'Got room for me?' I asked.

'Have we!' she exclaimed. 'I've just been dying to see you. Harvey is so busy with his mergers and his horrid old business that I don't ever get a chance to see him any more. You're a God-send.'

Harvey put his arm around his wife's waist. 'There, there, little girl,' he said, 'it won't be much longer, and then we'll take a vacation. We can go for a cruise somewhere. How about the South Seas?'

'Is that a promise?' she asked.

'That's a promise,' he told her so solemnly I felt certain he was lying.

'You've made promises before,' she pouted, 'but something new always came up in the business.'

'Well, it won't come up this time. I'll even sell the business before I get in another spell of work like this.'

I caught him glancing significantly at his partner.

'We've just finished dinner,' Mrs Pemberton explained to me, 'and Mr Bass and my husband are going back to their stuffy old office. How about going down and picking up your baggage now?'

'Anything you say,' I told her, leaving it up to her to take the lead. 'Come on then,' she invited. 'Harvey's car is out front. Mine's in the garage. We'll go get it out. Oh, you darling! I'm so glad to see you!' And she went into another clinch.

Harvey Pemberton regarded me with a patronizing smile. 'Olive's told me a lot about you, Pete,' he said. 'I'm looking forward to a chance to talk with you.'

Bass took a cigar from his pocket. 'Is Pete the one who did all the big game hunting down in Mexico?' he asked.

'That's the one,' Mrs Pemberton told him.

Bass said, 'You and I must have a good long chat some

time, young man. I used to be a forest ranger when I was just out of school. I was located up in the Upper Sespe, and the Pine Mountain country. I suppose you know the section.'

'I've hunted all over it,' I said.

He nodded. 'I was ranger there for three years. Well, come on, Harvey, let's go down and go over those figures.'

'We go out the back way,' Olive Pemberton told me, grabbing my hand and hurrying me out a side door. She skipped on ahead toward the garage. 'Hurry,' she said. 'They have a conference on at their office and I want to hear what it's about.'

She jerked open the garage door. I helped her into the car and she smiled her thanks as she adjusted herself in the seat. 'I like my feet free when I'm driving,' she said, pulling her skirt up to her knees.

She had pretty legs.

I climbed in beside her and she started the motor. We went out of there like a fire wagon charging down the main stem of a hick town. Her husband and Bass were just getting into their car as we hit the incline to the street. The car flattened down on its springs, then shot up in the air. I hung on. I heard rubber scream as she spun the wheel, waved her hand to her husband, and went streaking down the street.

'You always drive like that?' I asked.

'Most of the time,' she said. 'Sometimes I go faster.'

'No wonder you want your feet free,' I told her.

She glanced down at her legs, then her eyes were back on the road. 'I want to beat them there,' she explained. 'I've bribed the janitor and I have an office next to theirs.' She stepped harder on the gas, angrily.

'Hope I didn't scare you with my greeting,' she said, with a sidelong glance. 'I had to act cordial, you know.'

'I like cordiality,' I told her. 'It becomes you.'

She gave attention to her driving. It was the sort of driving which needed lots of attention. She reached the business section of town, hogged the traffic, crowded the signals at the intersections, and whipped the car into a parking lot. She said, 'Come on, Pete,' and led the way toward a seven-story building which apparently was the town's best in the way of office buildings.

'It's fortunate your name's really Pete,' she commented as we entered the building.

I nodded and let it go at that. I was sizing her up out of the corner of my eye. She was one of these supple women who seem to be just about half panther. She must have been around thirty-two or -three, but her figure and walk were what you'd expect to find on a woman in the early twenties. There was a peculiar husky note to her voice, and her eyes were just a little bit more than provocative.

The night elevators were on. The janitor came up in response to her ring. His face lit up like a Christmas tree when he saw her. He looked over at me and looked dubious.

'It's all right, Olaf,' she said. 'This man's helping me. Hurry up because my husband's coming.'

We got in the cage. Olaf slammed the door and sent us rattling upward, his eyes feasting on Olive's profile. I've seen dogs look at people with exactly that same expression – inarticulate love and a dumb, blind loyalty.

He let us out at the sixth floor. 'This way,' she said, and walked on ahead of me down the corridor.

I noticed the swing of her hips as she walked. I think she wanted me to – not that she gave a particular damn about me, she was simply one of those women who like to tease the animals – or was she making a play for me?

'No chance of the janitor selling you out?' I asked as she fitted a key in the lock.

'No,' she said.

'You seem to have a lot of faith in human nature,' I told her, as she clicked back the lock and snapped on lights in the office.

'I have,' she told me, 'in masculine nature. Men always play fair with me. It's women who double-cross me. I hate women.'

The office was bare of furnishings, save for a battered stenographer's desk, a couple of straightback chairs, an ash-tray and waste basket. Wires ran down from a hole in the plaster, to terminate in an electrical gadget. She opened a drawer in the desk, took out two head pieces and handed me one. 'When you hear my husband come in the next office,' she said, 'plug that in, and remember what you hear. I think things are coming to a show-down tonight.'

I sat across from her and nursed the last of my cigarette. 'Anything in particular I'm supposed to do about it?' I asked.

'Of course,' she said.

'What?' I asked.

'That's up to you.'

'Want me to bust things up with a club?' I asked.

She studied me with her dark, seductive eyes. 'I may as well be frank with you,' she said in that rich, throaty voice. 'I don't care a thing in the world about my husband. I don't think he cares any more about me. A separation is inevitable. When it happens I want my share of the property.'

'What's the property?' I asked her.

'Mostly a partnership interest,' she said. 'He's a free spender and he's been stepping around high, wide and handsome. After a man gets to be forty-three and starts stepping around, it takes money.

'So far, he's been just a mild sugar daddy. I haven't cared

particularly just so there was plenty for me to spend. But now he's put his neck in a noose. This Diane Locke is shrewd. She's too damn shrewd, or maybe somebody with brains is back of her. I think it must be a lawyer somewhere. Anyway, they have Harvey over a barrel. He needs money, lots of money. The only way he can get it is to sell his partnership interest. You heard that crack he made about selling out so he could take me on a cruise.'

I nodded.

'Well,' she said, 'if that's what's in the wind, I'm going to throw a lot of monkey wrenches in that machinery.'

I did a little thinking. 'The redhead,' I said, 'might open her bag, take out a nice, pearl-handled gun, and go rat-a-tat-tat. They have been known to do that, you know.'

It was just a feeler. I wanted to see what she'd say. She said it. 'That's all right, too. There's a big life insurance policy in my favor. But what I don't want is to have him stripped. He – Here they come now.'

I heard the elevator door clang. There were steps in the corridor, then I heard keys rattling and the door in the adjoining office creaked back and I heard the click of the light switch. Mrs Pemberton nodded to me, and I plugged in the jack and put the ear pieces over my head. She snapped a switch, and I could hear faint humming noises in the ear pieces. Then I heard a voice that I recognized as Bass's saying, 'But, Harvey, why the devil do you want to sell out?'

'I want to play a little bit,' Harvey Pemberton said. 'I want to have a real honeymoon with my wife before I'm too old to enjoy it. We've never traveled. I married her four years ago, when we were putting through that big hotel deal. And I've had my nose pushed against the grindstone ever since. We never had a honeymoon.'

'What are you going to do after you get back?'

'I don't know.'

'You could arrange things so you could take a honeymoon without selling out,' Bass said. 'I hate to lose you as a partner, Harvey.'

'No, I wouldn't leave a business behind in which I had all my money tied up,' Pemberton said. 'I'd worry about it so I'd be a rotten companion. I want to step out footloose and fancy-free.'

'One of the reasons I don't want you to do it right now,' Bass said, 'is that I'm rather short of money myself. I couldn't offer you anywhere near what your interest in the business is worth.'

'What could you offer?' Pemberton said, an edge to his voice.

'I don't know,' I heard Bass say.

'Oh, come,' Pemberton told him impatiently. 'You can't pull that stuff with me, Arthur. I told you this afternoon that I wanted to figure on some sort of a deal. You've had all afternoon to think it over.'

There was silence for several seconds, and I gathered that Bass was, perhaps, making figures on paper. I heard Harvey Pemberton say, 'I'm going to have an accountant work up a statement showing the status of the business and –'

'That doesn't have anything to do with it,' Bass said. 'It's not a question of what the business is worth, it's a question of what I can afford to pay without jeopardizing my working capital. I'll tell you frankly, Harvey, that I don't want you to sell. I don't want to lose you as a partner and you can't get anything like a fair value for your holdings at the present time. There's no one else you can sell them to. Under our articles of partnership, one partner has to give the other six months' notice before –'

'I understand all that,' Pemberton said impatiently. 'What's the price?'

'Ten thousand,' Bass said.

'Ten thousand!' Pemberton shouted. 'My God, you're crazy! The business is worth fifty thousand. I'm going to have an audit made in order to determine a fair figure. But I know my share's worth twenty-five. I'll take twenty for it, and that's the lowest price I'll even consider.'

There was relief in Bass's voice. 'That settles it then and I'm glad to hear it! You know, Pemberton, I was afraid you were in a jam over money matters and might have considered ten thousand dollars. It would be an awful mistake. I don't want you to sell.'

Pemberton started to swear. Bass said, 'Well, I'm glad we have an understanding on that, Harvey. Of course, I wouldn't try to exert any pressure to hold you here. In some ways it would be a good business deal for me to buy you out now. But I don't want to do it, either for my sake or yours. I'd have paid you every cent I could have scraped up, but – well, I'm glad you're staying. The business needs you, and I need you, and you need the business. Well, I'll be going. See you later. Good night.'

Over the electrical gadget came the sound of a slamming door. Pemberton yelled, 'Come back here, Arthur! I want to talk with you,' but there was no other sound. I exchanged glances with our client.

'You see,' she said, 'he's trying to sell the business. That vamp would get most of the money. He'd probably run away with her. I want you to stop that.'

'What's the program now?' I asked.

'I think he has an appointment with her,' she said. 'The janitor told me that he'd left instructions to pass a young woman to his office.'

Pretty soon I heard the clang of the elevator door, and light, quick steps in the corridor past our door, then a gentle tapping on the panels of the adjoining office. I put the head phones back on, and heard the sound of a door opening and closing.

'Did you bring the letters?' Harvey Pemberton asked.

A woman's voice said, 'Don't be such an old granny. Kiss me, and quit worrying about the letters. They're in a safe place.'

'You said you could put your hand on them any time,' Pemberton charged, 'and were going to bring them here to show me just what I'd written.'

'I brought you copies instead,' she said. 'My lawyer wouldn't let me take the originals.'

'Why not?'

'I don't know. I guess he doesn't trust me. Harvey, I don't want you to think that I'm utterly mercenary, but you broke my heart. It isn't money I'm after, dear, I want you. But you hurt me, and I went to that horrid lawyer, and he had me sign some papers, and now it seems I have to go through with it, unless you go away with me. That's what I want.'

'*My* lawyer tells me you can't sue a married man for breach of promise,' Pemberton interrupted. 'I think your lawyer is a shyster who's trying to stir up trouble and turn you into a blackmailer.'

'No, he isn't, Harvey. There's some wrinkle in the law. If a girl doesn't know a man's married and he conceals that fact from her, why then he can be sued for breach of promise, just the same as though he hadn't been married. Oh, Harvey, I don't want to deal with all these lawyers! I want you. Can't you divorce that woman and come with me?'

'Apparently not,' Harvey Pemberton said. 'Since you've

been such a little fool and signed your life away to this lawyer, he isn't going to let me get free. There's enough stuff in those letters to keep me from getting a divorce from my wife, and she won't get a divorce from me unless I turn over everything in the world to her. She wants to strip me clean. You want to do almost that.'

For a moment there was silence, then the sound of a woman sobbing.

Pemberton started speaking again. His voice rose and fell at regular intervals, and I gathered he was walking the floor and talking as he walked. 'Go ahead and sob,' he said. 'Sit there and bawl into your handkerchief! And if you want to know it, it looks fishy as hell to me. When I first met you on that steamboat, you didn't have any of this bawling complex. You wanted to play around.'

'You w-w-wanted to m-m-marry me!' she wailed.

'All right,' he told her, 'I was on the up-and-up on that, too. I thought my wife was going to get a divorce. Hell's fire, I didn't *have* to use marriage for bait. You know that. That came afterward. Then, when I break a date with you because of a business deal, you rush up to see this lawyer.'

'I went to him as a friend,' she said in a wailing, helpless voice. 'I'd known him for years. He told me you'd been t-t-trifling with me and I should get r-revenge. After all, all I want is just enough to get me b-b-back on my feet once more.'

Pemberton said, 'Add that to what your lawyer wants, and see where that leaves me. Why the hell don't you ditch the lawyer?'

'I c-can't. He made me sign papers.'

Once more there was silence, then Pemberton said, 'How the hell do I know you're on the level? You could have engineered this whole business.'

'You know me better than that,' she sobbed.

'I'm not so certain I do,' Pemberton told her. 'You were a pushover for me and now –'

Her voice came in good and strong then. 'All right, then,' she said, 'if you don't want the pill sugar-coated we'll make it bitter. I'm getting tired of putting on this sob-sister act for you. I never saw a sucker who was so damn dumb in my life. You seem to think a middle-aged old gander is going to get a sweet, innocent girl to fall for just your own sweet self. Bunk! If you'd been a good spender, taken what you wanted and left me with a few knick-knacks, I'd have thought you were swell. But you thought I was an innocent little kid who'd fall for this Model T line of yours. All right, get a load of this: You're being stood up. And what're you going to do about it? I have your letters. They show the kind of game you were trying to play. So quite stalling.'

'So that's it, is it?' he said. 'You've been a dirty double-crosser all along.'

'Oh, I'm a double-crosser, am I? Just a minute, Mr Harvey Pemberton, and I'll read from one of your letters. Figure how it will sound to the jury.

' "Remember, sweetheart, that except for the silly conventions of civilization, we are already man and wife. There is, of course, a ceremony to be performed, but I'll attend to that just as soon as I can arrange certain business details. It would hurt certain business plans which are rapidly coming to maturity if I should announce I was going to marry you right now. I ask you to have confidence in me, sweetheart, and to know that I cherish you. I could no more harm you than I could crush a beautiful rose. I love you, my sweetheart –" ' She broke off and said, 'God knows how much more of that drivel there is.'

'You dirty, double-crossing tramp,' he said.

Her voice sounded less loud. I gathered she'd moved over toward the door. 'Now then,' she said, 'quit stalling. You have twenty-four hours. Either put up or shut up.'

I heard the door slam, then the click of heels in the hall, and, after a moment, the clang of an elevator door.

All was silent in the other office.

I slipped the head pieces off my head.

'Well,' Mrs Pemberton said, 'there it is in a nutshell. I suppose he'll sell out to Bass for about half what his interest is worth and that little redhead will get it all.'

'How do you know she's redheaded?' I asked.

'I've seen her and I've had detectives on her tail turning up her past and trying to get something on her. I can't uncover a thing on her, though. She dressed the window for this play.'

'All right,' I told her, 'let your husband go ahead and fight. Even if he can't prove anything, a jury isn't going to give her so much in the line of damages.'

'It isn't that alone,' she said, 'it's a question of the letters. He writes foolish letters. Whenever he loses his head, he goes all the way. He can't learn to keep his fountain pen in his pocket. Remember that Bass & Pemberton have some rather influential clients. They can't carry out business unless those clients believe in the business acumen of the members of the partnership.'

'Those things blow over,' I told her. 'Your husband could take a trip to Europe.'

'You don't understand,' she said. 'He made a fool of himself once before. That's why Bass had a clause in the partnership contract. Each of them put in two thousand dollars when they started the partnership. The articles of partnership provide that neither can sell his interest without first giving six months' notice to his partner. And then there's some provision in the contract by which Bass can buy Harvey out by returning the original two thousand dollars to him if Harvey gets in any more trouble with women. I don't know the exact provision. Now then, I want you to nip this thing in the bud. Harvey's desperate. Something's got to be done within twenty-four hours.'

'All right,' I told her, 'I'll see what I can do. What's the girl's address?'

'Diane Locke, apartment 3A, forty-two fifteen Center Street. And it won't do you any good to try and frame her, because she's wise to all the tricks. I think she's a professional; but try and prove it.'

'One thing more,' I told her. 'I want the name of the lawyer.'

'You mean Diane Locke's lawyer?'

'Yes.'

'I can't give it to you.'

'Why not?'

'I don't know it,' she said. 'He's keeping very much in the background. He's some friend of the girl's. Probably he's afraid, he might be disbarred for participating in a blackmail action.'

'How long has this thing been going on?' I asked.

'You mean the affair with that redhead? It started –'

'No,' I said, 'I mean this,' indicating the office with a sweep of my hand.

'Since I couldn't get anywhere with the detective agency,' she said. 'Olaf, the janitor, is an electrician. He helped me rig things up. He got some old parts –'

'Think you can trust him?'

'With my life,' she said.

I lit a cigarette and said, 'How about the wash-room? Is it open?'

'I'll have to give you my key,' she told me, opening her handbag. Then she hesitated a second and said, 'I think it's in another purse. But the lock's mostly ornamental. Any key will work it. Or you can use the tip of a penknife.'

I looked down into her handbag. 'What's the idea of the gun?'

'For protection,' she said, closing the bag.

'All right,' I told her, 'pass it over. I'm your protection now. You'll get in trouble with that gun.'

She hesitated a moment while I held my hand out, then reluctantly took the gun from her purse and hesitated with it in her hand.

'But suppose you're not with me, and something should happen? Suppose he should find the wires and follow them in here and catch me?'

'Keep with me all the time,' I told her.

The business end of the gun waved around in a half-circle. 'Want me to go with you now?' she asked.

'Don't be a sap,' I told her. 'I'm going to the wash-room. I'll be right back.'

'And if my husband comes in while you're gone, I suppose I'm to tell him it's not fair, that you're seeing a man about a dog, and he mustn't choke me until you get back.'

I strode over to the door. 'Keep your plaything until I come back,' I said. 'When we go out, you either get rid of the gun, or get rid of me. You're the one who's paying the money, so you can take your choice.'

I crossed the office to the door, opened it, and pushed the catch so I could open the door from the outside. I wondered what would happen if Harvey Pemberton should make up his mind to go to the wash-room while I was in there, or should meet me in the corridor. I'd kill that chance by going to the floor below. I saw stairs to the right of the elevator, and went down.

The men's room was at the far end of the corridor. The first key on my ring did the trick.

Five minutes later, when I got back to Mrs Pemberton, I saw that she was nervous and upset.

'What's the matter?' I asked. 'Did something happen?'

She said in a nervous, strained voice, 'I was just thinking of what would happen if my husband ran into you in the corridor.'

I said, 'Well, he didn't.'

'You shouldn't take chances like that,' she told me.

I grinned. 'I didn't. I ran down the stairs for a couple of flights and used the room on the fourth floor.'

Her face showed relief. 'All right,' I told her, 'let's go. We'll pick up my baggage and then I'm going to take you home. Then, if you don't mind, I'll borrow your car. I have work to do.'

'Have you any plan?' she asked.

'I'm an opportunist.'

'All right,' she said, 'let's go. We'd better run down the stairs and ring the elevator from the lower floor.'

We started for the door. She clicked out the light.

'Just a minute,' I told her. 'You're forgetting something.'

'What?'

'The gun.'

'It's all right. I thought it over. I decided you were right about it, so I ditched the gun.'

'Where?'

'In the desk drawer.'

I switched the lights back on and went over to look.

'The upper right-hand drawer,' she said, her voice showing amusement.

I opened the drawer. The gun was there. I picked it up, started to put it in my pocket, then changed my mind and dropped it back in the drawer. 'Come on,' I told her, closing the drawer and switching off the lights.

We sneaked across the hall and down the flight of stairs to the lower floor. I rang for the elevator. Olaf brought the cage up and I took another look at him. He was a big raw-boned Swede with a bony nose, a drooping blond mustache, and dog eyes. His eyes never left Mrs Pemberton all the way down to the ground floor.

Mrs Pemberton kept her head turned away from him, toward the side of the elevator shaft, watching the doors creep by. When we got to the ground floor, she turned and looked at him. It was some look. His eyes glowed back at her like a couple of coals. Olaf opened the door, I took Mrs Pemberton's arm and we crossed over to the parking station.

'I'll drive,' I told her. 'I want to get accustomed to the car.'

I drove down to the station, got my baggage and drove Mrs Pemberton back out to the house. The butler carried my things up and showed me my room.

After he left, I opened my suit-case. There were two guns in it. I selected one with a shiny leather shoulder holster. I put it on under my coat and knocked on the door of Mrs Pemberton's room.

She opened the door and stood in the doorway. The light was behind her, throwing shadows of seductive curves through billowy, gossamer silk. I resolutely kept my eyes on her face. 'I'm going out,' I told her. 'Will you hear me when I come in?'

'Yes,' she said. 'I'll wait up.'

'If I cough when I pass your door, it means I have good

news for you. If I don't cough, it means things aren't going so well.'

She nodded, stepped toward me so that her lithe body was very close to mine. She put her hand on my arm and said in that peculiar, throaty voice of hers, 'Please be careful.'

I nodded and turned away. My eyes hadn't strayed once. Walking down the corridor and tiptoeing down the stairs, I reflected that I never had known a woman with that peculiar husky note in her voice who didn't like to tease the animals.

Forty-two fifteen Center Street was a three-story frame apartment house, the lower floor given over to stores. A doorway from the street opened on a flight of stairs. I tried the door, and it was unlocked.

I went back to sit in the car and think. It was queer the lawyer had never appeared in the picture except as a shadowy figure. No one knew his name. He was quoted freely, but he left it up to his client to do all the negotiating. Therefore, if the racket turned out to be successful, the client would be the one to collect the money. Then it would be up to her to pay the lawyer. That didn't sound right to me. It was like adding two and two and getting two as the answer.

I looked the block over. There was a little jewelry store in the first floor of the apartment house. It was closed up now, with a night light in the window, showing a few cheap wrist watches and some costume jewelry.

I drove around the corner and parked the car. A catch-all drugstore was open. I went in, bought some adhesive tape, a small bottle of benzine, a package of cotton, a writing pad and a police whistle. 'Got any cheap imitation pearls?' I asked the clerk.

He had some strings at forty-nine cents. I took one of

those. Then I went out to the car, cut the string of pearls and threw all but four of them away. I pulled a wad of cotton out of the box, put the four pearls in the cotton and stuffed the wad in my pocket. I popped the pasteboard off the back of the writing pad, cut two eyeholes in it and a place for my nose. I reinforced it with adhesive tape and left ends of adhesive tape on it so I could put it on at a moment's notice. Then I climbed the stairs of the apartment house and located apartment 3A.

There was a light inside the apartment. I could hear the sound of a radio, and gathered the door wasn't very thick. I took a small multiple-tool holder from my pocket and fitted a gimlet into the handle. I put a little grease on the point of the gimlet, bent over and went to work.

The best place to bore a hole in a paneled door is in the upper right- or left-hand corner of the lower panel. The wood is almost paper-thin there and doesn't take much of a hole to give a complete view of a room. Detectives have used it from time immemorial, but it's still a good trick. After the hole is bored, a little chewing gum keeps light from coming through the inside of the door and attracting the attention of a casual passer-by.

Making certain the corridor was deserted, I dropped to one knee and peeked through the hole I'd made. The girl was redheaded, all right. She was listening to the radio and reading a newspaper.

Watching through one hole to make certain that she didn't move in case my gimlet made any noise, I bored two more holes. That gave me a chance to see all of the apartment there was. I put a thin coating of chewing gum over each of the holes, went downstairs and waited for a moment when the sidewalk was deserted and there were no cars in sight on the street. Then I took the police whistle from my pocket and blew three shrill blasts. By the time the windows in the apartments commenced to come up, I'd ducked into the doorway and started up the stairs.

I held my pasteboard mask in my left hand. All I had to do was to raise it to my face, and the adhesive tape would clamp it into position. I backed up against the door of apartment 3A and knocked with my knuckles. When I heard steps coming toward the door, I slapped my left hand up to my face, putting the mask in position, and jerked the gun out of my shoulder holster. The redhead opened the door and I backed in, the gun menacing the corridor. Once inside of the door, I made a quick whirl, kicked the door shut and covered her with the gun.

'Not a peep out of you,' I said.

She'd put on a negligée and was holding it tightly about her throat. Her face was white.

'All right, sister,' I told her, 'get a load of this. If any copper comes wandering down the hallway, you go to the door to see what he wants. If he asks you if anyone's in here or if you've seen anyone in the corridor, tell him no. The reason you'll tell him no, is that I'm going to be standing just behind the door with this gun. They're never going to take me alive. I'd just as soon go out fighting as to be led up thirteen steps and dropped through a hole in the floor. Get it?'

She was white to the lips, but she nodded, her eyes large, round and dilated with fright.

'I stuck up that jewelry store downstairs,' I told her, 'and I've got some swag that's worth money. Now, I want some wrapping paper and some string. I'm going to drop that swag in the first mailbox I come to and let Uncle Sam take the responsibility of the delivery. Get me?'

She swallowed a couple of times and said, 'Y-yes.'

'And I'll tell you something else: Don't hold that filmy stuff so tight around you. I'm not going to bite you, but if a cop comes to the door and sees you all bundled up that way, he'll figure out what's happened. If there's a knock, I want you to open the door a crack and have that thing pretty well open in front, when you do. Then you can pull it shut when you see there's a man at the door and give a little squeal and say, "Oh, I thought it was Mamie!" Do you get that?'

'You're asking a lot of me,' she said.

I made motions with the business end of the gun. 'You've got a nice figure,' I said. 'It would be a shame to blow it in two. These are soft-nosed bullets. You'd have splinters from your spinal cord all mixed into your hip bone if I pulled this trigger. The cop in the doorway would get the next shot. Then I'd take a chance on the fire-escape.'

She didn't say anything and I jabbed at her with the gun. 'Come on, how about the wrapping paper?'

She opened a door into a little kitchenette, pulled out a drawer. There was brown paper and string in there. I said, 'Get over there away from the window; stand over there in the corner.'

I crossed over to the little card table. There was an ash-tray there with four or five cigarette ends in it and some burnt matches. I noticed that a couple of the matches had been broken in two. I pushed the tray to one side, spread the paper out, and took the cotton from my pocket.

When I opened the cotton, she saw the four big pearls nested in it and gave a little gasp. Standing eight or ten feet away as she was and seeing those pearls on the cotton, she felt she was looking at ready money.

'That all you took?' she asked in a voice that had a can't-we-be-friends note in it.

'Is that all I took?' I asked, and laughed, a nasty, sarcastic laugh. 'That jeweler,' I told her, 'has been trying to get those four pearls for a client for more than two years. They're perfectly matched pearls that came in from the South Seas, and, in case you want to know it, they didn't pay any duty. I know what I'm after before I heist a joint.'

I put the cotton around the pearls again, wrapped them in the paper, tied the paper with string and ostentatiously set my gun on the corner of the table while I took a fountain pen from my pocket to write an address on the package. I printed the first name which popped into my head, and a Los Angeles address. Then I reached in my pocket, took out my wallet and from it extracted a strip of postage stamps.

'What – what are they worth?' she asked.

'Singly,' I told her, 'they aren't worth over five thousand apiece, but the four of them taken together, with that perfect matching and luster, are worth forty grand in any man's dough.' I shot her a look to see if she thought there was anything phony about my appraisal. She didn't. Her eyes were commencing to narrow now as ideas raced through her head.

'I suppose,' she told me, 'you'll peddle them to a fence and only get about a tenth of what they're worth.'

'Well, a tenth of forty grand buys a lot of hamburgers,' I told her.

She moved over toward a small table, slid one hip up on that, and let the negligee slide carelessly open, apparently too much interested in the pearls to remember that she wasn't clothed for the street. She had plenty to look at, that girl.

'You make a working girl dizzy,' she said wistfully. 'Think how hard I'd have to work to make four thousand dollars.'

'Not with that shape.'

Indignantly she pulled the robe around her. Then she leaned forward, let the silk slip from her fingers and slide right back along the smooth line of her leg.

'I suppose it's wicked of me,' she said, 'but I can't help thinking what an awful shame it is to sell anything as valuable as that for a fraction of what it's worth. I should think you'd get yourself some good-looking female accomplice, someone who could really wear clothes. You could doll her up with some glad rags and show up in Santa Barbara or Hollywood, or perhaps in New Orleans. She could stay at a swell hotel, make friends, and finally confide to one of her gentlemen friends that she was temporarily embarrassed and wanted to leave some security with him and get a really good loan. Gosh, you know, there are lots of ways of playing a game like that.'

I frowned contemplatively. 'You've got something there, baby,' I told her. 'But it would take a girl who could wear clothes; it'd take a baby who'd be able to knock 'em dead and keep her head while she was doing it; it'd take a fast thinker, and it would take someone who'd be one hundred per cent loyal. Where are you going to find a moll like that?'

She got up off the table, gave a little shrug with her shoulders, and the negligee slipped down to the floor. She turned slowly around as though she'd been modeling the peach-colored underwear. 'I can wear clothes,' she said.

I let my eyes show suspicion. 'Yeah,' I told her. 'You sure got what it takes on that end, but how do I know you wouldn't cross me to the bulls if anybody came along and offered a reward?'

Her eyes were starry now. She came toward me. 'I don't double-cross people I like,' she said. 'I liked you from the minute I saw you – something in your voice, something in the way you look. I don't know what it is. When I fall, I fall fast and I fall hard. And I play the game all the way. You and I could go places together. I could put you up right here until the excitement's over. Then we could go places and –'

I said suspiciously, 'You aren't handing me a line?'

'Handing you a line!' she said scornfully. 'Do I look like the sort of girl who'd have to hand anyone a line? I'm not so dumb. I know I have a figure. But you don't see me living in a swell apartment with some guy footing the bills, do you? I'm just a working girl, plugging along and trying to be on the up-and-up. I'm not saying that I like it. I'm not even saying that I'm not sick of it. But I am telling you that you and I could go places together. You could use me and I'd stick.'

'Now, wait a minute, baby,' I temporized. 'Let me get this package stamped and think this thing over a minute. You sure have got me going. Cripes! I've been in stir where I didn't see a frail for months on end, and now you come along and dazzle me with a shape like that. Listen, baby, I –'

I raised the stamps to my tongue, licked them and started to put them on the package. The wet mucilage touched my thumb and the stamps stuck. I tried to shake my thumb loose and the stamps fell to the floor, windmilling around as they dropped. I swooped after the stamps, and sensed motion over on the other side of the table.

I straightened, to find myself staring into the business end of my gun, which she'd snatched up from the table.

'Now then, sucker,' she said, 'start reaching.'

I stood, muscles tensed, hands slowly coming up. 'Now, take it easy, baby. You wouldn't shoot me.'

'Don't think I wouldn't,' she told me. 'I'd shoot you in a minute. I'd tell the cops you'd busted in here after your stick-up and I distracted your attention long enough to grab your gun; that you made a grab for me and I acted in self-defense.'

'Now listen, baby,' I told her, keeping my hands up, 'let's be reasonable about this thing. I thought you and I were going away together. I'd show you London and Paris and –'

She laughed scornfully and said, 'What a sap I'd be to start traveling with a boob like you. A pair of pretty legs, and you forget all about your gun and leave it on the table while you chase postage stamps to the floor.'

'You going to call the cops?' I asked.

She laughed. 'Do I look dumb? I'm going to give you a chance to escape.'

'Why?'

'Because,' she said, 'I haven't got the heart to see a nice-looking young man like you go to jail. I'm going to call the cops and tell them I saw you in the corridor. I'll give you ten seconds start. That ten seconds will keep you from hanging around here, and calling the cops will put me in the clear in case anybody sees you.'

'Oh, I see,' I said sarcastically. 'You mean you're going to grab off the gravy.'

'Ideas don't circulate through that dome of yours very fast, do they?' she asked.

I made a lunge toward the paper parcel I'd wrapped up, but the gun snapped up to a level with my chest. Her eyes glittered. 'Don't crowd me, you fool!' she said. 'Of all the dumbhead plays you've made, that's the worst. I'll do it, and don't think I don't know how to shoot a gun, because I do.'

I backed slowly away.

'There's the door,' she said. 'Get going.' She started toward the telephone and said, 'I'm going to call the cops. You have ten seconds.'

I spilled a lot of cuss words, to make the act look good,

unlocked the door, jerked it open and jumped out into the corridor. I made pounding noises with my feet in the direction of the fire-escape and then tiptoed back. I heard a metallic click as she shot the bolt home in the door.

After waiting a couple of minutes, I dropped to one knee and peeked through the hole in the door. She was over at the table, ripping the wrappings from the parcel. I straightened, and pounded with my knuckles on the door.

'Police call,' I said in a deep gruff voice. 'Open up.'

Her voice sounded thick with sleep. 'What is it?'

'Police,' I said, and dropped again, to put an eye to the peep hole in the door.

She ran to a corner of the carpet, raised it, did something to the floor and then snatched up a kimono.

I pounded with my knuckles again.

'Coming,' she said drowsily.

She twisted back the bolt, opened the door about the width of a newspaper and asked, 'What do you want?'

I stood aside so she couldn't see me.

'We're looking for a man who robbed the jewelry store downstairs,' I growled in my throat. 'We think he came up here.'

'Well, he didn't.'

'Would you mind letting me in?'

She hesitated a moment, then said, 'Oh, very well, if you have to come in, I guess you have to. Just a minute. I'll put something on. . . . All right.'

She pulled the door back. I pushed my way into the room and kicked the door shut. She looked at me with wide, terror-stricken eyes, then jumped back and said, 'Listen, you can't pull this. I'll have the police here! I'll –'

I walked directly to the corner of the carpet. She flung herself at me. I pushed her off. I pulled back the corner of the carpet and saw nothing except floor. But I knew it was there and kept looking, pressing with my fingers. Suddenly I found it – a little cunningly joined section in the hardwood floor. I opened it. My package had been shoved in there, and down below it was a package of letters.

Bending down so that my body concealed just what I was doing, I pulled out pearls and letters and stuffed them in my inside coat pocket.

When I straightened, I found myself facing the gun.

'I told you you couldn't get away with this,' she warned. 'I'll claim you held up the jewelry store and then crashed the gate here. What're you going to do about that?'

'Nothing,' I told her, smiling. 'I have everything I came for.'

'I can kill you,' she said, 'and the police would give me a vote of thanks.'

'You could,' I told her, 'but nice girls don't go around killing men.'

I saw her face contort in a spasm of emotion. 'The hell they don't!' she said, and pulled the trigger.

The hammer clicked on an empty cylinder. She reinforced the index finger of her right hand with the index finger of her left. Her eyes were blazing. She clicked the empty cylinder six times and then threw the gun at me. I caught it by the barrel and side-stepped her rush. She tripped over a chair and fell on the couch.

'Take it easy,' I told her.

She raised her voice then and started to call me names. At the end of the first twenty seconds, I came to the conclusion I didn't know any words she didn't. I started for the door. She made a dash for the telephone and was yelling:

'Police headquarters!' into the transmitter as I closed the door and drifted noiselessly down the corridor.

In the hallway I pulled off the pasteboard mask, moistened a piece of cotton in the benzine and scrubbed off the bits of adhesive which had stuck to my face and forehead. I wadded the mask into a ball, walked around to my car and drove away.

I heard the siren of a police radio car when I was three blocks away. The machine roared by me, doing a good sixty miles an hour.

Walking down the corridor of the Pemberton home, I coughed as I passed Mrs Pemberton's door. I walked into my bedroom and waited. Nothing happened. I took out the letters and looked at them. They were plenty torrid. Some men like to put themselves on paper. Harvey Pemberton had indulged himself to the limit.

I heard a scratching noise on my door, then it slowly opened. Mrs Pemberton, walking as though she'd carefully rehearsed her entrance, came into the light of the room and pulled lacy things around her. 'My husband hasn't come in yet,' she said. 'But he may come in any minute.'

I looked her over. 'Even supposing that I'm your brother,' I said, 'don't you think he'd like it a lot better if you had on something a little more tangible?'

She said, 'I wear what I want. After all, you're my brother.'

'Well, go put on a bathrobe over that,' I told her, 'so I won't be so apt to forget it.'

She moved a step or two toward the door, then paused. 'You don't need to be so conventional,' she said.

'That's what you think.'

'I want to know what you've found out.'

'You're out in the clear,' I told her. 'All we need now is

to –' I broke off as I heard the sound of an automobile outside. There was a business-like snarl to the motor which I didn't like, and somebody wore off a lot of rubber as the car was slammed to a stop.

'That's Harvey now,' she said.

'Harvey wouldn't park his car at the curb in front, would he?' I asked.

'No,' she admitted.

'Get back to your room,' I told her.

'But I don't see what you're so –'

'Get started!' I said.

'Very well, Sir Galahad,' she told me.

She started down the corridor toward her room. I heard the pound of feet as someone ran around the house toward the back door. Then I heard feet on the stairs, crossing the porch, and the doorbell rang four or five times, long, insistent rings.

I slipped some shells into the empty chambers of my gun, switched off the lights, opened my door, picked up my bag and waited.

I heard Mrs Pemberton go to the head of the stairs, stand there, listening. After a moment I heard the rustle of her clothes as she started down. I stepped out to the hallway and stood still.

I heard her say, 'Who is it?' and a voice boom an answer through the closed door. 'Police,' it said. 'Open up.'

'But I – I don't understand.'

'Open up!'

She unlocked the door. I heard men coming into the corridor, then a man's voice say, 'I'm Lieutenant Sylvester. I want to talk with you. You're Mrs Pemberton?'

'Yes, but I can't understand what could bring you here at this hour. After all, Lieutenant, I'm –'

'I'm sorry,' the lieutenant interrupted, 'this is about your husband. When did you see him last?'

'Why, just this evening.'

'What time this evening?'

'Why, I don't know exactly.'

'Where did you see him last?'

'Will you please tell me the reason for these questions?'

'Where,' he repeated, 'did you see your husband last?'

'Well, if you insist on knowing, he was here for dinner and then left for the office about seven-thirty.'

'And you haven't seen him since?'

'No.'

The officer said, 'I'm sorry, Mrs Pemberton, but your husband's body was found on the floor of his office by the janitor about half an hour ago.'

'My husband's body!' she screamed.

'Yes, ma'am,' the lieutenant said. 'He'd been killed by two bullets fired from a thirty-two caliber automatic. The ejected shells were on the floor of his office. In an adjoining office, furnished with a dilapidated desk and a couple of chairs, we found a home-rigged microphone arrangement which would work as a dictograph. In the drawer of that desk we found the gun with which the murder had been committed. Now, Mrs Pemberton, what do you know about it?'

There was silence for a second or two, then she said in a thin, frightened voice, 'Why, I don't know anything about it.'

'What do you know about that office next to your husband's?'

'Nothing.'

'You've never been in there?'

This time she didn't hesitate. 'No,' she said, 'never. I don't know what makes you think I would be spying on my husband. Perhaps someone has hired detectives. *I* wouldn't know.'

I tiptoed back to my room, picked up my bag and started silently down the corridor toward the back stairs. I could hear the rumble of a man's voice from the front room, and, at intervals, the thin, shrill sound of Mrs Pemberton's half-hysterical answers.

I felt my way down the back stairs. There was a glass window in the back door, with a shade drawn over it. I raised a corner of the shade and peered through the glass. I could see the bulky figure of a man silhouetted against the lights which filtered in from the back yard. He was holding a sawed-off police riot gun in his hands.

I took a flash-light from my pocket and started exploring the kitchen. I found the door to the cellar, and went down. From the floor above came the scrape of chairs, then the noise of feet moving about the house.

There was a little window in the cellar. I scraped cobwebs away and shook off a couple of spiders I could feel crawling on my hand. I worked the catch on the sash and pulled it open. It dropped down on hinges and hung down on the inside. I pushed my bag out, breathed a prayer to Lady Luck, and gave a jump. My elbows caught on the cement. I wiggled and twisted, pulling myself up, and fighting to keep the side of the window from catching on my knees and coming up with me. I scrambled out to the lawn.

No one was watching this side of the house. I picked up my bag, tiptoed across the lawn and pushed my way through a hedge. In the next yard a dog commenced to bark. I turned back to the sidewalk and started walking fast. I looked back over my shoulder and saw lights coming on in the second story of the Pemberton house.

I walked faster.

*

From a pay station, I put in a long distance call for old E.B. Jonathan. E.B. didn't appreciate being called out of his slumber, but I didn't give him a chance to do any crabbing.

'Your client down here,' I told him, 'is having trouble.'

'Well,' he said, 'it can keep until morning.'

'No,' I told him, 'I don't think it can.'

'Why can't it?'

'She's going to jail.'

'What's she going to jail for?'

'Taking a couple of pot shots at her husband with a thirty-two automatic.'

'Did she hit him?'

'Dead center.'

'Where does that leave you?' Jonathan asked.

'As a fugitive from justice, talking from a pay station,' I told him. 'The janitor will testify that I was with her when she went up to the place, where the shooting occurred. The janitor is her dog. He lies down and rolls over when she snaps her fingers. She thinks it'd be nice to make me the goat.'

'You mean by blaming the shooting on you?'

'Exactly.'

'What makes you think so?'

'I'd trust some women a hell of a lot more than you do, and some women a hell of a lot less. This one I trust a lot less.'

'She's a client,' E.B. said testily. 'She wouldn't do that.'

'I know she's a client,' I told him. 'That may put whitewash all over her as far as you're concerned, but it doesn't as far as I'm concerned. I made her ditch the gun out of her handbag so she wouldn't be tempted to use it. I got my finger-prints on the gun doing it. When the going gets rough, she'll think of that, and the janitor in the building will swear to anything she suggests.'

He made clucking noises with his tongue against the roof of his mouth. 'I'll have Boniface drive down there right away,' he said. 'Where can Boniface find you?'

'Nowhere,' I said and hung up.

There was an all-night hamburger stand down by the depot. I ordered six hamburgers with plenty of onions and had them put in a bag to take out. I'd noticed there was a rooming-house across from the apartment where Diane Locke lived. I went there.

The landlady grumbled about the lateness of the hour, but I paid two days' rent in advance and she showed me a front room.

I said to her 'I work nights, and will be sleeping daytimes. Please don't let anyone disturb me.'

I told her I was Peter J. Gibbens from Seattle. She digested this sleepily and ambled away. I found a 'Do not Disturb' sign in the room which I hung on the door. I locked the door and went to bed.

About three o'clock in the afternoon, I sneaked out in the hallway for a reconnaissance. There were newspapers on the desk. I picked up one, left a nickel, and went back to the room.

My own picture stared at me from the front page. 'Peter Wennick, connected with prominent law firm in the metropolis, being sought for questioning by local police in connection with Pemberton murder.' This was in bold, black type.

It was quite an account: Mrs Pemberton had 'told all.' She had consulted the law firm in connection with some blackmail letters. The law firm had said I was a 'leg man and detective.' I had been sent down to investigate the situation and report on the evidence. She had taken me to the office, where, with a friendly janitor, she had rigged up a dictaphone. I had listened to a conversation between her husband and 'the woman in the case.'

On the pretext of leaving for the wash-room, I had thrown the night latch on the door of the office so I could return at any time. She had forgotten to put the night latch back on when we left. Therefore, I had left myself an opportunity to return and gain access to the room.

The janitor remembered when we had left. Something like an hour later, he had heard muffled sounds which could have been the two shots which were fired. He thought they had been the sounds of backfire from a truck. He'd been in the basement, reading. The sounds had apparently come from the alley, but might have been shots echoed back from the walls of an adjoining building. The medical authorities fixed the time of death as being probably half an hour to an hour and a half after we'd left the building.

Mrs Pemberton had insisted she'd gone home, and that I had immediately gone out. She didn't know where. I had returned, to tell her that I had good news for her, but before I could report, police had come to the house to question her in connection with her husband's death. I had made my escape through a cellar window while police were searching the house.

Arthur H. Bass, Pemberton's partner, had stated that Pemberton had been very much worried for the past few days, that he had announced it was necessary for him to raise immediate funds and had offered to sell his interest in the partnership business for much less than its value. Bass had reluctantly made a nominal offer, but had advised Pemberton not to accept it, and when Pemberton had refused to consider such a nominal amount, Bass had been jubilant because he didn't want to lose Pemberton as a partner. He had met Pemberton at Pemberton's request, to discuss the matter.

The district attorney announced that he had interviewed 'the woman in the case.' Inasmuch as she seemed to have been 'wronged' by Pemberton, and, inasmuch as a Peeping Tom who had tried to crash the gate of her apartment had caused her to place a call for the police at approximately the time Pemberton must have been killed, the police absolved her of all responsibility.

It seemed that this Peeping Tom, evidently trying to make a mash, had knocked at her door and advised her he had held up the jewelry store downstairs. She had promptly reported to the police, who had visited her apartment, to find her very much undressed, very much excited and shaken, and apparently sincere. Police records of the call showed that the police were actually in her apartment at the time the janitor had heard the sounds of what were undoubtedly the shots which took Pemberton's life.

Mrs Pemberton, the news account went on to say, could give no evidence in support of her alibi, but police were inclined to absolve her of blame, concentrating for the moment on a search for Pete Wennick, the leg man for the law firm.

Cedric L. Boniface, a member of the law firm, very much shocked at developments, had made a rush trip to the city and was staying at the Palace Hotel. So far, authorities had not let him talk to Mrs Pemberton, but they would probably do so at an early hour in the afternoon. Mr Boniface said he 'hoped Mr Wennick would be able to absolve himself.'

That was that.

Just for the fun of the thing, I turned to the Personals. It's a habit with me. I always read them in any paper. Under the heading: 'Too late to classify,' I came on one which interested me. It read simply: 'P.W. Can I help? Call on me for anything. M.D.'

Now there was a girl! Old E.B. Jonathan, with his warped, distorted, jaundiced idea of the sex, suspected all women except clients. Clients to him were sacred. I took women as I found them. Mae Devers would stick through thick and thin.

Mrs Pemberton had paraded around in revealing silks and had called me Sir Galahad when I'd told her to go put on a bathrobe. The minute the going got rough, she'd tossed me to the wolves. The question was whether she either killed her husband while I was in the wash-room or had gone back and killed him afterwards and deliberately imported me as the fall guy for the police. If she had, she'd made a damn good job of it.

Supper consisted of a couple of cold hamburgers. About five o'clock, I drew up a chair in front of the window and started watching. The redhead had accused me of being a Peeping Tom and now I was going to be one.

I didn't see Diane Locke come in or go out, and I didn't see anyone else I knew. After it got dark, a light came on in Diane's apartment. I sat there and waited. About nine o'clock I had another hamburger. I got tired of waiting and decided I'd force the play. I looked up the telephone number of Bass & Pemberton's office and memorized it. It was Temple 491. I shaved, combed my hair, put on a suit none of my new playmates had seen me wear, crossed the street, climbed the stairs of the apartment house and knocked on the door of apartment 3A.

Nothing happened at once. I dropped to one knee, scooped dried chewing gum out of the hole in the door and looked through. She was coming toward the door. And she had her clothes on.

I straightened as she came to the door, opened it, and asked, 'What is it?'

'I'm from the police,' I said in a thin, high, nasal voice this time. 'I'm trying to check up on that call you put through to police headquarters last night.'

'Yes?' she asked. She'd never seen me without a mask. 'What is it you wanted to know?'

'I'm trying to check your call,' I told her. 'If you don't mind, I'll come in.' I came in before she had a chance to mind. I walked over to the chair and sat down. She sat down in the other chair.

The chair I was sitting in was warm. 'Pardon me,' I said, 'was this your chair?'

'No. I was sitting in this one,' she told me.

She looked at me and said, 'I've seen you before. There's something vaguely familiar about your face. And I think I've heard your voice somewhere.'

I grinned across at her and said, 'I never contradict a lady, but if I'd ever met you, I'd remember it until I was a hundred and ten.'

She smiled at that and crossed her knees. I looked over at the ash-tray. There were two cigarette stubs on it. Both were smoldering. There was only one match in the tray. It was broken in two.

She followed the direction of my eyes, laughed, and pinched out the stubs. 'I'm always leaving cigarette stubs burning,' she said. 'What was it you wanted?'

I slid my hand under the lapel of my coat and loosened the gun. 'Miss Locke,' I said, 'you understand that the time element here is important. It's a question of when you placed that call to the police, as well as when the police got here. We want to check carefully on all those times. Now, in order to do that, I've been checking your calls with the telephone company. It seems that you put through a call to Temple 491 very shortly after you called the police. Can you tell me about that call?'

She studied her tinted fingernails for a minute, then raised her eyes and said, 'Yes, frankly, I can. I called Mr Pemberton.'

'Why did you call him?'

She said, 'I think you'll understand that I felt very close to Mr Pemberton in many ways. He had – well, he'd tricked me and betrayed me, but, nevertheless. . . . Oh, I just hated to make trouble for him. I called him to tell him I was sorry.'

'Did you talk with him?' My throat was getting irritated from straining my voice high.

Once more she hesitated, then said, 'No, he didn't answer the telephone.'

'The telephone company has you on a limited call basis,' I said. 'They report that the call was completed.'

Once more she studied her fingernails.

'Someone answered the phone,' she said, 'but said he was the janitor cleaning up the offices. So I hung up on him.'

That gave me all I wanted to know. I said, and I spoke in my own voice now, 'You know, it was a dirty trick they played on you, Diane. I don't think Bass cared whether you got anything out of it or not. He wanted Pemberton's interest in the partnership. In fact he had to have it because he'd been juggling funds. He was the mythical "lawyer" behind you. You're his woman and he put you up to playing Pemberton for a sucker, hoping Pemberton would be involved enough so he could put into effect that trick clause in the partnership agreement and buy him out for two thousand dollars. When Pemberton said he was going to have an auditor make a complete analysis of the books for the purpose of finding out what a half interest was worth, Bass went into a panic.'

She went white to her lips, but said nothing.

I went on: 'As soon as your "burglar" left and you found you'd lost the letters, you called Bass up and told him what had happened. He was in his private office, waiting for a call, waiting also for Pemberton to come back and accept his offer as a final last resort.

'But Bass was pretty smooth. He probably knew I wasn't Olive Pemberton's brother. He guessed I was a detective. That meant Olive was wise to the Diane business, and he was shrewd enough to figure there might be a dictograph running into Pemberton's office. He did a little exploring. The door to the adjoining office was unlocked, and he stepped in, looked the plant over, and found the gun. Obviously either Olive or I had left the gun there. It could be traced to one of us. It looked like a set-up. Bass took the gun with him, did the job and returned it.

'Killing Pemberton was his only out. Without the letters, his little blackmail scheme had fallen through. There'd be no money coming in to cover the shortage the audit would turn up. That meant he'd go to prison. Well, he'll go anyway, and he'll stay just long enough to be made ready for a pine box.'

By this time the redhead had recognized me, of course. 'You and your pearls,' she sneered, but the sneer was only a camouflage for the growing fright in her eyes.

'Now,' I went on, 'you're in Bass's way. Bass can't have the police knowing he was behind the blackmail business, and you can show he was. He'll have to try to get rid of both of us.'

'Arthur would never do anything like that,' she cried.

The closet door was in front of me. The bathroom door

was behind me. But a mirror in the closet door enabled me to see the bathroom one. I kept my eyes on these doors.

'He will, though,' I told her, 'and you know it. He's already killed once. Otherwise why did he come here tonight to tell you that under no circumstances were you to admit you'd talked with him over the telephone?'

She moistened her lips with her tongue. 'How do you know all these things?' she asked.

'I know them,' I told her, 'because I know that persons who have ever worked as forest rangers in the dry country make it an invariable habit to break their matches in two before they throw them away. I know that he was here the other night because there were broken matches in your ash-tray. He'd sent you up to put the screws on Harvey Pemberton. I know that he's here tonight. I know he was in the office last night. Just before you came in he'd been talking with Harvey Pemberton. I didn't hear him take the elevator, so I know he went in to his private office after he'd finished that talk. He was still there when I left. I'm Wennick.'

'But he wouldn't have done anything like that,' she said. 'Arthur couldn't.'

'But you did telephone right after those letters had been stolen, and told him about it, didn't you?'

'Yes,' she said, 'I –'

The door behind me opened a half inch. I saw the muzzle of the gun slowly creep out, but it wasn't until I had my fingers on the butt of my own gun that I realized the barrel wasn't pointing at me, but at her.

'Duck!' I yelled.

I think it was the sudden yell which frightened her half out of her wits. She didn't duck, but she recoiled from me as though I'd thrown a brick at her instead of my voice. The gun went off. The bullet whizzed through the air right where her head had been, and buried itself in the plaster. I whirled and shot, through the door. I saw the gun barrel waver. I shot again, and then an arm came into sight, drooping toward the floor. The gun fell from nerveless fingers, and Arthur Bass crashed full length into the room.

Old E.B. glowered at me with little, malevolent eyes which glittered from above the bluish-white pouches which puffed out from under his eyeballs. 'Wennick,' he said, 'you look like the devil!'

'I'm sorry,' I told him.

'You look dissipated.'

'I haven't shaved yet.'

'From all reports,' he said, 'you cleaned up this Pemberton murder case and were released by the police at Culverton with a vote of thanks, some time before ten o'clock yesterday evening. Cedric Boniface was in the law library, briefing the question of premeditation in connection with murder. He didn't know what had happened until after the police had obtained Bass's dying statement and you had left.'

I nodded.

'Now then,' E.B. said, 'why the hell is it that you didn't report to me?'

'I'm sorry,' I told him, 'but, after all, I have social engagements.'

'Social engagements!' he stormed. 'You were out with some woman!'

I nodded. 'I was out with a young lady,' I admitted, 'celebrating her birthday.'

He started cracking his knuckles. 'Out with a young lady!' he snorted. 'I had your apartment watched so I could be notified the minute you got in. You didn't get in until six o'clock this morning.'

RAYMOND CHANDLER

I'LL BE WAITING

AT ONE O'CLOCK in the morning, Carl, the night porter, turned down the last of three table lamps in the main lobby of the Windermere Hotel. The blue carpet darkened a shade or two and the walls drew back into remoteness. The chairs filled with shadowy loungers. In the corners were memories like cobwebs.

Tony Reseck yawned. He put his head on one side and listened to the frail, twittery music from the radio room beyond a dim arch at the far side of the lobby. He frowned. That should be his radio room after one a.m. Nobody should be in it. That red-haired girl was spoiling his nights.

The frown passed and a miniature of a smile quirked at the corners of his lips. He sat relaxed, a short, pale, paunchy, middle-aged man with long, delicate fingers clasped on the elk's tooth on his watch chain; the long delicate fingers of a sleight-of-hand artist, fingers with shiny, molded nails and tapering first joints, fingers a little spatulate at the ends. Handsome fingers. Tony Reseck rubbed them gently together and there was peace in his quiet sea-gray eyes.

The frown came back on his face. The music annoyed him. He got up with a curious litheness, all in one piece, without moving his clasped hands from the watch chain. At one moment he was leaning back relaxed, and the next he was standing balanced on his feet, perfectly still, so that the movement of rising seemed to be a thing perfectly perceived, an error of vision. . . .

He walked with small, polished shoes delicately across the blue carpet and under the arch. The music was louder. It contained the hot, acid blare, the frenetic, jittering runs of a jam session. It was too loud. The red-haired girl sat there and stared silently at the fretted part of the big radio cabinet as though she could see the band with its fixed professional grin and the sweat running down its back. She was curled up with her feet under her on a davenport which seemed to contain most of the cushions in the room. She was tucked among them carefully, like a corsage in the florist's tissue paper.

She didn't turn her head. She leaned there, one hand in a small fist on her peach-colored knee. She was wearing lounging pajamas of heavy ribbed silk embroidered with black lotus buds.

'You like Goodman, Miss Cressy?' Tony Reseck asked.

The girl moved her eyes slowly. The light in there was dim, but the violet of her eyes almost hurt. They were large, deep eyes without a trace of thought in them. Her face was classical and without expression.

She said nothing.

Tony smiled and moved his fingers at his sides, one by one, feeling them move. 'You like Goodman, Miss Cressy?' he repeated gently.

'Not to cry over,' the girl said tonelessly.

Tony rocked back on his heels and looked at her eyes. Large, deep, empty eyes. Or were they? He reached down and muted the radio.

'Don't get me wrong,' the girl said. 'Goodman makes money, and a lad that makes legitimate money these days is a lad you have to respect. But this jitterbug music gives me the backdrop of a beer flat. I like something with roses in it.'

'Maybe you like Mozart,' Tony said.

'Go on, kid me,' the girl said.

'I wasn't kidding you, Miss Cressy. I think Mozart was the greatest man that ever lived – and Toscanini is his prophet.'

'I thought you were the house dick.' She put her head back on a pillow and stared at him through her lashes.

'Make me some of that Mozart,' she added.

'It's too late,' Tony sighed. 'You can't get it now.'

She gave him another long lucid glance. 'Got the eye on me, haven't you, flatfoot?' She laughed a little, almost under her breath. 'What did I do wrong?'

Tony smiled his toy smile. 'Nothing, Miss Cressy. Nothing at all. But you need some fresh air. You've been five days in this hotel and you haven't been outdoors. And you have a tower room.'

She laughed again. 'Make me a story about it. I'm bored.'

'There was a girl here once had your suite. She stayed in the hotel a whole week, like you. Without going out at all, I mean. She didn't speak to anybody hardly. What do you think she did then?'

The girl eyed him gravely. 'She jumped her bill.'

He put his long delicate hand out and turned it slowly, fluttering the fingers, with an effect almost like a lazy wave breaking. 'Unh-uh. She sent down for her bill and paid it. Then she told the hop to be back in half an hour for her suitcases. Then she went out on her balcony.'

The girl leaned forward a little, her eyes still grave, one hand capping her peach-colored knee. 'What did you say your name was?'

'Tony Reseck.'

'Sounds like a hunky.'

'Yeah,' Tony said. 'Polish.'

'Go on, Tony.'

'All the tower suites have private balconies, Miss Cressy.

The walls of them are too low for fourteen stories above the street. It was a dark night, that night, high clouds.' He dropped his hand with a final gesture, a farewell gesture. 'Nobody saw her jump. But when she hit, it was like a big gun going off.'

'You're making it up, Tony.' Her voice was a clean dry whisper of sound.

He smiled his toy smile. His quiet sea-gray eyes seemed almost to be smoothing the long waves of her hair, 'Eve Cressy,' he said musingly. 'A name waiting for lights to be in.'

'Waiting for a tall dark guy that's no good, Tony. You wouldn't care why. I was married to him once. I might be married to him again. You can make a lot of mistakes in just one lifetime.' The hand on her knee opened slowly until the fingers were strained back as far as they would go. Then they closed quickly and tightly, and even in that dim light the knuckles shone like the little polished bones. 'I played him a low trick once. I put him in a bad place – without meaning to. You wouldn't care about that either. It's just that I owe him something.'

He leaned over softly and turned the knob on the radio. A waltz formed itself dimly on the warm air. A tinsel waltz, but a waltz. He turned the volume up. The music gushed from the loudspeaker in a swirl of shadowed melody. Since Vienna died, all waltzes are shadowed.

The girl put her hand on one side and hummed three or four bars and stopped with a sudden tightening of her mouth.

'Eve Cressy,' she said. 'It was in lights once. At a bum night club. A dive. They raided it and the lights went out.'

He smiled at her almost mockingly. 'It was no dive while you were there, Miss Cressy . . . That's the waltz the orchestra always played when the old porter walked up and down in front of the hotel entrance, all swelled up with his medals on his chest. *The Last Laugh*. Emil Jannings. You wouldn't remember that one, Miss Cressy.'

' "Spring, Beautiful Spring," ' she said. 'No, I never saw it.'

He walked three steps away from her and turned. 'I have to go upstairs and palm doorknobs. I hope I didn't bother you. You ought to go to bed now. It's pretty late.'

The tinsel waltz stopped and a voice began to talk. The girl spoke through the voice. 'You really thought something like that – about the balcony?'

He nodded. 'I might have,' he said softly. 'I don't any more.'

'No chance, Tony.' Her smile was a dim lost leaf. 'Come and talk to me some more. Redheads don't jump, Tony. They hang on – and wither.'

He looked at her gravely for a moment and then moved away over the carpet. The porter was standing in the archway that led to the main lobby. Tony hadn't looked that way yet, but he knew somebody was there. He always knew if anybody was close to him. He could hear the grass grow, like the donkey in *The Blue Bird*.

The porter jerked his chin at him urgently. His broad face above the uniform collar looked sweaty and excited. Tony stepped up close to him and they went together through the arch and out to the middle of the dim lobby.

'Trouble?' Tony asked wearily.

'There's a guy outside to see you, Tony. He won't come in. I'm doing a wipe-off on the plate glass of the doors and he comes up beside me, a tall guy. "Get Tony," he says, out of the side of his mouth.'

Tony said: 'Uh-huh,' and looked at the porter's pale blue eyes. 'Who was it?'

'Al, he said to say he was.'

Tony's face became as expressionless as dough. 'Okey.' He started to move off.

The porter caught his sleeve. 'Listen, Tony. You got any enemies?'

Tony laughed politely, his face still like dough.

'Listen, Tony.' The porter held his sleeve tightly. 'There's a big black car down the block, the other way from the hacks. There's a guy standing beside it with his foot on the running board. This guy that spoke to me, he wears a dark-colored, wrap-around overcoat with a high collar turned up against his ears. His hat's way low. You can't hardly see his face. He says, "Get Tony," out of the side of his mouth. You ain't got any enemies, have you, Tony?'

'Only the finance company,' Tony said. 'Beat it.'

He walked slowly and a little stiffly across the blue carpet, up the three shallow steps to the entrance lobby with the three elevators on one side and the desk on the other. Only one elevator was working. Beside the open doors, his arms folded, the night operator stood silent in a neat blue uniform with silver facings. A lean, dark Mexican named Gomez. A new boy, breaking in on the night shift.

The other side was the desk, rose marble, with the night clerk leaning on it delicately. A small neat man with a wispy reddish mustache and cheeks so rosy they looked rouged. He stared at Tony and poked a nail at his mustache.

Tony pointed a stiff index finger at him, folded the other three fingers tight to his palm, and flicked his thumb up and down on the stiff finger. The clerk touched the other side of his mustache and looked bored.

Tony went on past the closed and darkened newsstand and the side entrance to the drugstore, out to the brassbound plate-glass doors. He stopped just inside them and took a deep, hard breath. He squared his shoulders, pushed the doors open and stepped out into the cold damp night air.

The street was dark, silent. The rumble of traffic on Wilshire, two blocks away, had no body, no meaning. To the left were two taxis. Their drivers leaned against a fender, side by side, smoking. Tony walked the other way. The big dark car was a third of a block from the hotel entrance. Its lights were dimmed and it was only when he was almost up to it that he heard the gentle sound of its engine turning over.

A tall figure detached itself from the body of the car and strolled toward him, both hands in the pockets of the dark overcoat with the high collar. From the man's mouth a cigarette tip glowed faintly, a rusty pearl.

They stopped two feet from each other.

The tall man said, 'Hi, Tony. Long time no see.'

'Hello, Al. How's it going?'

'Can't complain.' The tall man started to take his right hand out of his overcoat pocket, then stopped and laughed quietly. 'I forgot. Guess you don't want to shake hands.'

'That don't mean anything,' Tony said. 'Shaking hands. Monkeys can shake hands. What's on your mind, Al?'

'Still the funny little fat guy, eh, Tony?'

'I guess.' Tony winked his eyes tight. His throat felt tight.

'You like your job back there?'

'It's a job.'

Al laughed his quiet laugh again. 'You take it slow, Tony. I'll take it fast. So it's a job and you want to hold it. Okey. There's a girl named Eve Cressy flopping in your quiet hotel. Get her out. Fast and right now.'

'What's the trouble?'

The tall man looked up and down the street. A man behind in the car coughed lightly. 'She's hooked with a wrong number. Nothing against her personal, but she'll lead trouble to you. Get her out, Tony. You got maybe an hour.'

'Sure,' Tony said aimlessly, without meaning.

Al took his hand out of his pocket and stretched it against Tony's chest. He gave him a light lazy push. 'I wouldn't be telling you just for the hell of it, little fat brother. Get her out of there.'

'Okey,' Tony said, without any tone in his voice.

The tall man took back his hand and reached for the car door. He opened it and started to slip in like a lean black shadow.

Then he stopped and said something to the men in the car and got out again. He came back to where Tony stood silent, his pale eyes catching a little dim light from the street.

'Listen, Tony. You always kept your nose clean. You're a good brother, Tony.'

Tony didn't speak.

Al leaned toward him, a long urgent shadow, the high collar almost touching his ears. 'It's trouble business, Tony. The boys won't like it, but I'm telling you just the same. This Cressy was married to a lad named Johnny Ralls. Ralls is out of Quentin two, three days, or a week. He did a three-spot for manslaughter. The girl put him there. He ran down an old man one night when he was drunk, and she was with him. He wouldn't stop. She told him to go in and tell it, or else. He didn't go in. So the Johns come for him.'

Tony said, 'That's too bad.'

'It's kosher, kid. It's my business to know. This Ralls flapped his mouth in stir about how the girl would be waiting for him when he got out, all set to forgive and forget, and he was going straight to her.'

Tony said, 'What's he to you?' His voice had a dry, stiff crackle, like thick paper.

Al laughed. 'The trouble boys want to see him. He ran a table at a spot on the Strip and figured out a scheme. He and another guy took the house for fifty grand. The other lad coughed up, but we still need Johnny's twenty-five. The trouble boys don't get paid to forget.'

Tony looked up and down the dark street. One of the taxi drivers flicked a cigarette stub in a long arc over the top of one of the cabs. Tony watched it fall and spark on the pavement. He listened to the quiet sound of the big car's motor.

'I don't want any part of it,' he said. 'I'll get her out.'

Al backed away from him, nodding. 'Wise kid. How's mom these days?'

'Okey,' Tony said.

'Tell her I was asking for her.'

'Asking for her isn't anything,' Tony said.

Al turned quickly and got into the car. The car curved lazily in the middle of the block and drifted back toward the corner. Its lights went up and sprayed on a wall. It turned a corner and was gone. The lingering smell of its exhaust drifted past Tony's nose. He turned and walked back to the hotel and into it. He went along to the radio room.

The radio still muttered, but the girl was gone from the davenport in front of it. The pressed cushions were hollowed out by her body. Tony reached down and touched them. He thought they were still warm. He turned the radio off and stood there, turning a thumb slowly in front of his body, his hand flat against his stomach. Then he went back through the lobby toward the elevator bank and stood beside a majolica jar of white sand. The clerk fussed behind a pebbled-glass screen at one end of the desk. The air was dead.

The elevator bank was dark. Tony looked at the indicator of the middle car and saw that it was at 14.

'Gone to bed,' he said under his breath.

The door of the porter's room beside the elevators opened and the little Mexican night operator came out in street clothes. He looked at Tony with a quiet sidewise look out of eyes the color of dried-out chestnuts.

'Good night, boss.'

'Yeah,' Tony said absently.

He took a thin dappled cigar out of his vest pocket and smelled it. He examined it slowly, turning it around in his neat fingers. There was a small tear along the side. He frowned at that and put the cigar away.

There was a distant sound and the hand on the indicator began to steal around the bronze dial. Light glittered up in the shaft and the straight line of the car floor dissolved the darkness below. The car stopped and the doors opened, and Carl came out of it.

His eyes caught Tony's with a kind of jump and he walked over to him, his head on one side, a thin shine along his pink upper lip.

'Listen, Tony.'

Tony took his arm in a hard swift hand and turned him. He pushed him quickly, yet somehow casually, down the steps to the dim main lobby and steered him into a corner. He let go of the arm. His throat tightened again, for no reason he could think of.

'Well?' he said darkly. 'Listen to what?'

The porter reached into a pocket and hauled out a dollar bill. 'He gimme this,' he said loosely. His glittering eyes looked past Tony's shoulder at nothing. They winked rapidly. 'Ice and ginger ale.'

'Don't stall,' Tony growled.

'Guy in Fourteen-B,' the porter said.

'Lemme smell your breath.'

The porter leaned toward him obediently.

'Liquor,' Tony said harshly.

'He gimme a drink.'

Tony looked down at the dollar bill. 'Nobody's in Fourteen-B. Not on my list,' he said.

'Yeah. There is.' The porter licked his lips and his eyes opened and shut several times. 'Tall dark guy.'

'All right,' Tony said crossly. 'All right. There's a tall dark guy in Fourteen-B and he gave you a buck and a drink. Then what?'

'Gat under his arm,' Carl said, and blinked.

Tony smiled, but his eyes had taken on the lifeless glitter of thick ice. 'You take Miss Cressy up to her room?'

Carl shook his head. 'Gomez. I saw her go up.'

'Get away from me,' Tony said between his teeth. 'And don't accept any more drinks from the guests.'

He didn't move until Carl had gone back into his cubby-hole by the elevators and shut the door. Then he moved silently up the three steps and stood in front of the desk, looking at the veined rose marble, the onyx pen set, the fresh registration card in its leather frame. He lifted a hand and smacked it down hard on the marble. The clerk popped out from behind the glass screen like a chipmunk coming out of its hole.

Tony took a flimsy out of his breast pocket and spread it on the desk. 'No Fourteen-B on this,' he said in a bitter voice.

The clerk wisped politely at his mustache. 'So sorry. You must have been out to supper when he checked in.'

'Who?'

'Registered as James Watterson, San Diego.' The clerk yawned.

'Ask for anybody?'

The clerk stopped in the middle of the yawn and looked at the top of Tony's head. 'Why yes. He asked for a swing band. Why?'

'Smart, fast and funny,' Tony said. 'If you like 'em that way.' He wrote on his flimsy and stuffed it back into his pocket. 'I'm going upstairs and palm doorknobs. There's four tower rooms you ain't rented yet. Get up on your toes, son. You're slipping.'

'I made out,' the clerk drawled, and completed his yawn. 'Hurry back, pop. I don't know how I'll get through the time.'

'You could shave that pink fuzz off your lip,' Tony said, and went across to the elevators.

He opened up a dark one and lit the dome light and shot the car up to fourteen. He darkened it again, stepped out and closed the doors. This lobby was smaller than any other, except the one immediately below it. It had a single blue-paneled door in each of the walls other than the elevator wall. On each door was a gold number and letter with a gold wreath around it. Tony walked over to 14A and put his ear to the panel. He heard nothing. Eve Cressy might be in bed asleep, or in the bathroom, or out on the balcony. Or she might be sitting there in the room, a few feet from the door, looking at the wall. Well, he wouldn't expect to be able to hear her sit and look at the wall. He went over to 14B and put his ear to that panel. This was different. There was a sound in there. A man coughed. It sounded somehow like a solitary cough. There were no voices. Tony pressed the small nacre button beside the door.

Steps came without hurry. A thickened voice spoke through the panel. Tony made no answer, no sound. The thickened voice repeated the question. Lightly, maliciously, Tony pressed the bell again.

Mr James Watterson, of San Diego, should now open the

door and give forth noise. He didn't. A silence fell beyond that door that was like the silence of a glacier. Once more Tony put his ear to the wood. Silence utterly.

He got out a master key on a chain and pushed it delicately into the lock of the door. He turned it, pushed the door inward three inches and withdrew the key. Then he waited.

'All right,' the voice said harshly. 'Come in and get it.'

Tony pushed the door wide and stood there, framed against the light from the lobby. The man was tall, black-haired, angular and white-faced. He held a gun. He held it as though he knew about guns.

'Step right in,' he drawled.

Tony went in through the door and pushed it shut with his shoulder. He kept his hands a little out from his sides, the clever fingers curled and slack. He smiled his quiet little smile.

'Mr Watterson?'

'And after that what?'

'I'm the house detective here.'

'It slays me.'

The tall, white-faced, somehow handsome and somehow not handsome man backed slowly into the room. It was a large room with a low balcony around two sides of it. French doors opened out on the little private open-air balcony that each of the tower rooms had. There was a grate set for a log fire behind a paneled screen in front of a cheerful davenport. A tall misted glass stood on a hotel tray beside a deep, cozy chair. The man backed toward this and stood in front of it. The large, glistening gun drooped and pointed at the floor.

'It slays me,' he said. 'I'm in the dump an hour and the house copper gives me the bus. Okey, sweetheart, look in the closet and bathroom. But she just left.'

'You didn't see her yet,' Tony said.

The man's bleached face filled with unexpected lines. His thickened voice edged toward a snarl. 'Yeah? Who didn't I see yet?'

'A girl named Eve Cressy.'

The man swallowed. He put his gun down on the table beside the tray. He let himself down into the chair backwards, stiffly, like a man with a touch of lumbago. Then he leaned forward and put his hands on his kneecaps and smiled brightly between his teeth. 'So she got here, huh? I didn't ask about her yet. I'm a careful guy. I didn't ask yet.'

'She's been here five days,' Tony said. 'Waiting for you. She hasn't left the hotel a minute.'

The man's mouth worked a little. His smile had a knowing tilt to it. 'I got delayed a little up north,' he said smoothly. 'You know how it is. Visiting old friends. You seem to know a lot about my business, copper.'

'That's right, Mr Ralls.'

The man lunged to his feet and his hand snapped at the gun. He stood leaning over, holding it on the table, staring. 'Dames talk too much,' he said with a muffled sound in his voice as though he held something soft between his teeth and talked through it.

'Not dames, Mr Ralls.'

'Huh?' The gun slithered on the hard wood of the table. 'Talk it up, copper. My mind reader just quit.'

'Not dames, guys. Guys with guns.'

The glacier silence fell between them again. The man straightened his body out slowly. His face was washed clean of expression, but his eyes were haunted. Tony leaned in front of him, a shortish plump man with a quiet, pale, friendly face and eyes as simple as forest water.

'They never run out of gas – those boys,' Johnny Ralls said, and licked at his lip. 'Early and late, they work. The old firm never sleeps.'

'You know who they are?' Tony said softly.

'I could maybe give nine guesses. And twelve of them would be right.'

'The trouble boys,' Tony said, and smiled a brittle smile.

'Where is she?' Johnny Ralls asked harshly.

'Right next door to you.'

The man walked to the wall and left his gun lying on the table. He stood in front of the wall, studying it. He reached up and gripped the grillwork of the balcony railing. When he dropped his hand and turned, his face had lost some of its lines. His eyes had a quieter glint. He moved back to Tony and stood over him.

'I've got a stake,' he said. 'Eve sent me some dough and I built it up with a touch I made up north. Case dough, what I mean. The trouble boys talk about twenty-five grand.' He smiled crookedly. 'Five C's I can count. I'd have a lot of fun making them believe that, I would.'

'What did you do with it?' Tony asked indifferently.

'I never had it, copper. Leave that lay. I'm the only guy in the world that believes it. It was a little deal that I got suckered on.'

'I'll believe it,' Tony said.

'They don't kill often. But they can be awful tough.'

'Mugs,' Tony said with a sudden bitter contempt. 'Guys with guns. Just mugs.'

Johnny Ralls reached for his glass and drained it empty. The ice cubes tinkled softly as he put it down. He picked his gun up, danced it on his palm, then tucked it, nose down, into an inner breast pocket. He stared at the carpet.

'How come you're telling me this, copper?'

'I thought maybe you'd give her a break.'

'And if I wouldn't?'

'I kind of think you will,' Tony said.

Johnny Ralls nodded quietly. 'Can I get out of here?'

'You could take the service elevator to the garage. You could rent a car. I can give you a card to the garage man.'

'You're a funny little guy,' Johnny Ralls said.

Tony took out a worn ostrich-skin billfold and scribbled on a printed card. Johnny Ralls read it, and stood holding it, tapping it against a thumbnail.

'I could take her with me,' he said, his eyes narrow.

'You could take a ride in a basket too,' Tony said. 'She's been here five days, I told you. She's been spotted. A guy I know called me up and told me to get her out of here. Told me what it was all about. So I'm getting you out instead.'

'They'll love that,' Johnny Ralls said. 'They'll send you violets.'

'I'll weep about it on my day off.'

Johnny Ralls turned his hand over and stared at the palm. 'I could see her, anyway. Before I blow. Next door to here, you said?'

Tony turned on his heel and started for the door. He said over his shoulder, 'Don't waste a lot of time, handsome. I might change my mind.'

The man said, almost gently: 'You might be spotting me right now, for all I know.'

Tony didn't turn his head. 'That's a chance you have to take.'

He went on to the door and passed out of the room. He shut it carefully, silently, looked once at the door of 14A and got into his dark elevator. He rode it down to the linen-room floor and got out to remove the basket that held the service elevator open at that floor. The door slid quietly shut. He held it so that it made no noise. Down the corridor, light came from the open door of the housekeeper's office. Tony got back into his elevator and went on down to the lobby.

The little clerk was out of sight behind his pebbled-glass screen, auditing accounts. Tony went through the main lobby and turned into the radio room. The radio was on again, soft. She was there, curled on the davenport again. The speaker hummed to her, a vague sound so low that what it said was as wordless as the murmur of trees. She turned her head slowly and smiled at him.

'Finished palming doorknobs? I couldn't sleep worth a nickel. So I came down again. Okey?'

He smiled and nodded. He sat down in a green chair and patted the plump brocade arms of it. 'Sure, Miss Cressy.'

'Waiting is the hardest kind of work, isn't it? I wish you'd talk to that radio. It sounds like a pretzel being bent.'

Tony fiddled with it, got nothing he liked, set it back where it had been.

'Beer-parlor drunks are all the customers now.'

She smiled at him again.

'I don't bother you being here, Miss Cressy?'

'I like it. You're a sweet little guy, Tony.'

He looked stiffly at the floor and a ripple touched his spine. He waited for it to go away. It went slowly. Then he sat back, relaxed again, his neat fingers clasped on his elk's tooth. He listened. Not to the radio – to far-off, uncertain things, menacing things. And perhaps to just the safe whir of wheels going away into a strange night.

'Nobody's all bad,' he said out loud.

The girl looked at him lazily. 'I've met two or three I was wrong on, then.'

He nodded. 'Yeah,' he admitted judiciously. 'I guess there's some that are.'

The girl yawned and her deep violet eyes half closed. She nestled back into the cushions. 'Sit there for a while, Tony. Maybe I could nap.'

'Sure. Not a thing for me to do. Don't know why they pay me.'

She slept quickly and with complete stillness, like a child. Tony hardly breathed for ten minutes. He just watched her, his mouth a little open. There was a quiet fascination in his limpid eyes, as if he was looking at an altar.

Then he stood up with infinite care and padded away under the arch to the entrance lobby and the desk. He stood at the desk listening for a little while. He heard a pen rustling out of sight. He went around the corner to the row of house phones in little glass cubbyholes. He lifted one and asked the night operator for the garage.

It rang three or four times and then a boyish voice answered: 'Windermere Hotel. Garage speaking.'

'This is Tony Reseck. That guy Watterson I gave a card to. He leave?'

'Sure, Tony. Half an hour almost. Is it your charge?'

'Yeah,' Tony said. 'My party. Thanks. Be seein' you.'

He hung up and scratched his neck. He went back to the desk and slapped a hand on it. The clerk wafted himself around the screen with his greeter's smile in place. It dropped when he saw Tony.

'Can't a guy catch up on his work?' he grumbled.

'What's the professional rate on Fourteen-B?'

The clerk stared morosely. 'There's no professional rate in the tower.'

'Make one. The fellow left already. Was there only an hour.'

'Well, well,' the clerk said airily. 'So the personality didn't click tonight. We get a skip-out.'

'Will five bucks satisfy you?'

'Friend of yours?'

'No. Just a drunk with delusions of grandeur and no dough.'

'Guess we'll have to let it ride, Tony. How did he get out?'

'I took him down the service elevator. You was asleep. Will five bucks satisfy you?'

'Why?'

The worn ostrich-skin wallet came out and a weedy five slipped across the marble. 'All I could shake him for,' Tony said loosely.

The clerk took the five and looked puzzled. 'You're the boss,' he said, and shrugged. The phone shrilled on the desk and he reached for it. He listened and then pushed it toward Tony. 'For you.'

Tony took the phone and cuddled it close to his chest. He put his mouth close to the transmitter. The voice was strange to him. It had a metallic sound. Its syllables were meticulously anonymous.

'Tony? Tony Reseck?'

'Talking.'

'A message from Al. Shoot?'

Tony looked at the clerk. 'Be a pal,' he said over the mouthpiece. The clerk flicked a narrow smile at him and went away. 'Shoot,' Tony said into the phone.

'We had a little business with a guy in your place. Picked him up scramming. Al had a hunch you'd run him out. Tailed him and took him to the curb. Not so good. Backfire.'

Tony held the phone very tight and his temples chilled with the evaporation of moisture. 'Go on,' he said. 'I guess there's more.'

'A little. The guy stopped the big one. Cold. Al – Al said to tell you goodbye.'

Tony leaned hard against the desk. His mouth made a sound that was not speech.

'Get it?' The metallic voice sounded impatient, a little bored. 'This guy had him a rod. He used it. Al won't be phoning anybody any more.'

Tony lurched at the phone, and the base of it shook on the rose marble. His mouth was a hard dry knot.

The voice said: 'That's as far as we go, bub. G'night.' The phone clicked dryly, like a pebble hitting a wall.

Tony put the phone down in its cradle very carefully, so as not to make any sound. He looked at the clenched palm of his left hand. He took a handkerchief out and rubbed the palm softly and straightened the fingers out with his other hand. Then he wiped his forehead. The clerk came around the screen again and looked at him with glinting eyes.

'I'm off Friday. How about lending me that phone number?'

Tony nodded at the clerk and smiled a minute frail smile. He put his handkerchief away and patted the pocket he had put it in. He turned and walked away from the desk, across the entrance lobby, down the three shallow steps, along the shadowy reaches of the main lobby, and so in through the arch to the radio room once more. He walked softly, like a man moving in a room where somebody is very sick. He reached the chair he had sat in before and lowered himself into it inch by inch. The girl slept on, motionless, in that curled-up looseness achieved by some women and all cats. Her breath made no slightest sound against the vague murmur of the radio.

Tony Reseck leaned back in the chair and clasped his hands on his elk's tooth and quietly closed his eyes.

DASHIELL HAMMETT

THE GATEWOOD CAPER

HARVEY GATEWOOD HAD issued orders that I was to be admitted as soon as I arrived, so it took me only a little less than fifteen minutes to thread my way past the door-keepers, office boys, and secretaries who filled up most of the space between the Gatewood Lumber Corporation's front door and the president's private office. His office was large, all mahogany and bronze and green plush, with a mahogany desk as big as a bed in the center of the floor.

Gatewood, leaning across the desk, began to bark at me as soon as the obsequious clerk who had bowed me in bowed himself out.

'My daughter was kidnaped last night! I want the gang that did it if it takes every cent I got!'

'Tell me about it,' I suggested.

But he wanted results, it seemed, and not questions, and so I wasted nearly an hour getting information that he could have given me in fifteen minutes.

He was a big bruiser of a man, something over 200 pounds of hard red flesh, and a czar from the top of his bullet head to the toes of his shoes that would have been at least number twelves if they hadn't been made to measure.

He had made his several millions by sandbagging every-body that stood in his way, and the rage he was burning up with now didn't make him any easier to deal with.

His wicked jaw was sticking out like a knob of granite and his eyes were filmed with blood – he was in a lovely frame of mind. For a while it looked as if the Continental Detective Agency was going to lose a client, because I'd made up my mind that he was going to tell me all I wanted to know, or I'd chuck the job.

But finally I got the story out of him.

His daughter Audrey had left their house on Clay Street at about 7 o'clock the preceding evening, telling her maid that she was going for a walk. She had not returned that night – though Gatewood had not known that until after he had read the letter that came this morning.

The letter had been from someone who said that she had been kidnaped. It demanded $50,000 for her release, and instructed Gatewood to get the money ready in hundred-dollar bills – so that there would be no delay when he was told the manner in which the money was to be paid over to his daughter's captors. As proof that the demand was not a hoax, a lock of the girl's hair, a ring she always wore, and a brief note from her, asking her father to comply with the demands, had been enclosed.

Gatewood had received the letter at his office and had telephoned to his house immediately. He had been told that the girl's bed had not been slept in the previous night and that none of the servants had seen her since she started out for her walk. He had then notified the police, turning the letter over to them, and a few minutes later he had decided to employ private detectives also.

'Now,' he burst out, after I had wormed these things out of him, and he had told me that he knew nothing of his daughter's associates or habits, 'go ahead and do something! I'm not paying you to sit around and talk about it!'

'What are you going to do?' I asked.

'Me? I'm going to put those — behind bars if it takes every cent I've got in the world!'

'Sure! But first you get that $50,000 ready, so you can give it to them when they ask for it.'

He clicked his jaw shut and thrust his face into mine.

'I've never been clubbed into doing anything in my life! And I'm too old to start now!' he said. 'I'm going to call these people's bluff!'

'That's going to make it lovely for your daughter. But, aside from what it'll do to her, it's the wrong play. Fifty thousand isn't a whole lot to you, and paying it over will give us two chances that we haven't got now. One when the payment is made – a chance either to nab whoever comes for it or get a line on them. And the other when your daughter is returned. No matter how careful they are, it's a cinch she'll be able to tell us something that will help us grab them.'

He shook his head angrily, and I was tired of arguing with him. So I left, hoping he'd see the wisdom of the course I had advised before it was too late.

At the Gatewood residence I found butlers, second men, chauffeurs, cooks, maids, upstairs girls, downstairs girls, and a raft of miscellaneous flunkies – he had enough servants to run a hotel.

What they told me amounted to this: the girl had not received a phone call, note by messenger or telegram – the time-honored devices for luring a victim out to a murder or abduction – before she left the house. She had told her maid that she would be back within an hour or two; but the maid had not been alarmed when her mistress failed to return all that night.

Audrey was the only child, and since her mother's death she had come and gone to suit herself. She and her father didn't hit it off very well together – their natures were too much alike, I gathered – and he never knew where she was.

There was nothing unusual about her remaining away all night. She seldom bothered to leave word when she was going to stay overnight with friends.

She was nineteen years old, but looked several years older, about five feet five inches tall, and slender. She had blue eyes, brown hair – very thick and long – was pale and very nervous. Her photographs, of which I took a handful, showed that her eyes were large, her nose small and regular and her chin pointed.

She was not beautiful, but in the one photograph where a smile had wiped off the sullenness of her mouth, she was at least pretty.

When she left the house she was wearing a light tweed skirt and jacket with a London tailor's label in them, a buff silk shirtwaist with stripes a shade darker, brown wool stockings, low-heeled brown oxfords, and an untrimmed gray felt hat.

I went up to her rooms – she had three on the third floor – and looked through all her stuff. I found nearly a bushel of photographs of men, boys, and girls; and a great stack of letters of varying degrees of intimacy, signed with a wide assortment of names and nicknames. I made notes of all the addresses I found.

Nothing in her rooms seemed to have any bearing on her abduction, but there was a chance that one of the names and addresses might be of someone who had served as a decoy. Also, some of her friends might be able to tell us something of value.

I dropped in at the Agency and distributed the names and addresses among the three operatives who were idle, sending them out to see what they could dig up.

Then I reached the police detectives who were working

on the case – O'Gar and Thode – by telephone, and went down to the Hall of Justice to meet them. Lusk, a post office inspector, was also there. We turned the job around and around, looking at it from every angle, but not getting very far. We were all agreed, however, that we couldn't take a chance on any publicity, or work in the open, until the girl was safe.

They had had a worse time with Gatewood than I – he had wanted to put the whole thing in the newspapers, with the offer of a reward, photographs and all. Of course, Gatewood was right in claiming that this was the most effective way of catching the kidnapers – but it would have been tough on his daughter if her captors happened to be persons of sufficiently hardened character. And kidnapers as a rule aren't lambs.

I looked at the letter they had sent. It was printed with pencil on ruled paper of the kind that is sold in pads by every stationery dealer in the world. The envelope was just as common, also addressed in pencil, and postmarked *San Francisco, September 20, 9 p.m.* That was the night she had been seized.

The letter read:

Sir:

We have your charming daughter and place a value of $50,000 upon her. You will get the money ready in $100 bills at once so there will be no delay when we tell you how it is to be paid over to us.

We beg to assure you that things will go badly with your daughter should you not do as you are told, or should you bring the police into this matter, or should you do anything foolish.

$50,000 is only a small fraction of what you stole while we were living in mud and blood in France for you, and we mean to get that much or else!

Three.

A peculiar note in several ways. They are usually written with a great pretense of partial illiterateness. Almost always there's an attempt to lead suspicion astray. Perhaps the ex-service stuff was there for that purpose – or perhaps not.

Then there was a postscript:

We know someone who will buy her even after we are through with her – in case you won't listen to reason.

The letter from the girl was written jerkily on the same kind of paper, apparently with the same pencil.

Daddy –

Please do as they ask! I am so afraid –

Audrey

A door at the other end of the room opened, and a head came through.

'O'Gar! Thode! Gatewood just called up. Get up to his office right away!'

The four of us tumbled out of the Hall of Justice and into a police car.

Gatewood was pacing his office like a maniac when we pushed aside enough hirelings to get to him. His face was hot with blood and his eyes had an insane glare in them.

'She just phoned me!' he cried thickly, when he saw us.

It took a minute or two to get him calm enough to tell us about it.

'She called me on the phone. Said, "Oh, Daddy! Do something! I can't stand this – they're killing me!" I asked her if she knew where she was, and she said, "No, but I can see Twin Peaks from here. There's three men and a woman, and –" And then I heard a man curse, and a sound as if he had struck her, and the phone went dead. I tried to get central to give me the number, but she couldn't! It's a damned outrage the way the telephone system is run. We pay enough for service, God knows, and we . . .'

O'Gar scratched his head and turned away from Gatewood. 'In sight of Twin Peaks! There are hundreds of houses that are!'

Gatewood meanwhile had finished denouncing the telephone company and was pounding on his desk with a paperweight to attract our attention.

'Have you people done anything at all?' he demanded.

I answered him with another question: 'Have you got the money ready?'

'No,' he said, 'I won't be held up by anybody!'

But he said it mechanically, without his usual conviction – the talk with his daughter had shaken him out of some of his stubbornness. He was thinking of her safety a little now instead of only his own fighting spirit.

We went at him hammer and tongs for a few minutes, and after a while he sent a clerk out for the money.

We split up the field then. Thode was to take some men from headquarters and see what he could find in the Twin Peaks end of town; but we weren't very optimistic over the prospects there – the territory was too large.

Lusk and O'Gar were to carefully mark the bills that the clerk brought from the bank, and then stick as close to Gatewood as they could without attracting attention. I was to go out to Gatewood's house and stay there.

The abductors had plainly instructed Gatewood to get the money ready immediately so that they could arrange to get it on short notice – not giving him time to communicate with anyone or make plans.

Gatewood was to get hold of the newspapers, give them the whole story, with the $10,000 reward he was offering for the abductors' capture, to be published as soon as the girl was safe – so we would get the help of publicity at the earliest possible moment without jeopardizing the girl.

The police in all the neighboring towns had already been notified – that had been done before the girl's phone message had assured us that she was held in San Francisco.

Nothing happened at the Gatewood residence all that evening. Harvey Gatewood came home early; and after dinner he paced his library floor and drank whiskey until bedtime, demanding every few minutes that we, the detectives in the case, do something besides sit around like a lot of damned mummies. O'Gar, Lusk, and Thode were out in the street, keeping an eye on the house and neighborhood.

At midnight Harvey Gatewood went to bed. I declined a bed in favor of the library couch, which I dragged over beside the telephone, an extension of which was in Gatewood's bedroom.

At 2.30 the telephone bell rang. I listened in while Gatewood talked from his bed.

A man's voice, crisp and curt: 'Gatewood?'

'Yes.'

'Got the dough?'

'Yes.'

Gatewood's voice was thick and blurred – I could imagine the boiling that was going on inside him.

'Good!' came the brisk voice. 'Put a piece of paper around it and leave the house with it, right away! Walk down Clay Street, keeping on the same side as your house. Don't walk too fast and keep walking. If everything's all right, and there's no elbows tagging along, somebody'll come up to you between your house and the waterfront. They'll have a handkerchief up to their face for a second, and then they'll let it fall to the ground.

'When you see that, you'll lay the money on the pavement, turn around, and walk back to your house. If the money isn't marked, and you don't try any fancy tricks, you'll get your daughter back in an hour or two. If you try to pull anything – remember what we wrote you! Got it straight?'

Gatewood sputtered something that was meant for an affirmative, and the telephone clicked silent.

I didn't waste any of my precious time tracing the call – it would be from a public telephone, I knew – but yelled up the stairs to Gatewood, 'You do as you were told, and don't try any foolishness!'

Then I ran out into the early morning air to find the police detectives and the post office inspector.

They had been joined by two plain-clothesmen, and had two automobiles waiting. I told them what the situation was, and we laid hurried plans.

O'Gar was to drive in one of the cars down Sacramento Street, and Thode, in the other, down Washington Street. These streets parallel Clay, one on each side. They were to drive slowly, keeping pace with Gatewood, and stopping at each cross street to see that he passed.

When he failed to cross within a reasonable time they were to turn up to Clay Street – and their actions from then on would have to be guided by chance and their own wits.

Lusk was to wander along a block or two ahead of Gatewood, on the opposite side of the street, pretending to be mildly intoxicated.

I was to shadow Gatewood down the street, with one

of the plain-clothesmen behind me. The other plain-clothesman was to turn in a call at headquarters for every available man to be sent to City Street. They would arrive too late, of course, and as likely as not it would take them some time to find us; but we had no way of knowing what was going to turn up before the night was over.

Our plan was sketchy enough, but it was the best we could do – we were afraid to grab whoever got the money from Gatewood. The girl's talk with her father that afternoon had sounded too much as if her captors were desperate for us to take any chances on going after them roughshod until she was out of their hands.

We had hardly finished our plans when Gatewood, wearing a heavy overcoat, left his house and turned down the street.

Farther down, Lusk, weaving along, talking to himself, was almost invisible in the shadows. There was no one else in sight. That meant that I had to give Gatewood at least two blocks' lead, so that the man who came for the money wouldn't tumble to me. One of the plain-clothesmen was half a block behind me, on the other side of the street.

We walked two blocks down, and then a chunky man in a derby hat came into sight. He passed Gatewood, passed me, went on.

Three blocks more.

A touring car, large, black, powerfully engined and with lowered curtains, came from the rear, passed us, went on. Possibly a scout. I scrawled its license number down on my pad without taking my hand out of my overcoat pocket.

Another three blocks.

A policeman passed, strolling along in ignorance of the game being played under his nose; and then a taxicab with a single male passenger. I wrote down its license number.

Four blocks with no one in sight ahead of me but Gatewood – I couldn't see Lusk any more.

Just ahead of Gatewood a man stepped out of a black doorway, turned around, called up to a window for someone to come down and open the door for him.

We went on.

Coming from nowhere, a woman stood on the sidewalk fifty feet ahead of Gatewood, a handkerchief to her face. It fluttered to the pavement.

Gatewood stopped, standing stiff-legged. I could see his right hand come up, lifting the side of the overcoat in which it was pocketed – and I knew his hand was gripped around a pistol.

For perhaps half a minute he stood like a statue. Then his left hand came out of his pocket, and the bundle of money fell to the sidewalk in front of him, where it made a bright blur in the darkness. Gatewood turned abruptly, and began to retrace his steps homeward.

The woman had recovered her handkerchief. Now she ran to the bundle, picked it up, and scuttled to the black mouth of an alley a few feet distant – a rather tall woman, bent, and in dark clothes from head to feet.

In the black mouth of the alley she vanished.

I had been compelled to slow up while Gatewood and the woman stood facing each other, and I was more than a block away now. As soon as the woman disappeared, I took a chance and started pounding my rubber soles against the pavement.

The alley was empty when I reached it.

It ran all the way through to the next street, but I knew that the woman couldn't have reached the other end before I got to this one. I carry a lot of weight these days, but I can still step a block or two in good time. Along both sides of the alley were the rears of apartment buildings, each with its back door looking blankly, secretively, at me.

The plain-clothesman who had been trailing behind me came up, then O'Gar and Thode in their cars, and soon, Lusk. O'Gar and Thode rode off immediately to wind through the neighboring streets, hunting for the woman. Lusk and the plain-clothesman each planted himself on a corner from which two of the streets enclosing the block could be watched.

I went through the alley, hunting vainly for an unlocked door, an open window, a fire escape that would show recent use – any of the signs that a hurried departure from the alley might leave.

Nothing!

O'Gar came back shortly with some reinforcements from headquarters that he had picked up, and Gatewood.

Gatewood was burning.

'Bungled the damn thing again! I won't pay your agency a nickel, and I'll see that some of these so-called detectives get put back in a uniform and set to walking beats!'

'What'd the woman look like?' I asked him.

'I don't know! I thought you were hanging around to take care of her! She was old and bent, kind of, I guess, but I couldn't see her face for her veil. I don't know! What the hell were you men doing? It's a damned outrage the way . . .'

I finally got him quieted down and took him home, leaving the city men to keep the neighborhood under surveillance. There were fourteen or fifteen of them on the job now, and every shadow held at least one.

The girl would head for home as soon as she was released and I wanted to be there to pump her. There was an excellent chance of catching her abductors before they got very far, if she could tell us anything at all about them

Home, Gatewood went up against the whiskey bottle again, while I kept one ear cocked at the telephone and the other at the front door. O'Gar or Thode phoned every half hour or so to ask if we'd heard from the girl.

They had still found nothing.

At 9 o'clock they, with Lusk, arrived at the house. The woman in black had turned out to be a man and got away.

In the rear of one of the apartment buildings that touched the alley – just a foot or so within the back door – they found a woman's skirt, long coat, hat and veil – all black. Investigating the occupants of the house, they had learned that an apartment had been rented to a young man named Leighton three days before.

Leighton was not home, when they went up to his apartment. His rooms held a lot of cold cigarette butts, an empty bottle, and nothing else that had not been there when he rented it.

The inference was clear; he had rented the apartment so that he might have access to the building. Wearing women's clothes over his own, he had gone out of the back door – leaving it unlatched behind him – to meet Gatewood. Then he had run back into the building, discarded his disguise and hurried through the building, out the front door, and away before we had our feeble net around the block – perhaps dodging into dark doorways here and there to avoid O'Gar and Thode in their cars.

Leighton, it seemed, was a man of about thirty, slender, about five feet eight or nine inches tall, with dark hair and eyes; rather good-looking, and well-dressed on the two occasions when people living in the building had seen him, in a brown suit and a light brown felt hat.

There was no possibility, according to both of the

detectives and the post office inspector, that the girl might have been held, even temporarily, in Leighton's apartment.

Ten o'clock came, and no word from the girl.

Gatewood had lost his domineering bull-headedness by now and was breaking up. The suspense was getting to him, and the liquor he had put away wasn't helping him. I didn't like him either personally or by reputation, but this morning I felt sorry for him.

I talked to the Agency over the phone and got the reports of the operatives who had been looking up Audrey's friends. The last person to see her had been an Agnes Dangerfield, who had seen her walking down Market Street near Sixth, alone, on the night of her abduction some time between 8.15 and 8.45. Audrey had been too far away from the Dangerfield girl to speak to her.

For the rest, the boys had learned nothing except that Audrey was a wild, spoiled youngster who hadn't shown any great care in selecting her friends – just the sort of girl who could easily fall into the hands of a mob of highbinders.

Noon struck. No sign of the girl. We told the newspapers to turn loose the story, with the added developments of the past few hours.

Gatewood was broken; he sat with his head in his hands, looking at nothing. Just before I left to follow a hunch I had, he looked up at me, and I'd never have recognized him if I hadn't seen the change take place.

'What do you think is keeping her away?' he asked.

I didn't have the heart to tell him what I had every reason to suspect, now that the money had been paid and she had failed to show up. So I stalled with some vague assurances and left.

I caught a cab and dropped off in the shopping district. I visited the five largest department stores, going to all the women's wear departments from shoes to hats, and trying to learn if a man – perhaps one answering Leighton's description – had been buying clothes in the past couple days that would fit Audrey Gatewood.

Failing to get any results, I turned the rest of the local stores over to one of the boys from the Agency, and went across the bay to canvass the Oakland stores.

At the first one I got action. A man who might easily have been Leighton had been in the day before, buying clothes of Audrey's size. He had bought lots of them, everything from lingerie to a coat, and – my luck was hitting on all cylinders – had had his purchases delivered to T. Offord, at an address on Fourteenth Street.

At the Fourteenth Street address, an apartment house, I found Mr and Mrs Theodore Offord's names in the vestibule for Apartment 202.

I had just found the apartment number when the front door opened and a stout, middle-aged woman in a gingham housedress came out. She looked at me a bit curiously, so I asked, 'Do you know where I can find the superintendent?'

'I'm the superintendent,' she said.

I handed her a card and stepped indoors with her. 'I'm from the bonding department of the North American Casualty Company' – a repetition of the lie that was printed on the card I had given her – 'and a bond for Mr Offord has been applied for. Is he all right so far as you know?' With the slightly apologetic air of one going through with a necessary but not too important formality.

'A bond? That's funny! He is going away tomorrow.'

'Well, I can't say what the bond is for,' I said lightly. 'We investigators just get the names and addresses. It may be for his present employer, or perhaps the man he is going to work for has applied for it. Or some firms have us look up prospective employees before they hire them, just to be safe.'

'Mr Offord, so far as I know, is a very nice young man,' she said, 'but he has been here only a week.'

'Not staying long, then?'

'No. They came here from Denver, intending to stay, but the low altitude doesn't agree with Mrs Offord, so they are going back.'

'Are you sure they came from Denver?'

'Well,' she said, 'they told me they did.'

'How many of them are there?'

'Only the two of them; they're young people.'

'Well, how do they impress you?' I asked, trying to get over the impression that I thought her a woman of shrewd judgement.

'They seem to be a very nice young couple. You'd hardly know they were in their apartment most of the time, they're so quiet. I'm sorry they can't stay.'

'Do they go out much?'

'I really don't know. They have their keys; and unless I should happen to pass them going in or out I'd never see them.'

'Then, as a matter of fact you couldn't say whether they stayed away all night some nights or not. Could you?'

She eyed me doubtfully – I was stepping way over my pretext now, but I didn't think it mattered – and shook her head. 'No, I couldn't say.'

'They have many visitors?'

'I don't know. Mr Offord is not –'

She broke off as a man came in quietly from the street, brushed past me, and started to mount the steps to the second floor.

'Oh, dear!' she whispered. 'I hope he didn't hear me talking about him. That's Mr Offord.'

A slender man in brown, with a light brown hat – Leighton, perhaps.

I hadn't seen anything of him except his back, nor he anything except mine. I watched him as he climbed the stairs. If he had heard the woman mention his name he would use the turn at the head of the stairs to sneak a look at me.

He did.

I kept my face stolid, but I knew him.

He was 'Penny' Quayle, a con man who had been active in the east four or five years before.

His face was as expressionless as mine. But he knew me.

A door on the second floor shut. I left the woman and started for the stairs.

'I think I'll go up and talk to him,' I told her.

Coming silently to the door of Apartment 202, I listened. Not a sound. This was no time for hesitation. I pressed the bell-button.

As close together as the tapping of three keys under the fingers of an expert typist, but a thousand times more vicious, came three pistol shots. And waist-high in the door of Apartment 202 were three bullet holes.

The three bullets would have been in my fat carcass if I hadn't learned years ago to stand to one side of strange doors when making uninvited calls.

Inside the apartment sounded a man's voice, sharp, commanding. 'Cut it, kid! For God's sake, not that!'

A woman's voice, shrill, bitter, spiteful, screaming blasphemies.

Two more bullets came through the door.

'Stop! No! No!' The man's voice had a note of fear in it now.

The woman's voice, cursing hotly. A scuffle. A shot that didn't hit the door.

I hurled my foot against the door, near the knob, and the lock broke away.

On the floor of the room, a man – Quayle – and a woman were tussling. He was bending over her, holding her wrists, trying to keep her down. A smoking pistol was in one of her hands. I got to it in a jump and tore it loose.

'That's enough!' I called to them when I was planted. 'Get up and receive company.'

Quayle released his antagonist's wrists, whereupon she struck at his eyes with curved, sharp-nailed fingers, tearing his cheek open. He scrambled away from her on hands and knees, and both of them got to their feet.

He sat down on a chair immediately, panting and wiping his bleeding cheek with a handkerchief.

She stood, hands on hips, in the center of the room, glaring at me. 'I suppose,' she spat, 'you think you've raised hell!'

I laughed – I could afford to.

'If your father is in his right mind,' I told her, 'he'll do it with a razor strap when he gets you home again. A fine joke you picked out to play on him!'

'If *you'd* been tied to him as long as I have and had been bullied and held down as much, I guess *you'd* do most anything to get enough money so that you could go away and live your own life.'

I didn't say anything to that. Remembering some of the business methods Harvey Gatewood had used – particularly some of his war contracts that the Department of Justice was still investigating – I suppose the worst that could be said about Audrey was that she was her father's own daughter.

'How'd you rap to it?' Quayle asked me, politely.

'Several ways,' I said. 'First, one of Audrey's friends saw her on Market Street between 8.15 and 8.45 the night she disappeared and your letter to Gatewood was postmarked 9 p.m. Pretty fast work. You should have waited a while before mailing it. I suppose she dropped it in the post office on her way over here?'

Quayle nodded.

'Then second,' I went on, 'there was that phone call of hers. She knew it took anywhere from ten to fifteen minutes to get her father on the wire at the office. If she had gotten to a phone while imprisoned, time would have been so valuable that she'd have told her story to the first person she got hold of – the switchboard operator, most likely. So that made it look as if, besides wanting to throw out that Twin Peaks line, she wanted to stir the old man out of his bull-headedness.

'When she failed to show up after the money was paid, I figured it was a sure bet that she had kidnaped herself. I knew that if she came back home after faking this thing, we'd find it out before we'd talked to her very long – and I figured she knew that too and would stay away.

'The rest was easy – I got some good breaks. We knew a man was working with her after we found the woman's clothes you left behind, and I took a chance on there being no one else in it. Then I figured she'd need clothes – she couldn't have taken any from home without tipping her mitt – and there was an even chance that she hadn't laid in a stock beforehand. She's got too many girl friends of the sort that do a lot of shopping to make it safe for her to have risked showing herself in stores. Maybe, then, the man would buy what she needed. And it turned out that he did, and that he was too lazy to carry away his purchases, or perhaps there were too many of them, and so he had them sent out. That's the story.'

Quayle nodded again.

'I was damned careless,' he said, and then, jerking a contemptuous thumb toward the girl, 'But what can you expect? She's had a skinful of hop ever since we started. Took all my time and attention keeping her from running wild and gumming the works. Just now was a sample – I told her you were coming up and she goes crazy and tries to add your corpse to the wreckage!'

The Gatewood reunion took place in the office of the captain of inspectors on the second floor of the Oakland City Hall, and it was a merry little party.

For over an hour it was a tossup whether Harvey Gatewood would die of apoplexy, strangle his daughter or send her off to the state reformatory until she was of age. But Audrey licked him. Besides being a chip off the old block, she was young enough to be careless of consequences, while her father, for all his bull-headedness, had had some caution hammered into him.

The card she beat him with was a threat of spilling everything she knew about him to the newspapers, and at least one of the San Francisco papers had been trying to get his scalp for years.

I don't know what she had on him, and I don't think he was any too sure himself; but with his war contracts still being investigated by the Department of Justice, he couldn't afford to take a chance. There was no doubt at all that she would have done as she threatened.

And so, together, they left for home, sweating hate for each other from every pore.

We took Quayle upstairs and put him in a cell, but he was too experienced to let that worry him. He knew that if the girl was to be spared, he himself couldn't very easily be convicted of anything.

I was glad it was over. It had been a tough caper.

AGATHA CHRISTIE

THE BLUE GERANIUM

'WHEN I WAS down here last year –' said Sir Henry Clithering, and stopped.

His hostess, Mrs Bantry, looked at him curiously.

The Ex-Commissioner of Scotland Yard was staying with old friends of his, Colonel and Mrs Bantry, who lived near St Mary Mead.

Mrs Bantry, pen in hand, had just asked his advice as to who should be invited to make a sixth guest at dinner that evening.

'Yes?' said Mrs Bantry encouragingly. 'When you were here last year? '

'Tell me,' said Sir Henry, 'do you know a Miss Marple?'

Mrs Bantry was surprised. It was the last thing she had expected.

'Know Miss Marple? Who doesn't! The typical old maid of fiction. Quite a dear, but hopelessly behind the times. Do you mean you would like me to ask *her* to dinner?'

'You are surprised?'

'A little, I must confess. I should hardly have thought you – but perhaps there's an explanation?'

'The explanation is simple enough. When I was down here last year we got into the habit of discussing unsolved mysteries – there were five or six of us – Raymond West, the novelist, started it. We each supplied a story to which we knew the answer, but nobody else did. It was supposed to be an exercise in the deductive faculties – to see who could get nearest the truth.'

'Well?'

'Like in the old story – we hardly realized that Miss Marple was playing; but we were very polite about it – didn't want to hurt the old dear's feelings. And now comes the cream of the jest. The old lady outdid us every time!'

'What?'

'I assure you – straight to the truth like a homing pigeon.'

'But how extraordinary! Why, dear old Miss Marple has hardly ever been out of St Mary Mead.'

'Ah! But according to her, that has given her unlimited opportunities of observing human nature – under the microscope as it were.'

'I suppose there's something in that,' conceded Mrs Bantry. 'One would at least know the petty side of people. But I don't think we have any really exciting criminals in our midst. I think we must try her with Arthur's ghost story after dinner. I'd be thankful if she'd find a solution to that.'

'I didn't know that Arthur believed in ghosts?'

'Oh! he doesn't. That's what worries him so. And it happened to a friend of his, George Pritchard – a most prosaic person. It's really rather tragic for poor George. Either this extraordinary story is true – or else –'

'Or else what?'

Mrs Bantry did not answer. After a minute or two she said irrelevantly:

'You know, I like George – everyone does. One can't believe that he – but people do do such extraordinary things.'

Sir Henry nodded. He knew, better than Mrs Bantry, the extraordinary things that people did.

So it came about that that evening Mrs Bantry looked round her dinner table (shivering a little as she did so, because the dining-room, like most English dining-rooms, was extremely cold) and fixed her gaze on the very upright old lady sitting on her husband's right. Miss Marple wore black lace mittens; an old lace fichu was draped round her shoulders and another piece of lace surmounted her white hair. She was talking animatedly to the elderly doctor, Dr Lloyd, about the Workhouse and the suspected shortcomings of the District Nurse.

Mrs Bantry marvelled anew. She even wondered whether Sir Henry had been making an elaborate joke – but there seemed no point in that. Incredible that what he had said could be really true.

Her glance went on and rested affectionately on her red-faced broad-shouldered husband as he sat talking horses to Jane Helier, the beautiful and popular actress. Jane, more beautiful (if that were possible) off the stage than on, opened enormous blue eyes and murmured at discreet intervals: 'Really?' 'Oh fancy!' 'How extraordinary!' She knew nothing whatever about horses and cared less.

'Arthur,' said Mrs Bantry, 'you're boring poor Jane to distraction. Leave horses alone and tell her your ghost story instead. You know . . . George Pritchard.'

'Eh, Dolly? Oh! but I don't know –'

'Sir Henry wants to hear it too. I was telling him something about it this morning. It would be interesting to hear what everyone has to say about it.'

'Oh, do!' said Jane. 'I love ghost stories.'

'Well –' Colonel Bantry hesitated. 'I've never believed much in the supernatural. But this –

'I don't think any of you know George Pritchard. He's one of the best. His wife – well, she's dead now, poor woman. I'll just say this much: she didn't give George any too easy a time when she was alive. She was one of those semi-invalids – I believe she had really something wrong with her, but whatever it was she played it for all it was worth. She was capricious, exacting, unreasonable. She complained from morning to night. George was expected to wait on her hand and foot, and every thing he did was always wrong and he got cursed for it. Most men, I'm fully convinced, would have hit her over the head with a hatchet long ago. Eh, Dolly, isn't that so?'

'She was a dreadful woman,' said Mrs Bantry with conviction. 'If George Pritchard had brained her with a hatchet, and there had been any woman on the jury, he would have been triumphantly acquitted.'

'I don't quite know how this business started. George was rather vague about it. I gather Mrs Pritchard had always had a weakness for fortune-tellers, palmists, clairvoyants – anything of that sort. George didn't mind. If she found amusement in it well and good. But he refused to go into rhapsodies himself, and that was another grievance.

'A succession of hospital nurses was always passing through the house, Mrs Pritchard usually becoming dissatisfied with them after a few weeks. One young nurse had been very keen on this fortune-telling stunt, and for a time Mrs Pritchard had been very fond of her. Then she suddenly fell out with her and insisted on her going. She had back another nurse who had been with her previously – an older woman, experienced and tactful in dealing with a neurotic patient. Nurse Copling, according to George, was a very good sort – a sensible woman to talk to. She put up with Mrs Pritchard's tantrums and nervestorms with complete indifference.

'Mrs Pritchard always lunched upstairs, and it was usual at lunch time for George and the nurse to come to some arrangement for the afternoon. Strictly speaking, the nurse went off from two to four, but "to oblige" as the phrase goes, she would sometimes take her time off after tea if

George wanted to be free for the afternoon. On this occasion, she mentioned that she was going to see a sister at Golders Green and might be a little late returning. George's face fell, for he had arranged to play a round of golf. Nurse Copling, however, reassured him.

'"We'll neither of us be missed, Mr Pritchard." A twinkle came into her eye. "Mrs Pritchard's going to have more exciting company than ours."

'"Who's that?"

'"Wait a minute," Nurse Copling's eyes twinkled more than ever. "Let me get it right. *Zarida, Psychic Reader of the Future.*"

'"Oh Lord!" groaned George. "That's a new one, isn't it?"

'"Quite new. I believe my predecessor, Nurse Carstairs, sent her along. Mrs Pritchard hasn't seen her yet. She made me write, fixing an appointment for this afternoon."

'"Well, at any rate, I shall get my golf," said George, and he went off with the kindliest feelings towards Zarida, the Reader of the Future.

'On his return to the house, he found Mrs Pritchard in a state of great agitation. She was, as usual, lying on her invalid couch, and she had a bottle of smelling-salts in her hand which she sniffed at frequent intervals.

'"George," she exclaimed. "What did I tell you about this house? The moment I came into it, I *felt* there was something wrong! Didn't I tell you so at the time?"

'Repressing his desire to reply, "You always do," George said, "No, can't say I remember it."

'"You never do remember anything that has to do with me. Men are all extraordinarily callous – but I really believe that you are even more insensitive than most."

'"Oh, come now, Mary dear, that's not fair."

'"Well, as I was telling you, this woman *knew* at once!

She – she actually blenched – if you know what I mean – as she came in at that door, and she said: "There is evil here – evil and danger. I feel it."

'Very unwisely George laughed.

' "Well, you have had your money's worth this afternoon."

'His wife closed her eyes and took a long sniff from her smelling-bottle.

' "How you hate me! You would jeer and laugh if I were dying."

'George protested and after a minute or two she went on.

' "You may laugh, but I shall tell you the whole thing. This house is definitely dangerous to me – the woman said so."

'George's formerly kind feeling towards Zarida underwent a change. He knew his wife was perfectly capable of insisting on moving to a new house if the caprice got hold of her.

' "What else did she say?" he asked.

' "She couldn't tell me very much. She was so upset. One thing she did say. I had some violets in a glass. She pointed at them and cried out:

' " 'Take those away. No blue flowers – never have blue flowers. *Blue flowers are fatal to you – remember that.*'

' "And you know," added Mrs Pritchard, "I always have told you that blue as a colour is repellent to me. I feel a natural instinctive sort of warning against it."

'George was much too wise to remark that he had never heard her say so before. Instead he asked what the mysterious Zarida was like. Mrs Pritchard entered with gusto upon a description.

' "Black hair in coiled knobs over her ears – her eyes were half closed – great black rims round them – she had a black veil over her mouth and chin – she spoke in a kind of singing voice with a marked foreign accent – Spanish, I think –"

'"In fact all the usual stock-in-trade," said George cheerfully.

'His wife immediately closed her eyes.

'"I feel extremely ill," she said. "Ring for nurse. Unkindness upsets me, as you know only too well."

'It was two days later that Nurse Copling came to George with a grave face.

'"Will you come to Mrs Pritchard, please. She has had a letter which upsets her greatly."

'He found his wife with the letter in her hand. She held it out to him.

'"Read it," she said.

'George read it. It was on heavily scented paper, and the writing was big and black.

'"*I have seen the Future. Be warned before it is too late. Beware of the Full moon. The Blue Primrose means Warning; the Blue Hollyhock means Danger; the Blue Geranium means Death. . . .*"

'Just about to burst out laughing, George caught Nurse Copling's eye. She made a quick warning gesture. He said rather awkwardly, "The woman's probably trying to frighten you, Mary. Anyway there aren't such things as blue primroses and blue geraniums."

'But Mrs Pritchard began to cry and say her days were numbered. Nurse Copling came out with George upon the landing.

'"Of all the silly tomfoolery," he burst out.

'"I suppose it is."

'Something in the nurse's tone struck him, and he stared at her in amazement.

'"Surely, nurse, you don't believe –"

'"No, no, Mr Pritchard. I don't believe in reading the future – that's nonsense. What puzzles me is the *meaning* of this. Fortune-tellers are usually out for what they can get. But this woman seems to be frightening Mrs Pritchard with no advantage to herself. I can't see the point. There's another thing –"

'"Yes?"

'"Mrs Pritchard says that something about Zarida was faintly familiar to her."

'"Well?"

'"Well, I don't like it, Mr Pritchard, that's all."

'"I didn't know you were so superstitious, nurse."

'"I'm not superstitious; but I know when a thing is fishy."

'It was about four days after this that the first incident happened. To explain it to you, I shall have to describe Mrs Pritchard's room –'

'You'd better let me do that,' interrupted Mrs Bantry. 'It was papered with one of these new wallpapers where you apply clumps of flowers to make a kind of herbaceous border. The effect is almost like being in a garden – though, of course, the flowers are all wrong. I mean they simply couldn't be in bloom all at the same time –'

'Don't let a passion for horticultural accuracy run away with you, Dolly,' said her husband. 'We all know you're an enthusiastic gardener.'

'Well, it *is* absurd,' protested Mrs Bantry. 'To have bluebells and daffodils and lupins and hollyhocks and Michaelmas daisies all grouped together.'

'Most unscientific,' said Sir Henry. 'But to proceed with the story.'

'Well, among these massed flowers were primroses, clumps of yellow and pink primroses and – oh go on, Arthur, this is your story –'

Colonel Bantry took up the tale.

'Mrs Pritchard rang her bell violently one morning. The household came running – thought she was in extremis; not at all. She was violently excited and pointing at the wall-paper; and there sure enough was *one blue primrose* in the midst of the others....'

'Oh!' said Miss Helier, 'how creepy!'

'The question was: Hadn't the blue primrose always been there? That was George's suggestion and the nurse's. But Mrs Pritchard wouldn't have it at any price. She had never noticed it till that very morning and the night before had been full moon. She was very upset about it.'

'I met George Pritchard that same day and he told me about it,' said Mrs Bantry. 'I went to see Mrs Pritchard and did my best to ridicule the whole thing; but without success. I came away really concerned, and I remember I met Jean Instow and told her about it. Jean is a queer girl. She said, "So she's really upset about it?" I told her that I thought the woman was perfectly capable of dying of fright – she was really abnormally superstitious.

'I remember Jean rather startled me with what she said next. She said, "Well, that might be all for the best, mightn't it?" And she said it so coolly, in so matter-of-fact a tone that I was really – well, shocked. Of course I know it's done nowadays – to be brutal and outspoken; but I never get used to it. Jean smiled at me rather oddly and said, "You don't like my saying that – but it's true. What use is Mrs Pritchard's life to her? None at all; and it's hell for George Pritchard. To have his wife frightened out of existence would be the best thing that could happen to him." I said, "George is most awfully good to her always." And she said, "Yes, he deserves a reward, poor dear. He's a very attractive person, George Pritchard. The last nurse thought so – the pretty one – what was her name? Carstairs. That was the cause of the row between her and Mrs P."

'Now I didn't like hearing Jean say that. Of course one had *wondered* –'

Mrs Bantry paused significantly.

'Yes, dear,' said Miss Marple placidly. 'One always does. Is Miss Instow a pretty girl? I suppose she plays golf?'

'Yes. She's good at all games. And she's nice-looking, attractive-looking, very fair with a healthy skin, and nice steady blue eyes. Of course we always have felt that she and George Pritchard – I mean if things had been different – they are so well suited to one another.'

'And they were friends?' asked Miss Marple.

'Oh yes. Great friends.'

'Do you think, Dolly,' said Colonel Bantry plaintively, 'that I might be allowed to go on with my story?'

'Arthur,' said Mrs Bantry resignedly, 'wants to get back to his ghosts.'

'I had the rest of the story from George himself,' went on the colonel. 'There's no doubt that Mrs Pritchard got the wind up badly towards the end of the next month. She marked off on a calendar the day when the moon would be full, and on that night she had both the nurse and then George into her room and made them study the wallpaper carefully. There were pink hollyhocks and red ones, but there were no blue amongst them. Then when George left the room she locked the door –'

'And in the morning there was a large blue hollyhock,' said Miss Helier joyfully.

'Quite right,' said Colonel Bantry. 'Or at any rate, nearly right. One flower of a hollyhock just above her head had turned blue. It staggered George; and of course the more it staggered him the more he refused to take the thing seriously. He insisted that the whole thing was some kind of practical joke. He ignored the evidence of the locked door and the fact that Mrs Pritchard discovered the change before anyone – even Nurse Copling – was admitted.

'It staggered George; and it made him unreasonable. His wife wanted to leave the house, and he wouldn't let her. He was inclined to believe in the supernatural for the first time, but he wasn't going to admit it. He usually gave in to his wife, but this time he wouldn't. Mary was not to make a fool of herself, he said. The whole thing was the most infernal nonsense.

'And so the next month sped away. Mrs Pritchard made less protest than one would have imagined. I think she was superstitious enough to believe that she couldn't escape her fate. She repeated again and again: "The blue primrose – warning. The blue hollyhock – danger. The blue geranium – *death*." And she would lie looking at the clump of pinky-red geraniums nearest her bed.

'The whole business was pretty nervy. Even the nurse caught the infection. She came to George two days before full moon and begged him to take Mrs Pritchard away. George was angry.

' "If all the flowers on that damned wall turned into blue devils it couldn't kill anyone!" he shouted.

' "It might. Shock has killed people before now."

' "Nonsense," said George.

'George has always been a shade pig-headed. You can't drive him. I believe he had a secret idea that his wife worked the changes herself and that it was all some morbid hysterical plan of hers.

'Well, the fatal night came. Mrs Pritchard locked her door as usual. She was very calm – in almost an exalted state of mind. The nurse was worried by her state – wanted to give her a stimulant, an injection of strychnine, but Mrs Pritchard refused. In a way, I believe, she was enjoying herself. George said she was.'

'I think that's quite possible,' said Mrs Bantry. 'There must have been a strange sort of glamour about the whole thing.'

'There was no violent ringing of a bell the next morning. Mrs Pritchard usually woke about eight. When, at eight-thirty, there was no sign from her, nurse rapped loudly on the door. Getting no reply, she fetched George, and insisted on the door being broken open. They did so with the help of a chisel.

'One look at the still figure on the bed was enough for Nurse Copling. She sent George to telephone for the doctor, but it was too late. Mrs Pritchard, he said, must have been dead at least eight hours. Her smelling salts lay by her hand on the bed, *and on the wall beside her one of the pinky-red geraniums was a bright deep blue.*'

'Horrible,' said Miss Helier with a shiver.

Sir Henry was frowning.

'No additional details?

Colonel Bantry shook his head, but Mrs Bantry spoke quickly.

'The gas.'

'What about the gas?' asked Sir Henry.

'When the doctor arrived there was a slight smell of gas, and sure enough he found the gas ring in the fireplace very slightly turned on; but so little that it couldn't have mattered.'

'Did Mr Pritchard and the nurse not notice it when they first went in?'

'The nurse said she did notice a slight smell. George said he didn't notice gas, but something made him feel very queer and overcome; but he put that down to shock – and probably it was. At any rate there was no question of gas poisoning. The smell was scarcely noticeable.'

'And that's the end of the story?'

'No, it isn't. One way and another, there was a lot of talk. The servants, you see, had overheard things – had heard, for instance, Mrs Pritchard telling her husband that he hated her and would jeer if she were dying. And also more recent remarks. She had said one day, apropos of his refusing to leave the house: "Very well, when I am dead, I hope everyone will realize that you have killed me." And as ill luck would have it, he had been mixing some weed killer for the garden paths the very day before. One of the younger servants had seen him and had afterwards seen him taking up a glass of hot milk to his wife.

'The talk spread and grew. The doctor had given a certificate – I don't know exactly in what terms – shock, syncope, heart failure, probably some medical term meaning nothing much. However the poor lady had not been a month in her grave before an exhumation order was applied for and granted.'

'And the result of the autopsy was nil, I remember,' said Sir Henry gravely. 'A case, for once, of smoke without fire.'

'The whole thing is really very curious,' said Mrs Bantry. 'That fortune-teller, for instance – Zarida. At the address where she was supposed to be, no one had ever heard of any such person!'

'She appeared once – out of the blue,' said her husband, 'and then utterly vanished. Out of the *blue* – that's rather good!'

'And what is more,' continued Mrs Bantry, 'little Nurse Carstairs, who was supposed to have recommended her, had never even heard of her.'

They looked at each other.

'It's a mysterious story,' said Dr Lloyd. 'One can make guesses; but to guess –'

He shook his head.

'Has Mr Pritchard married Miss Instow?' asked Miss Marple in her gentle voice.

'Now why do you ask that?' inquired Sir Henry.

Miss Marple opened gentle blue eyes.

'It seems to me so important,' she said. 'Have they married?'

Colonel Bantry shook his head.

'We – well, we expected something of the kind – but it's eighteen months now. I don't believe they even see much of each other.'

'That is important,' said Miss Marple. 'Very important.'

'Then you think the same as I do,' said Mrs Bantry. 'You think –'

'Now, Dolly,' said her husband. 'It's unjustifiable – what you're going to say. You can't go about accusing people without a shadow of proof.'

'Don't be so – so manly, Arthur. Men are always afraid to say *anything*. Anyway, this is all between ourselves. It's just a wild fantastic idea of mine that possibly – only *possibly* – Jean Instow disguised herself as a fortune-teller. Mind you, she may have done it for a joke. I don't for a minute think that she meant any harm; but if she did do it, and if Mrs. Pritchard was foolish enough to die of fright – well, that's what Miss Marple meant, wasn't it?'

'No, dear, not quite,' said Miss Marple. 'You see, if I were going to kill anyone – which, of course, I wouldn't dream of doing for a minute, because it would be very wicked, and besides I don't like killing – not even wasps, though I know it has to be, and I'm sure the gardener does it as humanely as possible. Let me see, what was I saying?'

'If you wished to kill anyone,' prompted Sir Henry.

'Oh yes. Well, if I did, I shouldn't be at all satisfied to trust to *fright*. I know one reads of people dying of it, but it seems a very uncertain sort of thing, and the most nervous people are far more brave than one really thinks they are. I should like something definite and certain, and make a thoroughly good plan about it.'

'Miss Marple,' said Sir Henry, 'you frighten me. I hope you will never wish to remove me. Your plans would be too good.'

Miss Marple looked at him reproachfully.

'I thought I had made it clear that I would never contemplate such wickedness,' she said. 'No, I was trying to put myself in the place of – er – a certain person.'

'Do you mean George Pritchard?' asked Colonel Bantry. 'I'll never believe it of George – though, mind you, even the nurse believes it. I went and saw her about a month afterwards, at the time of the exhumation. She didn't know how it was done – in fact, she wouldn't say anything at all – but it was clear enough that she believed George to be in some way responsible for his wife's death. She was convinced of it.'

'Well,' said Dr Lloyd, 'perhaps she wasn't so far wrong. And mind you, a nurse often *knows*. She can't say – she's got no proof – but she *knows*.'

Sir Henry leant forward.

'Come now, Miss Marple,' he said persuasively. 'You're lost in a daydream. Won't you tell us all about it?'

Miss Marple started and turned pink.

'I beg your pardon,' she said. 'I was just thinking about our District Nurse. A most difficult problem.'

'More difficult than the problem of the blue geranium?'

'It really depends on the primroses,' said Miss Marple.

'I mean, Mrs Bantry said they were yellow and pink. If it was a pink primrose that turned blue, of course, that fits in perfectly. But if it happened to be a yellow one –'

'It was a pink one,' said Mrs Bantry.

She stared. They all stared at Miss Marple.

'Then that seems to settle it,' said Miss Marple. She shook her head regretfully. 'And the wasp season and everything. And of course the gas.'

'It reminds you, I suppose, of countless village tragedies?' said Sir Henry.

'Not tragedies,' said Miss Marple. 'And certainly nothing criminal. But it does remind me a little of the trouble we are having with the District Nurse. After all, nurses are human beings, and what with having to be so correct in their behaviour and wearing those uncomfortable collars and being so thrown with the family – well, can you wonder that things sometimes happen?'

A glimmer of light broke upon Sir Henry.

'You mean Nurse Carstairs?

'Oh no. Not Nurse Carstairs. Nurse *Copling*. You see, she had been there before, and very much thrown with Mr Pritchard, who you say is an attractive man. I daresay she thought, poor thing – well, we needn't go into that. I don't suppose she knew about Miss Instow, and of course afterwards, when she found out, it turned her against him and she tried to do all the harm she could. Of course the letter really gave her away, didn't it?'

'What letter?'

'Well, she wrote to the fortune-teller at Mrs Pritchard's request, and the fortune-teller came, apparently in answer to the letter. But later it was discovered that there never had been such a person at that address. So that shows that Nurse Copling was in it. She only pretended to write – so what could be more likely than that *she* was the fortune-teller herself?'

'I never saw the point about the letter,' said Sir Henry. 'That's a most important point, of course.'

'Rather a bold step to take,' said Miss Marple, 'because Mrs Pritchard might have recognized her in spite of the disguise – though of course if she had, the nurse could have pretended it was a joke.'

'What did you mean,' said Sir Henry, 'when you said that if you were a certain person you would not have trusted to fright?'

'One couldn't be *sure* that way,' said Miss Marple. 'No, I think that the warnings and the blue flowers were, if I may use a military term,' she laughed self-consciously – 'just *camouflage*.'

'And the real thing?'

'I know,' said Miss Marple apologetically, 'that I've got wasps on the brain. Poor things, destroyed in their thousands – and usually on such a beautiful summer's day. But I remember thinking, when I saw the gardener shaking up the cyanide of potassium in a bottle with water, how like smelling-salts it looked. And if it were put in a smelling-salt bottle and substituted for the real one – well, the poor lady was in the habit of using her smelling-salts. Indeed you said they were found by her hand. Then, of course, while Mr Pritchard went to telephone to the doctor, the nurse would change it for the real bottle, and she'd just turn on the gas a little bit to mask any smell of almonds and in case anyone felt queer, and I always have heard that cyanide leaves no trace if you wait long enough. But, of course I may be wrong, and it may have been something entirely different in the bottle; but that doesn't really matter, does it?'

Miss Marple paused, a little out of breath.

Jane Helier leant forward and said, 'But the blue geranium, and the other flowers?'

'Nurses always have litmus paper, don't they?' said Miss Marple, 'for – well, for testing. Not a very pleasant subject. We won't dwell on it. I have done a little nursing myself.' She grew delicately pink. 'Blue turns red with acids, and red turns blue with alkalies. So easy to paste some red litmus over a red flower – near the bed, of course. And then, when the poor lady used her smelling-salts, the strong ammonia fumes would turn it blue. Really most ingenious. Of course, the geranium wasn't blue when they first broke into the room – nobody noticed it till afterwards. When nurse changed the bottles, she held the Sal Ammoniac against the wallpaper for a minute, I expect.'

'You might have been there, Miss Marple,' said Sir Henry.

'What worries me,' said Miss Marple, 'is poor Mr Pritchard and that nice girl, Miss Instow. Probably both suspecting each other and keeping apart – and life so very short.'

She shook her head.

'You needn't worry,' said Sir Henry. 'As a matter of fact I have something up my sleeve. A nurse has been arrested on a charge of murdering an elderly patient who had left her a legacy. It was done with cyanide of potassium substituted for smelling-salts. Nurse Copling trying the same trick again. Miss Instow and Mr Pritchard need have no doubts as to the truth.'

'Now isn't that nice?' cried Miss Marple. 'I don't mean about the new murder, of course. That's very sad, and shows how much wickedness there is in the world, and that if once you give way – which reminds me I *must* finish my little conversation with Dr Lloyd about the village nurse.'

SUSAN GLASPELL

A JURY OF HER PEERS

WHEN MARTHA HALE opened the storm-door and got a cut of the north wind, she ran back for her big woolen scarf. As she hurriedly wound that round her head her eye made a scandalized sweep of her kitchen. It was no ordinary thing that called her away – it was probably farther from ordinary than anything that had ever happened in Dickson County. But what her eye took in was that her kitchen was in no shape for leaving: her bread all ready for mixing, half the flour sifted and half unsifted.

She hated to see things half done; but she had been at that when the team from town stopped to get Mr Hale, and then the sheriff came running in to say his wife wished Mrs Hale would come too – adding, with a grin, that he guessed she was getting scarey and wanted another woman along. So she had dropped everything right where it was.

'Martha!' now came her husband's impatient voice. 'Don't keep folks waiting out here in the cold.'

She again opened the storm-door, and this time joined the three men and the one woman waiting for her in the big two-seated buggy.

After she had the robes tucked around her she took another look at the woman who sat beside her on the back seat. She had met Mrs Peters the year before at the county fair, and the thing she remembered about her was that she didn't seem like a sheriff's wife. She was small and thin and didn't have a strong voice. Mrs Gorman, sheriff's wife before Gorman went out and Peters came in, had a voice that somehow seemed to be backing up the law with every word. But if Mrs Peters didn't look like a sheriff's wife, Peters made it up in looking like a sheriff. He was to a dot the kind of man who could get himself elected sheriff – a heavy man with a big voice, who was particularly genial with the law-abiding, as if to make it plain that he knew the difference between criminals and non-criminals. And right there it came into Mrs Hale's mind, with a stab, that this man who was so pleasant and lively with all of them was going to the Wrights' now as a sheriff.

'The country's not very pleasant this time of year,' Mrs Peters at last ventured, as if she felt they ought to be talking as well as the men.

Mrs Hale scarcely finished her reply, for they had gone up a little hill and could see the Wright place now, and seeing it did not make her feel like talking. It looked very lonesome this cold March morning. It had always been a lonesome-looking place. It was down in a hollow, and the poplar trees around it were lonesome-looking trees. The men were looking at it and talking about what had happened. The county attorney was bending to one side of the buggy, and kept looking steadily at the place as they drew up to it.

'I'm glad you came with me,' Mrs Peters said nervously, as the two women were about to follow the men in through the kitchen door.

Even after she had her foot on the door-step, her hand on the knob, Martha Hale had a moment of feeling she could not cross the threshold. And the reason it seemed she couldn't cross it now was simply because she hadn't crossed it before. Time and time again it had been in her mind, 'I ought to go over and see Minnie Foster' – she still thought of her as Minnie Foster, though for twenty years she had been Mrs Wright. And then there was always something to do and Minnie Foster would go from her mind. But now she could come.

The men went over to the stove. The women stood close together by the door. Young Henderson, the county attorney, turned around and said, 'Come up to the fire, ladies.'

Mrs Peters took a step forward, then stopped. 'I'm not – cold,' she said.

And so the two women stood by the door, at first not even so much as looking around the kitchen.

The men talked for a minute about what a good thing it was the sheriff had sent his deputy out that morning to make a fire for them, and then Sheriff Peters stepped back from the stove, unbuttoned his outer coat, and leaned his hands on the kitchen table in a way that seemed to mark the beginning of official business. 'Now, Mr Hale,' he said in a sort of semi-official voice, 'before we move things about, you tell Mr Henderson just what it was you saw when you came here yesterday morning.'

The county attorney was looking around the kitchen.

'By the way,' he said, 'has anything been moved?' He turned to the sheriff. 'Are things just as you left them yesterday?'

Peters looked from cupboard to sink; from that to a small worn rocker a little to one side of the kitchen table.

'It's just the same.'

'Somebody should have been left here yesterday,' said the county attorney.

'Oh – yesterday,' returned the sheriff, with a little gesture as of yesterday having been more than he could bear to think of. 'When I had to send Frank to Morris Center for that man who went crazy – let me tell you, I had my hands full *yesterday.* I knew you could get back from Omaha by today, George, and as long as I went over everything here myself –'

'Well, Mr Hale,' said the county attorney, in a way of letting what was past and gone go, 'tell just what happened when you came here yesterday morning.'

Mrs Hale, still leaning against the door, had that sinking feeling of the mother whose child is about to speak a piece. Lewis often wandered along and got things mixed up in a story. She hoped he would tell this straight and plain, and not say unnecessary things that would just make things harder for Minnie Foster. He didn't begin at once, and she noticed that he looked queer – as if standing in that kitchen and having to tell what he had seen there yesterday morning made him almost sick.

'Yes, Mr Hale?' the county attorney reminded.

'Harry and I had started to town with a load of potatoes,' Mrs Hale's husband began.

Harry was Mrs Hale's oldest boy. He wasn't with them now, for the very good reason that those potatoes never got to town yesterday and he was taking them this morning, so he hadn't been home when the sheriff stopped to say he wanted Mr Hale to come over to the Wright place and tell the county attorney his story there, where he could point it all out. With all Mrs Hale's other emotions came the fear that maybe Harry wasn't dressed warm enough – they hadn't any of them realized how that north wind did bite.

'We come along this road,' Hale was going on, with a motion of his hand to the road over which they had just come, 'and as we got in sight of the house I says to Harry, "I'm goin' to see if I can't get John Wright to take a telephone." You see,' he explained to Henderson, 'unless I can get somebody to go in with me they won't come out this branch road except for a price *I* can't pay. I'd spoke to Wright about it once before; but he put me off, saying folks talked too much anyway, and all he asked was peace and quiet – guess you know about how much he talked himself. But I thought maybe if I went to the house and talked about it before his wife, and said all the women-folks liked the telephones, and that in this lonesome stretch of road it would be a good thing – well, I said to Harry that that was what I was going to say – though I said at the same time that I didn't know as what his wife wanted made much difference to John –'

Now, there he was! – saying things he didn't need to say. Mrs Hale tried to catch her husband's eye, but fortunately the county attorney interrupted with:

'Let's talk about that a little later, Mr Hale. I do want to talk about that, but I'm anxious now to get along to just what happened when you got here.'

When he began this time, it was very deliberately and carefully:

'I didn't see or hear anything. I knocked at the door. And still it was all quiet inside. I knew they must be up – it was past eight o'clock. So I knocked again, louder, and I thought I heard somebody say "Come in." I wasn't sure – I'm not sure yet. But I opened the door – this door,' jerking a hand toward the door by which the two women stood, 'and there, in that rocker' – pointing to it – 'sat Mrs Wright.'

Every one in the kitchen looked at the rocker. It came into Mrs Hale's mind that that rocker didn't look in the least like Minnie Foster – the Minnie Foster of twenty years before. It was a dingy red, with wooden rungs up the back, and the middle rung was gone, and the chair sagged to one side.

'How did she – look?' the county attorney was inquiring.

'Well,' said Hale, 'she looked – queer.'

'How do you mean – queer?'

As he asked it he took out a note-book and pencil. Mrs Hale did not like the sight of that pencil. She kept her eye fixed on her husband, as if to keep him from saying unnecessary things that would go into that note-book and make trouble.

Hale did speak guardedly, as if the pencil had affected him too.

'Well, as if she didn't know what she was going to do next. And kind of – done up.'

'How did she seem to feel about your coming?'

'Why, I don't think she minded – one way or other. She didn't pay much attention. I said, "Ho' do, Mrs Wright? It's cold, ain't it?" And she said, "Is it?" – and went on pleatin' at her apron.

'Well, I was surprised. She didn't ask me to come up to the stove, or to sit down, but just set there, not even lookin' at me. And so I said: "I want to see John."

'And then she – laughed. I guess you would call it a laugh.

'I thought of Harry and the team outside, so I said, a little sharp, "Can I see John?" "No," says she – kind of dull like. "Ain't he home?" says I. Then she looked at me. "Yes," says she, "he's home." "Then why can't I see him?" I asked her, out of patience with her now. "'Cause he's dead," says she, just as quiet and dull – and fell to pleatin' her apron. "Dead?" says I, like you do when you can't take in what you've heard.

'She just nodded her head, not getting a bit excited, but rockin' back and forth.

' "Why – where is he?" says I, not knowing *what* to say.

'She just pointed upstairs – like this' – pointing to the room above.

'I got up, with the idea of going up there myself. By this

time I didn't know what to do. I walked from there to here; then I says: "Why, what did he die of?"

'"He died of a rope around his neck," says she; and just went on pleatin' at her apron.'

Hale stopped speaking, and stood staring at the rocker, as if he were still seeing the woman who had sat there the morning before. Nobody spoke; it was as if every one were seeing the woman who had sat there the morning before.

'And what did you do then?' the county attorney at last broke the silence.

'I went out and called Harry. I thought I might – need help. I got Harry in, and we went upstairs.' His voice fell almost to a whisper. 'There he was – lying over the –'

'I think I'd rather have you go into that upstairs,' the county attorney interrupted, 'where you can point it all out. Just go on now with the rest of the story.'

'Well, my first thought was to get that rope off. It looked –'

He stopped, his face twitching.

'But Harry, he went up to him, and he said, "No, he's dead all right, and we'd better not touch anything." So we went downstairs.

'She was still sitting that same way. "Has anybody been notified?" I asked. "No," says she, unconcerned.

'"Who did this, Mrs Wright?" said Harry. He said it businesslike, and she stopped pleatin' at her apron. "I don't know," she says. "You don't *know*?" says Harry. "Weren't you sleepin' in the bed with him?" "Yes," says she, "but I was on the inside." "Somebody slipped a rope round his neck and strangled him, and you didn't wake up?" says Harry. "I didn't wake up," she said after him.

'We may have looked as if we didn't see how that could be, for after a minute she said, "I sleep sound."

'Harry was going to ask her more questions, but I said maybe that weren't our business; maybe we ought to let her tell her story first to the coroner or the sheriff. So Harry went fast as he could over to High Road – the Rivers' place, where there's a telephone.'

'And what did she do when she knew you had gone for the coroner?' The attorney got his pencil in his hand all ready for writing.

'She moved from that chair to this one over here' – Hale pointed to a small chair in the corner – 'and just sat there with her hands held together and looking down. I got a feeling that I ought to make some conversation, so I said I had come in to see if John wanted to put in a telephone; and at that she started to laugh, and then she stopped and looked at me – scared.'

At the sound of a moving pencil the man who was telling the story looked up.

'I dunno – maybe it wasn't scared,' he hastened; 'I wouldn't like to say it was. Soon Harry got back, and then Dr Lloyd came, and you, Mr Peters, and so I guess that's all I know that you don't.'

He said that last with relief, and moved a little, as if relaxing. Every one moved a little. The county attorney walked toward the stair door.

'I guess we'll go upstairs first – then out to the barn and around there.'

He paused and looked around the kitchen.

'You're convinced there was nothing important here?' he asked the sheriff. 'Nothing that would – point to any motive?'

The sheriff too looked all around, as if to re-convince himself.

'Nothing here but kitchen things,' he said, with a little laugh for the insignificance of kitchen things.

The county attorney was looking at the cupboard – a peculiar, ungainly structure, half closet and half cupboard, the upper part of it being built in the wall, and the lower part just the old-fashioned kitchen cupboard. As if its queerness attracted him, he got a chair and opened the upper part and looked in. After a moment he drew his hand away sticky.

'Here's a nice mess,' he said resentfully.

The two women had drawn nearer, and now the sheriff's wife spoke.

'Oh – her fruit,' she said, looking to Mrs Hale for sympathetic understanding. She turned back to the county attorney and explained: 'She worried about that when it turned so cold last night. She said the fire would go out and her jars might burst.'

Mrs Peters's husband broke into a laugh.

'Well, can you beat the women! Held for murder, and worrying about her preserves!'

The young attorney set his lips.

'I guess before we're through with her she may have something more serious than preserves to worry about.'

'Oh, well,' said Mrs Hale's husband, with good-natured superiority, 'women are used to worrying over trifles.'

The two women moved a little closer together. Neither of them spoke. The county attorney seemed suddenly to remember his manners – and think of his future.

'And yet,' said he, with the gallantry of a young politician, 'for all their worries, what would we do without the ladies?'

The women did not speak, did not unbend. He went to the sink and began washing his hands. He turned to wipe them on the roller towel – whirled it for a cleaner place.

'Dirty towels! Not much of a housekeeper, would you say, ladies?'

He kicked his foot against some dirty pans under the sink.

'There's a great deal of work to be done on a farm,' said Mrs Hale stiffly.

'To be sure. And yet' – with a little bow to her – 'I know there are some Dickson County farmhouses that do not have such roller towels.' He gave it a pull to expose its full length again.

'Those towels get dirty awful quick. Men's hands aren't always as clean as they might be.'

'Ah, loyal to your sex, I see,' he laughed. He stopped and gave her a keen look. 'But you and Mrs Wright were neighbors. I suppose you were friends, too.'

Martha Hale shook her head.

'I've seen little enough of her of late years. I've not been in this house – it's more than a year.'

'And why was that? You didn't like her?'

'I liked her well enough,' she replied with spirit. 'Farmers' wives have their hands full, Mr Henderson. And then' – She looked around the kitchen.

'Yes?' he encouraged.

'It never seemed a very cheerful place,' said she, more to herself than to him.

'No,' he agreed; 'I don't think any one could call it cheerful. I shouldn't say she had the home-making instinct.'

'Well, I don't know as Wright had, either,' she muttered.

'You mean they didn't get on very well?' he was quick to ask.

'No; I don't mean anything,' she answered, with decision. As she turned a little away from him, she added: 'But I don't think a place would be any the cheerfuler for John Wright's bein' in it.'

'I'd like to talk to you about that a little later, Mrs Hale,' he said. 'I'm anxious to get the lay of things upstairs now.'

He moved toward the stair door, followed by the two men.

'I suppose anything Mrs Peters does'll be all right?' the sheriff inquired. 'She was to take in some clothes for her, you know – and a few little things. We left in such a hurry yesterday.'

The county attorney looked at the two women whom they were leaving alone there among the kitchen things.

'Yes – Mrs Peters,' he said, his glance resting on the woman who was not Mrs Peters, the big farmer woman who stood behind the sheriff's wife. 'Of course Mrs Peters is one of us,' he said, in a manner of entrusting responsibility. 'And keep your eye out, Mrs Peters, for anything that might be of use. No telling; you women might come upon a clue to the motive – and that's the thing we need.'

Mr Hale rubbed his face after the fashion of a show man getting ready for a pleasantry.

'But would the women know a clue if they did come upon it?' he said; and, having delivered himself of this, he followed the others through the stair door.

The women stood motionless and silent, listening to the footsteps, first upon the stairs, then in the room above them.

Then, as if releasing herself from something strange, Mrs Hale began to arrange the dirty pans under the sink, which the county attorney's disdainful push of the foot had deranged.

'I'd hate to have men comin' into my kitchen,' she said testily – 'snoopin' around and criticizin'.'

'Of course it's no more than their duty,' said the sheriff's wife, in her manner of timid acquiescence.

'Duty's all right,' replied Mrs Hale bluffly; 'but I guess

that deputy sheriff that come out to make the fire might have got a little of this on.' She gave the roller towel a pull. 'Wish I'd thought of that sooner! Seems mean to talk about her for not having things slicked up when she had to come away in such a hurry.'

She looked around the kitchen. Certainly it was not 'slicked up.' Her eye was held by a bucket of sugar on a low shelf. The cover was off the wooden bucket, and beside it was a paper bag – half full.

Mrs Hale moved toward it.

'She was putting this in here,' she said to herself – slowly.

She thought of the flour in her kitchen at home – half sifted, half not sifted. She had been interrupted, and had left things half done. What had interrupted Minnie Foster? Why had that work been left half done? She made a move as if to finish it, – unfinished things always bothered her, – and then she glanced around and saw that Mrs Peters was watching her – and she didn't want Mrs Peters to get that feeling she had got of work begun and then – for some reason – not finished.

'It's a shame about her fruit,' she said, and walked toward the cupboard that the county attorney had opened, and got on the chair, murmuring: 'I wonder if it's all gone.'

It was a sorry enough looking sight, but 'Here's one that's all right,' she said at last. She held it toward the light. 'This is cherries, too.' She looked again. 'I declare I believe that's the only one.'

With a sigh, she got down from the chair, went to the sink, and wiped off the bottle.

'She'll feel awful bad, after all her hard work in the hot weather. I remember the afternoon I put up my cherries last summer.'

She set the bottle on the table, and, with another sigh,

started to sit down in the rocker. But she did not sit down. Something kept her from sitting down in that chair. She straightened – stepped back, and, half turned away, stood looking at it, seeing the woman who sat there 'pleatin' at her apron.'

The thin voice of the sheriff's wife broke in upon her: 'I must be getting those things from the front room closet.' She opened the door into the other room, started in, stepped back. 'You coming with me, Mrs Hale?' she asked nervously. 'You – you could help me get them.'

They were soon back – the stark coldness of that shut-up room was not a thing to linger in.

'My!' said Mrs Peters, dropping the things on the table and hurrying to the stove.

Mrs Hale stood examining the clothes the woman who was being detained in town had said she wanted.

'Wright was close!' she exclaimed, holding up a shabby black skirt that bore the marks of much making over. 'I think maybe that's why she kept so much to herself. I s'pose she felt she couldn't do her part; and then, you don't enjoy things when you feel shabby. She used to wear pretty clothes and be lively – when she was Minnie Foster, one of the town girls, singing in the choir. But that – oh, that was twenty years ago.'

With a carefulness in which there was something tender, she folded the shabby clothes and piled them at one corner of the table. She looked at Mrs Peters, and there was something in the other woman's look that irritated her.

'She don't care,' she said to herself. 'Much difference it makes to her whether Minnie Foster had pretty clothes when she was a girl.'

Then she looked again, and she wasn't so sure; in fact, she hadn't at any time been perfectly sure about Mrs Peters.

She had that shrinking manner, and yet her eyes looked as if they could see a long way into things.

'This all you was to take in?' asked Mrs Hale.

'No,' said the sheriff's wife; 'she said she wanted an apron. Funny thing to want,' she ventured in her nervous little way, 'for there's not much to get you dirty in jail, goodness knows. But I suppose just to make her feel more natural. If you're used to wearing an apron –. She said they were in the bottom drawer of this cupboard. Yes – here they are. And then her little shawl that always hung on the stair door.'

She took the small gray shawl from behind the door leading upstairs, and stood a minute looking at it.

Suddenly Mrs Hale took a quick step toward the other woman.

'Mrs Peters!'

'Yes, Mrs Hale?'

'Do you think she – did it?'

A frightened look blurred the other things in Mrs Peters's eyes.

'Oh, I don't know,' she said, in a voice that seemed to shrink away from the subject.

'Well, I don't think she did,' affirmed Mrs Hale stoutly. 'Asking for an apron, and her little shawl. Worryin' about her fruit.'

'Mr Peters says –' Footsteps were heard in the room above; she stopped, looked up, then went on in a lowered voice: 'Mr Peters says – it looks bad for her. Mr Henderson is awful sarcastic in a speech, and he's going to make fun of her saying she didn't – wake up.'

For a moment Mrs Hale had no answer. Then, 'Well, I guess John Wright didn't wake up – when they was slippin' that rope under his neck,' she muttered.

'No, it's *strange*,' breathed Mrs Peters. 'They think it was such a – funny way to kill a man.'

She began to laugh; at the sound of the laugh, abruptly stopped.

'That's just what Mr Hale said,' said Mrs Hale, in a resolutely natural voice. 'There was a gun in the house. He says that's what he can't understand.'

'Mr Henderson said, coming out, that what was needed for the case was a motive. Something to show anger – or sudden feeling.'

'Well, I don't see any signs of anger around here,' said Mrs Hale. 'I don't –'

She stopped. It was as if her mind tripped on something. Her eye was caught by a dish-towel in the middle of the kitchen table. Slowly she moved toward the table. One half of it was wiped clean, the other half messy. Her eyes made a slow, almost unwilling turn to the bucket of sugar and the half empty bag beside it. Things begun – and not finished.

After a moment she stepped back, and said, in that manner of releasing herself:

'Wonder how they're finding things upstairs? I hope she had it a little more red up up there. You know,' – she paused, and feeling gathered, – 'it seems kind of *sneaking*; locking her up in town and coming out here to get her own house to turn against her!'

'But, Mrs Hale,' said the sheriff's wife, 'the law is the law.'

'I s'pose 'tis,' answered Mrs Hale shortly.

She turned to the stove, saying something about that fire not being much to brag of. She worked with it a minute, and when she straightened up she said aggressively:

'The law is the law – and a bad stove is a bad stove. How'd you like to cook on this?' – pointing with the poker to the broken lining. She opened the oven door and started to express her opinion of the oven; but she was swept into her own thoughts, thinking of what it would mean, year after year, to have that stove to wrestle with. The thought of Minnie Foster trying to bake in that oven – and the thought of her never going over to see Minnie Foster –

She was startled by hearing Mrs Peters say: 'A person gets discouraged – and loses heart.'

The sheriff's wife had looked from the stove to the sink – to the pail of water which had been carried in from outside. The two women stood there silent, above them the footsteps of the men who were looking for evidence against the woman who had worked in that kitchen. That look of seeing into things, of seeing through a thing to something else, was in the eyes of the sheriff's wife now. When Mrs Hale next spoke to her, it was gently:

'Better loosen up your things, Mrs Peters. We'll not feel them when we go out.'

Mrs Peters went to the back of the room to hang up the fur tippet she was wearing. A moment later she exclaimed, 'Why, she was piecing a quilt,' and held up a large sewing basket piled high with quilt pieces.

Mrs Hale spread some of the blocks on the table.

'It's log-cabin pattern,' she said, putting several of them together. 'Pretty, isn't it?'

They were so engaged with the quilt that they did not hear the footsteps on the stairs. Just as the stair door opened Mrs Hale was saying:

'Do you suppose she was going to quilt it or just knot it?'

The sheriff threw up his hands.

'They wonder whether she was going to quilt it or just knot it!'

There was a laugh for the ways of women, a warming of

hands over the stove, and then the county attorney said briskly:

'Well, let's go right out to the barn and get that cleared up.'

'I don't see as there's anything so strange,' Mrs Hale said resentfully, after the outside door had closed on the three men – 'our taking up our time with little things while we're waiting for them to get the evidence. I don't see as it's anything to laugh about.'

'Of course they've got awful important things on their minds,' said the sheriff's wife apologetically.

They returned to an inspection of the blocks for the quilt. Mrs Hale was looking at the fine, even sewing, and preoccupied with thoughts of the woman who had done that sewing, when she heard the sheriff's wife say, in a queer tone:

'Why, look at this one.'

She turned to take the block held out to her.

'The sewing,' said Mrs Peters, in a troubled way. 'All the rest of them have been so nice and even – but – this one. Why, it looks as if she didn't know what she was about!'

Their eyes met – something flashed to life, passed between them; then, as if with an effort, they seemed to pull away from each other. A moment Mrs Hale sat there, her hands folded over that sewing which was so unlike all the rest of the sewing. Then she had pulled a knot and drawn the threads.

'Oh, what are you doing, Mrs Hale?' asked the sheriff's wife, startled.

'Just pulling out a stitch or two that's not sewed very good,' said Mrs Hale mildly.

'I don't think we ought to touch things,' Mrs Peters said, a little helplessly.

'I'll just finish up this end,' answered Mrs Hale, still in that mild, matter-of-fact fashion.

She threaded a needle and started to replace bad sewing with good. For a little while she sewed in silence. Then, in that thin, timid voice, she heard:

'Mrs Hale!'

'Yes, Mrs Peters?'

'What do you suppose she was so – nervous about?'

'Oh, *I* don't know,' said Mrs Hale, as if dismissing a thing not important enough to spend much time on. 'I don't know as she was – nervous. I sew awful queer sometimes when I'm just tired.'

She cut a thread, and out of the corner of her eye looked up at Mrs Peters. The small, lean face of the sheriff's wife seemed to have tightened up. Her eyes had that look of peering into something. But the next moment she moved, and said in her thin, indecisive way:

'Well, I must get those clothes wrapped. They may be through sooner than we think. I wonder where I could find a piece of paper – and string.'

'In that cupboard, maybe,' suggested Mrs Hale, after a glance around.

One piece of the crazy sewing remained unripped. Mrs Peters's back turned, Martha Hale now scrutinized that piece, compared it with the dainty, accurate sewing of the other blocks. The difference was startling. Holding this block made her feel queer, as if the distracted thoughts of the woman who had perhaps turned to it to try and quiet herself were communicating themselves to her.

Mrs Peters's voice roused her.

'Here's a bird-cage,' she said. 'Did she have a bird, Mrs Hale?'

'Why, I don't know whether she did or not.' She turned to look at the cage Mrs Peters was holding up. 'I've not been here in so long.' She sighed. 'There was a man round last year selling canaries cheap – but I don't know as she took one. Maybe she did. She used to sing real pretty herself.'

Mrs Peters looked around the kitchen.

'Seems kind of funny to think of a bird here.' She half laughed – an attempt to put up a barrier. 'But she must have had one – or why would she have a cage? I wonder what happened to it.'

'I suppose maybe the cat got it,' suggested Mrs Hale, resuming her sewing.

'No, she didn't have a cat. She's got that feeling some people have about cats – being afraid of them. When they brought her to our house yesterday, my cat got in the room, and she was real upset and asked me to take it out.'

'My sister Bessie was like that,' laughed Mrs Hale.

The sheriff's wife did not reply. The silence made Mrs Hale turn around. Mrs Peters was examining the bird-cage.

'Look at this door,' she said slowly. 'It's broke. One hinge has been pulled apart.'

Mrs Hale came nearer.

'Looks as if some one must have been – rough with it.'

Again their eyes met – startled, questioning, apprehensive. For a moment neither spoke nor stirred. Then Mrs Hale, turning away, said brusquely:

'If they're going to find any evidence, I wish they'd be about it. I don't like this place.'

'But I'm awful glad you came with me, Mrs Hale.' Mrs Peters put the bird-cage on the table and sat down. 'It would be lonesome for me – sitting here alone.'

'Yes, it would, wouldn't it?' agreed Mrs Hale, a certain determined naturalness in her voice. She picked up the sewing, but now it dropped in her lap, and she murmured in a different voice: 'But I tell you what I *do* wish, Mrs Peters. I wish I had come over sometimes when she was here. I wish – I had.'

'But of course you were awful busy, Mrs Hale. Your house – and your children.'

'I could've come,' retorted Mrs Hale shortly. 'I stayed away because it weren't cheerful – and that's why I ought to have come. I' – she looked around – 'I've never liked this place. Maybe because it's down in a hollow and you don't see the road. I don't know what it is, but it's a lonesome place, and always was. I wish I had come over to see Minnie Foster sometimes. I can see now –' She did not put it into words.

'Well, you mustn't reproach yourself,' counseled Mrs Peters. 'Somehow, we just don't see how it is with other folks till – something comes up.'

'Not having children makes less work,' mused Mrs Hale, after a silence, 'but it makes a quiet house – and Wright out to work all day – and no company when he did come in. Did you know John Wright, Mrs Peters?'

'Not to know him. I've seen him in town. They say he was a good man.'

'Yes – good,' conceded John Wright's neighbor grimly. 'He didn't drink, and kept his word as well as most, I guess, and paid his debts. But he was a hard man, Mrs Peters. Just to pass the time of day with him –' She stopped, shivered a little. 'Like a raw wind that gets to the bone.' Her eye fell upon the cage on the table before her, and she added, almost bitterly: 'I should think she would've wanted a bird!'

Suddenly she leaned forward, looking intently at the cage. 'But what do you s'pose went wrong with it?'

'I don't know,' returned Mrs Peters; 'unless it got sick and died.'

But after she said it she reached over and swung the broken door. Both women watched it as if somehow held by it.

'You didn't know – her?' Mrs Hale asked, a gentler note in her voice.

'Not till they brought her yesterday,' said the sheriff's wife.

'She – come to think of it, she was kind of like a bird herself. Real sweet and pretty, but kind of timid and – fluttery. How – she – did – change.'

That held her for a long time. Finally, as if struck with a happy thought and relieved to get back to everyday things, she exclaimed:

'Tell you what, Mrs Peters, why don't you take the quilt in with you? It might take up her mind.'

'Why, I think that's a real nice idea, Mrs Hale,' agreed the sheriff's wife, as if she too were glad to come into the atmosphere of a simple kindness. 'There couldn't possibly be any objection to that, could there? Now, just what will I take? I wonder if her patches are in here – and her things.'

They turned to the sewing basket.

'Here's some red,' said Mrs Hale, bringing out a roll of cloth. Underneath that was a box. 'Here, maybe her scissors are in here – and her things.' She held it up. 'What a pretty box! I'll warrant that was something she had a long time ago – when she was a girl.'

She held it in her hand a moment; then, with a little sigh, opened it.

Instantly her hand went to her nose.

'Why –!'

Mrs Peters drew nearer – then turned away.

'There's something wrapped up in this piece of silk,' faltered Mrs Hale.

'This isn't her scissors,' said Mrs Peters in a shrinking voice.

Her hand not steady, Mrs Hale raised the piece of silk. 'Oh, Mrs Peters!' she cried. 'It's –'

Mrs Peters bent closer.

'It's the bird,' she whispered.

'But, Mrs Peters!' cried Mrs Hale. '*Look* at it! Its neck – look at its neck! It's all – other side *to*.'

She held the box away from her.

The sheriff's wife again bent closer.

'Somebody wrung its neck,' said she, in a voice that was slow and deep.

And then again the eyes of the two women met – this time clung together in a look of dawning comprehension, of growing horror. Mrs Peters looked from the dead bird to the broken door of the cage. Again their eyes met. And just then there was a sound at the outside door.

Mrs Hale slipped the box under the quilt pieces in the basket, and sank into the chair before it. Mrs Peters stood holding to the table. The county attorney and the sheriff came in from outside.

'Well, ladies,' said the county attorney, as one turning from serious things to little pleasantries, 'have you decided whether she was going to quilt it or knot it?'

'We think,' began the sheriff's wife in a flurried voice, 'that she was going to – knot it.'

He was too preoccupied to notice the change that came in her voice on that last.

'Well, that's very interesting, I'm sure,' he said tolerantly. He caught sight of the bird-cage. 'Has the bird flown?'

'We think the cat got it,' said Mrs Hale in a voice curiously even.

He was walking up and down, as if thinking something out.

'Is there a cat?' he asked absently.

Mrs Hale shot a look up at the sheriff's wife.

'Well, not *now,*' said Mrs Peters. 'They're superstitious, you know; they leave.'

She sank into her chair.

The county attorney did not heed her. 'No sign at all of any one having come in from the outside,' he said to Peters, in the manner of continuing an interrupted conversation. 'Their own rope. Now let's go upstairs again and go over it, piece by piece. It would have to have been some one who knew just the –'

The stair door closed behind them and their voices were lost.

The two women sat motionless, not looking at each other, but as if peering into something and at the same time holding back. When they spoke now it was as if they were afraid of what they were saying, but as if they could not help saying it.

'She liked the bird,' said Martha Hale, low and slowly. 'She was going to bury it in that pretty box.'

'When I was a girl,' said Mrs Peters, under her breath, 'my kitten – there was a boy took a hatchet, and before my eyes – before I could get there –' She covered her face an instant. 'If they hadn't held me back I would have' – she caught herself, looked upstairs where footsteps were heard, and finished weakly – 'hurt him.'

Then they sat without speaking or moving.

'I wonder how it would seem,' Mrs Hale at last began, as if feeling her way over strange ground – 'never to have had any children around?' Her eyes made a slow sweep of the kitchen, as if seeing what that kitchen had meant through all the years. 'No, Wright wouldn't like the bird,' she said after that – 'a thing that sang. She used to sing. He killed that too.' Her voice tightened.

Mrs Peters moved uneasily.

'Of course we don't know who killed the bird.'

'I knew John Wright,' was Mrs Hale's answer.

'It was an awful thing was done in this house that night, Mrs Hale,' said the sheriff's wife. 'Killing a man while he slept – slipping a thing round his neck that choked the life out of him.'

Mrs Hale's hand went out to the bird-cage.

'His neck. Choked the life out of him.'

'We don't *know* who killed him,' whispered Mrs Peters wildly. 'We don't *know*.'

Mrs Hale had not moved. 'If there had been years and years of – nothing, then a bird to sing to you, it would be awful – still – after the bird was still.'

It was as if something within her not herself had spoken, and it found in Mrs Peters something she did not know as herself.

'I know what stillness is,' she said, in a queer, monotonous voice. 'When we homesteaded in Dakota, and my first baby died – after he was two years old – and me with no other then –'

Mrs Hale stirred.

'How soon do you suppose they'll be through looking for evidence?'

'I know what stillness is,' repeated Mrs Peters, in just that same way. Then she too pulled back. 'The law has got to punish crime, Mrs Hale,' she said in her tight little way.

'I wish you'd seen Minnie Foster,' was the answer, 'when she wore a white dress with blue ribbons, and stood up there in the choir and sang.'

The picture of that girl, the fact that she had lived neighbor to that girl for twenty years, and had let her die for lack of life, was suddenly more than she could bear.

'Oh, I *wish* I'd come over here once in a while!' she cried. 'That was a crime! That was a crime! Who's going to punish that?'

'We mustn't take on,' said Mrs Peters, with a frightened look toward the stairs.

'I might 'a' *known* she needed help! I tell you, it's *queer*, Mrs Peters. We live close together, and we live far apart. We all go through the same things – it's all just a different kind of the same thing! If it weren't – why do you and I *understand*? Why do we *know* – what we know this minute?'

She dashed her hand across her eyes. Then, seeing the jar of fruit on the table, she reached for it and choked out:

'If I was you I wouldn't *tell* her her fruit was gone! Tell her it *ain't*. Tell her it's all right – all of it. Here – take this in to prove it to her! She – she may never know whether it was broke or not.'

She turned away.

Mrs Peters reached out for the bottle of fruit as if she were glad to take it – as if touching a familiar thing, having something to do, could keep her from something else. She got up, looked about for something to wrap the fruit in, took a petticoat from the pile of clothes she had brought from the front room, and nervously started winding that round the bottle.

'My!' she began, in a high, false voice, 'it's a good thing the men couldn't hear us! Getting all stirred up over a little thing like a – dead canary.' She hurried over that. 'As if that could have anything to do with – with – My, wouldn't they *laugh*?'

Footsteps were heard on the stairs.

'Maybe they would,' muttered Mrs Hale – 'maybe they wouldn't.'

'No, Peters,' said the county attorney incisively; 'it's all perfectly clear, except the reason for doing it. But you know juries when it comes to women. If there was some definite thing – something to show. Something to make a story about. A thing that would connect up with this clumsy way of doing it.'

In a covert way Mrs Hale looked at Mrs Peters. Mrs Peters was looking at her. Quickly they looked away from each other. The outer door opened and Mr Hale came in.

'I've got the team round now,' he said. 'Pretty cold out there.'

'I'm going to stay here awhile by myself,' the county attorney suddenly announced. 'You can send Frank out for me, can't you?' he asked the sheriff. 'I want to go over everything. I'm not satisfied we can't do better.'

Again, for one brief moment, the two women's eyes found one another.

The sheriff came up to the table.

'Did you want to see what Mrs Peters was going to take in?'

The county attorney picked up the apron. He laughed.

'Oh, I guess they're not very dangerous things the ladies have picked out.'

Mrs Hale's hand was on the sewing basket in which the box was concealed. She felt that she ought to take her hand off the basket. She did not seem able to. He picked up one of the quilt blocks which she had piled on to cover the box. Her eyes felt like fire. She had a feeling that if he took up the basket she would snatch it from him.

But he did not take it up. With another little laugh, he turned away, saying:

'No; Mrs Peters doesn't need supervising. For that matter, a sheriff's wife is married to the law. Ever think of it that way, Mrs Peters?'

Mrs Peters was standing beside the table. Mrs Hale shot a look up at her; but she could not see her face. Mrs Peters had turned away. When she spoke, her voice was muffled.

'Not – just that way,' she said.

'Married to the law!' chuckled Mrs Peters's husband. He moved toward the door into the front room, and said to the county attorney:

'I just want you to come in here a minute, George. We ought to take a look at these windows.'

'Oh – windows,' said the county attorney scoffingly.

'We'll be right out, Mr Hale,' said the sheriff to the farmer, who was still waiting by the door.

Hale went to look after the horses. The sheriff followed the county attorney into the other room. Again – for one moment – the two women were alone in that kitchen.

Martha Hale sprang up, her hands tight together, looking at that other woman, with whom it rested. At first she could not see her eyes, for the sheriff's wife had not turned back since she turned away at that suggestion of being married to the law. But now Mrs Hale made her turn back. Her eyes made her turn back. Slowly, unwillingly, Mrs Peters turned her head until her eyes met the eyes of the other woman. There was a moment when they held each other in a steady, burning look in which there was no evasion nor flinching. Then Martha Hale's eyes pointed the way to the basket in which was hidden the thing that would make certain the conviction of the other woman – that woman who was not there and yet who had been there with them all through the hour.

For a moment Mrs Peters did not move. And then she

did it. With a rush forward, she threw back the quilt pieces, got the box, tried to put in in her handbag. It was too big. Desperately she opened it, started to take the bird out. But there she broke – she could not touch the bird. She stood helpless, foolish.

There was a sound of a knob turning in the inner door. Martha Hale snatched the box from the sheriff's wife, and got it in the pocket of her big coat just as the sheriff and the county attorney came back into the kitchen.

'Well, Henry,' said the county attorney facetiously, 'at least we found out that she was not going to quilt it. She was going to – what is it you call it, ladies?'

Mrs Hale's hand was against the pocket of her coat.

'We call it – knot it, Mr Henderson.'

G.K. CHESTERTON

THE BLUE CROSS

could not be certain; nobody could be certain about Flambeau.

It is many years now since this colossus of crime suddenly ceased keeping the world in a turmoil; and when he ceased, as they said after the death of Roland, there was a great quiet upon the earth. But in his best days (I mean, of course, his worst) Flambeau was a figure as statuesque and international as the Kaiser. Almost every morning the daily paper announced that he had escaped the consequences of one extraordinary crime by committing another. He was a Gascon of gigantic stature and bodily daring; and the wildest tales were told of his outbursts of athletic humour; how he turned the *juge d'instruction* upside down and stood him on his head, 'to clear his mind'; how he ran down the Rue de Rivoli with a policeman under each arm. It is due to him to say that his fantastic physical strength was generally employed in such bloodless though undignified scenes; his real crimes were chiefly those of ingenious and wholesale robbery. But each of his thefts was almost a new sin, and would make a story by itself. It was he who ran the great Tyrolean Dairy Company in London, with no dairies, no cows, no carts, no milk, but with some thousand subscribers. These he served by the simple operation of moving the little milk-cans outside people's doors to the doors of his own customers. It was he who had kept up an unaccountable and close correspondence with a young lady whose whole letter-bag was intercepted, by the extraordinary trick of photographing his messages infinitesimally small upon the slides of a microscope. A sweeping simplicity, however, marked many of his experiments. It is said he once repainted all the numbers in a street in the dead of night merely to divert one traveller into a trap. It is quite certain that he invented a portable pillar-box, which he put up at corners in quiet suburbs on the chance of strangers dropping postal orders into it. Lastly he was known to be a startling acrobat; despite his huge figure, he could leap like a grasshopper and melt into the tree-tops like a monkey. Hence the great Valentin, when he set out to find Flambeau, was perfectly well aware that his adventures would not end when he had found him.

But how was he to find him? On this the great Valentin's ideas were still in process of settlement.

There was one thing which Flambeau, with all his dexterity of disguise, could not cover, and that was his singular height. If Valentin's quick eye had caught a tall applewoman, a tall grenadier, or even a tolerably tall duchess, he might have arrested them on the spot. But all along his train there was nobody that could be a disguised Flambeau, any more than a cat could be a disguised giraffe. About the people on the boat he had already satisfied himself; and the people picked up at Harwich or on the journey limited themselves with certainty to six. There was a short railway official travelling up to the terminus, three fairly short market-gardeners picked up two stations afterwards, one very short widow lady going up from a small Essex town, and a very short Roman Catholic priest going up from a small Essex village. When it came to the last case, Valentin gave it up and almost laughed. The little priest was so much the essence of those Eastern flats: he had a face as round and dull as a Norfolk dumpling; he had eyes as empty as the North Sea; he had several brown-paper parcels which he was quite incapable of collecting. The Eucharistic Congress had doubtless sucked out of their local stagnation many such creatures, blind and helpless, like moles disinterred. Valentin was a sceptic in the severe style of France, and could have no love for priests. But he could have pity for them, and this one might have provoked pity in anybody. He had a large, shabby umbrella, which constantly fell on the floor. He did not seem to know which was the right end of his return ticket. He explained with a mooncalf simplicity to everybody in the carriage that he had to be careful, because he had something made of real silver 'with blue stones' in one of his brown-paper parcels. His quaint blending of Essex flatness with saintly simplicity continuously amused the Frenchman till the priest arrived (somehow) at Stratford with all his parcels, and came back for his umbrella. When he did the last, Valentin even had the good-nature to warn him not to take care of the silver by telling everybody about it. But to whomever he talked, Valentin kept his eye open for someone else; he looked out steadily for anyone, rich or poor, male or female, who was well up to six feet; for Flambeau was four inches above it.

He alighted at Liverpool Street, however, quite conscientiously secure that he had not missed the criminal so far. He then went to Scotland Yard to regularize his position and arrange for help in case of need; he then lit another cigarette and went for a long stroll in the streets of London. As he was walking in the streets and squares beyond Victoria, he paused suddenly and stood. It was a quaint, quiet square, very typical of London, full of an accidental stillness. The tall, flat houses round looked at once prosperous and uninhabited; the square of shrubbery in the centre looked as deserted as a green Pacific islet. One of the four sides was much higher than the rest, like a dais; and the line of this side was broken by one of London's admirable accidents – a restaurant that looked as if it had strayed from Soho. It was an unreasonably attractive object, with dwarf plants in pots and long, striped blinds of lemon yellow and white. It stood specially high above the street, and in the usual patchwork way of London, a flight of steps from the street ran up to meet the front door almost as a fire-escape might run up to a first-floor window. Valentin stood and smoked in front of the yellow-white blinds and considered them long.

The most incredible thing about miracles is that they happen. A few clouds in heaven do come together into the staring shape of one human eye. A tree does stand up in the landscape of a doubtful journey in the exact and elaborate shape of a note of interrogation. I have seen both these things myself within the last few days. Nelson does die in the instant of victory; and a man named Williams does quite accidentally murder a man named Williamson; it sounds like a sort of infanticide. In short, there is in life an element of elfin coincidence which people reckoning on the prosaic may perpetually miss. As it has been well expressed in the paradox of Poe, wisdom should reckon on the unforeseen.

Aristide Valentin was unfathomably French; and the French intelligence is intelligence specially and solely. He was not 'a thinking machine'; for that is a brainless phrase of modern fatalism and materialism. A machine only is a machine because it cannot think. But he was a thinking man, and a plain man at the same time. All his wonderful successes, that looked like conjuring, had been gained by plodding logic, by clear and commonplace French thought. The French electrify the world not by starting any paradox, they electrify it by carrying out a truism. They carry a truism so far – as in the French Revolution. But exactly because Valentin understood reason, he understood the limits of reason. Only a man who knows nothing of motors talks of motoring without petrol; only a man who knows nothing of reason talks of reasoning without strong, undisputed first principles. Here he had no strong first principles. Flambeau had been missed at Harwich; and if he was in London at all, he might be anything from a tall tramp on Wimbledon Common to a tall toastmaster at the Hôtel Métropole. In such a naked state of nescience, Valentin had a view and a method of his own.

In such cases he reckoned on the unforeseen. In such cases, when he could not follow the train of the reasonable, he coldly and carefully followed the train of the unreasonable. Instead of going to the right places – banks, police-stations, rendezvous – he systematically went to the wrong places; knocked at every empty house, turned down every *cul de sac*, went up every lane blocked with rubbish, went round every crescent that led him uselessly out of the way. He defended this crazy course quite logically. He said that if one had a clue this was the worst way; but if one had no clue at all it was the best, because there was just the chance that any oddity that caught the eye of the pursuer might be the same that had caught the eye of the pursued. Somewhere a man must begin, and it had better be just where another man might stop. Something about that flight of steps up to the shop, something about the quietude and quaintness of the restaurant, roused all the detective's rare romantic fancy and made him resolve to strike at random. He went up the steps, and sitting down by the window, asked for a cup of black coffee.

It was half-way through the morning, and he had not breakfasted; the slight litter of other breakfasts stood about on the table to remind him of his hunger; and adding a poached egg to his order, he proceeded musingly to shake some white sugar into his coffee, thinking all the time about Flambeau. He remembered how Flambeau had escaped, once by a pair of nail scissors, and once by a house on fire; once by having to pay for an unstamped letter, and once by getting people to look through a telescope at a comet that might destroy the world. He thought his detective brain as good as the criminal's, which was true. But he fully realized the disadvantage. 'The criminal is the creative artist; the detective only the critic,' he said with a sour smile, and lifted his coffee cup to his lips slowly, and put it down very quickly. He had put salt in it.

He looked at the vessel from which the silvery powder had come; it was certainly a sugar-basin; as unmistakably meant for sugar as a champagne-bottle for champagne. He wondered why they should keep salt in it. He looked to see if there were any more orthodox vessels. Yes, there were two salt-cellars quite full. Perhaps there was some speciality in the condiment in the salt-cellars. He tasted it; it was sugar. Then he looked round at the restaurant with a refreshed air of interest, to see if there were any other traces of that singular artistic taste which puts the sugar in the salt-cellars and the salt in the sugar-basin. Except for an odd splash of some dark fluid on one of the white-papered walls, the whole place appeared neat, cheerful and ordinary. He rang the bell for the waiter.

When that official hurried up, fuzzy-haired and somewhat blear-eyed at that early hour, the detective (who was not without an appreciation of the simpler forms of humour) asked him to taste the sugar and see if it was up to the high reputation of the hotel. The result was that the waiter yawned suddenly and woke up.

'Do you play this delicate joke on your customers every morning?' inquired Valentin. 'Does changing the salt and sugar never pall on you as a jest?'

The waiter, when this irony grew clearer, stammeringly assured him that the establishment had certainly no such intention; it must be a most curious mistake. He picked up the sugar-basin and looked at it; he picked up the salt-cellar and looked at that, his face growing more and more bewildered. At last he abruptly excused himself, and hurrying away, returned in a few seconds with the proprietor. The proprietor also examined the sugar-basin and then the salt-cellar; the proprietor also looked bewildered.

Suddenly the waiter seemed to grow inarticulate with a rush of words.

'I zink,' he stuttered eagerly, 'I zink it is those two clergymen.'

'What two clergymen?'

'The two clergymen,' said the waiter, 'that threw soup at the wall.'

'Threw soup at the wall?' repeated Valentin, feeling sure this must be some Italian metaphor.

'Yes, yes,' said the attendant excitedly, and pointing at the dark splash on the white paper; 'threw it over there on the wall.'

Valentin looked his query at the proprietor, who came to his rescue with fuller reports.

'Yes, sir,' he said, 'it's quite true, though I don't suppose it has anything to do with the sugar and salt. Two clergymen came in and drank soup here very early, as soon as the shutters were taken down. They were both very quiet, respectable people; one of them paid the bill and went out; the other, who seemed a slower coach altogether, was some minutes longer getting his things together. But he went at last. Only, the instant before he stepped into the street he deliberately picked up his cup, which he had only half emptied, and threw the soup slap on the wall. I was in the back room myself, and so was the waiter; so I could only rush out in time to find the wall splashed and the shop empty. It didn't do any particular damage, but it was confounded cheek; and I tried to catch the men in the street. They were too far off though; I only noticed they went round the corner into Carstairs Street.'

The detective was on his feet, hat settled and stick in hand. He had already decided that in the universal darkness of his mind he could only follow the first odd finger that pointed; and this finger was odd enough. Paying his bill and clashing the glass doors behind him, he was soon swinging round into the other street.

It was fortunate that even in such fevered moments his eye was cool and quick. Something in a shop-front went by him like a mere flash; yet he went back to look at it. The shop was a popular greengrocer and fruiterer's, an array of goods set out in the open air and plainly ticketed with their names and prices. In the two most prominent compartments were two heaps, of oranges and of nuts respectively. On the heap of nuts lay a scrap of cardboard, on which was written in bold, blue chalk, 'Best tangerine oranges, two a penny.' On the oranges was the equally clear and exact description, 'Finest Brazil nuts, 4d. a lb.' M. Valentin looked at these two placards and fancied he had met this highly subtle form of humour before, and that somewhat recently. He drew the attention of the red-faced fruiterer, who was looking rather sullenly up and down the street, to this inaccuracy in his advertisements. The fruiterer said nothing, but sharply put each card into its proper place. The detective, leaning elegantly on his walking-cane, continued to scrutinize the shop. At last he said: 'Pray excuse my apparent irrelevance, my good sir, but I should like to ask you a question in experimental psychology and the association of ideas.'

The red-faced shopman regarded him with an eye of menace; but he continued gaily, swinging his cane. 'Why,' he pursued, 'why are two tickets wrongly placed in a greengrocer's shop like a shovel hat that has come to London for a holiday? Or, in case I do not make myself clear, what is the mystical association which connects the idea of nuts marked as oranges with the idea of two clergymen, one tall and the other short?'

The eyes of the tradesman stood out of his head like a snail's; he really seemed for an instant likely to fling himself upon the stranger. At last he stammered angrily: 'I don't know what you 'ave to do with it, but if you're one of their friends, you can tell 'em from me that I'll knock their silly 'eads off, parsons or no parsons, if they upset my apples again.'

'Indeed?' asked the detective, with great sympathy. 'Did they upset your apples?'

'One of 'em did,' said the heated shopman; 'rolled 'em all over the street. I'd 'ave caught the fool but for havin' to pick 'em up.'

'Which way did these parsons go?' asked Valentin.

'Up that second road on the left-hand side, and then across the square,' said the other promptly.

'Thanks,' said Valentin, and vanished like a fairy. On the other side of the second square he found a policeman, and said: 'This is urgent, constable; have you seen two clergymen in shovel hats?'

The policeman began to chuckle heavily. 'I 'ave, sir; and if you arst me, one of 'em was drunk. He stood in the middle of the road that bewildered that –'

'Which way did they go?' snapped Valentin.

'They took one of them yellow buses over there,' answered the man; 'them that go to Hampstead.'

Valentin produced his official card and said very rapidly: 'Call up two of your men to come with me in pursuit,' and crossed the road with such contagious energy that the ponderous policeman was moved to almost agile obedience. In a minute and a half the French detective was joined on the opposite pavement by an inspector and a man in plain clothes.

'Well, sir,' began the former, with smiling importance, 'and what may –?'

Valentin pointed suddenly with his cane. 'I'll tell you on the top of that omnibus,' he said, and was darting and dodging across the tangle of the traffic. When all three sank panting on the top seats of the yellow vehicle, the inspector said: 'We could go four times as quick in a taxi.'

'Quite true,' replied their leader placidly, 'if we only had an idea of where we were going.'

'Well, where *are* you going?' asked the other, staring.

Valentin smoked frowningly for a few seconds; then, removing his cigarette, he said: 'If you *know* what a man's doing, get in front of him; but if you want to guess what he's doing, keep behind him. Stray when he strays; stop when he stops; travel as slowly as he. Then you may see what he saw and may act as he acted. All we can do is to keep our eyes skinned for a queer thing.'

'What sort of a queer thing do you mean?' asked the inspector.

'Any sort of queer thing,' answered Valentin, and relapsed into obstinate silence.

The yellow omnibus crawled up the northern roads for what seemed like hours on end; the great detective would not explain further, and perhaps his assistants felt a silent and growing doubt of his errand. Perhaps, also, they felt a silent and growing desire for lunch, for the hours crept long past the normal luncheon hour, and the long roads of the North London suburbs seemed to shoot out into length after length like an infernal telescope. It was one of those journeys on which a man perpetually feels that now at last he must have come to the end of the universe, and then finds he has only come to the beginning of Tufnell Park. London died away in draggled taverns and dreary scrubs, and then was unaccountably born again in blazing high streets and blatant hotels. It was like passing through thirteen separate vulgar cities all just touching each other. But though the winter twilight was already threatening the road ahead of them, the Parisian detective still sat silent and watchful, eyeing the frontage of the streets that slid by on either side. By the time they had left Camden Town behind, the policemen were nearly asleep; at least, they gave something like a jump as Valentin leapt erect, struck a hand on each man's shoulder, and shouted to the driver to stop.

They tumbled down the steps into the road without realizing why they had been dislodged; when they looked round for enlightenment they found Valentin triumphantly pointing his finger towards a window on the left side of the road. It was a large window, forming part of the long façade of a gilt and palatial public-house; it was the part reserved for respectable dining, and labelled 'Restaurant.' This window, like all the rest along the frontage of the hotel, was of frosted and figured glass, but in the middle of it was a big, black smash, like a star in the ice.

'Our cue at last,' cried Valentin, waving his stick; 'the place with the broken window.'

'What window? What cue?' asked his principal assistant. 'Why, what proof is there that this has anything to do with them?'

Valentin almost broke his bamboo stick with rage.

'Proof!' he cried. 'Good God! the man is looking for proof! Why, of course, the chances are twenty to one that it has *nothing* to do with them. But what else can we do? Don't you see we must either follow one wild possibility or else go home to bed?' He banged his way into the restaurant, followed by his companions, and they were soon seated at a late luncheon at a little table, and looking at the star of smashed glass from the inside. Not that it was very informative to them even then.

'Got your window broken, I see,' said Valentin to the waiter, as he paid his bill.

'Yes, sir,' answered the attendant, bending busily over the change, to which Valentin silently added an enormous tip. The waiter straightened himself with mild but unmistakable animation.

'Ah, yes, sir,' he said. 'Very odd thing, that, sir.'

'Indeed? Tell us about it,' said the detective with careless curiosity.

'Well, two gents in black came in,' said the waiter; 'two of those foreign parsons that are running about. They had a cheap and quiet little lunch, and one of them paid for it and went out. The other was just going out to join him when I looked at my change again and found he'd paid me more than three times too much. "Here," I says to the chap who was nearly out of the door, "you've paid too much." "Oh," he says, very cool, "have we?" "Yes," I says, and picks up the bill to show him. Well, that was a knock-out.'

'What do you mean?' asked his interlocutor.

'Well, I'd have sworn on seven Bibles that I'd put 4s. on that bill. But now I saw I'd put 14s., as plain as paint.'

'Well?' cried Valentin, moving slowly, but with burning eyes, 'and then?'

'The parson at the door he says, all serene, "Sorry to confuse your accounts, but it'll pay for the window." "What window?" I says. "The one I'm going to break," he says, and smashed that blessed pane with his umbrella.'

All the inquirers made an exclamation; and the inspector

said under his breath: 'Are we after escaped lunatics?' The waiter went on with some relish for the ridiculous story:

'I was so knocked silly for a second, I couldn't do anything. The man marched out of the place and joined his friend just round the corner. Then they went so quick up Bullock Street that I couldn't catch them, though I ran round the bars to do it.'

'Bullock Street,' said the detective, and shot up that thoroughfare as quickly as the strange couple he pursued.

Their journey now took them through bare brick ways like tunnels; streets with few lights and even with few windows; streets that seemed built out of the blank backs of everything and everywhere. Dusk was deepening, and it was not easy even for the London policemen to guess in what exact direction they were treading. The inspector, however, was pretty certain that they would eventually strike some part of Hampstead Heath. Abruptly one bulging and gas-lit window broke the blue twilight like a bull's-eye lantern; and Valentin stopped an instant before a little garish sweet-stuff shop. After an instant's hesitation he went in; he stood amid the gaudy colours of the confectionery with entire gravity and bought thirteen chocolate cigars with a certain care. He was clearly preparing an opening; but he did not need one.

An angular, elderly young woman in the shop had regarded his elegant appearance with a merely automatic inquiry; but when she saw the door behind him blocked with the blue uniform of the inspector, her eyes seemed to wake up.

'Oh,' she said, 'if you've come about that parcel, I've sent it off already.'

'Parcel!' repeated Valentin; and it was his turn to look inquiring.

‘I mean the parcel the gentleman left – the clergyman gentleman.’

‘For goodness’ sake,’ said Valentin, leaning forward with his first real confession of eagerness, ‘for Heaven’s sake tell us what happened exactly.’

‘Well,’ said the woman, a little doubtfully, ‘the clergymen came in about half an hour ago and bought some peppermints and talked a bit, and then went off towards the Heath. But a second after, one of them runs back into the shop and says, “Have I left a parcel?” Well, I looked everywhere and couldn’t see one; so he says, “Never mind; but if it should turn up, please post it to this address,” and he left me the address and a shilling for my trouble. And sure enough, though I thought I’d looked everywhere, I found he’d left a brown-paper parcel, so I posted it to the place he said. I can’t remember the address now; it was somewhere in Westminster. But as the thing seemed so important, I thought perhaps the police had come about it.’

‘So they have,’ said Valentin shortly. ‘Is Hampstead Heath near here?’

‘Straight on for fifteen minutes,’ said the woman, ‘and you’ll come right out on the open.’ Valentin sprang out of the shop and began to run. The other detectives followed him at a reluctant trot.

The street they threaded was so narrow and shut in by shadows that when they came out unexpectedly into the void common and vast sky they were startled to find the evening still so light and clear. A perfect dome of peacock-green sank into gold amid the blackening trees and the dark violet distances. The glowing green tint was just deep enough to pick out in points of crystal one or two stars. All that was left of the daylight lay in a golden glitter across the edge of Hampstead and that popular hollow which is called the Vale of Health. The holiday makers who roam this region had not wholly dispersed: a few couples sat shapelessly on benches; and here and there a distant girl still shrieked in one of the swings. The glory of heaven deepened and darkened around the sublime vulgarity of man; and standing on the slope and looking across the valley, Valentin beheld the thing which he sought.

Among the black and breaking groups in that distance was one especially black which did not break – a group of two figures clerically clad. Though they seemed as small as insects, Valentin could see that one of them was much smaller than the other. Though the other had a student's stoop and an inconspicuous manner, he could see that the man was well over six feet high. He shut his teeth and went forward, whirling his stick impatiently. By the time he had substantially diminished the distance and magnified the two black figures as in a vast microscope, he had perceived something else; something which startled him, and yet which he had somehow expected. Whoever was the tall priest, there could be no doubt about the identity of the short one. It was his friend of the Harwich train, the stumpy little *curé* of Essex whom he had warned about his brown-paper parcels.

Now, so far as this went, everything fitted in finally and rationally enough. Valentin had learned by his inquiries that morning that a Father Brown from Essex was bringing up a silver cross with sapphires, a relic of considerable value, to show some of the foreign priests at the congress. This undoubtedly was the 'silver with blue stones'; and Father Brown undoubtedly was the little greenhorn in the train. Now there was nothing wonderful about the fact that what Valentin had found out Flambeau had also found out; Flambeau found out everything. Also there was nothing wonderful in the fact that when Flambeau heard of a sapphire cross he should try to steal it; that was the most natural thing in all natural history. And most certainly there was nothing wonderful about the fact that Flambeau should have it all his own way with such a silly sheep as the man with the umbrella and the parcels. He was the sort of man whom anybody could lead on a string to the North Pole; it was not surprising that an actor like Flambeau, dressed as another priest, could lead him to Hampstead Heath. So far the crime seemed clear enough; and while the detective pitied the priest for his helplessness, he almost despised Flambeau for condescending to so gullible a victim. But when Valentin thought of all that had happened in between, of all that had led him to his triumph, he racked his brains for the smallest rhyme or reason in it. What had the stealing of a blue-and-silver cross from a priest from Essex to do with chucking soup at wallpaper? What had it to do with calling nuts oranges, or with paying for windows first and breaking them afterwards? He had come to the end of his chase; yet somehow he had missed the middle of it. When he failed (which was seldom), he had usually grasped the clue, but nevertheless missed the criminal. Here he had grasped the criminal, but still he could not grasp the clue.

The two figures that they followed were crawling like black flies across the huge green contour of a hill. They were evidently sunk in conversation, and perhaps did not notice where they were going; but they were certainly going to the wilder and more silent heights of the Heath. As their pursuers gained on them, the latter had to use the undignified attitudes of the deer-stalker, to crouch behind clumps of trees and even to crawl prostrate in deep grass. By these ungainly ingenuities the hunters even came close enough to the quarry to hear the murmur of the discussion, but no word could be distinguished except the word 'reason' recurring frequently in a high and almost childish voice. Once, over an abrupt dip of land and a dense tangle of thickets, the detectives actually lost the two figures they were following. They did not find the trail again for an agonizing ten minutes, and then it led round the brow of a great dome of hill overlooking an amphitheatre of rich and desolate sunset scenery. Under a tree in this commanding yet neglected spot was an old ramshackle wooden seat. On this seat sat the two priests still in serious speech together. The gorgeous green and gold still clung to the darkening horizon; but the dome above was turning slowly from peacock-green to peacock-blue, and the stars detached themselves more and more like solid jewels. Mutely motioning to his followers, Valentin contrived to creep up behind the big branching tree, and, standing there in deathly silence, heard the words of the strange priests for the first time.

After he had listened for a minute and a half, he was gripped by a devilish doubt. Perhaps he had dragged the two English policemen to the wastes of a nocturnal heath on an errand no saner than seeking figs on thistles. For the two priests were talking exactly like priests, piously, with learning and leisure, about the most aerial enigmas of theology. The little Essex priest spoke the more simply, with his round face turned to the strengthening stars; the other talked with his head bowed, as if he were not even worthy to look at them. But no more innocently clerical conversation could have been heard in any white Italian cloister or black Spanish cathedral.

The first he heard was the tail of one of Father Brown's sentences, which ended: '. . . what they really meant in the Middle Ages by the heavens being incorruptible.'

The taller priest nodded his bowed head and said:

'Ah, yes, these modern infidels appeal to their reason; but who can look at those millions of worlds and not feel that there may well be wonderful universes above us where reason is utterly unreasonable?'

'No,' said the other priest; 'reason is always reasonable, even in the last limbo, in the lost borderland of things. I know that people charge the Church with lowering reason, but it is just the other way. Alone on earth, the Church makes reason really supreme. Alone on earth, the Church affirms that God Himself is bound by reason.'

The other priest raised his austere face to the spangled sky and said:

'Yet who knows if in that infinite universe –?'

'Only infinite physically,' said the little priest, turning sharply in his seat, 'not infinite in the sense of escaping from the laws of truth.'

Valentin behind his tree was tearing his finger-nails with silent fury. He seemed almost to hear the sniggers of the English detectives whom he had brought so far on a fantastic guess only to listen to the metaphysical gossip of two mild old parsons. In his impatience he lost the equally elaborate answer of the tall cleric, and when he listened again it was again Father Brown who was speaking:

'Reason and justice grip the remotest and the loneliest star. Look at those stars. Don't they look as if they were single diamonds and sapphires? Well, you can imagine any mad botany or geology you please. Think of forests of adamant with leaves of brilliants. Think the moon is a blue moon, a single elephantine sapphire. But don't fancy that all that frantic astronomy would make the smallest difference to the reason and justice of conduct. On plains of opal, under cliffs cut out of pearl, you would still find a notice-board, "Thou shalt not steal." '

Valentin was just in the act of rising from his rigid and crouching attitude and creeping away as softly as might be, felled by the one great folly of his life. But something in the very silence of the tall priest made him stop until the latter spoke. When at last he did speak, he said simply, his head bowed and his hands on his knees:

'Well, I still think that other worlds may perhaps rise higher than our reason. The mystery of heaven is unfathomable, and I for one can only bow my head.'

Then, with brow yet bent and without changing by the faintest shade his attitude or voice, he added:

'Just hand over that sapphire cross of yours, will you? We're all alone here, and I could pull you to pieces like a straw doll.'

The utterly unaltered voice and attitude added a strange violence to that shocking change of speech. But the guarder of the relic only seemed to turn his head by the smallest section of the compass. He seemed still to have a somewhat foolish face turned to the stars. Perhaps he had not understood. Or, perhaps, he had understood and sat rigid with terror.

'Yes,' said the tall priest, in the same low voice and in the same still posture, 'yes, I am Flambeau.'

Then, after a pause, he said:

'Come, will you give me that cross?'

'No,' said the other, and the monosyllable had an odd sound.

Flambeau suddenly flung off all his pontifical pretensions. The great robber leaned back in his seat and laughed low but long.

'No,' he cried; 'you won't give it me, you proud prelate. You won't give it me, you little celibate simpleton. Shall I tell you why you won't give it me? Because I've got it already in my own breast-pocket.'

The small man from Essex turned what seemed to be a dazed face in the dusk, and said, with the timid eagerness of 'The Private Secretary':

'Are – are you sure?'

Flambeau yelled with delight.

'Really, you're as good as a three-act farce,' he cried. 'Yes, you turnip, I am quite sure. I had the sense to make a duplicate of the right parcel, and now, my friend, you've got the duplicate, and I've got the jewels. An old dodge, Father Brown – a very old dodge.'

'Yes,' said Father Brown, and passed his hand through his hair with the same strange vagueness of manner. 'Yes, I've heard of it before.'

The colossus of crime leaned over to the little rustic priest with a sort of sudden interest.

'*You* have heard of it?' he asked. 'Where have *you* heard of it?'

'Well, I mustn't tell you his name, of course,' said the little man simply. 'He was a penitent, you know. He had lived prosperously for about twenty years entirely on duplicate brown-paper parcels. And so, you see, when I began to suspect you, I thought of this poor chap's way of doing it at once.'

'Began to suspect me?' repeated the outlaw with increased intensity. 'Did you really have the gumption to suspect me just because I brought you up to this bare part of the heath?'

'No, no,' said Brown with an air of apology. 'You see, I suspected you when we first met. It's that little bulge up the sleeve where you people have the spiked bracelet.'

'How in Tartarus,' cried Flambeau, 'did you ever hear of the spiked bracelet?'

'Oh, one's little flock, you know!' said Father Brown, arching his eyebrows rather blankly. 'When I was a curate in Hartlepool, there were three of them with spiked bracelets. So, as I suspected you from the first, don't you see, I made sure that the cross should go safe, anyhow. I'm afraid I watched you, you know. So at last I saw you change the parcels. Then, don't you see, I changed them back again. And then I left the right one behind.'

'Left it behind?' repeated Flambeau, and for the first time there was another note in his voice beside his triumph.

'Well, it was like this,' said the little priest, speaking in the same unaffected way. 'I went back to that sweet-shop and asked if I'd left a parcel, and gave them a particular address if it turned up. Well, I knew I hadn't; but when I went away again I did. So, instead of running after me with that valuable parcel, they have sent it flying to a friend of mine in Westminster.' Then he added rather sadly: 'I learnt that, too, from a poor fellow in Hartlepool. He used to do it with handbags he stole at railway stations, but he's in a monastery now. Oh, one gets to know, you know,' he added, rubbing his head again with the same sort of desperate apology. 'We can't help being priests. People come and tell us these things.'

Flambeau tore a brown-paper parcel out of his inner pocket and rent it in pieces. There was nothing but paper and sticks of lead inside it. He sprang to his feet with a gigantic gesture, and cried:

'I don't believe you. I don't believe a bumpkin like you could manage all that. I believe you've still got the stuff on you, and if you don't give it up – why, we're all alone, and I'll take it by force!'

'No,' said Father Brown simply, and stood up also; 'you won't take it by force. First, because I really haven't still got it. And, second, because we are not alone.'

Flambeau stopped in his stride forward.

'Behind that tree,' said Father Brown, pointing, 'are two strong policemen and the greatest detective alive. How did they come here, do you ask? Why, I brought them, of course! How did I do it? Why, I'll tell you if you like! Lord bless you, we have to know twenty such things when we work among the criminal classes! Well, I wasn't sure you were a thief, and it would never do to make a scandal against one of our own clergy. So I just tested you to see if anything would make you show yourself. A man generally makes a small scene if he finds salt in his coffee; if he doesn't, he has some reason for keeping quiet. I changed the salt and sugar, and *you* kept quiet. A man generally objects if his bill is three times too big. If he pays it, he has some motive for passing unnoticed. I altered your bill, and *you* paid it.'

The world seemed waiting for Flambeau to leap like a tiger. But he was held back as by a spell; he was stunned with the utmost curiosity.

'Well,' went on Father Brown, with lumbering lucidity, 'as you wouldn't leave any tracks for the police, of course somebody had to. At every place we went to, I took care to do something that would get us talked about for the rest of the day. I didn't do much harm – a splashed wall, spilt apples, a broken window; but I saved the cross, as the cross will always be saved. It is at Westminster by now. I rather wonder you didn't stop it with the Donkey's Whistle.'

'With the what?' asked Flambeau.

'I'm glad you've never heard of it,' said the priest, making a face. 'It's a foul thing. I'm sure you're too good a man for a Whistler. I couldn't have countered it even with the Spots myself; I'm not strong enough in the legs.'

'What on earth are you talking about?' asked the other.

'Well, I did think you'd know the Spots,' said Father

Brown, agreeably surprised. 'Oh, you can't have gone so very wrong yet!'

'How in blazes do you know all these horrors?' cried Flambeau.

The shadow of a smile crossed the round, simple face of his clerical opponent.

'Oh, by being a celibate simpleton, I suppose,' he said. 'Has it never struck you that a man who does next to nothing but hear men's real sins is not likely to be wholly unaware of human evil? But, as a matter of fact, another part of my trade, too, made me sure you weren't a priest.'

'What?' asked the thief, almost gaping.

'You attacked reason,' said Father Brown. 'It's bad theology.'

And even as he turned away to collect his property, the three policemen came out from under the twilight trees. Flambeau was an artist and a sportsman. He stepped back and swept Valentin a great bow.

'Do not bow to me, *mon ami*,' said Valentin, with silver clearness. 'Let us both bow to our master.'

And they both stood an instant uncovered, while the little Essex priest blinked about for his umbrella.

ARTHUR CONAN DOYLE

SILVER BLAZE

'I AM AFRAID, Watson, that I shall have to go,' said Holmes, as we sat down together to our breakfast one morning.

'Go! Where to?'

'To Dartmoor – to King's Pyland.'

I was not surprised. Indeed, my only wonder was that he had not already been mixed up in this extraordinary case, which was the one topic of conversation through the length and breadth of England. For a whole day my companion had rambled about the room with his chin upon his chest and his brows knitted, charging and recharging his pipe with the strongest black tobacco, and absolutely deaf to any of my questions or remarks. Fresh editions of every paper had been sent up by our newsagent only to be glanced over and tossed down into a corner. Yet, silent as he was, I knew perfectly well what it was over which he was brooding. There was but one problem before the public which could challenge his powers of analysis, and that was the singular disappearance of the favourite for the Wessex Cup, and the tragic murder of its trainer. When, therefore, he suddenly announced his intention of setting out for the scene of the drama, it was only what I had both expected and hoped for.

'I should be most happy to go down with you if I should not be in the way,' said I.

'My dear Watson, you would confer a great favour upon me by coming. And I think that your time will not be misspent, for there are points about this case which promise to make it an absolutely unique one. We have, I think, just time to catch our train at Paddington, and I will go further into the matter upon our journey. You would oblige me by bringing with you your very excellent field-glass.'

And so it happened that an hour or so later I found myself in the corner of a first-class carriage, flying along, *en route* for Exeter, while Sherlock Holmes, with his sharp, eager face framed in his ear-flapped travelling-cap, dipped rapidly into the bundle of fresh papers which he had procured at Paddington. We had left Reading far behind us before he thrust the last of them under the seat, and offered me his cigar-case.

'We are going well,' said he, looking out of the window, and glancing at his watch. 'Our rate at present is fifty-three and a half miles an hour.'

'I have not observed the quarter-mile posts,' said I.

'Nor have I. But the telegraph posts upon this line are sixty yards apart, and the calculation is a simple one. I presume that you have already looked into this matter of the murder of John Straker and the disappearance of Silver Blaze?'

'I have seen what the *Telegraph* and the *Chronicle* have to say.'

'It is one of those cases where the art of the reasoner should be used rather for the sifting of details than for the acquiring of fresh evidence. The tragedy has been so uncommon, so complete, and of such personal importance to so many people that we are suffering from a plethora of surmise, conjecture, and hypothesis. The difficulty is to detach the framework of fact – of absolute, undeniable fact – from the embellishments of theorists and reporters. Then, having established ourselves upon this sound basis, it is our duty to see what inferences may be drawn, and which are the special points upon which the whole mystery turns. On Tuesday evening I received telegrams, both from Colonel Ross, the owner of the horse, and from Inspector Gregory, who is looking after the case, inviting my co-operation.'

'Tuesday evening!' I exclaimed. 'And this is Thursday morning. Why did you not go down yesterday?'

'Because I made a blunder, my dear Watson – which is, I am afraid, a more common occurrence than anyone would think who only knew me through your memoirs. The fact is that I could not believe it possible that the most remarkable horse in England could long remain concealed, especially in so sparsely inhabited a place as the north of Dartmoor. From hour to hour yesterday I expected to hear that he had been found, and that his abductor was the murderer of John Straker. When, however, another morning had come and I found that, beyond the arrest of young Fitzroy Simpson, nothing had been done, I felt that it was time for me to take action. Yet in some ways I feel that yesterday has not been wasted.'

'You have formed a theory then?'

'At least I have a grip of the essential facts of the case. I shall enumerate them to you, for nothing clears up a case so much as stating it to another person, and I can hardly expect your co-operation if I do not show you the position from which we start.'

I lay back against the cushions, puffing at my cigar, while Holmes, leaning forward, with his long thin forefinger checking off the points upon the palm of his left hand, gave me a sketch of the events which had led to our journey.

'Silver Blaze,' said he, 'is from the Isonomy stock, and holds as brilliant a record as his famous ancestor. He is now in his fifth year, and has brought in turn each of the prizes of the turf to Colonel Ross, his fortunate owner. Up to the time of the catastrophe he was first favourite for the Wessex Cup, the betting being three to one on. He has always, however, been a prime favourite with the racing public, and has never yet disappointed them, so that even at short odds enormous sums of money have been laid upon him. It is obvious, therefore, that there were many people who had the strongest interest in preventing Silver Blaze from being there at the fall of the flag next Tuesday.

'This fact was, of course, appreciated at King's Pyland, where the Colonel's training stable is situated. Every precaution was taken to guard the favourite. The trainer, John Straker, is a retired jockey, who rode in Colonel Ross's colours before he became too heavy for the weighing-chair. He has served the Colonel for five years as jockey, and for seven as trainer, and has always shown himself to be a zealous and honest servant. Under him were three lads, for the establishment was a small one, containing only four horses in all. One of these lads sat up each night in the stable, while the others slept in the loft. All three bore excellent characters. John Straker, who is a married man, lived in a small villa about two hundred yards from the stables. He has no children, keeps one maid-servant, and is comfortably off. The country round is very lonely, but about half a mile to the north there is a small cluster of villas which have been built by a Tavistock contractor for the use of invalids and others who may wish to enjoy the pure Dartmoor air. Tavistock itself lies two miles to the west, while across the moor, also about two miles distant, is the larger training establishment of Capleton, which belongs to Lord Backwater, and is managed by Silas Brown. In every other direction the moor is a complete wilderness, inhabited only by a few roaming gipsies. Such was the general situation last Monday night, when the catastrophe occurred.

'On that evening the horses had been exercised and watered as usual, and the stables were locked up at nine o'clock. Two of the lads walked up to the trainer's house, where they had supper in the kitchen, while the third, Ned Hunter, remained on guard. At a few minutes after nine the maid, Edith Baxter, carried down to the stables his supper, which consisted of a dish of curried mutton. She took no liquid, as there was a water-tap in the stables, and it was the rule that the lad on duty should drink nothing else. The maid carried a lantern with her, as it was very dark, and the path ran across the open moor.

'Edith Baxter was within thirty yards of the stables when a man appeared out of the darkness and called to her to stop. As he stepped into the circle of yellow light thrown by the lantern she saw that he was a person of gentlemanly bearing, dressed in a grey suit of tweed with a cloth cap. He wore gaiters, and carried a heavy stick with a knob to it. She was most impressed, however, by the extreme pallor of his face and by the nervousness of his manner. His age, she thought, would be rather over thirty than under it.

' "Can you tell me where I am?" he asked. "I had almost made up my mind to sleep on the moor when I saw the light of your lantern."

' "You are close to the King's Pyland training stables," she said.

' "Oh, indeed! What a stroke of luck!" he cried. "I understand that a stable boy sleeps there alone every night. Perhaps that is his supper which you are carrying to him. Now I am sure that you would not be too proud to earn the price of a new dress, would you?" He took a piece of white paper folded up out of his waistcoat pocket. "See that the boy has this tonight, and you shall have the prettiest frock that money can buy."

'She was frightened by the earnestness of his manner, and ran past him to the window through which she was accustomed to hand the meals. It was already open, and Hunter was seated at the small table inside. She had begun to tell him of what had happened, when the stranger came up again.

' "Good evening," said he, looking through the window, "I wanted to have a word with you." The girl has sworn that as he spoke she noticed the corner of the little paper packet protruding from his closed hand.

' "What business have you here?" asked the lad.

' "It's business that may put something into your pocket," said the other. "You've two horses in for the Wessex Cup – Silver Blaze and Bayard. Let me have the straight tip, and you won't be a loser. Is it a fact that at the weights Bayard could give the other a hundred yards in five furlongs, and that the stable have put their money on him?"

' "So you're one of those damned touts," cried the lad. "I'll show you how we serve them in King's Pyland." He sprang up and rushed across the stable to unloose the dog. The girl fled away to the house, but as she ran she looked back, and saw that the stranger was leaning through the window. A minute later, however, when Hunter rushed out with the hound he was gone, and though the lad ran all round the buildings he failed to find any trace of him.'

'One moment!' I asked. 'Did the stable boy, when he ran out with the dog, leave the door unlocked behind him?'

'Excellent, Watson; excellent!' murmured my companion. 'The importance of the point struck me so forcibly, that I sent a special wire to Dartmoor yesterday to clear the matter up. The boy locked the door before he left it. The window, I may add, was not large enough for a man to get through.

'Hunter waited until his fellow-grooms had returned, when he sent a message up to the trainer and told him what had occurred. Straker was excited at hearing the account, although he does not seem to have quite realized its true significance. It left him, however, vaguely uneasy, and Mrs Straker, waking at one in the morning, found that he was dressing. In reply to her inquiries, he said that he could not sleep on account of his anxiety about the horses, and that he intended to walk down to the stables to see that all was well. She begged him to remain at home, as she could hear the rain pattering against the windows, but in spite of her entreaties he pulled on his large mackintosh and left the house.

'Mrs Straker awoke at seven in the morning, to find that her husband had not yet returned. She dressed herself hastily, called the maid, and set off for the stables. The door was open; inside, huddled together upon a chair, Hunter was sunk in a state of absolute stupor, the favourite's stall was empty, and there were no signs of his trainer.

'The two lads who slept in the chaff-cutting loft above the harness-room were quickly roused. They had heard nothing during the night, for they are both sound sleepers. Hunter was obviously under the influence of some powerful drug; and, as no sense could be got out of him, he was left to sleep it off while the two lads and the two women ran out in search of the absentees. They still had hopes that the trainer had for some reason taken out the horse for early exercise, but on ascending the knoll near the house, from which all the neighbouring moors were visible, they not only could see no signs of the favourite, but they perceived something which warned them that they were in the presence of a tragedy.

'About a quarter of a mile from the stables, John Straker's

overcoat was flapping from a furze bush. Immediately beyond there was a bowl-shaped depression in the moor, and at the bottom of this was found the dead body of the unfortunate trainer. His head had been shattered by a savage blow from some heavy weapon, and he was wounded in the thigh, where there was a long, clean cut, inflicted evidently by some very sharp instrument. It was clear, however, that Straker had defended himself vigorously against his assailants, for in his right hand he held a small knife, which was clotted with blood up to the handle, while in his left he grasped a red and black silk cravat, which was recognized by the maid as having been worn on the preceding evening by the stranger who had visited the stables.

'Hunter, on recovering from his stupor, was also quite positive as to the ownership of the cravat. He was equally certain that the same stranger had, while standing at the window, drugged his curried mutton, and so deprived the stables of their watchman.

'As to the missing horse, there were abundant proofs in the mud which lay at the bottom of the fatal hollow, that he had been there at the time of the struggle. But from that morning he has disappeared; and although a large reward has been offered, and all the gipsies of Dartmoor are on the alert, no news has come of him. Finally an analysis has shown that the remains of his supper, left by the stable lad, contain an appreciable quantity of powdered opium, while the people of the house partook of the same dish on the same night without any ill effect.

'Those are the main facts of the case stripped of all surmise and stated as baldly as possible. I shall now recapitulate what the police have done in the matter.

'Inspector Gregory, to whom the case has been committed, is an extremely competent officer. Were he but gifted with imagination he might rise to great heights in his profession. On his arrival he promptly found and arrested the man upon whom suspicion naturally rested. There was little difficulty in finding him, for he was thoroughly well known in the neighbourhood. His name, it appears, was Fitzroy Simpson. He was a man of excellent birth and education, who had squandered a fortune upon the turf, and who lived now by doing a little quiet and genteel bookmaking in the sporting clubs of London. An examination of his betting-book shows that bets to the amount of five thousand pounds had been registered by him against the favourite.

'On being arrested he volunteered the statement that he had come down to Dartmoor in the hope of getting some information about the King's Pyland horses, and also about Desborough, the second favourite, which was in charge of Silas Brown, at the Capleton stables. He did not attempt to deny that he had acted as described upon the evening before, but declared that he had no sinister designs, and had simply wished to obtain first-hand information. When confronted with the cravat he turned very pale, and was utterly unable to account for its presence in the hand of the murdered man. His wet clothing showed that he had been out in the storm of the night before, and his stick, which was a Penang lawyer, weighted with lead, was just such a weapon as might, by repeated blows, have inflicted the terrible injuries to which the trainer had succumbed.

'On the other hand, there was no wound upon his person, while the state of Straker's knife would show that one, at least, of his assailants must bear his mark upon him. There you have it all in a nutshell, Watson, and if you can give me any light I shall be infinitely obliged to you.'

I had listened with the greatest interest to the statement

which Holmes, with characteristic clearness, had laid before me. Though most of the facts were familiar to me, I had not sufficiently appreciated their relative importance, nor their connection with each other.

'Is it not possible,' I suggested, 'that the incised wound upon Straker may have been caused by his own knife in the convulsive struggles which follow any brain injury?'

'It is more than possible; it is probable,' said Holmes. 'In that case, one of the main points in favour of the accused disappears.'

'And yet,' said I, 'even now I fail to understand what the theory of the police can be.'

'I am afraid that whatever theory we state has very grave objections to it,' returned my companion. 'The police imagine, I take it, that this Fitzroy Simpson, having drugged the lad, and having in some way obtained a duplicate key, opened the stable door, and took out the horse, with the intention, apparently, of kidnapping him altogether. His bridle is missing, so that Simpson must have put it on. Then, having left the door open behind him, he was leading the horse away over the moor, when he was either met or overtaken by the trainer. A row naturally ensued, Simpson beat out the trainer's brains with his heavy stick without receiving any injury from the small knife which Straker used in self-defence, and then the thief either led the horse on to some secret hiding-place, or else it may have bolted during the struggle, and be now wandering out on the moors. That is the case as it appears to the police, and improbable as it is, all other explanations are more improbable still. However, I shall very quickly test the matter when I am once upon the spot, and until then I really cannot see how we can get much further than our present position.'

It was evening before we reached the little town of

Tavistock, which lies, like the boss of a shield, in the middle of the huge circle of Dartmoor. Two gentlemen were awaiting us at the station; the one a tall fair man with lion-like hair and beard, and curiously penetrating light blue eyes, the other a small alert person, very neat and dapper, in a frock-coat and gaiters, with trim little side-whiskers and an eyeglass. The latter was Colonel Ross, the well-known sportsman, the other Inspector Gregory, a man who was rapidly making his name in the English detective service.

'I am delighted that you have come down, Mr Holmes,' said the Colonel. 'The Inspector here has done all that could possibly be suggested; but I wish to leave no stone unturned in trying to avenge poor Straker, and in recovering my horse.'

'Have there been any fresh developments?' asked Holmes.

'I am sorry to say that we have made very little progress,' said the Inspector. 'We have an open carriage outside, and as you would no doubt like to see the place before the light fails, we might talk it over as we drive.'

A minute later we were all seated in a comfortable landau and were rattling through the quaint old Devonshire town. Inspector Gregory was full of his case, and poured out a stream of remarks, while Holmes threw in an occasional question or interjection. Colonel Ross leaned back with his arms folded and his hat tilted over his eyes, while I listened with interest to the dialogue of the two detectives. Gregory was formulating his theory, which was almost exactly what Holmes had foretold in the train.

'The net is drawn pretty close round Fitzroy Simpson,' he remarked, 'and I believe myself that he is our man. At the same time, I recognize that the evidence is purely circumstantial, and that some new development may upset it.'

'How about Straker's knife?'

'We have quite come to the conclusion that he wounded himself in his fall.'

'My friend Dr Watson made that suggestion to me as we came down. If so, it would tell against this man Simpson.'

'Undoubtedly. He has neither a knife nor any sign of a wound. The evidence against him is certainly very strong. He had a great interest in the disappearance of the favourite, he lies under the suspicion of having poisoned the stable boy, he was undoubtedly out in the storm, he was armed with a heavy stick, and his cravat was found in the dead man's hand. I really think we have enough to go before a jury.'

Holmes shook his head. 'A clever counsel would tear it all to rags,' said he. 'Why should he take the horse out of the stable? If he wished to injure it, why could he not do it there? Has a duplicate key been found in his possession? What chemist sold him the powdered opium? Above all, where could he, a stranger to the district, hide a horse, and such a horse as this? What is his own explanation as to the paper which he wished the maid to give to the stable boy?'

'He says that it was a ten-pound note. One was found in his purse. But your other difficulties are not so formidable as they seem. He is not a stranger to the district. He has twice lodged at Tavistock in the summer. The opium was probably brought from London. The key, having served its purpose, would be hurled away. The horse may lie at the bottom of one of the pits or old mines upon the moor.'

'What does he say about the cravat?'

'He acknowledges that it is his, and declares that he had lost it. But a new element has been introduced into the case which may account for his leading the horse from the stable.'

Holmes pricked up his ears.

'We have found traces which show that a party of gipsies encamped on Monday night within a mile of the spot where the murder took place. On Tuesday they were gone. Now, presuming that there was some understanding between Simpson and these gipsies, might he not have been leading the horse to them when he was overtaken, and may they not have him now?'

'It is certainly possible.'

'The moor is being scoured for these gipsies. I have also examined every stable and outhouse in Tavistock, and for a radius of ten miles.'

'There is another training stable quite close, I understand?'

'Yes, and that is a factor which we must certainly not neglect. As Desborough, their horse, was second in the betting, they had an interest in the disappearance of the favourite. Silas Brown, the trainer, is known to have had large bets upon the event, and he was no friend to poor Straker. We have, however, examined the stables, and there is nothing to connect him with the affair.'

'And nothing to connect this man Simpson with the interests of the Capleton stable?'

'Nothing at all.'

Holmes leaned back in the carriage and the conversation ceased. A few minutes later our driver pulled up at a neat little red-brick villa with overhanging eaves, which stood by the road. Some distance off, across a paddock, lay a long grey-tiled outbuilding. In every other direction the low curves of the moor, bronze-coloured from the fading ferns, stretched away to the skyline, broken only by the steeples of Tavistock, and by a cluster of houses away to the westward, which marked the Capleton stables. We all sprang out with the exception of Holmes, who continued to lean back with his eyes fixed upon the sky in front of him, entirely absorbed in his own thoughts. It was only when I touched his arm that he roused himself with a violent start and stepped out of the carriage.

'Excuse me,' said he, turning to Colonel Ross, who had looked at him in some surprise. 'I was day-dreaming.' There was a gleam in his eyes and a suppressed excitement in his manner which convinced me, used as I was to his ways, that his hand was upon a clue, though I could not imagine where he had found it.

'Perhaps you would prefer at once to go on to the scene of the crime, Mr Holmes?' said Gregory.

'I think that I should prefer to stay here a little and go into one or two questions of detail. Straker was brought back here, I presume?'

'Yes, he lies upstairs. The inquest is tomorrow.'

'He has been in your service some years, Colonel Ross?'

'I have always found him an excellent servant.'

'I presume that you made an inventory of what he had in his pockets at the time of his death, Inspector?'

'I have the things themselves in the sitting-room, if you would care to see them.'

'I should be very glad.'

We all filed into the front room, and sat round the central table, while the Inspector unlocked a square tin box and laid a small heap of things before us. There was a box of vestas, two inches of tallow candle, an ADP briar-root pipe, a pouch of sealskin with half an ounce of long-cut cavendish, a silver watch with a gold chain, five sovereigns in gold, an aluminium pencil-case, a few papers, and an ivory-handled knife with a very delicate inflexible blade marked Weiss & Co., London.

'This is a very singular knife,' said Holmes, lifting it up and examining it minutely. 'I presume, as I see blood-stains upon it, that it is the one which was found in the dead man's grasp. Watson, this knife is surely in your line.'

'It is what we call a cataract knife,' said I.

'I thought so. A very delicate blade devised for very delicate work. A strange thing for a man to carry with him upon a rough expedition, especially as it would not shut in his pocket.'

'The tip was guarded by a disc of cork which we found beside his body,' said the Inspector. 'His wife tells us that the knife had lain for some days upon the dressing-table, and that he had picked it up as he left the room. It was a poor weapon, but perhaps the best that he could lay his hand on at the moment.'

'Very possible. How about these papers?'

'Three of them are receipted hay-dealers' accounts. One of them is a letter of instructions from Colonel Ross. This other is a milliner's account for thirty-seven pounds fifteen, made out by Madame Lesurier, of Bond Street, to William Darbyshire. Mrs Straker tells us that Darbyshire was a friend of her husband's, and that occasionally his letters were addressed here.'

'Madame Darbyshire had somewhat expensive tastes,' remarked Holmes, glancing down the account. 'Twenty-two guineas is rather heavy for a single costume. However, there appears to be nothing more to learn, and we may now go down to the scene of the crime.'

As we emerged from the sitting-room a woman who had been waiting in the passage took a step forward and laid her hand upon the Inspector's sleeve. Her face was haggard, and thin, and eager; stamped with the print of a recent horror.

'Have you got them? Have you found them?' she panted.

'No, Mrs Straker; but Mr Holmes, here, has come from London to help us, and we shall do all that is possible.'

'Surely I met you in Plymouth, at a garden party, some little time ago, Mrs Straker,' said Holmes.

'No, sir; you are mistaken.'

'Dear me; why, I could have sworn to it. You wore a costume of dove-coloured silk with ostrich feather trimming.'

'I never had such a dress, sir,' answered the lady.

'Ah; that quite settles it,' said Holmes; and, with an apology, he followed the Inspector outside. A short walk across the moor took us to the hollow in which the body had been found. At the brink of it was the furze bush upon which the coat had been hung.

'There was no wind that night, I understand,' said Holmes.

'None; but very heavy rain.'

'In that case the overcoat was not blown against the furze bushes, but placed there.'

'Yes, it was laid across the bush.'

'You fill me with interest. I perceive that the ground has been trampled up a good deal. No doubt many feet have been there since Monday night.'

'A piece of matting has been laid here at the side, and we have all stood upon that.'

'Excellent.'

'In this bag I have one of the boots which Straker wore, one of Fitzroy Simpson's shoes, and a cast horseshoe of Silver Blaze.'

'My dear Inspector, you surpass yourself!'

Holmes took the bag, and descending into the hollow he pushed the matting into a more central position. Then stretching himself upon his face and leaning his chin upon his hands he made a careful study of the trampled mud in front of him.

'Halloa!' said he, suddenly, 'what's this?'

It was a wax vesta, half burned, which was so coated with mud that it looked at first like a little chip of wood.

'I cannot think how I came to overlook it,' said the Inspector, with an expression of annoyance.

'It was invisible, buried in the mud. I only saw it because I was looking for it.'

'What! You expected to find it?'

'I thought it not unlikely.' He took the boots from the bag and compared the impressions of each of them with marks upon the ground. Then he clambered up to the rim of the hollow and crawled about among the ferns and bushes.

'I am afraid that there are no more tracks,' said the Inspector. 'I have examined the ground very carefully for a hundred yards in each direction.'

'Indeed!' said Holmes, rising, 'I should not have the impertinence to do it again after what you say. But I should like to take a little walk over the moors before it grows dark, that I may know my ground tomorrow, and I think that I shall put this horseshoe into my pocket for luck.'

Colonel Ross, who had shown some signs of impatience at my companion's quiet and systematic method of work, glanced at his watch.

'I wish you would come back with me, Inspector,' said he. 'There are several points on which I should like your advice, and especially as to whether we do not owe it to the public to remove our horse's name from the entries for the Cup.'

'Certainly not,' cried Holmes, with decision, 'I should let the name stand.'

The Colonel bowed. 'I am very glad to have had your opinion, sir,' said he. 'You will find us at poor Straker's house when you have finished your walk, and we can drive together into Tavistock.'

He turned back with the Inspector, while Holmes and I walked slowly across the moor. The sun was beginning to sink behind the stables of Capleton, and the long sloping plain in front of us was tinged with gold, deepening into rich, ruddy brown where the faded ferns and brambles caught the evening light. But the glories of the landscape were all wasted upon my companion, who was sunk in the deepest thought.

'It's this way, Watson,' he said, at last. 'We may leave the question of who killed John Straker for the instant, and confine ourselves to finding out what has become of the horse. Now, supposing that he broke away during or after the tragedy, where could he have gone to? The horse is a very gregarious creature. If left to himself, his instincts would have been either to return to King's Pyland or go over to Capleton. Why should he run wild upon the moor? He would surely have been seen by now. And why should gipsies kidnap him? These people always clear out when they hear of trouble, for they do not wish to be pestered by the police. They could not hope to sell such a horse. They would run a great risk and gain nothing by taking him. Surely that is clear.'

'Where is he, then?'

'I have already said that he must have gone to King's Pyland or to Capleton. He is not at King's Pyland, therefore he is at Capleton. Let us take that as a working hypothesis, and see what it leads us to. This part of the moor, as the Inspector remarked, is very hard and dry. But it falls away towards Capleton, and you can see from here that there is a long hollow over yonder, which must have been very wet on Monday night. If our supposition is correct, then the horse must have crossed that, and there is the point where we should look for his tracks.'

We had been walking briskly during this conversation, and a few more minutes brought us to the hollow in question. At Holmes' request I walked down the bank to the right, and he to the left, but I had not taken fifty paces before I heard him give a shout, and saw him waving his hand to me. The track of a horse was plainly outlined in the soft earth in front of him, and the shoe which he took from his pocket exactly fitted the impression.

'See the value of imagination,' said Holmes. 'It is the one quality which Gregory lacks. We imagined what might have happened, acted upon the supposition, and find ourselves justified. Let us proceed.'

We crossed the marshy bottom and passed over a quarter of a mile of dry, hard turf. Again the ground sloped and again we came on the tracks. Then we lost them for half a mile, but only to pick them up once more quite close to Capleton. It was Holmes who saw them first, and he stood pointing with a look of triumph upon his face. A man's track was visible beside the horse's.

'The horse was alone before,' I cried.

'Quite so. It was alone before. Halloa! what is this?'

The double track turned sharp off and took the direction of King's Pyland. Holmes whistled, and we both followed along after it. His eyes were on the trail, but I happened to look a little to one side, and saw to my surprise the same tracks coming back again in the opposite direction.

'One for you, Watson,' said Holmes, when I pointed it out; 'you have saved us a long walk which would have brought us back on our own traces. Let us follow the return track.'

We had not to go far. It ended at the paving of asphalt which led up to the gates of the Capleton stables. As we approached a groom ran out from them.

'We don't want any loiterers about here,' said he.

'I only wished to ask a question,' said Holmes, with his finger and thumb in his waistcoat pocket. 'Should I be too early to see your master, Mr Silas Brown, if I were to call at five o'clock tomorrow morning?'

'Bless you, sir, if anyone is about he will be, for he is always the first stirring. But here he is, sir, to answer your questions for himself. No, sir, no; it's as much as my place is worth to let him see me touch your money. Afterwards, if you like.'

As Sherlock Holmes replaced the half-crown which he had drawn from his pocket, a fierce-looking elderly man strode out from the gate with a hunting-crop swinging in his hand,

'What's this, Dawson?' he cried. 'No gossiping! Go about your business! And you – what the devil do you want here?'

'Ten minutes' talk with you, my good sir,' said Holmes, in the sweetest of voices.

'I've no time to talk to every gadabout. We want no strangers here. Be off, or you may find a dog at your heels.'

Holmes leaned forward and whispered something in the trainer's ear. He started violently and flushed to the temples.

'It's a lie!' he shouted. 'An infernal lie!'

'Very good! Shall we argue about it here in public, or talk it over in your parlour?'

'Oh, come in if you wish to.'

Holmes smiled. 'I shall not keep you more than a few minutes, Watson,' he said. 'Now, Mr Brown, I am quite at your disposal.'

It was quite twenty minutes, and the reds had all faded into greys before Holmes and the trainer reappeared. Never have I seen such a change as had been brought about in Silas Brown in that short time. His face was ashy pale, beads of perspiration shone upon his brow, and his hands shook until the hunting-crop wagged like a branch in the wind. His bullying, overbearing manner was all gone too, and he cringed along at my companion's side like a dog with its master.

'Your instructions will be done. It shall be done,' said he.

'There must be no mistake,' said Holmes, looking round at him. The other winced as he read the menace in his eyes.

'Oh, no, there shall be no mistake. It shall be there. Should I change it first or not?'

Holmes thought a little and then burst out laughing.

'No, don't,' said he. 'I shall write to you about it. No tricks now or—'

'Oh, you can trust me, you can trust me!'

'You must see to it on the day as if it were your own.'

'You can rely upon me.'

'Yes, I think I can. Well, you shall hear from me tomorrow.' He turned upon his heel, disregarding the trembling hand which the other held out to him, and we set off for King's Pyland.

'A more perfect compound of the bully, coward, and sneak than Master Silas Brown I have seldom met with,' remarked Holmes, as we trudged along together.

'He has the horse, then?'

'He tried to bluster out of it, but I described to him so exactly what his actions had been upon that morning, that he is convinced that I was watching him. Of course, you observed the peculiarly square toes in the impressions, and that his own boots exactly corresponded to them. Again, of course, no subordinate would have dared to have done such a thing. I described to him how when, according to his custom, he was the first down, he perceived a strange horse wandering over the moor; how he went out to it, and his astonishment at recognizing from the white forehead which has given the favourite its name that chance had put in his power the only horse which could beat the one upon which he had put his money. Then I described how his first impulse had been to lead him back to King's Pyland, and how the devil had shown him how he could hide the horse until the race was over, and how he had led it back and concealed it at Capleton. When I told him every detail he gave it up, and thought only of saving his own skin.'

'But his stables had been searched.'

'Oh, an old horse-faker like him has many a dodge.'

'But are you not afraid to leave the horse in his power now, since he has every interest in injuring it?'

'My dear fellow, he will guard it as the apple of his eye. He knows that his only hope of mercy is to produce it safe.'

'Colonel Ross did not impress me as a man who would be likely to show much mercy in any case.'

'The matter does not rest with Colonel Ross. I follow my own methods, and tell as much or as little as I choose. That is the advantage of being unofficial. I don't know whether you observed it, Watson, but the Colonel's manner has been just a trifle cavalier to me. I am inclined now to have a little amusement at his expense. Say nothing to him about the horse.'

'Certainly not, without your permission.'

'And, of course, this is all quite a minor case compared with the question of who killed John Straker.'

'And you will devote yourself to that?'

'On the contrary, we both go back to London by the night train.'

I was thunderstruck by my friend's words. We had only been a few hours in Devonshire, and that he should give up an investigation which he had begun so brilliantly was quite incomprehensible to me. Not a word more could I draw from him until we were back at the trainer's house. The Colonel and the Inspector were awaiting us in the parlour.

'My friend and I return to town by the midnight express,' said Holmes. 'We have had a charming little breath of your beautiful Dartmoor air.'

The Inspector opened his eyes, and the Colonel's lips curled in a sneer.

'So you despair of arresting the murderer of poor Straker,' said he.

Holmes shrugged his shoulders. 'There are certainly grave difficulties in the way,' said he. 'I have every hope, however, that your horse will start upon Tuesday, and I beg that you will have your jockey in readiness. Might I ask for a photograph of Mr John Straker?'

The Inspector took one from an envelope in his pocket and handed it to him.

'My dear Gregory, you anticipate all my wants. If I might ask you to wait here for an instant, I have a question which I should like to put to the maid.'

'I must say that I am rather disappointed in our London consultant,' said Colonel Ross, bluntly, as my friend left the room. 'I do not see that we are any further than when he came.'

'At least, you have his assurance that your horse will run,' said I.

'Yes, I have his assurance,' said the Colonel, with a shrug of his shoulders. 'I should prefer to have the horse.'

I was about to make some reply in defence of my friend, when he entered the room again.

'Now, gentlemen,' said he, 'I am quite ready for Tavistock.'

As we stepped into the carriage one of the stable lads held

the door open for us. A sudden idea seemed to occur to Holmes, for he leaned forward and touched the lad upon the sleeve.

'You have a few sheep in the paddock,' he said. 'Who attends to them?'

'I do, sir.'

'Have you noticed anything amiss with them of late?'

'Well, sir, not of much account; but three of them have gone lame, sir.'

I could see that Holmes was extremely pleased, for he chuckled and rubbed his hands together.

'A long shot, Watson; a very long shot!' said he, pinching my arm. 'Gregory, let me recommend to your attention this singular epidemic among the sheep. Drive on, coachman!'

Colonel Ross still wore an expression which showed the poor opinion which he had formed of my companion's ability, but I saw by the Inspector's face that his attention had been keenly aroused.

'You consider that to be important?' he asked.

'Exceedingly so.'

'Is there any other point to which you would wish to draw my attention?'

'To the curious incident of the dog in the night-time.'

'The dog did nothing in the night-time.'

'That was the curious incident,' remarked Sherlock Holmes.

Four days later Holmes and I were again in the train bound for Winchester, to see the race for the Wessex Cup. Colonel Ross met us, by appointment, outside the station, and we drove in his drag to the course beyond the town. His face was grave and his manner was cold in the extreme.

'I have seen nothing of my horse,' said he.

'I suppose that you would know him when you saw him?' asked Holmes.

The Colonel was very angry. 'I have been on the turf for twenty years, and never was asked such a question as that before,' said he. 'A child would know Silver Blaze with his white forehead and his mottled off foreleg.'

'How is the betting?'

'Well, that is the curious part of it. You could have got fifteen to one yesterday, but the price has become shorter and shorter, until you can hardly get three to one now.'

'Hum!' said Holmes. 'Somebody knows something, that is clear!'

As the drag drew up in the enclosure near the grandstand, I glanced at the card to see the entries. It ran:

Wessex Plate. 50 sovs. each, h ft, with 1,000 sovs. added, for four- and five-year-olds. Second £300. Third £200. New course (one mile and five furlongs).

1. Mr Heath Newton's The Negro (red cap, cinnamon jacket).
2. Colonel Wardlaw's Pugilist (pink cap, blue and black jacket).
3. Lord Backwater's Desborough (yellow cap and sleeves).
4. Colonel Ross's Silver Blaze (black cap, red jacket).
5. Duke of Balmoral's Iris (yellow and black stripes).
6. Lord Singleford's Rasper (purple cap, black sleeves).

'We scratched our other one and put all hopes on your word,' said the Colonel. 'Why, what is that? Silver Blaze favourite?'

'Five to four against Silver Blaze!' roared the ring. 'Five to four against Silver Blaze! Fifteen to five against Desborough! Five to four on the field!'

'There are the numbers up,' I cried. 'They are all six there.'

'All six there! Then my horse is running,' cried the Colonel, in great agitation. 'But I don't see him. My colours have not passed.'

'Only five have passed. This must be he.'

As I spoke a powerful bay horse swept out from the weighing enclosure and cantered past us, bearing on its back the well-known black and red of the Colonel.

'That's not my horse,' cried the owner. 'That beast has not a white hair upon its body. What is this that you have done, Mr Holmes?'

'Well, well, let us see how he gets on,' said my friend, imperturbably. For a few minutes he gazed through my field-glass. 'Capital! An excellent start!' he cried suddenly. 'There they are, coming round the curve!'

From our drag we had a superb view as they came up the straight. The six horses were so close together that a carpet could have covered them, but half-way up the yellow of the Capleton stable showed to the front. Before they reached us, however, Desborough's bolt was shot, and the Colonel's horse, coming away with a rush, passed the post a good six lengths before its rival, the Duke of Balmoral's Iris making a bad third,

'It's my race anyhow,' gasped the Colonel, passing his hand over his eyes. 'I confess that I can make neither head nor tail of it. Don't you think that you have kept up your mystery long enough, Mr Holmes?'

'Certainly, Colonel. You shall know everything. Let us all go round and have a look at the horse together. Here he is,' he continued, as we made our way into the weighing enclosure where only owners and their friends find admittance. 'You have only to wash his face and his leg in spirits of wine and you will find that he is the same old Silver Blaze as ever.'

'You take my breath away!'

'I found him in the hands of a faker, and took the liberty of running him just as he was sent over.'

'My dear sir, you have done wonders. The horse looks very fit and well. It never went better in its life. I owe you a thousand apologies for having doubted your ability. You have done me a great service by recovering my horse. You would do me a greater still if you could lay your hands on the murderer of John Straker.'

'I have done so,' said Holmes, quietly.

The Colonel and I stared at him in amazement. 'You have got him! Where is he, then?'

'He is here.'

'Here! Where?'

'In my company at the present moment.'

The Colonel flushed angrily. 'I quite recognize that I am under obligations to you, Mr Holmes,' said he, 'but I must regard what you have just said as either a very bad joke or an insult.'

Sherlock Holmes laughed. 'I assure you that I have not associated you with the crime, Colonel,' said he; 'the real murderer is standing immediately behind you!'

He stepped past and laid his hand upon the glossy neck of the thoroughbred.

'The horse!' cried both the Colonel and myself.

'Yes, the horse. And it may lessen his guilt if I say that it was done in self-defence, and that John Straker was a man who was entirely unworthy of your confidence. But there goes the bell; and as I stand to win a little on this next race, I shall defer a more lengthy explanation until a more fitting time.'

*

We had the corner of a Pullman car to ourselves that evening as we whirled back to London, and I fancy that the journey was a short one to Colonel Ross as well as to myself, as we listened to our companion's narrative of the events which had occurred at the Dartmoor training stables upon that Monday night, and the means by which he had unravelled them.

'I confess,' said he, 'that any theories which I had formed from the newspaper reports were entirely erroneous. And yet there were indications there, had they not been overlaid by other details which concealed their true import. I went to Devonshire with the conviction that Fitzroy Simpson was the true culprit, although, of course, I saw that the evidence against him was by no means complete.

'It was while I was in the carriage, just as we reached the trainer's house, that the immense significance of the curried mutton occurred to me. You may remember that I was distrait, and remained sitting after you had all alighted. I was marvelling in my own mind how I could possibly have overlooked so obvious a clue.'

'I confess,' said the Colonel, 'that even now I cannot see how it helps us.'

'It was the first link in my chain of reasoning. Powdered opium is by no means tasteless. The flavour is not disagreeable, but it is perceptible. Were it mixed with any ordinary dish, the eater would undoubtedly detect it, and would probably eat no more. A curry was exactly the medium which would disguise this taste. By no possible supposition could this stranger, Fitzroy Simpson, have caused curry to be served in the trainer's family that night, and it is surely too monstrous a coincidence to suppose that he happened to come along with powdered opium upon the very night when a dish happened to be served which would disguise the flavour. That is unthinkable. Therefore Simpson becomes eliminated from the case, and our attention centres upon Straker and his wife, the only two people who could have chosen curried mutton for supper that night. The opium was added after the dish was set aside for the stable boy, for the others had the same for supper with no ill effects. Which of them, then, had access to that dish without the maid seeing them?

'Before deciding that question I had grasped the significance of the silence of the dog, for one true inference invariably suggests others. The Simpson incident had shown me that a dog was kept in the stables, and yet, though someone had been in and had fetched out a horse, he had not barked enough to arouse the two lads in the loft. Obviously the midnight visitor was someone whom the dog knew well.

'I was already convinced, or almost convinced, that John Straker went down to the stables in the dead of the night and took out Silver Blaze. For what purpose? For a dishonest one, obviously, or why should he drug his own stable boy? And yet I was at a loss to know why. There have been cases before now where trainers have made sure of great sums of money by laying against their own horses, through agents, and then prevented them from winning by fraud. Sometimes it is a pulling jockey. Sometimes it is some surer and subtler means. What was it here? I hoped that the contents of his pockets might help me to form a conclusion.

'And they did so. You cannot have forgotten the singular knife which was found in the dead man's hand, a knife which certainly no sane man would choose for a weapon. It was, as Dr Watson told us, a form of knife which is used for the most delicate operations known in surgery. And it was to be used for a delicate operation that night. You must know, with your wide experience of turf matters, Colonel Ross, that it is possible to make a slight nick upon the tendons of a horse's ham, and to do it subcutaneously so as to leave absolutely no trace. A horse so treated would develop a slight lameness which would be put down to a strain in exercise or a touch of rheumatism, but never to foul play.'

'Villain! Scoundrel!' cried the Colonel.

'We have here the explanation of why John Straker wished to take the horse out on to the moor. So spirited a creature would have certainly roused the soundest of sleepers when it felt the prick of the knife. It was absolutely necessary to do it in the open air.'

'I have been blind!' cried the Colonel. 'Of course, that was why he needed the candle, and struck the match.'

'Undoubtedly. But in examining his belongings, I was fortunate enough to discover, not only the method of the crime, but even its motives. As a man of the world, Colonel, you know that men do not carry other people's bills about in their pockets. We have most of us quite enough to do to settle our own. I at once concluded that Straker was leading a double life, and keeping a second establishment. The nature of the bill showed that there was a lady in the case, and one who had expensive tastes. Liberal as you are with your servants, one hardly expects that they can buy twenty-guinea walking dresses for their women. I questioned Mrs Straker as to the dress without her knowing it, and having satisfied myself that it had never reached her, I made a note of the milliner's address, and felt that by calling there with Straker's photograph, I could easily dispose of the mythical Darbyshire.

'From that time on all was plain. Straker had led out the horse to a hollow where his light would be invisible. Simpson, in his flight, had dropped his cravat, and Straker had picked it up with some idea, perhaps, that he might use it in securing the horse's leg. Once in the hollow he had got behind the horse, and had struck a light, but the creature, frightened at the sudden glare, and with the strange instinct of animals feeling that some mischief was intended, had lashed out, and the steel shoe had struck Straker full on the forehead. He had already, in spite of the rain, taken off his overcoat in order to do his delicate task, and so, as he fell, his knife gashed his thigh. Do I make it clear?'

'Wonderful!' cried the Colonel. 'Wonderful! You might have been there.'

'My final shot was, I confess, a very long one. It struck me that so astute a man as Straker would not undertake this delicate tendon-nicking without a little practice. What could he practise on? My eyes fell upon the sheep, and I asked a question which, rather to my surprise, showed that my surmise was correct.'

'You have made it perfectly clear, Mr Holmes.'

'When I returned to London I called upon the milliner, who at once recognized Straker as an excellent customer, of the name of Darbyshire, who had a very dashing wife with a strong partiality for expensive dresses. I have no doubt that this woman had plunged him over head and ears in debt, and so led him into this miserable plot.'

'You have explained all but one thing,' cried the Colonel. 'Where was the horse?'

'Ah, it bolted and was cared for by one of your neighbours. We must have an amnesty in that direction, I think. This is Clapham Junction, if I am not mistaken, and we shall be in Victoria in less than ten minutes. If you care to smoke a cigar in our rooms, Colonel, I shall be happy to give you any other details which might interest you.'

BRET HARTE

THE STOLEN CIGAR CASE

I FOUND HEMLOCK JONES in the old Brook Street lodgings, musing before the fire. With the freedom of an old friend I at once threw myself in my usual familiar attitude at his feet, and gently caressed his boot. I was induced to do this for two reasons: one, that it enabled me to get a good look at his bent, concentrated face, and the other, that it seemed to indicate my reverence for his superhuman insight. So absorbed was he even then, in tracking some mysterious clue, that he did not seem to notice me. But therein I was wrong – as I always was in my attempt to understand that powerful intellect.

'It is raining,' he said, without lifting his head.

'You have been out, then?' I said quickly.

'No. But I see that your umbrella is wet, and that your overcoat has drops of water on it.'

I sat aghast at his penetration. After a pause he said carelessly, as if dismissing the subject: 'Besides, I hear the rain on the window. Listen.'

I listened. I could scarcely credit my ears, but there was the soft pattering of drops on the panes. It was evident there was no deceiving this man!

'Have you been busy lately?' I asked, changing the subject. 'What new problem – given up by Scotland Yard as inscrutable – has occupied that gigantic intellect?'

He drew back his foot slightly, and seemed to hesitate ere he returned it to its original position. Then he answered wearily: 'Mere trifles – nothing to speak of. The Prince Kupoli has been here to get my advice regarding the disappearance of certain rubies from the Kremlin; the Rajah of Pootibad, after vainly beheading his entire bodyguard, has been obliged to seek my assistance to recover a jeweled sword. The Grand Duchess of Pretzel-Brauntswig is desirous of discovering where her husband was on the night of February 14; and last night' – he lowered his voice slightly – 'a lodger in this very house, meeting me on the stairs, wanted to know why they didn't answer his bell.'

I could not help smiling – until I saw a frown gathering on his inscrutable forehead.

'Pray remember,' he said coldly, 'that it was through such an apparently trivial question that I found out Why Paul Ferroll Killed His Wife, and What Happened to Jones!'

I became dumb at once. He paused for a moment, and then suddenly changing back to his usual pitiless, analytical style, he said: 'When I say these are trifles, they are so in comparison to an affair that is now before me. A crime has been committed, – and, singularly enough, against myself. You start,' he said. 'You wonder who would have dared to attempt it. So did I; nevertheless, it has been done. *I* have been *robbed*!'

'*You* robbed! You, Hemlock Jones, the Terror of Peculators!' I gasped in amazement, arising and gripping the table as I faced him.

'Yes! Listen. I would confess it to no other. But *you* who have followed my career, who know my methods; you, for whom I have partly lifted the veil that conceals my plans from ordinary humanity, – you, who have for years rapturously accepted my confidences, passionately admired my inductions and inferences, placed yourself at my beck and call, become my slave, groveled at my feet, given up your practice except those few unremunerative and rapidly decreasing patients to whom, in moments of abstraction over *my* problems, you have administered strychnine for quinine and arsenic for Epsom salts; you, who have sacrificed anything and everybody to me, – *you* I make my confidant!'

I arose and embraced him warmly, yet he was already so engrossed in thought that at the same moment he mechanically placed his hand upon his watch chain as if to consult the time. 'Sit down,' he said. 'Have a cigar?'

'I have given up cigar smoking,' I said.

'Why?' he asked.

I hesitated, and perhaps colored. I had really given it up because, with my diminished practice, it was too expensive. I could afford only a pipe. 'I prefer a pipe,' I said laughingly. 'But tell me of this robbery. What have you lost?'

He arose, and planting himself before the fire with his hands under his coat-tails, looked down upon me reflectively for a moment. 'Do you remember the cigar case presented to me by the Turkish Ambassador for discovering the missing favorite of the Grand Vizier in the fifth chorus girl at the Hilarity Theatre? It was that one. I mean the cigar case. It was incrusted with diamonds.'

'And the largest one had been supplanted by paste,' I said.

'Ah,' he said, with a reflective smile, 'you know that?'

'You told me yourself. I remember considering it a proof of your extraordinary perception. But, by Jove, you don't mean to say you have lost it?'

He was silent for a moment. 'No; it has been stolen, it is true, but I shall still find it. And by myself alone! In your profession, my dear fellow, when a member is seriously ill, he does not prescribe for himself, but calls in a brother doctor. Therein we differ. I shall take this matter in my own hands.'

'And where could you find better?' I said enthusiastically. 'I should say the cigar case is as good as recovered already.'

'I shall remind you of that again,' he said lightly. 'And now, to show you my confidence in your judgment, in spite of my determination to pursue this alone, I am willing to listen to any suggestions from you.'

He drew a memorandum book from his pocket and, with a grave smile, took up his pencil.

I could scarcely believe my senses. He, the great Hemlock Jones, accepting suggestions from a humble individual like myself! I kissed his hand reverently, and began in a joyous tone:

'First, I should advertise, offering a reward; I should give the same intimation in handbills, distributed at the "pubs" and the pastry-cooks'. I should next visit the different pawnbrokers; I should give notice at the police station. I should examine the servants. I should thoroughly search the house and my own pockets. I speak relatively,' I added, with a laugh. 'Of course I mean *your* own.'

He gravely made an entry of these details.

'Perhaps,' I added, 'you have already done this?'

'Perhaps,' he returned enigmatically.

'Now, my dear friend,' he continued, putting the notebook in his pocket and rising, 'would you excuse me for a few moments? Make yourself perfectly at home until I return; there may be some things,' he added with a sweep of his hand toward his heterogeneously filled shelves, 'that may interest you and while away the time. There are pipes and tobacco in that corner.'

Then nodding to me with the same inscrutable face he left the room. I was too well accustomed to his methods to think much of his unceremonious withdrawal, and made no doubt he was off to investigate some clue which had suddenly occurred to his active intelligence.

Left to myself I cast a cursory glance over his shelves. There were a number of small glass jars containing earthy substances, labeled 'Pavement and Road Sweepings,' from the principal thoroughfares and suburbs of London, with the sub-directions 'for identifying foot-tracks.' There were several other jars, labeled 'Fluff from Omnibus and Road Car Seats,' 'Cocoanut Fibre and Rope Strands from Mattings in Public Places,' 'Cigarette Stumps and Match Ends from Floor of Palace Theatre, Row A, 1 to 50.' Everywhere were evidences of this wonderful man's system and perspicacity.

I was thus engaged when I heard the slight creaking of a door, and I looked up as a stranger entered. He was a rough-looking man, with a shabby overcoat and a still more disreputable muffler around his throat and the lower part of his face. Considerably annoyed at his intrusion, I turned upon him rather sharply, when, with a mumbled, growling apology for mistaking the room, he shuffled out again and closed the door. I followed him quickly to the landing and saw that he disappeared down the stairs. With my mind full of the robbery, the incident made a singular impression upon me. I knew my friend's habit of hasty absences from his room in his moments of deep inspiration; it was only too probable that, with his powerful intellect and magnificent perceptive genius concentrated on one subject, he should be careless of his own belongings, and no doubt even forget to take the ordinary precaution of locking up his drawers. I tried one or two and found that I was right, although for some reason I was unable to open one to its fullest extent. The handles were sticky, as if some one had opened them with dirty fingers. Knowing Hemlock's fastidious cleanliness, I resolved to inform him of this circumstance, but I forgot it, alas! until – but I am anticipating my story.

His absence was strangely prolonged. I at last seated myself by the fire, and lulled by warmth and the patter of the rain on the window, I fell asleep. I may have dreamt, for during my sleep I had a vague semi-consciousness as of hands being softly pressed on my pockets – no doubt induced by the story of the robbery. When I came fully to my senses, I found Hemlock Jones sitting on the other side of the hearth, his deeply concentrated gaze fixed on the fire.

'I found you so comfortably asleep that I could not bear to awaken you,' he said, with a smile.

I rubbed my eyes. 'And what news?' I asked. 'How have you succeeded?'

'Better than I expected,' he said, 'and I think,' he added, tapping his note-book, 'I owe much to *you*.'

Deeply gratified, I awaited more. But in vain. I ought to have remembered that in his moods Hemlock Jones was reticence itself. I told him simply of the strange intrusion, but he only laughed.

Later, when I arose to go, he looked at me playfully. 'If you were a married man,' he said, 'I would advise you not to go home until you had brushed your sleeve. There are a few short brown sealskin hairs on the inner side of your forearm, just where they would have adhered if your arm had encircled a sealskin coat with some pressure!'

'For once you are at fault,' I said triumphantly; 'the hair is my own, as you will perceive; I have just had it cut at the hairdresser's, and no doubt this arm projected beyond the apron.'

He frowned slightly, yet, nevertheless, on my turning to go he embraced me warmly – a rare exhibition in that man of ice. He even helped me on with my overcoat and pulled out and smoothed down the flaps of my pockets. He was particular, too, in fitting my arm in my overcoat sleeve, shaking the sleeve down from the armhole to the cuff with his deft fingers. 'Come again soon!' he said, clapping me on the back.

'At any and all times,' I said enthusiastically; 'I only ask ten minutes twice a day to eat a crust at my office, and four hours' sleep at night, and the rest of my time is devoted to you always, as you know.'

'It is indeed,' he said, with his impenetrable smile.

Nevertheless, I did not find him at home when I next called. One afternoon, when nearing my own home, I met him in one of his favorite disguises, – a long blue swallow-tailed coat, striped cotton trousers, large turn-over collar, blacked face, and white hat, carrying a tambourine. Of course to others the disguise was perfect, although it was known to myself, and I passed him – according to an old understanding between us – without the slightest recognition, trusting to a later explanation. At another time, as I was making a professional visit to the wife of a publican at the East End, I saw him, in the disguise of a broken-down artisan, looking into the window of an adjacent pawn-shop. I was delighted to see that he was evidently following my suggestions, and in my joy I ventured to tip him a wink; it was abstractedly returned.

Two days later I received a note appointing a meeting at his lodgings that night. That meeting, alas! was the one memorable occurrence of my life, and the last meeting I ever had with Hemlock Jones! I will try to set it down calmly, though my pulses still throb with the recollection of it.

I found him standing before the fire, with that look upon his face which I had seen only once or twice in our acquaintance – a look which I may call an absolute concatenation of inductive and deductive ratiocination – from which all that was human, tender, or sympathetic was absolutely discharged. He was simply an icy algebraic symbol! Indeed, his whole being was concentrated to that extent that his clothes fitted loosely, and his head was absolutely so much reduced in size by his mental compression that his hat tipped back from his forehead and literally hung on his massive ears.

After I had entered he locked the doors, fastened the windows, and even placed a chair before the chimney. As I watched these significant precautions with absorbing interest, he suddenly drew a revolver and, presenting it to my temple, said in low, icy tones:

'Hand over that cigar case!'

Even in my bewilderment my reply was truthful, spontaneous, and involuntary.

'I haven't got it,' I said.

He smiled bitterly, and threw down his revolver. 'I expected that reply! Then let me now confront you with something more awful, more deadly, more relentless and convincing than that mere lethal weapon, – the damning inductive and deductive proofs of your guilt!' He drew from his pocket a roll of paper and a note-book.

'But surely,' I gasped, 'you are joking! You could not for a moment believe –'

'Silence! Sit down!' I obeyed.

'You have condemned yourself,' he went on pitilessly. 'Condemned yourself on my processes, – processes familiar to you, applauded by you, accepted by you for years! We will go back to the time when you first saw the cigar case. Your expressions,' he said in cold, deliberate tones, consulting his paper, were, "How beautiful! I wish it were mine." This was your first step in crime – and my first indication.

From "I *wish* it were mine" to "I *will* have it mine," and the mere detail, "*How can* I make it mine?" the advance was obvious. Silence! But as in my methods it was necessary that there should be an overwhelming inducement to the crime, that unholy admiration of yours for the mere trinket itself was not enough. You are a smoker of cigars.'

'But,' I burst out passionately, 'I told you I had given up smoking cigars.'

'Fool!' he said coldly, 'that is the *second* time you have committed yourself. Of course you told me! What more natural than for you to blazon forth that prepared and unsolicited statement to *prevent* accusation. Yet, as I said before, even that wretched attempt to cover up your tracks was not enough. I still had to find that overwhelming, impelling motive necessary to affect a man like you. That motive I found in the strongest of all impulses – Love, I suppose you would call it,' he added bitterly, 'that night you called! You had brought the most conclusive proofs of it on your sleeve.'

'But –' I almost screamed.

'Silence!' he thundered. 'I know what you would say. You would say that even if you had embraced some Young Person in a sealskin coat, what had that to do with the robbery? Let me tell you, then, that that sealskin coat represented the quality and character of your fatal entanglement! You bartered your honor for it – that stolen cigar case was the purchaser of the sealskin coat!

'Silence! Having thoroughly established your motive, I now proceed to the commission of the crime itself. Ordinary people would have begun with that – with an attempt to discover the whereabouts of the missing object. These are not *my* methods.'

So overpowering was his penetration that, although

I knew myself innocent, I licked my lips with avidity to hear the further details of this lucid exposition of my crime.

'You committed that theft the night I showed you the cigar case, and after I had carelessly thrown it in that drawer. You were sitting in that chair, and I had arisen to take something from that shelf. In that instant you secured your booty without rising. Silence! Do you remember when I helped you on with your overcoat the other night? I was particular about fitting your arm in. While doing so I measured your arm with a spring tape measure, from the shoulder to the cuff. A later visit to your tailor confirmed that measurement. It proved to be *the exact distance between your chair and that drawer*!'

I sat stunned.

'The rest are mere corroborative details! You were again tampering with the drawer when I discovered you doing so! Do not start! The stranger that blundered into the room with a muffler on – was myself! More, I had placed a little soap on the drawer handles when I purposely left you alone. The soap was on your hand when I shook it at parting. I softly felt your pockets, when you were asleep, for further developments. I embraced you when you left – that I might feel if you had the cigar case or any other articles hidden on your body. This confirmed me in the belief that you had already disposed of it in the manner and for the purpose I have shown you. As I still believed you capable of remorse and confession, I twice allowed you to see I was on your track: once in the garb of an itinerant negro minstrel, and the second time as a workman looking in the window of the pawnshop where you pledged your booty.'

'But,' I burst out, 'if you had asked the pawnbroker, you would have seen how unjust –'

'Fool!' he hissed, 'that was one of *your* suggestions – to

search the pawnshops! Do you suppose I followed any of your suggestions, the suggestions of the thief? On the contrary, they told me what to avoid.'

'And I suppose,' I said bitterly, 'you have not even searched your drawer?'

'No,' he said calmly.

I was for the first time really vexed. I went to the nearest drawer and pulled it out sharply. It stuck as it had before, leaving a part of the drawer unopened. By working it, however, I discovered that it was impeded by some obstacle that had slipped to the upper part of the drawer, and held it firmly fast. Inserting my hand, I pulled out the impeding object. It was the missing cigar case! I turned to him with a cry of joy.

But I was appalled at his expression. A look of contempt was now added to his acute, penetrating gaze. 'I have been mistaken,' he said slowly; 'I had not allowed for your weakness and cowardice! I thought too highly of you even in your guilt! But I see now why you tampered with that drawer the other night. By some inexplicable means – possibly another theft – you took the cigar case out of pawn and, like a whipped hound, restored it to me in this feeble, clumsy fashion. You thought to deceive me, Hemlock Jones! More, you thought to destroy my infallibility. Go! I give you your liberty. I shall not summon the three policemen who wait in the adjoining room – but out of my sight forever!'

As I stood once more dazed and petrified, he took me firmly by the ear and led me into the hall, closing the door behind him. This reopened presently, wide enough to permit him to thrust out my hat, overcoat, umbrella, and overshoes, and then closed against me forever!

I never saw him again. I am bound to say, however, that thereafter my business increased, I recovered much of my old practice, and a few of my patients recovered also. I became rich. I had a brougham and a house in the West End. But I often wondered, pondering on that wonderful man's penetration and insight, if, in some lapse of consciousness, I had not really stolen his cigar case!

JAMES McLEVY

LONG LOOKED-FOR, COME AT LAST

ONE OF THE least strange circumstances in my life is, that I seldom ever had any great desire to get hold of a worthy character without having it gratified. How that most adroit of all thieves, Adam M'Donald, did flutter my laurels! If ever there was a man who interfered with my night's rest, it was that man. For twenty-five years he had laid contributions on the good folks of Edinburgh; and yet, such was his caution, dexterity, and boldness, that he escaped trouble. Often apprehended, he was so successful in non-recognitions, alibis, and scapegoats, that he foiled every one. As my reputation increased, so increased my regret at his. At one time he was the aim and object of all my ambition. Yea, I would have given all my fame, to have it to earn again by the capture of that one man. We knew each other perfectly well, often met, and looked at each other, saying, as plainly as looks could do, 'I know you love me, M'Levy, but I am coy, and will never submit to your embraces' – 'Why will you not eat, Adam? the apple is sweet; and, if it should be the price of your soul, I will be a gentle master over you.' It wouldn't do.

If I was a gentleman in charge, he was a gentleman at large. If I was curious in my changes of place, Adam was everywhere, and yet nowhere. If I was up to a thing, Adam was up to twenty things. If I was burning to catch Adam, as only one article, Adam was zealous to catch many articles without being caught himself. If I was vexed with disappointment, Adam was comfortable in success. Never was an

Adam more envied than he was by me, and never an Adam more difficult to tempt.

It is said, that if you 'wait *long enough* to become tenant of a house, you may sleep in the king's palace.' I would have waited a hundred years to get possession of this man; but, probably, my good angel, Chance, thought I had waited long enough when the period came to fifteen years. Yet that was not the whole time of his triumphs, for that had extended to twenty-five – yea, he had been great when I was little, famous when I was unknown. And surely these fifteen years were enough. I certainly thought so, and some other detectives among the gods must have been of the same opinion; for in January 1835 it was reported to us that a gentleman had, on the previous evening, been robbed in the High Street of a gold watch, and it was suspected that the famous Adam was the skilful artist. To whom should this great business have been committed by Serjeant-major Ramage but to me, his natural rival in fame? Yes, that commission was the very pride of my life; and I set about its execution as if it had been a power of attorney to possess myself of a thousand a-year.

Yet the very boon was at first like a mockery. The suspicion against him was a mere gossamer web of floating surmises. No one would swear to him, and he was so defiant that I could not apprehend him without evidence to support my interference with the liberty of a British-born subject. I was pestered with advices, – a kind of contribution I never valued much, for, though they cost nothing to give, they are often dear to receive. One of the weaknesses of the regular celebrities is a kind of pride of a clever achievement, which (however unlikely it may appear to ordinary thinkers) leads them, as if by a fatality, to the scene of their triumph – ay, to the very repetition of the same act in the same place.

Admitted that it is a weakness, I have often found it my strength. It will scarcely be believed, that at a quarter to seven of that evening when I got my commission, I was posted in the entry to Milne Square, in the almost certain expectation of Adam figuring again thereabout, and in the same way. There I stood, while Mulholland went with some message to Princes Street; and, before he returned, whom did I see pass, going east, but my friend Kerr, road-officer at Jock's Lodge – groggy, but not unable to take some care of himself? I knew he had a gold watch, which he guarded by a chain round his neck. No sooner had he passed, than I saw Adam, and a faithful friend, Ebenezer Chisholm, following and watching the unsteady prey from the middle of the High Street. My heart would have leapt, if I had not something else to do with its ordinary pulses, – and I could have wished even these to be calmer.

I do not say that it was a rather rebellious state of my case that made me in an instant old as ninety, and lame as palsy. With what difficulty and straining of nature I made across the street, eyeing all the while the victim and his followers. I saw them leave the middle of the street and betake themselves to the pavement, about the door of M'Intosh's snuff-shop, where they laid hold of Kerr, no doubt, as friends, each taking an arm of him, to help him on, and save him from robbers. At sight of this I got young again, my palsy left me, and I planted myself under the pend of Blackfriars Wynd. May Heaven forgive me for my adjuration, that that man, Adam M'Donald, should at that moment be put into my hands. Surely I might be forgiven the prayer when the prayer would be answered, but then it would not be till they took him to the King's Park, on his way home, where they could do their business undisturbed. Would they be fools enough to attempt a robbery of a road-officer, on the principal street of the city? Answer – I have already stated my ridiculed calculation. I saw them leave the pavement at a point opposite to the very pend below which I stood. In an instant, the feet were taken from Kerr, he was thrown flat on his back, with a sound of his head against the granite which reached my ears. Chisholm held him down; Adam, whirling the gold chain over the victim's head, rolled it up in his hand, along with the watch, and bolted, – Chisholm, at the same instant, making for the dense parts of the Canongate. But whither did Adam bolt? Into my very arms! Yes; I received him joyfully as a long lost friend. But that ingratitude, of which I have complained so often! The moment I clutched him, he commenced a struggle with me, which, if I had not been of the strength I am, would have ended in his escape. Excepting once, I never encountered so tough a job. The moment we closed in the strife, I could see his face marked with the traits of a demon, while a spluttering of words, mixed with foam, assaulted me otherwise than in the ear – 'M'Levy, the devil of all devils!' responded to, without the foam, 'Adam M'Donald, my love of all loves!' Nor did my grip, nor even my blandishments, calm him. He swung himself from side to side in sudden writhings, breathed more laboriously, flared upon me more luminously with his flaming eyes, which I could see in the dark; and yet he could not get away. I answered every movement by an action equal and contrary, and, as the crowd increased, his determination at length began to be less resolute. Yes, I had nearly conquered this hero of twenty-five years' triumphs, when Mulholland, having returned from Princes Street, and seeing a crowd down the High Street, made up, and laid his helping hand on my antagonist.

'Adam M'Donald,' said I.

'Adam M'Donald!' echoed he, in wonder.

'Long looked-for, come at last,' rejoined I.

'Yes, you have caught a man,' said Adam, with a bitter sneer; 'but nothing else. I defy you. I have done nothing that's wrong, and have no man's property.'

'Here is the watch,' said a man of the name of M'Gregor, who kept a tavern at the head of the wynd; 'I was standing at my door when the robber came rushing in, and the moment you closed I heard the clink of something at my foot. On taking it up, I found it to be this watch. I give it to you, Mr M'Levy.'

'I know nothing of it,' cried Adam; 'you cannot prove it was ever in my possession.'

'I saw you throw down Mr Kerr on the street,' cried a woman, looking into M'Donald's face.

'It's a lie,' cried the infuriated demon.

'He's lying there yet, man,' persisted the woman.

And it was true, for Kerr had been so stunned by the fall, added to his state of drunkenness, that he lay where he fell, and the rush to the wynd so confused the people that some short time elapsed before he was looked after. Just as we emerged from the wynd with our prisoner, they were assisting Kerr up. We left him in good hands, and proceeded with our prisoner to the office. I never was very fond of crowds to witness my captures, but in this case I thought I could understand a little of that feeling delighted in by mighty conquerors, crowned poets, and such celebrities in their way. We have all at times our portion of pride, and who knows, when I don't deny, but that when now taking Adam M'Donald to my stronghold I felt myself to be as great a man as any of them; for when had a conqueror watched fifteen years for his enemy? When had a poet taken as long to write his poem? The only difference between us was, that, while these think they are working for immortality, I did not just come to the conclusion that the capture of Adam M'Donald by M'Levy would be celebrated by anniversaries or jubilees. Not that I did not think that future ages, thus neglectful, would be ungrateful, if not foolish, but that I did not want to dwell upon it.

But there we are with our prisoner before Captain Stewart, after this something like ovation, as they call it, but of the meaning whereof I am doubtful; not so of my captain's reception of one who had been so long as a lion in his way; for no sooner did he cast his eyes on Adam than he exclaimed –

'Here at last! but, M'Levy,' he whispered, 'you have committed a grave error.'

'Not at all.'

'We have no evidence that it was he who robbed the gentleman last night.'

'No more we have; but he has robbed another tonight, and, see, there's the evidence – no other than the watch of Mr Kerr, the road-officer.'

'And where was the deed done?'

'Where, amidst all laughter, I said it would be – in the High Street.'

'Most wonderful!'

I don't think so. They tell us that truth is very simple, and that lies are very knotty. I have yet a way of getting at the road where men are likely to travel, and there I meet them. I told you that robbers and thieves have a yearning for the places where their pride has been flattered, and so you see it is. Even Adam, the cunningest fox that ever went back to the same roost, with his ears along his neck, his eyes like fire, and his mouth all a-watering for the second hen, couldn't go against the common nature anyhow. But we have Chisholm to get – his henchman, a foxy-headed fellow too, who held Kerr down while Adam swept the chain over his head. I must complete my work.

But, here, as I went down the High Street again with Mulholland, I saw our difficulty in so far as Chisholm was concerned, for I doubted whether anyone saw *him* in the fray. He had learned of Adam, and knew of alibis, and scape-goats, and all the rest of the resources of men who put themselves in a position where they *must* be greater vaga-bonds still. So it was. We found he had gone into a publican's house in Carnegie Street, where he had collected a number of sympathizers, who were ready to swear that he was there drinking at six o'clock, – as so he might have been, – and thereafter, till long past the hour of the robbery, so that it was impossible he could have been engaged in it. Yet I was not daunted; we went to his house, and found him in bed by the side of his wife (?), who, the moment she knew our message, insisted that he had never been out of the house since six o'clock.

'That's true,' he rejoined.

'An alibi everywhere,' said I. 'Your wife swears to your having been here; the man in the public-house in Carnegie Street, and half-a-dozen others, say you were there; and I saw you, with my blear eyes, in the High Street robbing Kerr at eight. You were thus in three places at one time!'

And my man was actually inclined to abuse my religion, because I would not admit he was a god. I confess this roused me a little, and being, besides, impatient of his delay, I seized him perhaps more harshly than I am in the habit of treating my prodigals to get them out of the troughs of the swine, and give them bread and water in place of husks. Yet he was disobedient and struggled; then began one of those scenes which in my trade are unavoidable, and very disagreeable to a quiet man like me, who, if I had occupied the place of Simpson, would have done as he did with his children, – clapped them with the one hand, as kindly grooms do restive fillies, and put the kench over the head with the other. The wife clung to him and screamed; her fine black hair – and she was a regular beauty all over – falling over her back and shoulders, quite in the Jane Shore way, and looking, as it lay upon her white skin – where shall I get anything like it? – but what would be the use if I should try it, when I am satisfied you could detect nothing to come up to it anywhere, except in Mohammed's showroom of temptation? Then her arms were fixed round his neck, and I could see one or two rings, which should have been in my keeping, shining on fingers that were just as fine as any lady's; and why not? for she was 'a fancy', and wrought none; and so she held on, crying and weeping, as the tears rolled down on a face so pure in its colour, and so delicately tipt off in the curved nose, with the nostrils wide from excitement, and the thin lips open too, and shewing equally fine teeth, that my heart began to give way, though not a melter. Somehow or other, he liked the grip of this lava-Venus better than mine, and no great wonder, I suspect; and as she clung to him, and he to her, I could not separate them anyhow, until Mulholland, getting to the back of the bed, drew her to him, while I pulled him out.

'Hold her on,' said I.

A request which my assistant – very modest man as he was – did not disobey, but he had no easy task, for the creature, who had got hysterical, writhed in his large hands like a beautiful serpent; till, at last exhausted, she sank in his arms, with her face turned up to him, and her beseeching eyes so fixed on his, that he afterwards declared, that if it had been possible to save Chisholm, he would at that moment have given two weeks' pay (40s.) to send him back to so faithful a creature. But I had something else to mind.

'Get on your breeches, sir.'

But my prisoner was slow indeed; never before, I believe, did a man dress so slowly, with the exception, of course, of those who dress for the last home, under the impression that the clothes are to go, without a testament, to him who finishes all toilets with the hempen cravat. Yet there was excuse for him, which one might have found in his eyes, fixed as they were on the girl, as she lay still, as if dead, in the arms of Mulholland, and, it may be, not to be seen by him again, whose first step out would be in the direction of Norfolk Island.

I might notice all this, and have some qualms about my heart as I thought how strange it is that vice makes 'no gobs' at good looks, but gets into very beautiful temples. Even Chisholm was himself a good specimen of the higher sort of the higher animals, and really the two should not have been what they were, nor where they were. But no help; away he must trudge. Mulholland laid the poor girl gently on the bed, and left her alone, but with little of that glory she might have been encompassed with in another quarter, if more fortunately fated.

M'Donald was easily disposed of at the trial before the High Court, but it was a tough job with Chisholm, who, with his witnesses from Carnegie Street, battled for his alibi in noble style. No use; they got a lifetime of the other hemisphere.

EDGAR ALLAN POE

THE PURLOINED LETTER

Nil sapientiæ odiosius acumine nimio. – *Seneca*

AT PARIS, JUST after dark one gusty evening in the autumn of 18—, I was enjoying the twofold luxury of meditation and a meerschaum, in company with my friend, C. Auguste Dupin, in his little back library, or book-closet, *au troisième*, No. 33 *Rue Dunôt, Faubourg St Germain*. For one hour at least we had maintained a profound silence; while each, to any casual observer, might have seemed intently and exclusively occupied with the curling eddies of smoke that oppressed the atmosphere of the chamber. For myself, however, I was mentally discussing certain topics which had formed matter for conversation between us at an earlier period of the evening; I mean the affair of the Rue Morgue, and the mystery attending the murder of Marie Rogêt. I looked upon it, therefore, as something of a coincidence, when the door of our apartment was thrown open and admitted our old acquaintance, Monsieur G—, the Prefect of the Parisian police.

We gave him a hearty welcome; for there was nearly half as much of the entertaining as of the contemptible about the man, and we had not seen him for several years. We had been sitting in the dark, and Dupin now arose for the purpose of lighting a lamp, but sat down again, without doing so, upon G.'s saying that he had called to consult us, or rather to ask the opinion of my friend, about some official business which had occasioned a great deal of trouble.

'If it is any point requiring reflection,' observed Dupin, as he forbore to enkindle the wick, 'we shall examine it to better purpose in the dark.'

'That is another of your odd notions,' said the Prefect, who had the fashion of calling everything 'odd' that was beyond his comprehension, and thus lived amid an absolute legion of 'oddities.'

'Very true,' said Dupin, as he supplied his visitor with a pipe, and rolled toward him a comfortable chair.

'And what is the difficulty now?' I asked. 'Nothing more in the assassination way, I hope?'

'Oh, no; nothing of that nature. The fact is, the business is *very* simple indeed, and I make no doubt that we can manage it sufficiently well ourselves; but then I thought Dupin would like to hear the details of it, because it is so excessively *odd*.'

'Simple and odd,' said Dupin.

'Why, yes; and not exactly that either. The fact is, we have all been a good deal puzzled because the affair *is* so simple, and yet baffles us altogether.'

'Perhaps it is the very simplicity of the thing which puts you at fault,' said my friend.

'What nonsense you *do* talk!' replied the Prefect, laughing heartily.

'Perhaps the mystery is a little *too* plain,' said Dupin.

'Oh, good heavens! who ever heard of such an idea?'

'A little *too* self-evident.'

'Ha! ha! ha! – ha! ha! ha! – ho! ho! ho!' roared our visitor, profoundly amused, 'oh, Dupin, you will be the death of me yet!'

'And what, after all, *is* the matter on hand?' I asked.

'Why, I will tell you,' replied the Prefect, as he gave a long, steady, and contemplative puff, and settled himself in his chair. 'I will tell you in a few words; but, before I begin, let me caution you that this is an affair demanding the greatest secrecy, and that I should most probably lose the position I now hold, were it known that I confided it to any one.'

'Proceed,' said I.

'Or not,' said Dupin.

'Well, then; I have received personal information, from a very high quarter, that a certain document of the last importance has been purloined from the royal apartments. The individual who purloined it is known; this beyond a doubt; he was seen to take it. It is known, also, that it still remains in his possession.'

'How is this known?' asked Dupin.

'It is clearly inferred,' replied the Prefect, 'from the nature of the document, and from the non-appearance of certain results which would at once arise from its passing *out* of the robber's possession – that is to say, from his employing it as he must design in the end to employ it.'

'Be a little more explicit,' I said.

'Well, I may venture so far as to say that the paper gives its holder a certain power in a certain quarter where such power is immensely valuable.' The Prefect was fond of the cant of diplomacy.

'Still I do not quite understand,' said Dupin.

'No? Well; the disclosure of the document to a third person, who shall be nameless, would bring in question the honor of a personage of most exalted station; and this fact gives the holder of the document an ascendancy over the illustrious personage whose honor and peace are so jeopardized.'

'But this ascendancy,' I interposed, 'would depend upon the robber's knowledge of the loser's knowledge of the robber. Who would dare –'

'The thief,' said G., 'is the Minister D—, who dares all things, those unbecoming as well as those becoming a man. The method of the theft was not less ingenious than bold. The document in question – a letter, to be frank – had been received by the personage robbed while alone in the royal *boudoir*. During its perusal she was suddenly interrupted by the entrance of the other exalted personage from whom especially it was her wish to conceal it. After a hurried and vain endeavor to thrust it in a drawer, she was forced to place it, open it was, upon a table. The address, however, was uppermost, and, the contents thus unexposed, the letter escaped notice. At this juncture enters the Minister D—. His lynx eye immediately perceives the paper, recognizes the handwriting of the address, observes the confusion of the personage addressed, and fathoms her secret. After some business transactions, hurried through in his ordinary manner, he produces a letter somewhat similar to the one in question, opens it, pretends to read it, and then places it in close juxtaposition to the other. Again he converses, for some fifteen minutes, upon the public affairs. At length, in taking leave, he takes also from the table the letter to which he had no claim. Its rightful owner saw, but, of course, dared not call attention to the act, in the presence of the third personage who stood at her elbow. The minister decamped; leaving his own letter – one of no importance – upon the table.'

'Here, then,' said Dupin to me, 'you have precisely what you demand to make the ascendancy complete – the robber's knowledge of the loser's knowledge of the robber.'

'Yes,' replied the Prefect; 'and the power thus attained has, for some months past, been wielded, for political purposes, to a very dangerous extent. The personage robbed is more thoroughly convinced, every day, of the necessity of reclaiming her letter. But this, of course, cannot be done openly. In fine, driven to despair, she has committed the matter to me.'

'Than whom,' said Dupin, amid a perfect whirlwind of smoke, 'no more sagacious agent could, I suppose, be desired, or even imagined.'

'You flatter me,' replied the Prefect; 'but it is possible that some such opinion may have been entertained.'

'It is clear,' said I, 'as you observe, that the letter is still in the possession of the minister; since it is this possession, and not any employment of the letter, which bestows the power. With the employment the power departs.'

'True,' said G.; 'and upon this conviction I proceeded. My first care was to make thorough search of the minister's hotel; and here my chief embarrassment lay in the necessity of searching without his knowledge. Beyond all things, I have been warned of the danger which would result from giving him reason to suspect our design.'

'But,' said I, 'you are quite *au fait* in these investigations. The Parisian police have done this thing often before.'

'Oh, yes; and for this reason I did not despair. The habits of the minister gave me, too, a great advantage. He is frequently absent from home all night. His servants are by no means numerous. They sleep at a distance from their master's apartment, and, being chiefly Neapolitans, are readily made drunk. I have keys, as you know, with which I can open any chamber or cabinet in Paris. For three months a night has not passed, during the greater part of which I have not been engaged, personally, in ransacking the D— Hotel. My honor is interested, and, to mention a great secret, the reward is enormous. So I did not abandon the search until I had become fully satisfied that the thief is a more astute man than myself. I fancy that I have investigated every nook and corner of the premises in which it is possible that the paper can be concealed.'

'But is it not possible,' I suggested, 'that although the letter may be in possession of the minister, as it unquestionably is, he may have concealed it elsewhere than upon his own premises?'

'This is barely possible,' said Dupin. 'The present peculiar condition of affairs at court, and especially of those intrigues in which D— is known to be involved, would render the instant availability of the document – its susceptibility of being produced at a moment's notice – a point of nearly equal importance with its possession.'

'Its susceptibility of being produced?' said I.

'That is to say, of being *destroyed*,' said Dupin.

'True,' I observed; 'the paper is clearly then upon the premises. As for its being upon the person of the minister, we may consider that as out of the question.'

'Entirely,' said the Prefect. 'He has been twice waylaid, as if by foot-pads, and his person rigidly searched under my own inspection.'

'You might have spared yourself this trouble,' said Dupin. 'D—, I presume, is not altogether a fool, and, if not, must have anticipated these waylayings, as a matter of course.'

'Not *altogether* a fool,' said G., 'but then he is a poet, which I take to be only one remove from a fool.'

'True,' said Dupin, after a long and thoughtful whiff from his meerschaum, 'although I have been guilty of certain doggerel myself.'

'Suppose you detail,' said I, 'the particulars of your search.'

'Why, the fact is, we took our time, and we searched *everywhere*. I have had long experience in these affairs. I took the entire building, room by room; devoting the nights of a whole week to each. We examined, first, the furniture of each apartment. We opened every possible drawer; and I presume you know that, to a properly trained police-agent, such a thing as a "*secret*" drawer is impossible. Any man is a dolt who permits a "secret" drawer to escape him in a search of this kind. The thing is *so* plain. There is a certain amount of bulk – of space – to be accounted for in every cabinet. Then we have accurate rules. The fiftieth part of a line could not escape us. After the cabinets we took the chairs. The cushions we probed with the fine long needles you have seen me employ. From the tables we removed the tops.'

'Why so?'

'Sometimes the top of a table, or other similarly arranged piece of furniture, is removed by the person wishing to conceal an article; then the leg is excavated, the article deposited within the cavity, and the top replaced. The bottoms and tops of bedposts are employed in the same way.'

'But could not the cavity be detected by sounding?' I asked.

'By no means, if, when the article is deposited, a sufficient wadding of cotton be placed around it. Besides, in our case, we were obliged to proceed without noise.'

'But you could not have removed – you could not have taken to pieces *all* articles of furniture in which it would have been possible to make a deposit in the manner you mention. A letter may be compressed into a thin spiral roll, not differing much in shape or bulk from a large knitting-needle, and in this form it might be inserted into the rung of a chair, for example. You did not take to pieces all the chairs?'

'Certainly not; but we did better – we examined the rungs of every chair in the hotel, and, indeed, the jointings of every description of furniture, by the aid of a most powerful microscope. Had there been any traces of recent disturbance we should not have failed to detect it instantly. A single grain of gimlet-dust, for example, would have been as obvious as an apple. Any disorder in the gluing – any unusual gaping in the joints – would have sufficed to insure detection.'

'I presume you looked to the mirrors, between the boards and the plates, and you probed the beds and the bedclothes, as well as the curtains and carpets.'

'That of course; and when we had absolutely completed every particle of the furniture in this way, then we examined the house itself. We divided its entire surface into compartments, which we numbered, so that none might be missed; then we scrutinized each individual square inch throughout the premises, including the two houses immediately adjoining, with the microscope, as before.'

'The two houses adjoining!' I exclaimed; 'you must have had a great deal of trouble.'

'We had; but the reward offered is prodigious.'

'You include the *grounds* about the houses?'

'All the grounds are paved with brick. They gave us comparatively little trouble. We examined the moss between the bricks, and found it undisturbed.'

'You looked among D—'s papers, of course, and into the books of the library?'

'Certainly; we opened every package and parcel; we not only opened every book, but we turned over every leaf in each volume, not contenting ourselves with a mere shake, according to the fashion of some of our police officers. We also measured the thickness of every book-*cover*, with the most accurate admeasurement, and applied to each the most jealous scrutiny of the microscope. Had any of the bindings been recently meddled with, it would have been utterly impossible that the fact should have escaped observation.

Some five or six volumes, just from the hands of the binder, we carefully probed, longitudinally, with the needles.'

'You explored the floors beneath the carpets?'

'Beyond doubt. We removed every carpet, and examined the boards with the microscope.'

'And the paper on the walls?'

'Yes.'

'You looked into the cellars?'

'We did.'

'Then,' I said, 'you have been making a miscalculation, and the letter is *not* upon the premises, as you suppose.'

'I fear you are right there,' said the Prefect. 'And now, Dupin, what would you advise me to do?'

'To make a thorough research of the premises.'

'That is absolutely needless,' replied G—. 'I am not more sure that I breathe than I am that the letter is not at the hotel.'

'I have no better advice to give you,' said Dupin. 'You have, of course, an accurate description of the letter?'

'Oh, yes!' – And here the Prefect, producing a memorandum-book, proceeded to read aloud a minute account of the internal, and especially of the external, appearance of the missing document. Soon after finishing the perusal of this description, he took his departure, more entirely depressed in spirits than I had ever known the good gentleman before.

In about a month afterward he paid us another visit, and found us occupied very nearly as before. He took a pipe and a chair and entered into some ordinary conversation. At length I said:

'Well, but G., what of the purloined letter? I presume you have at last made up your mind that there is no such thing as overreaching the Minister?'

'Confound him, say I – yes; I made the re-examination. However, as Dupin suggested – but it was all labor lost, as I knew it would be.'

'How much was the reward offered, did you say?' asked Dupin.

'Why, a very great deal – a *very* liberal reward – I don't like to say how much, precisely; but one thing I *will* say, that I wouldn't mind giving my individual check for fifty thousand francs to any one who could obtain me that letter. The fact is, it is becoming of more and more importance every day; and the reward has been lately doubled. If it were trebled, however, I could do no more than I have done.'

'Why, yes,' said Dupin, drawlingly, between the whiffs of his meerschaum, 'I really – think, G., you have not exerted yourself – to the utmost in this matter. You might – do a little more, I think, eh?'

'How? – in what way?'

'Why – puff, puff – you might – puff, puff – employ counsel in the matter, eh? – puff, puff, puff. Do you remember the story they tell of Abernethy?'

'No; hang Abernethy!'

'To be sure! hang him and welcome. But, once upon a time, a certain rich miser conceived the design of spunging upon this Abernethy for a medical opinion. Getting up, for this purpose, an ordinary conversation in a private company, he insinuated his case to the physician, as that of an imaginary individual.

' "We will suppose," said the miser, "that his symptoms are such and such; now, doctor, what would *you* have directed him to take?"

' "Take!" said Abernethy, "why, take *advice*, to be sure." '

'But,' said the Prefect, a little discomposed, '*I* am *perfectly* willing to take advice, and to pay for it. I would *really* give fifty thousand francs to any one who would aid me in the matter.'

'In that case,' replied Dupin, opening a drawer, and producing a check-book, 'you may as well fill me up a check for the amount mentioned. When you have signed it, I will hand you the letter.'

I was astounded. The Prefect appeared absolutely thunderstricken. For some minutes he remained speechless and motionless, looking incredulously at my friend with open mouth, and eyes that seemed starting from their sockets; then apparently recovering himself in some measure, he seized a pen, and after several pauses and vacant stares, finally filled up and signed a check for fifty thousand francs, and handed it across the table to Dupin. The latter examined it carefully and deposited it in his pocket-book; then, unlocking an *escritoire*, took thence a letter and gave it to the Prefect. This functionary grasped it in a perfect agony of joy, opened it with a trembling hand, cast a rapid glance at its contents, and then, scrambling and struggling to the door, rushed at length unceremoniously from the room and from the house, without having uttered a syllable since Dupin had requested him to fill up the check.

When he had gone, my friend entered into some explanations.

'The Parisian police,' he said, 'are exceedingly able in their way. They are persevering, ingenious, cunning, and thoroughly versed in the knowledge which their duties seem chiefly to demand. Thus, when G— detailed to us his mode of searching the premises at the Hotel D—, I felt entire confidence in his having made a satisfactory investigation – so far as his labors extended.'

'So far as his labors extended?' said I.

'Yes,' said Dupin. 'The measures adopted were not only

the best of their kind, but carried out to absolute perfection. Had the letter been deposited within the range of their search, these fellows would, beyond a question, have found it.'

I merely laughed – but he seemed quite serious in all that he said.

'The measures, then,' he continued, 'were good in their kind, and well executed; their defect lay in their being inapplicable to the case and to the man. A certain set of highly ingenious resources are, with the Prefect, a sort of Procrustean bed, to which he forcibly adapts his designs. But he perpetually errs by being too deep or too shallow for the matter in hand; and many a school-boy is a better reasoner than he. I knew one about eight years of age, whose success at guessing in the game of "even and odd" attracted universal admiration. This game is simple, and is played with marbles. One player holds in his hand a number of these toys, and demands of another whether that number is even or odd. If the guess is right, the guesser wins one; if wrong, he loses one. The boy to whom I allude won all the marbles of the school. Of course he had some principle of guessing; and this lay in mere observation and admeasurement of the astuteness of his opponents. For example, an arrant simpleton is his opponent, and, holding up his closed hand, asks, "Are they even or odd?" Our school-boy replies, "odd," and loses; but upon the second trial he wins, for he then says to himself: "The simpleton had them even upon the first trial, and his amount of cunning is just sufficient to make him have them odd upon the second; I will therefore guess odd"; – he guesses odd, and wins. Now, with a simpleton a degree above the first, he would have reasoned thus: "This fellow finds that in the first instance I guessed odd, and, in the second, he will propose to himself, upon the first impulse, a simple variation from even to odd, as did the first simpleton; but then a second thought will suggest that this is too simple a variation, and finally he will decide upon putting it even as before. I will therefore guess even"; – he guesses even, and wins. Now this mode of reasoning in the school-boy, whom his fellows termed "lucky," – what, in its last analysis, is it?'

'It is merely,' I said, 'an identification of the reasoner's intellect with that of his opponent.'

'It is,' said Dupin; 'and, upon inquiring of the boy by what means he effected the *thorough* identification in which his success consisted, I received answer as follows: "When I wish to find out how wise, or how stupid, or how good, or how wicked is any one, or what are his thoughts at the moment, I fashion the expression of my face, as accurately as possible, in accordance with the expression of his, and then wait to see what thoughts or sentiments arise in my mind or heart, as if to match or correspond with the expression." This response of the school-boy lies at the bottom of all the spurious profundity which has been attributed to Rochefoucault, to La Bougive, to Machiavelli, and to Campanella.'

'And the identification,' I said, 'of the reasoner's intellect with that of his opponent, depends, if I understand you aright, upon the accuracy with which the opponent's intellect is admeasured.'

'For its practical value it depends upon this,' replied Dupin; 'and the Prefect and his cohort fail so frequently, first, by default of this identification, and, secondly, by ill-admeasurement, or rather through non-admeasurement, of the intellect with which they are engaged. They consider only their *own* ideas of ingenuity; and, in searching for any thing hidden, advert only to the modes in which *they* would have hidden it. They are right in this much – that their own ingenuity is a faithful representative of that of *the mass*; but when the cunning of the individual felon is diverse in character from their own, the felon foils them, of course. This always happens when it is above their own, and very usually when it is below. They have no variation of principle in their investigations; at best, when urged by some unusual emergency – by some extraordinary reward – they extend or exaggerate their old modes of *practice*, without touching their principles. What, for example, in this case of D—, has been done to vary the principle of action? What is all this boring, and probing, and sounding, and scrutinizing with the microscope, and dividing the surface of the building into registered square inches – what is it all but an exaggeration *of the application* of the one principle or set of principles of search, which are based upon the one set of notions regarding human ingenuity, to which the Prefect, in the long routine of his duty, has been accustomed? Do you not see he has taken it for granted that *all* men proceed to conceal a letter, not exactly in a gimlet-hole bored in a chair-leg, but, at least, in *some* out-of-the-way hole or corner suggested by the same tenor of thought which would urge a man to secrete a letter in a gimlet-hole bored in a chair-leg? And do you not see also, that such *recherchés* nooks for concealment are adapted only for ordinary occasions, and would be adopted only by ordinary intellects; for, in all cases of concealment, a disposal of the article concealed – a disposal of it in this *recherché* manner, – is, in the very first instance, presumable and presumed; and thus its discovery depends, not at all upon the acumen, but altogether upon the mere care, patience, and determination of the seekers; and where the case is of importance – or, what amounts to the same thing in the political eyes, when the reward is of magnitude, – the qualities in question have *never* been known to fail.

You will now understand what I meant in suggesting that, had the purloined letter been hidden anywhere within the limits of the Prefect's examination – in other words, had the principle of its concealment been comprehended within the principles of the Prefect – its discovery would have been a matter altogether beyond question. This functionary, however, has been thoroughly mystified; and the remote source of his defeat lies in the supposition that the Minister is a fool, because he has acquired renown as a poet. All fools are poets; this the Prefect *feels*; and he is merely guilty of a *non distributio medii* in thence inferring that all poets are fools.'

'But is this really the poet?' I asked. 'There are two brothers, I know; and both have attained reputation in letters. The Minister I believe has written learnedly on the Differential Calculus. He is a mathematician, and no poet.'

'You are mistaken; I know him well; he is both. As poet *and* mathematician, he would reason well; as mere mathematician, he could not have reasoned at all, and thus would have been at the mercy of the Prefect.'

'You surprise me,' I said, 'by these opinions, which have been contradicted by the voice of the world. You do not mean to set at naught the well-digested idea of centuries. The mathematical reason has long been regarded as *the* reason *par excellence*.'

' "*Il y a à parier*," replied Dupin, quoting from Chamfort, ' "*que toute idée publique, toute convention reçue, est une sottise, car elle a convenue au plus grand nombre*." The mathematicians, I grant you, have done their best to promulgate the popular error to which you allude, and which is none the less an error for its promulgation as truth. With an art worthy a better cause, for example, they have insinuated the term "analysis" into application to algebra. The French are the originators of this particular deception; but if a term is of any importance – if words derive any value from applicability – then "analysis" conveys "algebra" about as much as, in Latin, "*ambitus*" implies "ambition," "*religio*" "religion," or "*homines honesti*" a set of *honorable* men.'

'You have a quarrel on hand, I see,' said I, 'with some of the algebraists of Paris; but proceed.'

'I dispute the availability, and thus the value, of that reason which is cultivated in any especial form other than the abstractly logical. I dispute, in particular, the reason educed by mathematical study. The mathematics are the science of form and quantity; mathematical reasoning is merely logic applied to observation upon form and quantity. The great error lies in supposing that even the truths of what is called *pure* algebra are abstract or general truths. And this error is so egregious that I am confounded at the universality with which it has been received. Mathematical axioms are *not* axioms of general truth. What is true of *relation* – of form and quantity – is often grossly false in regard to morals, for example. In this latter science it is very usually *un*true that the aggregated parts are equal to the whole. In chemistry also the axiom fails. In the consideration of motive it fails; for two motives, each of a given value, have not, necessarily, a value when united, equal to the sum of their values apart. There are numerous other mathematical truths which are only truths within the limits of *relation*. But the mathematician argues from his finite truths, through habit, as if they were of an absolutely general applicability – as the world indeed imagines them to be. Bryant, in his very learned "Mythology," mentions an analogous source of error, when he says that "although the pagan fables are not believed, yet we forget ourselves continually, and make inferences from them as existing realities." With the algebraists, however, who are pagans themselves, the "pagan fables" *are* believed, and the inferences are made, not so much through lapse of memory as through an unaccountable addling of the brains. In short, I never yet encountered the mere mathematician who would be trusted out of equal roots, or one who did not clandestinely hold it as a point of his faith that $x^2 + px$ was absolutely and unconditionally equal to q. Say to one of these gentlemen, by way of experiment, if you please, that you believe occasions may occur where $x^2 + px$ is *not* altogether equal to q, and, having made him understand what you mean, get out of his reach as speedily as convenient, for, beyond doubt, he will endeavor to knock you down.

'I mean to say,' continued Dupin, while I merely laughed at his last observations, 'that if the Minister had been no more than a mathematician, the Prefect would have been under no necessity of giving me this check. I knew him, however, as both mathematician and poet, and my measures were adapted to his capacity, with reference to the circumstances by which he was surrounded. I knew him as a courtier, too, and as a bold *intriguant.* Such a man, I considered, could not fail to be aware of the ordinary policial modes of action. He could not have failed to anticipate – and events have proved that he did not fail to anticipate – the waylayings to which he was subjected. He must have foreseen, I reflected, the secret investigations of his premises. His frequent absences from home at night, which were hailed by the Prefect as certain aids to his success, I regarded only as *ruses,* to afford opportunity for thorough search to the police, and thus the sooner to impress them with the conviction to which G—, in fact, did finally arrive – the conviction that the letter was not upon the premises. I felt, also, that the whole train of thought, which I was at some pains in detailing to you just now, concerning the invariable principle of policial action in searches for articles concealed – I felt that this whole train of thought would necessarily pass through the mind of the minister. It would imperatively lead him to despise all the ordinary *nooks* of concealment. *He* could not, I reflected, be so weak as not to see that the most intricate and remote recess of his hotel would be as open as his commonest closets to the eyes, to the probes, to the gimlets, and to the microscopes of the Prefect. I saw, in fine, that he would be driven, as a matter of course, to *simplicity*, if not deliberately induced to it as a matter of choice. You will remember, perhaps, how desperately the Prefect laughed when I suggested, upon our first interview, that it was just possible this mystery troubled him so much on account of its being so *very* self-evident.'

'Yes,' said I, 'I remember his merriment well. I really thought he would have fallen into convulsions.'

'The material world,' continued Dupin, 'abounds with very strict analogies to the immaterial; and thus some color of truth has been given to the rhetorical dogma, that metaphor, or simile, may be made to strengthen an argument as well as to embellish a description. The principle of the *vis inertiæ*, for example, seems to be identical in physics and metaphysics. It is not more true in the former, that a large body is with more difficulty set in motion than a smaller one, and that its subsequent *momentum* is commensurate with this difficulty, than it is, in the latter, that intellects of the vaster capacity, while more forcible, more constant, and more eventful in their movements than those of inferior grade, are yet the less readily moved, and more embarrassed, and full of hesitation in the first few steps of their progress. Again: have you ever noticed which of the street signs, over the shop doors, are the most attractive of attention?'

'I have never given the matter a thought,' I said.

'There is a game of puzzles,' he resumed, 'which is played upon a map. One party playing requires another to find a given word – the name of town, river, state, or empire – any word, in short, upon the motley and perplexed surface of the chart. A novice in the game generally seeks to embarrass his opponents by giving them the most minutely lettered names; but the adept selects such words as stretch, in large characters, from one end of the chart to the other. These, like the over-largely lettered signs and placards of the street, escape observation by dint of being excessively obvious; and here the physical oversight is precisely analogous with the moral inapprehension by which the intellect suffers to pass unnoticed those considerations which are too obtrusively and too palpably self-evident. But this is a point, it appears, somewhat above or beneath the understanding of the Prefect. He never once thought it probable, or possible, that the minister had deposited the letter immediately beneath the nose of the whole world, by way of best preventing any portion of that world from perceiving it.

'But the more I reflected upon the daring, dashing, and discriminating ingenuity of D—; upon the fact that the document must always have been *at hand*, if he intended to use it to good purpose; and upon the decisive evidence, obtained by the Prefect, that it was not hidden within the limits of that dignitary's ordinary search – the more satisfied I became that, to conceal this letter, the minister had resorted to the comprehensive and sagacious expedient of not attempting to conceal it at all.

'Full of these ideas, I prepared myself with a pair of green spectacles, and called one fine morning, quite by accident, at the Ministerial hotel. I found D— at home, yawning, lounging, and dawdling, as usual, and pretending to be in the last extremity of *ennui*. He is, perhaps, the most really energetic human being now alive – but that is only when nobody sees him.

'To be even with him, I complained of my weak eyes, and lamented the necessity of the spectacles, under cover of which I cautiously and thoroughly surveyed the whole apartment, while seemingly intent only upon the conversation of my host.

'I paid especial attention to a large writing-table near which he sat, and upon which lay confusedly, some miscellaneous letters and other papers, with one or two musical instruments and a few books. Here, however, after a long and very deliberate scrutiny, I saw nothing to excite particular suspicion.

'At length my eyes, in going the circuit of the room, fell upon a trumpery filigree card-rack of pasteboard, that hung dangling by a dirty blue ribbon, from a little brass knob just beneath the middle of the mantel-piece. In this rack, which had three or four compartments, were five or six visiting cards and a solitary letter. This last was much soiled and crumpled. It was torn nearly in two, across the middle – as if a design, in the first instance, to tear it entirely up as worthless, had been altered, or stayed, in the second. It had a large black seal, bearing the D— cipher *very* conspicuously, and was addressed, in a diminutive female hand, to D—, the minister, himself. It was thrust carelessly, and even, as it seemed, contemptuously, into one of the uppermost divisions of the rack.

'No sooner had I glanced at this letter than I concluded it to be that of which I was in search. To be sure, it was, to all appearance, radically different from the one of which the Prefect had read us so minute a description. Here the seal was large and black, with the D— cipher; there it was small and red, with the ducal arms of the S— family. Here, the address, to the minister, was diminutive and feminine; there the superscription, to a certain royal personage, was markedly bold and decided; the size alone formed a point of correspondence. But, then, the *radicalness* of these differences, which was excessive; the dirt; the soiled and torn condition of the paper, so inconsistent with the *true* methodical habits of D—, and so suggestive of a design to delude the beholder into an idea of the worthlessness of the document; – these things, together with the hyperobtrusive situation of this document, full in the view of every visitor, and thus exactly in accordance with the conclusions to which I had previously arrived; these things, I say, were strongly corroborative of suspicion, in one who came with the intention to suspect.

'I protracted my visit as long as possible, and, while I maintained a most animated discussion with the minister, upon a topic which I knew well had never failed to interest and excite him, I kept my attention really riveted upon the letter. In this examination, I committed to memory its external appearance and arrangement in the rack; and also fell, at length, upon a discovery which set at rest whatever trivial doubt I might have entertained. In scrutinizing the edges of the paper, I observed them to be more *chafed* than seemed necessary. They presented the *broken* appearance which is manifested when a stiff paper, having been once folded and pressed with a folder, is refolded in a reversed direction, in the same creases or edges which had formed the original fold. This discovery was sufficient. It was clear to me that the letter had been turned, as a glove, inside out, re-directed and re-sealed. I bade the minister good-morning, and took my departure at once, leaving a gold snuff-box upon the table.

'The next morning I called for the snuff-box, when we resumed, quite eagerly, the conversation of the preceding day. While thus engaged, however, a loud report, as if of a pistol, was heard immediately beneath the windows of the hotel, and was succeeded by a series of fearful screams, and the shoutings of a terrified mob. D— rushed to a casement, threw it open, and looked out. In the meantime I stepped to the card-rack, took the letter, put it in my pocket, and replaced it by a *facsimile*, (so far as regards externals) which I had carefully prepared at my lodgings – imitating the D— cipher, very readily, by means of a seal formed of bread.

'The disturbance in the street had been occasioned by the frantic behavior of a man with a musket. He had fired it among a crowd of women and children. It proved, however, to have been without ball, and the fellow was suffered to go his way as a lunatic or a drunkard. When he had gone, D— came from the window, whither I had followed him immediately upon securing the object in view. Soon afterward I bade him farewell. The pretended lunatic was a man in my own pay.'

'But what purpose had you,' I asked, 'in replacing the letter by a facsimile? Would it not have been better, at the first visit, to have seized it openly, and departed?'

'D—,' replied Dupin, 'is a desperate man, and a man of nerve. His hotel, too, is not without attendants devoted to his interests. Had I made the wild attempt you suggest, I might never have left the Ministerial presence alive. The good people of Paris might have heard of me no more. But I had an object apart from these considerations. You know my political prepossessions. In this matter, I act as a partisan of the lady concerned. For eighteen months the Minister has had her in his power. She has now him in hers – since, being unaware that the letter is not in his possession, he will proceed with his exactions as if it was. Thus will he inevitably commit himself, at once, to his political destruction. His downfall, too, will not be more precipitate than awkward. It is all very well to talk about the *facilis descensus Averni*; but in all kinds of climbing, as Catalani said of singing, it is far more easy to get up than to come down. In the present instance I have no sympathy – at least no pity – for him who descends. He is that *monstrum horrendum*, an unprincipled man of genius. I confess, however, that I should like very well to know the precise character of his thoughts, when, being defied by her whom the Prefect terms "a certain personage," he is reduced to opening the letter which I left for him in the card-rack.'

'How? Did you put any thing particular in it?'

'Why – it did not seem altogether right to leave the interior blank – that would have been insulting. D—, at Vienna once, did me an evil turn, which I told him, quite good-humoredly, that I should remember. So, as I knew he would feel some curiosity in regard to the identity of the person who had outwitted him, I thought it a pity not to give him a clew. He is well acquainted with my MS., and I just copied into the middle of the blank sheet the words –

– Un dessein si funeste,
S'il n'est digne d'Atrée, est digne de Thyeste.

They are to be found in Crébillon's "Atrée."'

ACKNOWLEDGMENTS

JORGE LUIS BORGES: 'Death and the Compass by Jorge Luis Borges, translated by James E. Irby, from *Labyrinths*, copyright © 1962, 1964 by New Directions Publishing Corp. Reprinted by permission of New Directions Publishing Corporation and Pollinger Limited.

RAYMOND CHANDLER: 'I'll Be Waiting' from *The Simple Art of Murder* by Raymond Chandler. Copyright © 1950 by Raymond Chandler, renewed 1978 by Helga Greene. Reprinted by permission of Houghton Mifflin Harcourt Publishing Company. All rights reserved.

AGATHA CHRISTIE: 'The Blue Geranium' from *The Thirteen Problems*, published by William Collins, 1932. © Agatha Christie Limited 1932.

E. S. GARDNER: 'Leg Man' © 1938, 1966, E. S. Gardner.

DASHIELL HAMMETT: 'The Gatewood Caper' from *The Big Knockover* by Dashiell Hammett. Copyright © 1923, renewed. Published by permission of the Dashiell Hammett Property Trust. 'The Gatewood Caper' from *The Big Knockover* by Dashiell Hammett. Reprinted with permission from Random House, Inc.

H. F. KEATING: 'Inspector Ghote and the Miracle Baby' from *Great Law and Order Stories*, ed. John Mortimer. © H. R. F. Keating 1990. Reprinted with permission from Peters, Fraser & Dunlop.

SARA PARETSKY: 'The Takamoku *Joseki*' from *V. I. For Short*

(Hamish Hamilton, 1995). Reprinted with permission from David Grossman Literary Agency.

'The Takamoku *Joseki*' copyright © 1983 by Sara Paretsky. First published in *Alfred Hitchcock's Mystery Magazine*. Reprinted with permission from Dominick Abel Literary Agency, Inc.

IAN RANKIN: 'Window of Opportunity' from *Beggars Banquet* by Ian Rankin. Reprinted with permission from Robinson Literary Agency Limited.

RUTH RENDELL: 'People Don't Do Such Things' from *The Fallen Curtain and Other Stories* by Ruth Rendell, published by Century. Reprinted by permission of The Random House Group Limited.

GEORGES SIMENON: 'Mademoiselle Berthe and her Lover' taken from *Maigret's Pipe*, translated by Jean Stewart. Published by Hamish Hamilton, 1977 © G. Simenon 1947.

Everyman's Pocket Classics are
typeset in the classic typeface Garamond and
printed on acid-free, cream-wove paper
with a sewn, full-cloth binding.